The

CW00801292

by

Geraint Roberts

First impression 2020

Cover design: Geraint Roberts

ISBN:
9781838135805

To David Haven reugld ddo y Nadolig blwyddyn [handwritten inscription]

Foreword

I enjoy using what are, perhaps, lesser known historical events to my work. Thus, the industrial components of Aberystwyth; the harbour, the developing railways and the local metal mining industry, are key backdrops to this story. Dafydd himself is the son of Owain, a lead miner protagonist in the first three novels that I ever wrote. As a backdrop to these, I used the history of Frongoch mine, near Pontrhydygroes. It is a place I had studied in my academic life but found had more to offer than geology. Slowly, Owain's story took shape and Dafydd's tale opened up in its own right.

By the Banks of the Rheidol ended in 1905 with Dafydd on his way to a new life. Now, the story enter the tumultuous period of the first world war.

For this novel, I am indebted to my sister, Deborah Lea, for her stoic work in the minefield of proof reading and Andrew 'Ted' Foulds for fixing some technical inaccuracies in my characters escapades on the rails. The cover is inspired by an old photograph, providing a period image that could be in a multitude of venues. The graphics have been compiled by Gareth Jones, who has patiently tweaked and tweaked and tweaked again without once complaining. The country maps were adapted from www.d-map.com, a free resource! (Merci beaucoup, mes amies!)

The belief and support of my mother, Rita Roberts and my wife, Aile Roberts has been unwavering and I would also like to pay tribute to the family of the Vale of Rheidol railway. That band of railwaymen and women are the true lifeblood of the operation and make it such a compelling place to work.

Although the roles portrayed by the characters are real, the characters themselves are fictional. However, the background historical settings are wherever possible, based on real events. Anything to the contrary is purely coincidental

NB I <u>have</u> chosen to use spellings of some Welsh place-names as they would have appeared at the time. This does not reflect on how I feel they should be spelt or pronounced in modern Wales.

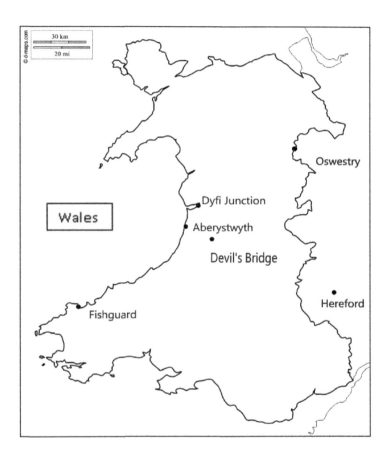

Wales

30 km
20 mi

Oswestry

Dyfi Junction

Aberystwyth

Devil's Bridge

Fishguard

Hereford

Western Front in Belgium

Ypres

Poperinge

Borre

Hazebrouck

Belgium

30 km
20 mi

© d-maps.com

4

Chapter One

The Return
(1915)

There was something triumphant in the train's approach to Aberystwyth. It raced up Commins Bank before shooting round the curve into the Rheidol valley like a bagatelle and then finally speeding towards the town. A quick whistle to Llanbadarn Church, a hiss of steam acknowledging Plascrug Castle, then quickly coasting past the engine shed and the throat of the goods yard to the bustling station.

Dafydd was sure that if the engine had arms, they would have been outstretched crying:

'Look at me! Here I am! I have returned!'

That was certainly how he felt. His time across the border at Oswestry, though enjoyable, had felt like an exile. Now he was back with something to show for it. Passed fireman and a transfer back to his hometown. The pain of the past was washed clean out of him.

Dafydd grinned in anticipation of a warm cup of coffee at his sister's cafe. He left the platform then stopped abruptly, as the sight of a woman with curly fair hair made him miss his step. He waited for her to look up with a beautiful wide smile... The woman turned towards him and Dafydd relaxed. It was not who he thought it was. *Besides*, he thought. *I'm past that time. I'm mature now.*

Oswestry had been good to him. The wound to his heart had healed.

The small station forecourt provided limited shelter from the sun, as Dafydd made his way to the street outside. The shops had lowered their canopies to allow people to walk in the shade. Dafydd quickly took advantage of this to cool down. He walked down the street, fondly admiring the way its end appeared to touch the blue sky. Halfway along, he turned off and made for the cafe.

The smile that greeted him as he walked through the door mirrored the sunshine outside. His younger sister, Angharad, rushed forward to hug him and kiss his cheek. The assembled customers affected a genteel air of embarrassment, but this was lost on the girl as she drew him into the small cafe.

Dafydd ignored the chorus of gasps and tuts of disapproval from the customers and looked towards the proprietor of the cafe. The bushy moustache almost hid the smile, but the pleasure still shone from his eyes. A small cough preceded his welcome greeting, a legacy of the years spent mining lead in the Ceredigion Mountains, far from the shores of his native Italy.

'Daveed,' he said, his baritone voice still stumbling over the Welsh name.

'Hello Donato,' Dafydd said. 'I am sorry to disturb your cafe.'

'For why? You are always welcome. A visit?'

'No, my friend. I have moved. Been sent down to Aber shed as passed fireman. It means I'm a fireman in name and I can also drive unimportant trains or shunting sometimes when needed, until I learn the road and get some experience, like.'

Donato smiled. 'I understand. You have new job, a better job. And a home perhaps? You stay with us?'

Dafydd shook his head. 'I have lodgings already.'

'The old lady in Trefechan? Yes, yes. She always looked out for you. Sioned is in the back, go see her. We talk later. Please, go.'

Dafydd moved through to the back of the small cafe and into a parlour. Sioned looked up from the fireplace, where she was brushing the grate.

She quickly got up to greet her brother, brushing her hands clean of the coal dust. Her slow warm smile matched the embrace of welcome.

'You didn't tell them.' Dafydd said.

'I thought the surprise would be worth it,' Sioned replied. 'I could have heard Angharad all the way to the promenade just now. You did not leave much behind?'

'Nothing. Not much to pack. Oh, I see... Smart you are there. I got no sweetheart if that's what you're thinking.'

'Just looking out for you, *bach*. I'll have you down church then, doffing your cap at the spinsters!'

Dafydd smiled and kissed her cheek. 'I'm over her, it's past. All done now. I have too much to look forward to dwell on back then.'

She stepped back and looked at him with a sigh, before pecking him on the cheek.

'If you say so. Where you staying?'

'Greenfield Street. A room in one of them new terraced houses.'

'Not Mrs Lewis in Trefechan? She always been good to you.' She arched her eyebrows and his shoulders collapsed at the discovery of the lie.

'Alright, I lied, Mrs Lewis. She's part of the past, so maybe I should be staying somewhere else, then?'

'Well, you know we can squeeze you in, if you're stuck?'

'Thanks, cariad. If you don't mind, I'll stay by the river.'

'You Trefechan Turkeys are a law unto yourselves, Daf bach!'

'You're not over busy?' Dafydd asked.

'No, nothing the others can't handle and young Owain is asleep also.'

She moved to the kettle and Dafydd looked on in approval. For someone six months after giving birth, his sister looked good for it, but he knew she was tired.

Sioned came back with a tray containing two cups of tea and a plate of bara brith, which Dafydd gratefully accepted.

'So, tell me what you been doing, Daf. It's been nearly five years and we haven't seen you up to now.'

'I been having fun,' Dafydd replied with a hint of a boyish grin. 'I been taught how to fire, proper like and I been learning the roads from Whitchurch all the way to here and up the coast. I know when to talk and when to shovel. And I fired just about every kind of loco the Cambrian's got.' There was a boyish glee underpinning his words and she smiled.

'You and your toys,' Sioned said gently.

Dafydd paused and looked at his sister's poker face.

'Oh alright, girl, truth is, I'm happy doing what I'm doing. It's hard, but you can't have it all your own way now, can you?'

There was a pause and Dafydd looked at a circling bubble on his tea.

'I'm past her now, Sioned. Honest, I am looking forward.'

'She hurt you so much, *cariad*,' Sioned replied.

'I was a fool, Sioned. I made her wait for me until she was on the door of the workhouse.'

'That's no excuse for her taking another woman's husband to bed.'

'Well it is when you are penniless.'

'Aye, they have a name for that and all.'

'Don't.' The word spoken softly, was of sadness, stripped of anger.

It was Sioned's turn to stare at her cup.

'I'm sorry, but it changed you, Daf. You were full of spirit before and then you went in yourself. You've not been over here for five years. Five years, *cariad*! And I know you've been in town on trains, so don't tell me otherwise. They say you don't go further than the shed and keep your head down when in the station, as if you're hiding. Don't deny it!'

'Alright Sioned.'

'Dad understands you know, even though it meant he never sees you.'

'It's not her fault!'

'That you don't come here? I'm sorry, Dafydd, we'll never agree on that score. She's the talk of the town that one, walking round as if she owns the place. Being the lover of a rich man doesn't put you above your station in life.'

'Alright Sioned!' Dafydd snapped and the noise in the parlour dropped to only the hiss and crackle of the logs on the fire.

'I'm glad you told me you were coming,' Sioned finally said. 'I am still surprised you did come, but I am glad for it and all.'

'I'm sorry, Sioned. I know you're angry with her and I'm angry with me and all. I lost a lot of time worrying about it, but now things have changed. Moving down a different path now, I am.'

'Well if you say so, so what will you be doing now at the shed?'

Dafydd perked up with the chance to talk about his work.

'I'll be firing and covering driving. Mostly freight, some local passenger. Been bumped up the links a bit to cover them that's joined up for the war. Everyone's short of good men and now railways is a reserved occupation, I'm happy to have got the chance.'

'Good.'

He sighed. 'I got to go, Sioned. I have to report to the shed and make ready.'

'Course you have, *cariad*. Well, come over for Sunday and I'll have a place set for you at lunch.'

'I will.'

They moved out of the parlour and back to the cafe. Angharad moved to give him a quick hug and Donato nodded with a grin.

Dafydd felt the warmth of the greetings. For a moment, a wave of regret washed over him as he thought of the years he had wasted in exile. He had missed the love of his family. There was no time for regret. He had done what had needed to be done at the time. Now he just had to carry on and make the best of it.

He walked through the cafe and paid attention to the customers. One or two knew him or at least that he was family. Their smiles were warm, and he welcomed them with a nod.

He reached the door and looked out onto the street. There was the gentle bustle of everyday life. A horse cart went by, the driver shouting a greeting to a window cleaner, pushing his barrow. Ladies window shopped, looking at fine clothes for sale, despite the Kaiser's shadow over the world.

Dafydd's gaze was drawn to a lady walking down the road. He admired the way she strolled confidently down the pavement, basket under one arm. Her smile disarmed all the hostile gazes in her path, creating an impermeable wall to all who would cast scorn. He stood admiring her for a while, before his brain suddenly went numb with the shock of recognition. His hands tingled and the base of his spine went rigid.

'Moving on, *cariad*,' Sioned whispered from behind him. 'Moving on.'

Chapter Two

Reunion

The terraced house in Trefechan looked cosy and warm in the cold September wind, as Dafydd stood outside. By rights he shouldn't have been there. He still cursed himself that he had tried to lie about it. Why bother? Because he was moving forward in his life and he didn't want to be seen reliving the past. He hesitated, before knocking on the door. After a few minutes before he heard shuffling footsteps and an old lady opened the door.

'Mrs Owen.'

'Dafydd,' she grunted. 'Well, come in. I can't stand here when I've got busy things to do.'

She turned and walked back down the hallway and he followed her inside.

'You're in your normal room, but don't get comfortable. As soon as I get another lodger, you're sharing.'

Dafydd sighed. Despite the ghosts that played on his mind from before, he felt he was finally back at home, it was a good feeling.

'Do you want a *panad*?'

'No. *Diolch*, I had tea at my sister's. I need to get to the engine shed now, in a minute.'

'That's alright then. I'll have some supper ready for you.' She paused. 'It will be good to have company.'

'It's been a bit quiet, has it?'

'Town's a bit quiet, cariad. Everyone's gone off to war. Twelve months have gone, and they've not come back in a hurry.'

11

'Well, I work in a restricted job, Mrs Lewis. They need the likes of me to get the coal to Jellicoe's fleet. I'm not going anywhere in a hurry.'

Mrs Lewis smiled. 'No? Well that will be nice. Some went from the railway anyway, but there's enough out in France already in my mind.'

Dafydd sighed. 'Actually, I'm a bit tired and I've no need to go to shed just now. I think I'll take a walk around, sort my bearings out like.'

'You do that, Dafydd cariad. Then you come back, and I'll have some tea and bara brith on the go.'

Dafydd smiled at the thought as he went through the door. He quickly made his way through the small group of terraces to the riverside and gazed at the scene. Across the river and behind a retaining wall was the tell-tale chimney of a small locomotive smoking away quietly outside a shed. A football ground lay to the right, bounded by a railway bridge. Looking the other way, Dafydd could make out the sails and masts of ships that lay behind the Trefechan Bridge in the harbour. Straight ahead were the new terraced houses in Aberystwyth, pointing towards the direction of the livestock market. A smell of fermenting hops filled the air. Dafydd felt warm with the happiness of returning to the town. He was back in Trefechan, a Turkey once more. He took a deep breath of contentment and sighed.

Then a wave of sadness passed over him. The bridge was where Gwen had found him destitute and took him in. The lime kilns in the harbour were where they ate baked potatoes on a summer's evening. The hill behind, where he had had his moment of passion with her. The arches of the bridge under which he had fought Gwen's cousin after he found the man was an arsonist and murderer.

He quickly looked away to the railway engine. Behind it lay the small narrow-gauge railway station for Devil's Bridge. It was the place where he had found out that Gwen had become the mistress of one of the town's richest men.

Behind the football ground, in the distance was the pond, where he had pleaded with her to come with him to England and she had agreed, only to desert him at the train he left on.

Being back in Trefechan came with a price to pay. The pain of never having found his happiness. His chest tightened and his stomach felt ill, as the memories washed over him like a harsh tide.

He stepped back with the impact. Dafydd realised that Sioned was right. It was time to move on; time to find a new path with a brighter future. Even in a world tainted by war.

He stared at the flowing water for a long time but finding no answers, made his way back to the house.

He went straight inside the hall and down the side of the stairs to the kitchen at the back. Mrs Owen was nowhere to be seen, although she could be heard moving something upstairs. A lady sat at the small table of the kitchen sipping tea. Her hair was covered with a large hat tied under the chin with ribbons. The puffed sleeves and long skirts of her dress spoke of money. Dafydd looked at the beautiful face, the blonde curling hair and brown eyes, the glorious smile that always lit the room like a morning sun. His heart sank like a ship in mid-ocean, at the mercy of a storm.

'Hello *cariad*,' Gwen said. 'Where you been hiding then?'

****

Dafydd's chest tightened once more. His breathing was heavy and laboured. He knew that seeing her again would hurt for days after. He felt angry that he had been so willing to believe that all those feelings had passed, angry that it had all been proven to be an illusion. Although his soul screamed at him to tell her his feelings, his mind slammed the door to the vulnerability that would bring.

It was not the time and looking at her finery, there was no longer any point. Many years back she had chosen her path and it wasn't the same as his. The fever subsided but the pain settled into a dull ache.

'You know well enough what I been up to,' Dafydd replied, a little bit too sharply for his own liking. 'What you doing here then? Not the circle you move in these days, I expect?'

'You're right of course. But I heard you had come back, and I had to see you.'

'Why?'

The silence echoed like a slap.

'I wanted to see you,' she said quietly.

Dafydd took a deep breath and nodded. 'You're looking well.'

He felt the understatement in his heart.

'Thank you,' she replied. 'Please, I made you tea.'

Dafydd looked forlornly at the teapot encased in its cosy.

'I thought you understood,' Gwen said.

'I know why you went, but now you have done that, I don't see why you are looking back,' Dafydd replied.

She sighed and looked away.

'We all have choices, cariad. Some are harder than others.'

You did well out of yours, Dafydd thought sourly, biting back the words. He was upset, but more in anger at himself for his feelings. It was still painful to realise she was never going to be part of his life the way he wanted.

He looked at the proffered teacup, desperately yearning for the earth to swallow him up. It was a futile thought.

'I'll tell you now what I should have done back then. You rescued me from the gutter and set me back on the road. When you were in difficulty, I wasn't there for you. It hurts me now and it is something that will never sit well with me. I am truly sorry, but I can only say that my feelings for you have never changed. I was fool enough to believe they had, but I was wrong.

So, I am glad you're well and I'm happy you are happy and all, but don't get upset if I'm not looking pleased to see you.'

There was a long silence, as Dafydd wondered where the hell he had found that speech and the voice to deliver it. Gwen was playing with a teaspoon and the tension seemed unbearable.

'I hoped that you had settled down and all.' she finally said.

'Yes, well,' Dafydd muttered. 'I never been one with the women. Never had the words.'

Gwen raised her eyebrows but did not reply.

'Look,' Dafydd said. 'I can see you are happy. I really am glad for that. I'd be less of a man if I wasn't. It's just... hard.'

The word '*cariad*' stuck in his throat. Gwen nodded slowly.

'I know. You have great qualities, Dafydd. Most would behave badly in your place. You're more of a gentleman than a gentleman himself. I made a mistake coming here, for I did not know I would cause so much pain. I am truly sorry.'

She stood up swiftly and went over to gently kiss his cheek.

'Try not to think bad of me. Don't judge me too hard I beg you. I'll see myself out.'

She got up and left Dafydd staring out of the window.

'*I want to be angry,*' he muttered to himself. '*I want to throw something. I want to bury myself.*'

Mrs Owen shuffled into the room a few minutes later and started cleaning the table. For a second, she looked so much older as she smiled sadly at him.

'She got it wrong, Dafydd *bach*. She should have said not to judge yourself too harshly.'

****

Dafydd walked across the Trefechan Bridge into Aberystwyth. The ghosts still stood sentry in various places, but for now they would not venture out of the shadows. He walked past the new terraced housing towards the livestock market on what was called Smithfield Road.

The road ended in a maze of railway lines. The railway to Carmarthen stretched past the goods sidings. Behind lay the narrow-gauge line to Devil's Bridge, where Dafydd had first been employed as a fireman. He quickly located a path of wooden boards and cinder, leading to the engine shed.

The shed wasn't a bad size, Dafydd thought. Maybe not as big as Machynlleth, definitely not a patch on Oswestry. But it was to be home soon enough for him, so he felt he'd best get used to the change.

A small rain shower began to pick up and Dafydd quickened his pace. A bit of damp wouldn't harm him and perhaps the cool rain would help numb the pain he still nursed in his heart. He looked at the rain trickling down the slate roof of the shed. Perhaps he didn't need that much cooling down, he thought, so he started to jog. As he reached the office door, he nearly collided with a burly man dressed in the grey-blue overalls of an engineman.

'Watch where you're going!' the man snapped.

'Sorry there,' Dafydd replied. 'It was a bit wet.'

'You English are soft,' the man replied, leaving Dafydd speechless. The more for the fact that they were speaking Welsh at the time.

The door to the foreman's office was open and a man sat behind the desk. He beckoned Dafydd inside.

'I remember you from the Rheidol railway,' the man said after introductions. 'Jenkins! Come in.'

The burly man was standing at the door.

'This is your new fireman, Jenkins.'

A flicker of emotion at the corner of Jenkins' mouth showed his distaste.

'An Englishman?'

'I was born in the Ystwyth valley,' Dafydd replied calmer than he felt.

'A country boy? Even worse. Any chance you know how to fire?'

'Let's hope so,' Dafydd replied in an even tone. He'd had his fill of bullies in his time and wasn't in the mood for another.

'You're up in the links ahead of your time,' the foreman said. 'What with losing people to the war and all. But Oswestry says you are a good worker, as do many of the drivers. You got a chance here, take it. One of the cleaners will knock you up tomorrow, give you time to get here.'

For some reason, Gwen appeared in his mind. He quickly tried to suppress the thought. Not now, he thought. Not ever again.

'Well then?' Jenkins had been talking at Dafydd, his face a picture of expectation. Without thinking, Dafydd nodded. There was a grunt of approval and Dafydd breathed a small sigh of relief.

'Until tomorrow then,' the foreman said. Dafydd left and went back to the house. He felt weary from the day and its twists and turns. Perhaps an early night would help, though he feared his mind would be awake thinking of Gwen for most of it.

Chapter Three

Jenkins

The early morning silence was shattered by a knock on the door. A normal, but painful routine for Dafydd, to be up before dawn. He stumbled to the window and lifted it to look out. A young voice came from the gloom below.

'I was sent to wake you.'

'I'm awake, *bach*. What time is it?'

'Four o'clock. I'm running a bit late.'

'What's your name, son?'

'Aled Lewis,' came the reluctant reply. '*Please* don't say I'm late.'

'You were here in plenty of time, Aled Lewis. Don't you fret there.'

Dafydd went to the wash basin and splashed his face with cold water. His clothes were ready on the chair and he quickly dressed, then went downstairs to find Mrs. Owen putting bacon on a plate. A mug of tea steamed on the table, Dafydd's breath steamed in response.

'You can't make a habit of this, Mrs. Owen.'

'Well, maybe I can and maybe I can't, but you're as much family to me and I'll do what I want for that.'

The frank admission had Dafydd wondering if she had been drinking. Even though Mrs. Owen was Band of Hope.

He squeezed her arm in thanks and got a grunt in reply. *That's more like it*, he thought.

By the time Jenkins had turned up to the freight engine. the fire had been lit by the fire raiser. It had come on a long way from the newspaper taper, the coal slowly being added to build it up and the boiler was now beginning to make small popping sounds as Dafydd added more fuel to raise the heat and give the steam engine voice. .

Jenkins grabbed his oil can and walked around the engine, topping up. He then returned, depositing his flask on a metal ridge behind the regulator and unscrewing the cup to pour a brew.

'Not bad, that,' he nodded at the fire. His voice begrudged the compliment.

'More to come,' Dafydd replied.

'There'd better be. Do you know what loco she is?'

Dafydd nodded. 'An Aston large goods.'

'What do you reckon?'

'Best I've had so far.'

Jenkins laughed. 'You fired an express yet?'

Dafydd shook his head.

'You'll be doing one with me soon enough. Now can you shovel to Welshpool?'

'I reckon.'

'Go to it then.'

Dafydd kept his head down and tried to avoid glimpsing the flask of tea. He kicked himself for forgetting his own. It was unlikely he would be offered any by Jenkins.

The grumpy driver took the engine off shed and into the goods yard. Dafydd went to couple the engine to its train, silently thanking the fire raiser for giving the engine a good head of steam. He thanked the shunter for gathering a tidy rake of trucks. Less chance for Jenkins to find fault, Dafydd thought gloomily. He coupled up the engine and then moved back into the cab to find Jenkins with the firebox door wide open.

'Look in there and tell me where the cold spots are.'

Dafydd felt it was always funny to talk of cold spots in a roaring fire, but with his colleague's lack of a sense of humour, his thoughts were best left unsaid.

' Middle to the left and a bit either side of the front.'

Jenkins nodded. 'See to it then.'

Dafydd wasn't sure if he was going to be able to put up with the stilted tone for long, but he settled to shovel more coal into the fire. His actions were smooth, and he found his targets with ease, it helped alleviate the 'welcome' he was receiving. He leant out of the cab to collect the token from the signalman as they passed the box. The man grinned back.

'Good luck, son!'

There was sympathy in the voice. *I'm going to need it*, Dafydd thought, before springing back into focus and he looked ahead.

'Plascrug crossing, clear!' he shouted.

There was no answer. The engine slipped on damp rails and Jenkins slammed the regulator shut with a curse. Dafydd thought of Gwen, looking so beautiful in her fine clothes, as she sat in Mrs Owen's kitchen. He shovelled another load of coal into the firebox.

'Where do you think you are throwing that?' Jenkins bellowed.

It was going to be a long day.

****

'Some people have a joy in their heart,' Donato said, before sipping his coffee. 'Others have a struggle to find it.'

He sat outside the back of the cafe with Dafydd at an old table, looking at the strip of garden with its crude vegetable patch.

'Your father, he love to make a vegetable grow.'

'He do all this himself?'

'No, your Uncle Gwilym also. He get a share and we all eat well. Bella catch mice and she get fish for it.'

Dafydd looked at the tortoiseshell cat, which was walking towards them, tail up in greeting. Dafydd leant to tickle her ears, as she rose up on her back legs, purring in appreciation.

'You're right, Donato. But why me, eh?'

'They put you with a master. Perhaps this is good thing, no?'

Dafydd pulled a face. 'Well perhaps I'll learn. Not looking forward to him flogging me up Talerddig Bank every day, mind. What about you, anyhow? You're a master, book learner. Speak a few more languages than me. To me, you look as if you live way below yourself, but you seem happy?'

'That I do not patronise you, perhaps? This is the word, I think. I know how you are, Daveed. I think this Jenkins just need to know you a little.'

'Why are you here, Donato?'

Donato shrugged. 'I was once lost in love. I once lost love. Frongoch was hiring men from Bergamo. I went with them and I found a love once more.'

He sat back with his cup of coffee at his lips and a ghost of a smile appeared.

'Frongoch was not a happy place in the end, much trouble with Welsh and Italians. Sioned was in danger for knowing me and so we come here. Some luck, some hard work and still we are here. Angharad of course, she is a great help.'

He smiled as Angharad approached to collect empty cups. She flushed as her name was spoken.

'*Hisht* your noise!' she said. 'We're getting busy again.'

'Okay, I come, then you rest.'

'I'd better leave,' Dafydd said. 'Need to be on shift later.'

Although the conversation was light and the company warm. Dafydd felt a gap from Donato's simple words.

'*I was once lost in love. I once lost love.*'

All he could think was '*Where do I go from here?*'

****

It was with a great patience that Dafydd continued firing for Jenkins. It felt as if nothing was good enough for the man, Time and time again, Dafydd bit his tongue, ducked down and got on with it. He needed the work to focus on and not dwell on broken dreams of long ago that whispered to him at every opportunity. As he sat in the garden with Donato, Dafydd could only feel peace, a haven from the anguish.

'Dafydd, you can't keep dwelling on it,' Sioned's voice broke through his thoughts. Donato had got up to leave and Dafydd's sister came to sit in his place.

'What you on about now, Sioni?'

'Gwen, *cariad*. You can't just sit here thinking of her. She's gone.'

'Who says I was?' Dafydd replied.

Sioned sighed. 'I'm not the little girl in Trisant anymore, Dafydd. The spark in you died when you saw her again.'

Dafydd stared at the cat, which was oblivious to it all, as it washed itself.

'You know she came to visit me. Just to see how I was and hoping we would be friends.'

Sioned rolled her eyes. '*Iesu*! Either she is very ignorant or very cruel. She's poison, that one…'

'Perhaps I should move, get a transfer to Mach shed.'

Sioned stood up and kissed his forehead. 'Perhaps you should think about yourself in this. You've got a good job here. At least you're not off to France.'

'Yes, and I get some unkindly looks these days from folk. I should pin my 'reserved occupation' badge to my forehead. People look on me as if I am running away...'

'Many have sons and husbands over there, Dafydd and now realise how much danger they are in. It wasn't settled by Christmas last year and it won't be for ages now. Look, here you got a good, safe job, good town and a good teacher, if a bit harsh at times. Try and think of what is happening in your life that is good. The moment you stop worrying about stuff, it all sorts itself out on its own. Stay where you are. Anyone who wishes a man to go across to France is a fool!'

'Dangerous talk in this land,' Dafydd replied.

'People die out there. They are not coming back to argue with me.'

****

Dafydd ate with Mrs. Owen in silence, even though he enjoyed the taste of the food and the company. There was nothing to say, and inwardly he cursed himself. This was supposed to be his moment, yet here he was with his mind in turmoil.

He noticed a dustpan and brush to one side, the dust was still in the pan, as was a large grey-white feather. He stared at it, as his heart sank. Mrs Owen stared at him and then moved quickly to throw the contents of the pan onto the fire.

'Seagulls are always shedding their feathers,' she muttered.

Dafydd shrugged. He knew the feather was a message meant for him.

'I think this is a bad area for birds losing their feathers.'

She stopped and gazed at the fire. 'Don't go to war, Dafydd *cariad*. I can't afford to lose another to soldiering.'

'Mr Owen?'

'Went south to fight the Boer. I never even got to bury him. You're needed by here; don't you listen to them fools!'

'I was a fool to come back, Mrs Owen. I thought I had moved on.'

'There's nothing that should make you want to throw away your own life.'

'There's nothing for me here.'

'There can be, you just have to heal, that's all.'

Dafydd went to hug her and she wept in his arms.

'There you are,' she said as her sobbing subsided. 'Even old Mrs Owen needs a *cwtch* now and again. Now go find someone to come and *cwtch* you.'

****

The weather had changed, and a week of torrential rain had made the fields around Machynlleth look like ponds. Dafydd always thanked the foresight of the construction engineers to have raised the track bed. The land was so flat and the Dyfi so active on that day, that it looked ready to re-establish Machynlleth as the ancient port of old. *Owain Glyndwr would have been proud of that*, Dafydd thought. He would not voice it out loud. He knew his driver was no audience.

They had taken the local stopping train out from Aberystwyth to Oswestry and were coming back on an evening run. Jenkins had been his normal taciturn self, but at least Dafydd now had his flask of tea on the shelf behind the regulator. It felt like progress, as they ambled along through a deluge of rain.

'They do say it's the war,' Dafydd said, as they waited in Machynlleth station for the all-clear back to Aberystwyth. 'All the gun smoke makes them clouds and its more there for the raining.'

Jenkins chose not to comment. *It's alright for you*, Dafydd thought. *Sat inside your cosy cab and me half-soaked reaching for the coal*. The tarpaulin covered the gap to the tender only so far and Dafydd needed to wade in to dig some up from the back. Jenkins had decided there was no need for stocking up.

Jenkins edged the engine forward and tapped the regulator with his fingers. As they slowed towards the approach for Dovey Junction, he uttered a mild curse. Dafydd looked ahead and spied the faint gleam of rails in the evening gloom. They seemed to end in a lake.

'The Dovey is high,' Jenkins shouted. 'Tide is up, spring one at that. We're in for a wet one tonight.'

'What do we do?' Dafydd asked.

'Well, the signal's set. We've got the road and I've a warm chair back home to look forward to. Damned if water'll stop me.' It was almost a snarl in response.

Dafydd looked across and for once received an answering grin. Jenkins was enjoying himself.

'The secret, Dafydd bach, is not to make a bow wave. You get the tokens and keep the fire nice and hot. I'll do the rest.'

The train slowed and Dafydd marvelled at the way they began to cut through the water like a sailing ship. They were nearing Dovey Junction and the water was just below the platform. Dafydd shook his head, *surely, they couldn't prevail?*

'Token!' Jenkins shouted and Dafydd quickly looked out to the station, where two men stood on the platform. One held a metal loop. Dafydd took his solid metal key-shaped token and stuffed it into a pouch of a similar loop and leaned out extending the wire. He'd never been sailing, but he was sure it must be like this.

'You're not showing navigation lights,' said one of the men as he slipped his arm through the metal loop. Dafydd let go.

'If you get stuck, we'll put a tow rope on you and claim salvage!' said the other 'Hazard to shipping you'll be!'

Dafydd reversed the exercise, taking the loop with the new token onto his shoulder.

'You think I've never heard that one before?' Jenkins shouted back.

The men only grinned back. One waded across to the signal box and Dafydd soon saw the signal ahead was green to go. Jenkins had not stopped and Dafydd breathed a sigh of relief. The train would have derailed if the signalman had not acted fast enough. Nobody else seemed worried though, it seemed like they all were treating it as a normal event.

They carried on down the line. The water was now washing the top steps of the locomotive, occasionally splashing through the gap between tender and engine. They were making headway, but he had to make sure the fire was hot enough to keep them going. He opened the firebox door and put his shovel over the top of the entrance to shield his eyes from the white glare of the fire. Identifying some cold spots, he quickly shovelled in some coal and slammed the door shut. Looking out, he noticed they were now wreathed in steam.

'Leave it for now,' Jenkins said. 'She's enough to be hot enough.'

It felt like hours, but soon the straight to Glandyfi station was in sight and they were exchanging tokens again. The river appeared to have over-run the land, but all the while, Jenkins kept peering out of the cab, with one hand on the regulator.

As they moved through the rocks at Ynys Hir, he nodded in satisfaction and then with a sharp blast of the whistle, set the engine at a faster pace. Dafydd looked down again, but the water was only around the rails, and he shook his head in wonder.

'She's steady now,' Jenkins said as they entered a cutting. 'You keep an eye on her and I'll sort out this firebox.'

Dafydd was crestfallen. Now he wasn't even trusted to do his own job. Was that his worth? Jenkins took back the regulator as they came into Ynyslas station and Dafydd took the tokens in a sour mood. He just wanted to be away from it all.

As they finally arrived in Aberystwyth and ran the engine around to the front of the train, Dafydd had convinced himself that Jenkins had shown him his true opinion of his firing skills. It wasn't good.

They moved to refuel and handed over the engine to James James, a young passed cleaner. He was a good man, a fast worker, but cheeky with it. Dafydd knew James was good enough to fire, but that was only if his cheek didn't hold him back.

'A good journey, Daf?'

'Bit wet, James bach, we were sailing across Dovey Junction at one point.'

'Duw, I've heard of that but never known anyone to do it. How was old grumpy balls then?'

Dafydd smiled despite his mood. James was always one for lifting his spirits. They helped each other out at the classes that were run once a week for those trying to learn to be drivers.

'How was he? He was fine, I was awful. Jenks had me standing there minding the engine while he stoked up the fire after we'd got out of the water. He obviously doesn't trust me.'

James's jaw dropped. 'He gave you the regulator! Bloody hell, man! Do you know what that means?'

'He thinks I'm useless,' Dafydd snapped.

'Hardly. Jenkins never gives anyone the regulator. He said he never trusted no-one. And he fired for you? Dafydd bach, he's treating you like royalty!'

Dafydd walked back home with a warm glow. He finally felt respected. He couldn't wait to tell Mrs. Owen, though in his heart he knew there was another woman he longed to rush and tell.

Chapter Four

White feather

He had been up since before dawn coaxing the engine to life. The iron beast now bubbled, hissed and spluttered like an impatient kettle, waiting like a greyhound to be let loose on the long trek from Aberystwyth to Oswestry on the English border. Dafydd polished the motif on the locomotive tender. The Cambrian Railways badge buffed up as proud as he felt. Now, after all these years, he was on a Top Link and firing the express train. One of the best of the best.

Today was so special to him and everything had been perfect so far. The morning was glorious and crisp, as only May could provide. It wasn't going to be too hot, at least not beyond the furnace heat of the avaricious fire of the engine. The weather looked as if it would hold and Dafydd was sure he was going to enjoy the day.

His reverie was broken by a tap on the shoulder. A lady leant forward to hand him something. Her dress and large hat spoke of comfort and wealth. Indeed, Dafydd's first impression was he was being handed a tip. It was not unheard of, some believing it would lead to greater punctuality.

It wasn't coins or paper notes that he held and for a brief instant, Dafydd felt it was some lucky token. Again, this was not unknown practice in his line of work. He opened his hand to look and his brain numbed as if he had been hit from behind, when he gazed on the small white feather.

In the background, he could vaguely hear her words washing over him like the whisper of a morning breeze.

'In memory of our brave boys, who are fighting in France whilst you choose to stay at home,' her tone was laced with sickly sweetness.

Dafydd returned to the cab, to find Jenkins, his driver, motionless. He was holding a similar feather between his thumb and forefinger. Even under the layers of grease and grime, the man looked paler, as he gently placed the feather against the small lens window that looked forward down the engine.

'Let's be off then,' he said quietly. 'We've got a service to run.'

The signalman had walked over to give the token to proceed.

'Why the long faces, boys?' He said by way of greeting. 'These Aston engines make easy work of Talerddig.'

'We've been given the white feather,' Dafydd replied and the signalman rolled his eyes in despair.

'Yes, there are a lot of them about. Women of leisure that got nothing better to do. They'd prefer to see you away fighting the foreign foe than doing some hard, honest graft. They pay no attention to the war service badge we wear.'

'Well trains don't run themselves,' Dafydd grumbled. 'We're short of men as it is without those who joined up at the start.'

'There's talk of women being brought in to fill the gaps,' the signalman said. He roared with laughter at the thought and Dafydd smiled. At the back of his mind though, he had visions of his eldest sister working a train. He had no doubts she would manage it well and it made him feel uneasy.

The journey began and Dafydd began to concentrate on the job at hand. There was no question he would have his work cut out, especially going up Talerddig Bank. No time for memories of silly women now. He hoped he had left a dose of grease on her dainty white linen gloves.

Jenkins looked straight ahead without a word. Even by the next token swap at Bow Street, he appeared oblivious to the world.

Llanfihangel came and went with no change in his mood. Dafydd moved as if to shovel some more coal from the back of the tender. It was not needed after such a short distance, but he found the open space more desirable than the company and Jenkins could be snappy at the best of times. Top Link men always acted as if they were princes, but this silent treatment was not normal, even for him.

The engine roared its approval as they raced down Borth Bank and around a long curve. Borth village itself loomed ahead. In the light of the morning sun, the combination of small fishermen's houses and large hotels looked quite pretty against the background of the long strand. Normally, Dafydd would welcome the sight, but today he was too busy and too troubled.

The silent Jenkins was still closed to him, the man's knuckles white on the regulator. Dafydd knew better than to break the silence without a valid reason. He quickly checked the water glass, topped up more from the tender and shovelled a few more loads of coal into the firebox.

It sat badly with Dafydd that many of his friends had taken up the call to arms. A buzz of excitement had swept through the land, taking away the young and old. Those eager for adventure and those fed up with their lot and needing a new beginning from their mundane lives had gone. It was all a bizarre carnival and soon the ghoulish gossips were revelling in the weekly casualty lists, looking out for the names of many known sons of the parish and talking of them to idle away the days.

Dafydd looked at each name with despair. These were men he had known, who would never smile again. Whose mothers would nurse their grief and whose sweethearts would feel only pain with every morning sunrise.

Then there were the white feather women, who thought they could shame people into joining up. He was in a reserved occupation, meaning and he was needed more at home working the trains than in joining up. He even sported an enamel badge to that effect.

It didn't stop the mutterings or the looks on the street as he went by. In his heart, he questioned what had allowed him this privilege. He was no coward, but war seemed so absolute. Dafydd still wanted time to live and love.

Jenkins eased the regulator and the engine moved off towards the small halt at Ynyslas. Dafydd had never fired one of these beasts before and it seemed to quiver like a greyhound to Jenkins' touch. He quickly fed the fire to get ready for the stretch alongside the estuary.

They slowed for the road crossing and trundled towards the lonely platforms, devoid of life except for the signalman waiting with the next token. As they passed, the man called out.

'Jenkins? Is that you, you old goat?'

Jenkins looked straight ahead without a word and Dafydd began to feel uneasy. This was his day, his moment of triumph. The next level up from Top Link fireman was to qualify as a driver, and he so wanted his hand on the regulator. He tried to focus on his favourite part of the journey.

The train picked up speed and Dafydd prepared himself. He needed to keep his mind clear for where the marshland had edged the track out of shape. In his hand, he held a small bag of Reckits Blue, ready to fling on the track, to be used as a marker for the platelayers to knock the rails back. Dafydd's eyes would gaze on the hills of Merioneth and the calm waters of Aberdyfi. He would feel the wind in his hair. All the while he waited for the dip or sway that would signify a problem.

In his mind, he was on a boat, gently rocking on the waves of the estuary. He thought of fish grilling on the fire. Then his imaginary boat moved towards the estuary mouth and the waters became choppier.

31

Dafydd broke out of his daydream as the train lurched from side to side. He threw down the Reckits and then hung onto the tender. What he heard next was the last thing he expected.

Jenkins bellowed a curse and brought the engine to a complete standstill. This shocked Dafydd, for Jenkins was a teetotaller, a god-fearing chapel boy. Yet he cursed like a trooper, as he brought his train to a halt in the Dyfi marshes. Glandyfi lay a few miles distant, and it appealed to Dafydd like a haven from the dark storm now set on Jenkins' face.

'Come on Daf, we're off!'

Jenkins was halfway down the steps of the cab before Dafydd realised. He quickly followed, more out of curiosity than anything else. Dafydd had seen the woman get on the train and he feared Jenkins would now do something against his nature that he would regret. He caught up with the man, who was walking purposefully down the track past the train, the small white feather fluttering in one hand.

'Where you off to?' Dafydd asked, having to repeat himself as Jenkins made no effort to reply the first time.

'Back there,' came the surly reply. 'I've had enough of all this.'

'Come on man,' Dafydd started, but Jenkins brushed straight past him.

People began to open carriage windows to look at what was happening. As they reached the second coach, a window opened ahead of them and the lady peered out.

'What is the problem?' she asked.

'No problem, madam,' Jenkins replied with courtesy. 'I've been thinking about your words and you are right. We are being far too selfish doing this job whilst so many brave men have left to fight in France. We're off to join up and make the difference.'

'Why don't you wait until you finish your work?' she asked.

'My conscience tells me I have waited far too long' came the reply. 'There is a recruitment centre in the village hall. No time to waste, people are dying out there and we must defeat the Kaiser before he causes any more trouble, mustn't we?'

Jenkins continued to walk on and Dafydd followed, wondering if he was telling the truth. The woman called out to Jenkins' back.

'But who will drive the train?'

Jenkins stopped and scratched his chin. 'That's a point, eh? Who will drive the trains now? Who will help the passengers reach their destinations? Who will take the soldiers to and from the ports, who will take the coal to the docks at Portsmouth and Scapa Flow, for the Navy to go out and beat the Kaiser's ships? Or deliver the armaments for the men to fight with? Who will do all this if we are all at the front fighting?'

Jenkins took a deep breath and looked up to the lady. His words became more deliberate, his manner calm but cool.

'Perhaps not everyone can be a soldier, but there is a need to support those who are. I was a soldier once. When I was young, I fought the Boer. I watched my friends die in a foreign land. Don't you dare say to me I am a coward!'

There was a long pause as the two locked gazes, before the lady quietly withdrew and closed her window.

Jenkins took a deep breath and scanned the land around. The rolling green hills, and the acres of marsh along the placid waters of the river Dyfi. The sky was still a glorious pink.

'I'm wondering about the fire,' Dafydd said softly. 'Perhaps it may need a few shovels of coal on it.'

Jenkins looked over and gave a lukewarm smile.

'You're right, Dafydd bach. Smoke's looking a bit wrong now. Best sort it out, we've a few minutes to make up but we'll give it a good shot, eh?'

He waved to the guard. 'It's alright Jones, we thought one of the pipes was leaky, but she's good.'

'Course it is,' came the terse reply. 'And now we're losing time.'

'We'll be fine now,' Jenkins said to Dafydd. 'You'll see. Don't fret, I'll help you shovel our way up Talerddig Bank today. The way I'm feeling, we'll not need a banking engine. No-one's going to say you were late on your first express.'

Dafydd followed his driver back. Jenkins was right. Someone had to stay behind to make sure that things got through. To support the army in its fight. The problem was that Dafydd no longer believed he was the man to do that job...

****

'That bloody white feather! We're being punished for that bloody woman!'

Jenkins was ranting all the way to the Vale of Rheidol shed. Dafydd hid his smile, for deep inside he was happy, it was like coming home and not that far from the lodgings for him at the end of the day either.

'And this heap of junk and all,' Jenkins said with a dirty look at the engine.

Dafydd's heart lifted at the sight of the little engine, Rheidol, which stood in front of them. The engine that Dafydd had learnt to fire on. The little coffee pot that had changed Dafydd's life from a labourer at Talybont to a railwayman on the *lein fach* to Devil's Bridge.

'And all because of that woman, I should have left her on the marshes,' Jenkins blustered through Dafydd's dreams.

'Look, go and get yourself a *panad* of tea and leave this to me,' Dafydd said.

Jenkins stopped in surprise; Dafydd had never spoken to him like that before. Quite possibly it was the first time anyone had.

'I know this old girl, she's like an old friend. I fired her when she was on the old Plynlimon and Hafan and then when we were building the Rheidol line. I'll get her set up; you can take it easy.'

Jenkins stared at him for a long time before he finally nodded.

'Right you are then,' he said and walked off. Dafydd gave a sigh of surprise mixed with relief.

'Hello, old girl,' he said to the engine and she hissed gently back at him as he checked her over. The fire was not over high, so Dafydd built it up before tapping the gauges to check the pressure. Topping up with water, he then went to find some decent lumps of spare coal to store in front of the cab. That done, he stood back and looked around the spartan cab. The regulator was such a tiny lever compared to the large bar he was used to in the large engines. Everything appeared in miniature and Dafydd realised how far he had moved on from his days as a fledgling; back when he had fired the small engine as it pulled the construction train up the valley, to the navvies building the line. Jenkins climbed into the cab again.

'All good?'

'All fine. I built her up with a large fire, so there's no stoking before Glanyrafon.'

'The boys say you really did help build the line.'

'Yes, that's right. I spent a long time in this cab.'

'Well, you can take her up then.'

Dafydd stood mouth agape and he shook his head.

'I won't say it again.'

'Alright, you keep an eye on the left side and ... enjoy the view!'

Dafydd stopped. In his panic, he was telling Jenkins his job.

'Well, you know what to do,' he said lamely. There was no response.

Dafydd nodded to himself. There was a letter in his pocket that he had picked up in the morning but hadn't had time to read. He didn't know who it was from, but that revelation would have to wait a bit longer.

'Come on now,' Jenkins was saying. 'It's the milk train. There's few people on it who want to go up the valley and this little girl is simpler than even those Metropolitan tanks the Cambrian wasted money on. It's a chance for you to show your skills - and for me to have a rest.'

Dafydd was shocked. Not only was this the longest speech he had ever heard from Jenkins, but the man was being genial. Dafydd gave a long blast from the whistle and eased the locomotive out from the shed. The echo in the wooden structure reminded Dafydd of chapel.

'That's woken up the town,' Jenkins said. 'And deafened them who are preparing that engine number one.'

'Sorry!' Dafydd shouted back playfully. Jenkins stared ahead.

Rheidol rolled and rattled its way out of Aberystwyth with the almost empty train. Dafydd revelled in every shudder. The feel of being in control and the affection he held for the engine made him forget his worries.

'This little monster rocks like a jig,' Jenkins shouted. 'Why do people like her so much?'

'She's a little marvel. She'll go anywhere and always give her best.'

Jenkins turned away. He said little for the rest of the journey. Dafydd was quite happy looking ahead. He had no time to check the view, although in his mind he knew it would be stunning in the morning sun. They approached the final curve, past water mills and woodland before surging through a cutting and into the station.

Dafydd was hit by a wave of melancholia as he spied the small shack of a station ahead.

He brought the train in, ran the engine around to the other end and moved off to get water. He started to prepare, but Jenkins cut in.

'Take a few minutes off, I'll do all that.'

Dafydd needed no second invitation and walked off through the cutting entrance to the station yard to stare at the Rheidol valley beyond. A flash of pain seared through his mind as memories gathered of past events.

'She's all ready and waiting,' Jenkins' voice broke through the painful thoughts, as the man walked towards him. 'So Dafydd *bach*, you took this one up line like you were born to handle her. Now you're looking like you've been to a funeral.'

Dafydd went to reply, then stopped sharply as the words choked in his throat. He swallowed deeply.

'Here my dream died. I never thought I would feel this bad coming back, but there we are.'

'Alright son,' Jenkins said quietly. 'You can tell me or not. It's up to you.'

Dafydd groaned. 'I fell in love, I really did, but I never got close enough. I mean, every time I did, it was like something was there to pull us apart. This old engine has been more of a girlfriend than I've ever had.' He laughed sadly. 'I mean I saw her on the old Plynlimon tramway when she were called Talybont. Then when I got an apprenticeship at Bagnall's, she came back there, and I went off with her down to this line for the building of it.'

He looked away and bit his knuckles.

'When I came back, I couldn't find Gwen anywhere. Then one day, they ran a special train up here and all the *crachach* were on it. One man brought his mistress, it was my Gwen. And I had to fire the bloody train up here and back...'

'Alright son, she wasn't worth it, obviously.'

Dafydd shook his head. 'She had waited until she was almost in the workhouse. She was forced into service and caught her master's eye, who…. I don't blame her. It's just… I came back here, Mr Jenkins, thinking I was over her, but the first moment I saw her again, I knew it were a lie. And now this…'

He held out a letter, which Jenkins took. Resorting to a small pair of reading glasses from his top pocket, he began to read.

My Dear Dafydd

I was so pleased to see you again after all this time. You look so well and so changed from the runaway youth I met at Trefechan Bridge that day. I am glad that you finally found a trade and learnt to forgive yourself.

I will say that not a day went by without me thinking about you and what had become of you. So much that when I heard you were back, I had to run to see you again. In this I was wrong, and I am so sorry that I caused you pain by doing so. I wish I could make you happy, but I know this is not possible. Please remember that I will always hold you in great affection.

Warm regards

Gwen

Jenkins handed the letter back slowly.

'I have been thinking long and hard about it, Mr Jenkins. I enjoy the firing with you, and I am better for it now. I don't fret about them white feathers, but I need to escape from here and perhaps the Army is the answer. Maybe I will find release there.'

'Bit drastic if you ask me, Dafydd *bach*. Think long and hard about it. I'm sure I can get you a transfer to Mach shed or even a move to the North Western Railway on the North coast?'

Dafydd's lips trembled as he slowly shook his head. Jenkins nodded.

'Now I won't stand in your way if that's your thoughts. But sleep on it one more night and if there's nothing for it, go to the biggest recruitment station in town and tell them you are wanting the Royal Engineers. Forget the Welsh regiments, I would hate to see your talent go to waste. You love this job and they will need your skills out there; you mark my words.'

Chapter Five

Crossed Wires (1916)

Dear Dafydd,

I am so shocked and upset that you joined up. This is all my fault. I should never have called. I swear I did not want to hurt you. If there was anything I could do to change things, you know I would.

If anything happens, I will never forgive myself. Please let me know that you are safe and well.

Take care

Gwen

Dear Gwen

I am fine. Please don't blame yourself. I need to go and help do my bit in France. I'm going there now, but I am not allowed to tell you where. I will write some more when I get there. What you can do for me is keep writing to me, because this will be an odd time and I need to hear some normal stories from home.

I hope you are both well and happy.

Dafydd

The train lurched to a stop for what felt like the hundredth time to Dafydd. He had given up on the idea of catching any sleep, in the sweaty, musty, claustrophobic compartment coach filled with khaki clad men.

Once more he pulled at the neck of his tunic, to stop it digging into his chin. He turned around cap in his hands and stared at the Royal Engineers badge. He was lucky and by God did he know it. The recruiting officer in Aberystwyth had taken his details, before remarking.

'I'm putting you forward for the railway division, son. You are lucky you came to the main recruiting station, a village one would have had you in the foot regiments without so much as a by-your-leave.'

Dafydd thought about his luck. Longmoor camp had been a confused muddle. He had spent most of the time square bashing and digging trenches. What railway work there had been was just basic shunting that even a station pilot would have done in his sleep. He had been told he was being sent back to the Cambrian, yet on the morning of his journey home, he was given new orders.

Dafydd was tired. His driver at Longmoor had been hopeless. One time, Dafydd had had to lean across him to snap shut the drain cocks on the engine and stop the incessant steam blast.

The man looked ashen. 'I'm sorry, I'm just a track ganger really. I only said I could drive to get into this unit. I don't want to be sent to the front.' he finished with a terrified whisper.

Dafydd had taken over driving the locomotive and directing the man, where and when to shovel the coal. In time, he was found out and Dafydd was reprimanded for not reporting the subterfuge. The hapless rogue driver was sent back to the track gang.

'At least he got his wish,' Dafydd mused.

The train stopped again and Dafydd yawned. *How far was Southampton anyway?* He didn't even know where it was, save that it was obviously on the coast, as the boat from France was waiting there.

41

The conversation in the carriage was lively enough, though Dafydd had no desire to join in with it. He was a foreigner, a Welsh-speaking outsider in a sea of English voices. He was being sent out as a replacement, rather than part of a unit and all those that would have offered the hand of friendship appeared to have been left behind long ago at Longmoor barracks.

Dafydd didn't mind the English talk. He had learnt enough from growing up around the lead mines and working on the railway. He was happier in his mother tongue but could follow well enough what was being said.

The conversations were bright and loud, with lots of banter being thrown about. Dafydd looked at the men as they carried on, noting how the bravado hid a lot of nervousness, the tension only broken by the teasing. A bottle was being passed around the carriage. Dafydd stared out of the window as a chorus of 'Goodbye-ee' rang through for the umpteenth time.

'Here, drink this.'

Dafydd looked to find the snout of the open bottle close to his face. The man offering it was smiling, which seemed to dim with uncertainty as Dafydd stared back for a while.

'What's the matter, chum?'

Dafydd took the bottle and a small swig. It was hard liquor and his eyes narrowed. He exhaled sharply.

'Thank you.'

A cheer went up and the bottle passed on. The stranger clapped Dafydd on the shoulder. 'A Welshman? Well you don't get many of them to the pound here. Do you speak English?' Dafydd nodded. 'Where are you bound, me duck?'

'Boulogne.'

The man shrugged. 'It's all foreign to me. We're the Northumberlands, but in truth, me and me mates are frum Nottingham, like. We was given a choice of regiments, as the Sherwoods was full and they needed us to fill in where there's gaps. We chose the Northumberlands. Simple really - Newcastle play in the same colours as County. Smoke?'

Dafydd shook his head. The man took a roll-up from a Woodbine tin and bent to light it.

'So, who you with, mate?' he said blowing a cloud of blue smoke.

'Engineers. Railway division. Don't know any more than that.'

'Railways? Why didn't you stay at home? Nice cushy number, that one.'

Dafydd paused. 'Lloyd George asked me to go and shovel coal in a foreign land, I suppose.'

The soldier chuckled. 'Well, you Welshies stick together, don't you? You could have picked somewhere warm though.'

'Warm enough in the cab with the fire going,' Dafydd replied.

'I never thought of that. Here lads, this one's shovelling coal for us so we can stick one on the Jerries.'

There was a smatter of laughter. The man smiled, patted Dafydd's shoulder and moved to talk to his friends. Dafydd felt glad of the break, but at the same time he felt a pang of regret that he was alone in a crowd once again.

The soldiers began to sing 'Blaydon Races' and Dafydd went back to staring out of the window. The bravado couldn't hide the fact they were all scared of the unknown that lay ahead. Dafydd spoke to no-one else for the rest of the journey, choosing to join the ranks of sullen resignation. He tried to sleep and let the banter wash over him.

****

The port was in chaos. A forest of rifles, slung on shoulders, milled around the dockside. Corporals who had finally found their vocation in life stood screaming orders to the masses.

Dafydd stepped back and listened carefully, straining for the name of his destination to be shouted out. He moved quickly to join a line making for a gangplank. He wondered where he might grab a cup of tea when an over-eager corporal button-holed him.

'You sure you want Boo-Loyn?'

Dafydd nodded.

'Where's your rifle then?'

Dafydd turned his shoulder to show the railway corps badge on his lapel.

'He's Welsh, corp. He won't answer you.' a familiar voice from the line piped up.

'Bloody Taffs,' the corporal muttered and moved on.

Dafydd looked down the line to see the soldier from the train. The man gave a cheery wave in reply before turning back to his friends.

The journey was uneventful. The overcrowding meant he was forced to sit on the ship's wooden deck and watch the world go by. It helped overcome any feelings of nausea, although some were more delicate. At least they have a clear run to the handrail up here, Dafydd thought. Better than those lodged below decks.

The voyage became monotonous. Dafydd looked at the faint outline of land on the horizon and wondered what it would all come to. Not for the first time was he doubting his impulsive move to the army. He thought of his family and the cafe and once again asked himself why he had left them.

Then Gwen's face appeared into his daydream and his eyes closed with pain. Tears welled up and he wished he couldn't open his eyes again or at least until they had dried. The rhythm of the ship and the time spent travelling was making him feel drowsy and before long he was dozing.

Boulogne was worse than the docks in England, as far as Dafydd was concerned. The massed crowds were still a chaotic spectacle, but as so many ships appeared to be disembarking their human cargo at the same time, it was inevitable.

The corporals marshalling the soldiers at the dockside were barking orders at the docile but surly mass of khaki, like incompetent sheepdogs.

Farther down the docks, Dafydd spied a small tank engine moving slowly towards a ship with a flat wagon. A field gun was suspended in mid- air waiting to be winched onto the truck.

The engine looked British in outline, although the crew wore blue serge. The letters 'R O D' could be seen on the side of the tank engine where it was washed of some of its grime. It looked as if it was going to be a long tedious process and Dafydd wondered if it wasn't more of an attractive place to be than what lay ahead, for most of the people surrounding him.

'Get in line!'

A voice bawled at breaking point through Dafydd's musing and made him start.

'I'm Engineers. Where do I go?' Dafydd asked.

'In that bloody line. You daft or something?'

He grabbed a bewildered Dafydd and pushed him into the middle of a queue.

'Stay there!'

'Like to see him fight in the bloody trenches,' someone close by muttered. 'He wouldn't last bloody five minutes.'

The line of men seemed endless, but in time, Dafydd could see it snaking towards a warehouse. As he tried to relax and watch the small shunting engine, a car horn blurted out and he turned to find a khaki coloured car approaching at speed. A few of the men had to jump out of the way as it drove on regardless. A driver sat impassively at the front and two officers relaxed in the back looking straight ahead. They left in the wake of a torrent abuse from the throng.

It took hours, but as the line moved on, Dafydd saw that inside their destination warehouse, three desks were sited in the middle. Behind each, a sergeant sat with a sheaf of papers scribbling away.

When it came to Dafydd's turn, he looked down at the sergeant and saw that his face radiated extreme boredom. The fingers of his right hand drummed in irritation.

'Name?' he snapped.

'Dafydd Thomas.'

The man's furrowed eyebrows darkened and Dafydd watched him write the word 'David'.

'It's Dafydd.'

'Occupation,' the sergeant curtly scythed through the argument.

'Railway Corps, engineers.'

The man looked up and gave a withering stare. 'Occupation.'

The animosity threw Dafydd and he blankly looked back at him.

'What do you do? Are you a driver?'

'I done some driving at Longmoor,' Dafydd replied helpfully. 'But I'm normally firing on the Cambrian.'

The sergeant did not look up again as he scribbled away. He tore off a piece of paper.

'Go there for further instructions. Next.'

Dafydd felt upset at the impersonal nature of the man and began to get angry. Everyone was being sent to the front to risk their lives, while some sergeant on a cushy number was treating them like dirt. He turned to tell the man what he thought.

The sergeant's left sleeve was empty and pinned to his tunic. A deep scar crept up his face to the ear. The man looked up and stared back at Dafydd almost in challenge. For a second, they locked gazes then Dafydd nodded to the man.

'Thank you, sergeant,' he muttered. He turned and began his search for the wine warehouse on the address. He hoped it was full of bottles, he felt like he needed a drink.

****

He was one of a dozen in the warehouse, mostly track workers. All just wanting their sleep. Sacking was commandeered for rough billets. Dafydd found a niche where a wine barrel was missing in a stack. He grabbed some sacking to feather his nest and then jumped up to sit back in the impromptu armchair. It got him little sleep and his back was on fire when he was roused by a corporal.

They were put on a train moving east. Dafydd observed the train crew as they walked past him on the platform. They spoke French to each other, which made Dafydd more confused. If French drivers still worked the railway, what was he doing here? Dafydd managed to grab a corner seat and drifted off to sleep again.

The journey was very haphazard, but Dafydd managed to keep the momentum of the catnap going until the train jolted to a halt with such a force that Dafydd was nearly thrown from his seat.

He looked out of the window at the fields, it was like he hadn't left England.

'You're a cool one,' his neighbour remarked. 'All of us are as nervous as hell, but you are sleeping like nothing' s happening.'

'It's because I'm tired, bach,' Dafydd replied. 'And all I'm doing is the same job as I'm doing back home.'

He didn't want to talk and certainly didn't need a cigarette from the amount of tobacco smoke in the air. He reached for his side pocket to retrieve the letter, he still got a thrill from reading.

Dear Daf,

I hope this finds you well. I know the square bashing must be boring, but at least you get out in the fresh air! And you are still on your engines, doing what you enjoy. Keep safe, we all think about you and pray for your quick return, cariad. Stay lucky.

Sioned.

The training at Longmoor involved a lot of marching day and night in the parade yard - or so it had felt. Just square bashing. The one time he had been on an engine was to move a coach of top brass around the camp. Most of his colleagues had been sent back home on reserve.

Lucky? Dafydd didn't feel it.

Chapter Six

Flanders

'We're here,' the neighbour nudged him. Dafydd looked out at the station, past the scrum of kit bags and bodies as people made ready to get off.

He looked around for station signs, they appeared absent.

'Where are we?' he asked.

'Borre,' came the reply. 'Looks like a dump and all. Lives up to its name right enough.'

Dafydd looked at a maze of lines leading from the station. A few columns of smoke gave the impression of activity. An overeager corporal came to shoo him down the platform. As soon as it was clear where Dafydd was bound, he was given precise directions by a nonchalant jerk of the thumb and left alone.

Dafydd slung his kit bag over his shoulder and set off down the platform and onto a cinder path to the depot. A wiry grey-haired sergeant came out of a lean-to and intercepted him.

'Thomas sir, reporting for duty.'

'That's fine, but you call me sergeant son.'

'Sorry sir, sergeant.'

'You're late, son,'

Dafydd was speechless, as he checked his watch.

'By about two bloody years,' the sergeant replied.

'I came as quick as I could, sergeant.'

A ghost of a smile played on the man's lips.

'You're also a corporal, so get some stripes from stores. Your billet is over there. Find a spare bunk and God help you if you snore.'

'What? Behind the trucks?'

The sergeant laughed. 'In the trucks. Try and pick the one the horses haven't slept in. Are you ready to learn the road? Well, no choice. Take that engine, it's off to Wipers. Go tell the crew to call out the route as they go.'

'Wipers?'

'Ieper, Ypres. Whatever you want to call it.'

'But that's the front.'

'This is a war, son. What do you expect? Captain is too busy for you now; you can report to him on your way back. Which railway are you?'

'Cambrian.'

'Well, we're a mixed bunch here, Mainly Great Eastern and Great Northern. A couple of Lankys. No company rivalries or you'll answer to me. See to it then.'

The sergeant moved off and Dafydd took off his kit bag, resting it at his feet. The area was bustling with active locomotives. It was tidy in appearance, but what made it alien to Dafydd he realised, was not the flow of khaki clad people everywhere. The town looked different to him. The rooves were redder and the buildings perhaps more angular. All the time, there was a rumble of thunder in the background a long way off.

'Oi, Thomas! Don't you know there's a war on?'

The sergeant's shout broke through Dafydd's reverie and with a sigh he shouldered his kit bag and made for his billet.

He found an empty bunk in a truck that faintly smelt of horse manure, then went off to find the freight engine that was standing in a siding. Wisps of steam curled from the wheels up to the steps of the cab as Dafydd approached from the rear. In the evening light, he could see the letters WD overprinted on the livery of the owning company. The khaki brown colour of the engine made Dafydd think of sewers.

He was looking forward to his bunk, as the long journey had caught up with him. There was a sound of someone shovelling coal in the cab. Dafydd hoped the crew weren't French, he didn't feel up to trying to speak a third language, not yet anyhow.

Dafydd looked inside the cab and spied a short, wiry man with a handlebar moustache digging at the coal with what seemed like pure venom. A roll-up was lodged behind his ear, waiting for his moment of rest. The man glared at everything he looked at and Dafydd groaned inwardly at the thought of sharing the footplate with someone so angry with the world.

'So what you looking at, son?' the man snapped without stopping work.

'I'm supposed to join you to learn the road,' Dafydd replied evenly. He wasn't going to provoke a fight, but he sure as hell wasn't in the mood to be pushed around.

'Well, you best come up then.'

Dafydd climbed into the cab and looked around. He didn't feel it was a bad place for space or shelter. It felt a bit like the goods engines back home.

'Looks alright this old girl,' Dafydd said cheerfully. 'Scottish one?'

The fireman shovelled in a bit more coal, checked the gauges and shut the firebox door.

'She's Belgian, son. Designed by McIntosh, the Caledonian man. She's like a Jumbo, but with a Westinghouse brake. You here to gossip or to learn the road, sapper?'

'I'm a corporal,' Dafydd replied evenly. 'And I'm here to fire.'

The man had grabbed an old broom and was sweeping the coal dust off the cab floor.

'Well, I'm the fireman here, son. We've been told to train a driver and no fireman that I know makes corporal, so seems to me you're either not well briefed or you're wet behind the ears. Which is it to be?'

He grabbed an oil can, climbed down to the track and moved to the front of the engine. Dafydd sighed and looked around the cab. The controls all made sense, a slightly different layout to that on the Cambrian engines. Nothing he couldn't master. What worried Dafydd more was that although he knew how to drive, he had not done much of it. If he made a hash of it, would they send him to the front?

A movement at the cab steps saw a newcomer climb up into the cab. A stocky man who struggled with his footing. In the end, he crawled onto the cab floor and slowly pulled himself up, staggering for a few steps to keep himself steady. He squinted at Dafydd and a wave of alcoholic breath washed over him as the man slurred.

'Oo are you then?'

'I'm Corporal Thomas, here to learn the road.'

The man blew his cheeks out before looking to stagger towards the cab side, slapping his hand until he managed to pull down a wooden seat at the second attempt and collapsed onto it.

'Well, it's a straight road,' he said, his hand flapping around at nothing. 'Just follow the rails and you'll get there.'

The fireman had climbed back into the cab and was looking at the driver with contempt.

'And you watch out for this one,' the driver sniggered. 'Tom Hebdyke. A real bad egg and shit stirrer. Never trust Northerners, Taff. Wanky Lanky Yorky, he is'

Tom muttered and grabbed a shovel, moving to the tender.

'Never trust 'em,' the driver continued, his cheeks turning redder as he grew more excited. 'Was a driver once, that one. Got pulled down to fireman for fighting in the ranks. Should have been shot, ain't that right, you Northern bastard?'

Tom took a few quick steps forward and smacked the driver across the jaw. He grabbed the man by the hair and pulled his head back. The driver was giggling, despite the pain.

'Ooh I got you now, Hebdyke! You're for it, matey. Striking a superior officer with a witness looking on. That's mutiny! They'll shoot yer or you'll be up the front and over the top with a Jerry bayonet up your arse, with the rest of them.'

'Listen, you cockney shithouse,' Tom growled back. 'You're standing here drunk on parade and unable to carry out your duties. That's dereliction. You could be shot at dawn or sent up t'front just as easy. So, I suggest you go sit in t'tender and sleep it off and we'll say no more 'bout it, Sam Cartwright.'

The two men glared at each other for a long time, before Cartwright smiled and stood up. He stumbled into a mock bow and grinned at Dafydd before he climbed over the coal pile and disappeared behind it. The faint sounds of him singing 'Pop goes the Weasel' could be heard, as Tom turned to Dafydd.

'Right then son, you're on. You drive and I'll have to teach you t'road as I go.'

'Tom, I can't. I mean, I can, but I'm a fireman just passed. Back home I'm only starting out, like.'

Tom thumped the cab with his fist and muttered a curse. 'But you're down as a driver!'

'Don't know why, Tom. At Longmoor I was a fireman. I helped a driver once, but he were a fake and I took over. I don't know; at the port they asked me and he was pushing like. 'Have you driven? Have you driven?'

Tom put his fist to his head and then chuckled.

'So, there's you, a new fireman as a driver and me ten years driving top link expresses on t' Lanky, as a fireman. It's not much better a mix than that, lad.'

He stepped forward and clapped Dafydd on the shoulder.

'It's up to you, son. I'll not drive for th'army again. Not after what they done to me. You can drive and I'll teach you t'road and what to do and I'll get some peace from that cockney arsehole. What do you say?'

Dafydd hesitated and Tom frowned.

'Chance of a lifetime, son. Don't waste it.'

Dafydd nodded and gave a nervous smile. 'Alright.'

'What's your name, son?'

'Dafydd Thomas.'

'You'll be David before us war's out. Military is not that good at listening.'

'Call me Daf then.'

'Alright Daf,' Tom peered out of one of the cab spectacle windows. 'We've got the road. Now it's time you found your feet.' He unscrewed the tender brake and shouted. 'Brake's off.'

Dafydd grabbed the gear to put the engine into forward and put his hand on the regulator. He couldn't resist the tingle of pleasure that thrilled down his arm. The regulator was stiff and as he slowly increased the pressure, it suddenly bucked up. The engine appeared to give a great sigh before a throaty chuff of disappointment. Then it bucked and a rapid chuffing sound was made as the wheels slipped on the rail.

'Regulator off,' Tom shouted. 'Ok, you're moving now. Inches only, but now you know the measure of the regulator. Take it easy and have another try.'

The second attempt was smoother and Dafydd breathed a huge sigh of relief, nodding to the signalman as they passed.

'Clear on the crossing!' Tom shouted and they were soon rumbling over it and away.

The sky was grey, but the sun was doing its best to break through the clouds. A white circle in the shadows. The line was clear ahead and Dafydd looked behind at the freight trucks. The guard waved back from the safety of the birdcage vantage point above his van. Dafydd ventured a quick look into the tender and saw the crumpled form of Cartwright fast asleep with his head back and mouth open. Dafydd imagined the snores. Images swept into his mind, of sneaking into the village pub as a child. Seeing an old timer slumped in the corner, jug in hand.

'You'll need to ease her off a bit,' Tom said. 'Don't worry over Cartwright, I'll rouse him before we get to t'Wipers. Let the loco do t' work for you, she's a good lass this one.'

Dafydd felt more relaxed as the journey continued. He let Tom do all the talking and looked out for landmarks around the track. There was a bleakness about the place and for a second, Dafydd was at a loss to put his finger on it.

'It should be greener...' he muttered.

Although nature had begun to make its return to the land, it was still patchy. Dead hulks of trees, leafless and forlorn stood like withered sentinels in a pock-marked land that should have been neat farm fields. A long ridge lay in the distance, like a shadow on the horizon. What grass there was only showed in small clumps. Rubble and shattered walls stood in place of what had once been proud buildings.

'Keep your eye on the road. Crossings clear, you need to take her down a notch or she'll run away from you.' Tom's voice broke through the reverie.

Despite what they had seen in the papers, it didn't look too bad to Dafydd.

'You'll need to open her up for the climb here.'

Dafydd looked ahead, thinking of the green valleys on the climb to Talerddig in the middle of Wales. He gave a start as he broke his daydream. He so wanted to be back there. Aberystwyth felt such a haven in comparison to this. He dreamed of the cafe and Harri's laughter showering him like a peal of bells. Then he was looking into Gwen's eyes...

'Don't worry for the smoke, lad. That's my problem, you just keep her going.'

'Signal's against us here,' Dafydd said and eased the loco down, bringing them to a halt with a smooth manner.

'You can tell you're new over here, son.'

'Why's that?'

'You care about the way you stop and start. All the guards will love you.'

'How long do we normally wait?' Dafydd asked.

'Could be minutes, could be hours.' Tom shrugged. 'Could be anything. Congestion, damaged track from gunfire, retreat. Some RTO can't manage the line, more like.'

'What of our passenger? He's had a right skinfull.'

Tom laughed. 'He'll be out for hours yet. If not, I'll just have to lay him out again, eh?'

He picked up his broom to sweep the coal dust off the cab floor. It seemed to Dafydd that Tom always needed to be busy.

'When I were a green 'un, like you, I'd have struggled to do what you just done.'

'Good teacher, you are,' Dafydd replied.

There was a silence, as the two men set about their tasks, whilst struggling for something to say. Eventually, Dafydd reached into his pocket.

'Chocolate?'

'Aye,' Tom replied, taking the proffered piece. 'Happen I will. Five Boys chocolate? Now that's one I haven't seen in a while.'

'I made a mess of the start of the run and no mistake,' Dafydd complained.

'You were nervous, son. Thrown in t'deep end with a bastard for a fireman...'

'No, you've been fine, Tom.'

'Careful lad or they'll pair you off with me as soon as you can spit. Someone tried to bully me, someone that had made trouble all around and I stood up to him. And I paid the price. Now no-one'll work with me.'

'I'll work with you, Tom,' Dafydd replied then added quickly. 'We can pool our pay and share it equal, like. Only fair then, isn't it?'

'You're a rum 'un,' said Tom as he rubbed his thumb across his lined forehead. But I think you're alright. We'll get by, you and me.'

'Well, isn't this cosy?' Cartwright's voice lumbered from the tender. 'What will the CO think of this?'

Dafydd flushed as he turned to face the man.

'They're not going to know. Because I'll have you up before the redcaps for drunkenness and assaulting an officer. You'll be too busy at the punishment block to think.'

'How you gonna do that? I didn't hit you, Taff.'

'No, but Tom will back me up. Then we'll say that you attacked both of us and we had to tie you down.'

'I saw that,' came a voice. The guard had appeared at the cab steps. 'If they ask, Cartwright, I saw it. Face up to it, you sleep today off, then you get on with the war. Nobody gets any bother.'

Cartwright scowled and swore.

'You get that one for free. Next one will cost you,' Tom said. 'Now keep out of t'way.'

'You've got the road, had it a while,' the guard said to Dafydd. 'Let's finish this run, so I can get meself a brew - or better.'

'There,' said Tom as the guard retreated. 'Told you, you'd make friends. If Old Morris sticks by you, you've got everyone. Let's get sorted. If there's time, I think you should get to know Wipers, see what we're up against.'

Dafydd coaxed the engine onwards. It did not feel it needed much persuasion. As he looked forward along the locomotive body, his eyes were drawn to the khaki mud colour of the engine once more. It was such a contrast from the sleek-black silhouette of Cambrian engines. The ground around him appeared pock-marked again with more holes, many filled with water.

Now Dafydd caught sight of a ditch. As they approached, he saw it appeared to be a zigzag of lines. Was it an open sewer? Dafydd felt dirty, just thinking about it. Then he was past it, and the images of duckboards, sandbags and debris had him realising that he had seen his first trench complex.

The scene continued to be that of devastation. Pockmarks abounded, Dafydd thought there seemed to be holes than patches of level ground and everywhere was mud. More charred trees skeletal in their appearance blurred past him.

'Was that a front line?' Dafydd shouted.

'No, it was set up as a defensive line,' Tom replied. 'In case they needed to fall back. Blown to buggery by t'German guns now. Look over there at that mess. Artillery set up there to pound German lines. Only t'Germans got wind of where they were first.'

Dafydd felt cold, as he saw a heap of debris. Mangled barbed wire spiralled above the ragged layers of burst sandbags and an upturned cart. Dafydd could almost feel the pain. He spied a horse carcase, the legs sticking upwards.

'I guess the horses were left to rot?' Dafydd said.

'Doubt it, there's precious little food for t'Belgian folk that's left here. Good to be a railwayman, son. Don't forget that, you'd be out there else.'

Dafydd felt numb, he'd had a glimpse of an image and it stuck fast with him. A flash of khaki, a torn sleeve from a uniform. It hadn't looked empty.

They moved on and the road ahead seemed to be heading towards a large flat empty space. It was grey, but then everywhere appeared grey on the landscape. It was beginning to spit with rain, which only added to the gloom.

Dafydd spied sidings ahead, containing several wagons. A goods spur, in the middle of nowhere. The burnt-out rubble-strewn shells of buildings were slowly increasing in number. Dafydd wondered if it had been a village once, around the railway or perhaps bigger.

'You're at th'edge of Wipers town centre,' Tom shouted. 'This is as far as we go.'

'This is the station?' Dafydd asked.

'Aye and now I need my flamin' brew!'

Dafydd looked at the heaps of rubble that had once been dwellings. Beams and posts stuck out of the nearest one at a crazy angle. Debris was everywhere. He briefly felt irritated that nobody had bothered to clear the mess. Then he realised the rumbling sound in the distance was still there. Looking out on the horizon, he saw a cloud of smoke, followed by another puff and another.

'It's not Liverpool Street, Taff,' Cartwright said from the tender. 'Welcome to hell.'

'If this is hell,' Tom said. 'Think of what the poor buggers at t'front are going through. We'll be off to a siding now. We won't go any further. The Jerries love t'main station so much; it's on their daily list for shelling. We'll get th'engine coaled and watered and then wait for t'next duty. Probably just taking th'empties back, but to be honest, you never know.'

They were stuck for a while, Tom kept himself busy by sweeping the cab floor yet again and tidying. Dafydd grabbed an oil can and went track-side to check the motion of the engine and its lubrication. He may as well have arrived on the moon; the landscape was so alien. He fingered a letter in his pocket and, as soon as he was able, reached for Sioned's message. He wanted to see the words and feel the warmth in them. To think of home and family. He stiffened as he looked at the envelope; he had taken out Gwen's letter instead. The ache started in his heart once more. He knew it would hurt, but once more he read the message, and the memories flooded back.

'We've got t'road, son. Let's go off and rest this old girl. If we get some rest time ourselves here, I'll show you Wipers.'

Dafydd quickly resisted the temptation to run his fingers over the words and carefully put the letter back in his pocket.

'Alright, Tom, I'll be with you now.'

Now wasn't the time to wallow in past hurt, he had a job to fulfil and much to learn. He would take the engine back to Borre, to Berlin itself as far as he cared. If he was to be a driver, he'd work to be the best there was. Then he'd go back home, and they'd all look at him differently. He could see their faces, although try as he might not to, the proudest face in his daydream was Gwen's.

Chapter Seven

Wipers

Dear Dafydd,

I hope this finds you well wherever you are. I'm still worried for you, so just keep your head down and stay behind the lines for my sake. The master of the house is now over in France also with the Royal Welch. There are no men left here, bar the old, the infirm and the foolish.

I see your sister from time to time. She disapproves of me and I don't blame her. Angharad smiles at me, but the world smiles with her. I do not see Donato, but town is good for talk and he is known for his hard work and helping others.

I hope this finds you well, I hope this finds you. If it does, please let me know you are alright. I worry about those I know who are in France. Please keep yourself safe. I do care, cariad.

Gwen

Dafydd held the letter out. A part of him wanted to put it in the firebox. But he knew it wouldn't happen.

'How the 'ell did they know I was here?' he said. 'I arrive at Borre. I'm five minutes there then off on a train to bloody Wipers and someone gives me a letter at Poperinge. How did they know?'

'Simple, son,' Tom replied. 'You're on t'railway, you're Welsh and it sat there knowing at some point it'd catch you. You'd be at one shed or t'other.'

The pair had finished off and been sent into Ypres city for stores whilst they waited for the next run.

'Right Daf, a bit of scran and we'll be ready for the return. You had an easy start. I've known it to take three times that.'

Tom took them through paths between the piles of rubble, that resembled a giant building site. Dafydd noticed that a small line of local people were standing on the side of the path, selling whatever they could.

'I didn't think the Belgies had anything left to sell,' he said. Tom smiled grimly.

'You'd be surprised. Not everything is destroyed. Most things, but there's still fields as can be worked in pockets. Trenches move position so slowly that them locals adapt as best they can. Man's got to live.'

He went to an old woman, selling a small bag of apples and bought two, passing one to Dafydd.

'There's some as would haggle, but these folk are desperate.'

Dafydd looked at an old fragmented church tower. The great gothic arches were now reduced to the windowsills in places. He thought of the mediaeval castle back home in Aberystwyth. Sandcastles on the beach, trampled on then smoothed by the sea sprung to mind, though it seemed the Germans had done a better job.

'Must have been a nice church,' he said. Tom snorted.

'Church? It was the bloody cloth Hall, been there for 700 years until we came along. The Belgians were proud as hell of it. Now just look at it. If you need to remember why we are here, remember this street. Remember these people.'

A group of Tommies stood outside a house waiting, joking and smoking.

'Is that where we can get food?'

Tom spat. 'No, that's where those as can't wait until they are home go dip their wick. Remember that and all, the levels people are forced down to for surviving.'

'Do you hate the Germans, Tom?'

Tom paused, then reached for a tobacco tin in his lapel pocket and took out a pre-made roll-up, putting it behind one ear.

'Do I hate Germans? No. Armies? Too bloody right. They've all forgotten why they're here. I want you to take this scene in, son. Treat them Belgies with respect. Army looks down on them and if that's so, what the bloody hell are we here for?'

They found a canteen and quickly digested the watery broth that was on offer.

'There's more in this tea than the soup,' Dafydd complained.

Tom removed his hat to scratch his balding pate, before grabbing the roll-up from behind his ear. He lit up and sat back blowing out a satisfying drag of smoke.

'Get used to it, son. It's hardly the Ritz. Makes a change from Bully Beef at any road.'

'Is Cartwright going to be a problem?'

'Now? No. Later? Who knows? Not everyone's to be trusted here.'

'So, what's Borre like then?'

Tom scratched his ear. 'Didn't they tell you? We're moving to Poperinge. New base, closer to the front.'

'Nobody's told me nothing.'

'Welcome to war, son. Welcome to war.'

On their return, Dafydd was handed another letter. He recognised the writing. He decided it would wait for the end of the day, when all the madness had finished.

Dear Gwen,

I hope you are well. I am writing to let you know I am safe. We are in ־ר־ר־ר־ר־ר־ר. It is a lovely town - or was once. The work is fine but never a change from home, just more of it. I hope you are being looked after and the boy is well. Be yourself and be proud.

Dafydd

****

Dear Dafydd,

I was so pleased to get your letter. Write to me again as soon as you can. I'm wishing I could turn back time and undo things, but there we are. Now the master is gone, the mistress of the house has sent me away. She pays for my lodging, which is something, so I'm back with Mrs. Owen in Trefechan and with less of the finery, but more of the love!

Next time you are back, bring some potatoes and we'll go bake them at the lime kiln. The world is so grim now. Too much that comes out is black these days. There is no laughter, no joy in the place, no pierrots at the castle, no donkeys on the promenade. No tourists paddle along the seashore. The pier is quiet, save for the injured staying here in their blue uniforms. I feel so sad for them. Perhaps I should become an auxiliary nurse and help them. Scrubbing floors would be a good way of paying for my sins...'

Be a nurse, Dafydd thought. *Your smile would cure many ills.* Once again, he cursed himself that he had written back, but he could not have done otherwise.

There was no way he could stop himself. However bitter-sweet it felt, it was still a comfort. He couldn't help feeling the warmth of knowing she cared, even if he was aware it wasn't to the level he wanted. Dafydd held the pair of socks enclosed.

They would be on his feet pretty soon. He wondered if he would ever take them off.

'So, this is the run then? Wipers and back?'

Tom shook his head.

'Hardly, this may be double track, but when there's a build-up, there's a jam of trains. Ammo, guns, troops one-way. Empties and casualties, t'other. There's two of these lines going forward and many lines in-between. Then who knows when they may decide to build another relief line. There's more track around here than roads, as they're all blown to buggery and mud.'

'Well, I wasn't expecting a holiday. Where's Cartwright?'

'Don't know, don't care. If he's not here when we get the off, he can go to hell and suffer the consequences for all I care. Here, see this Rupert coming our way? He's an RTO - regional Train operative. He'll give us the orders for our next run. Wherever and whenever that will be...'

'You're taking empties back to Hazebrouck,' the officer said on his arrival. 'Then await further orders.'

'Where's Driver Cartwright?' asked Dafydd.

'Already gone, said you were his relief.'

Tom gave Dafydd a knowing glance.

'Right you are sir. We're ready for it. Chance to fill our urns with tea before?'

'Yes, you'd best be quick. It's a busy road and you'll have a few waiting stops on the way.'

They arrived back at Borre five hours later. Dafydd was glad of the dark that hid the ruined landscape. The charred remnants of trees that dotted the fields, the angry sea of mud criss-crossed by trenches, duckboards and debris. The small pools of muddy water and the overall feeling of death and pain.

'I'm for me bunk,' Tom said on arrival.

'No, you're not!' the voice of the station RTO came from the platform. 'Company has moved to Poperinge, all packed up and ready. You can turn this one round and take her over there.'

Tom slammed his shovel into the coal.

'Careful, Sapper,' the RTO snapped.

'I'm stoking her up sir, that's all. We ran the fire down to make it easier to put her away.'

'Alright, see you're safe and get ready for the road.' The officer left and Tom threw his shovel down to the floor.

Tom, do you want the regulator?' Dafydd asked. 'You can take over and say I'm worn out. Give you a rest, won't it? I'll shovel.'

Tom sighed. 'No son, you're alright, I've said I'll never drive here again. One more leg then and the cattle truck will seem like t'Ritz after all. Off we go then.'

'Why are we moving to Poperinge, do you think?'

'No idea, son. There's no rhyme nor reason when it gets to us. No notice, no explanation, we just do.'

Chapter Eight

Poperinge

Dear Gwen,

I hope you are well. It's all very confusing here. I can't tell you much about why, but I think a lot of it is because I'm new. Just to say I'm safe and well and made new friends. Tom, my fireman is a good man. He's very supportive. Yes, I'm a driver now. Not the best, but Tom helps me out. I have got your socks and I am wearing them now. They are very warm and remind me of home…

They remind me of you, Dafydd thought sadly. He wished he was telling her this, not writing it.

'Is that to your sweetheart?' Tom asked.

'No, just a friend,' Dafydd replied too quickly.

'Are you sure?' Tom asked, tapping his pipe to his nose. 'Your eyes say different.'

'Alright boy, you got me. It's the girl I've loved for years but have never been with,' *bar once,* Dafydd thought to himself and the pain rose in his chest.

I should have taken her to Stafford. I should never have left her.

'Why've you never gone past that? What are you now, thirty?'

'Thirty-six. Because I never got over her. Still haven't.'

'Why? She still a spinster?'

'She went into service, then became a mistress.'

'And you still have owt to do with her?'

Dafydd sighed. 'It was my fault. I should have taken her with me when I got an apprenticeship. She was forced to choose service or the workhouse.'

'Do you feel guilty?'

'I don't know.'

'Would she have gone with yer?'

'I suppose not.'

'Then it were her choice, son.'

Dafydd sighed. It was an argument he could not counter. It would not stop him writing though.

...Them houses in Trefechan are good and sturdy. Keep you warm at night. Look after you and your child and don't worry about the rest. If you get stuck, go ask Donato for help. Tell him I sent you, show him this letter...

'Tell her the wagon you bunk in smells of horse shit. the crew you share it with smells of horse shit and your daily ration tastes of bloody horse shit,' Tom muttered, moving to his bunk and rolling to one side, his back to the world. 'Welcome to Poperinge.'

****

'Talbot House,' Tom pointed to a large town house on the cobbled street. It had an oblong frontage and large slightly recessed windows. A welcoming lamp hung outside, slim and curved, a handle at one end and a spout at the other. Dafydd thought the place looked quite ordinary, although there was little activity around it, apart from the odd coming and going of a soldier, placing his hat back on his head as he left.

'Are you sure it's not a top-class brothel?' Dafydd asked. Tom boomed a laugh in reply.

'What? Toc H? I don't think the Reverend would approve.'

'Reverend?'

'Tubby Clayton. He runs the place as a club for men on leave to come and relax. For them at the front, it's a break from the reality of the horrors.'

'Is this going to be our gaff then?'

Tom shook his head. 'You picking up Tommy slang already? No, we'll get precious time away from that horse box. They'll want us on call all t'time, especially when there's a push on and they want all things moved ter t'front. We'll come here when we can, though. It's worth it.'

Tom nodded towards a man that was approaching them.

'Jim,' he acknowledged. Dafydd was surprised to see it was their sergeant.

'Lads,' he said with a nod and made towards a steep flight of stairs.

Tom indicated for Dafydd to move to another room, where a few comfortable chairs were arranged in a haze of blue pipe smoke, a calling card from a previous occupant. Tom took to an armchair and gestured to Dafydd to sit also.

'There's a few rules here,' Tom said. 'For first, everyone's equal. This is a Christian building and Tubby's got it set as read. Everyone's equal here, in God's eyes, so there's no ranks.'

'What?'

'Did you not see the sign at the door? *All rank abandon ye, who enter here.* Them's the rules, son. You can call Sergeant Macrae, "Jim" here, but do it outside and you're for the high jump!'

Dafydd nodded. He was so comfortable in the armchair, that he would have agreed to anything at that moment.

'Secondly, these people respect us, so we respect them. If you're not clean and presentable, if you're lousy – you're not coming in.'

Dafydd knew he wasn't suffering from lice, but Tom's words still made him want to itch.

'There's three floors here for us. Ground floor, you can relax and chat, drink tea and all, that sort of thing. First floor is your library. You can go and lose yourself in books and forget what's going on.'

Dafydd thought about the idea of being on his own in a quiet place. Whilst they had sat, a dozen people had been in and out, all wearing an expression of calm. It was almost unbearable how happy those who came through the door looked. Just a release. One looked ready to cry.

'Top floor is your chapel,' Tom was saying. 'If you need to talk ter t'big man upstairs, you go there.'

'You mean Tubby?'

'I mean Tubby's boss. Come on lad. I'll get you a cuppa. Tin cup will be washed and clean in here by those as have used them. Have a look around.'

Dafydd nodded and made for the stairs, electing to start at the very top of the building. The room he found himself in was quiet and empty. A series of benches arranged like pews filled the room. A large aisle led to a cloth-covered altar. A drape above focussed his eyes to it. A single tall cross took pride of place to the side of this, fixed to the wall. A man knelt in front of the altar with his head bowed. On hearing Dafydd, he turned.

'Sorry sir,' Dafydd muttered.

The man smiled. 'No rank here, my boy. Welcome to Toc H.' He got up and walked towards Dafydd with his hand outstretched in greeting.

'Tubby's the name, how are you?'

'Dafydd Thomas, sir,' Dafydd said quickly, wincing at the mistake. Without thinking, he checked his hand for grease and wiped them on his trousers. The man smiled again.

'It takes a while to get used to and don't worry, I've seen dirt before. Welshman? I thought your boys were further south.'

'Engineers, si...Tubby. Railway Operating Division. I drive trains.'

'The dream of many a young boy. So how do you find it here?'

'I've just been to Ypres.'

'I understand, David. Please feel free to stay for as long as you wish. I have my own moments of reflection here.' Dafydd blinked in incomprehension and the reverend looked around his domain, for a moment looking sad.

'Here, I can give thanks that I am miles from the trenches and that I have the means to provide small comforts for those who do not have this luxury.'

He started packing away a keyboard in a suitcase. 'However, it would be very remiss of me not to go out and see our men in the trenches from time to time. I am thankful that this little bellows organ packs away nicely. You're new here, aren't you?'

Dafydd nodded. 'Yes, but you must get them all the time, coming in like me.'

'Yes, we do, it's the way people scour the place with their eyes, taking it all in.'

Dafydd gazed at the rows of benches, the tall cross on the wall and the semi-circular low windows, flooding the room with light at either side of the altar.

'I suppose you are right. It's just so peaceful here.'

'Yes, my boy, that's the point. I'll leave you to your own reflections and I hope to see you again.'

Dafydd sat down on a bench and looked ahead at everything and nothing. The reverend's manner had been so disarming that Dafydd had felt the urge to tell him about Gwen. About his hopes and fears for a future together. The deep realisation that his dreams would probably founder in the end. Within himself he knew it would not be resolved, but neither would it go away. He sat and took in the feelings of peace from the room. It helped ease the pain.

When he finally turned around, Dafydd saw about a dozen soldiers behind him, all lost in their own thoughts. He made as quiet a retreat as possible and went to find Tom.

Tom was outside in the garden, dozing away under a large tree. For once the day was warm and sunny, although in the shade of the tree, the cool breeze gave the air a gentle bite. Dafydd felt he could sit there all day and catch up with his sleep.

'Happy?' Tom asked.

'Yes,' Dafydd said.

'Told you. We've got some time now still before we're due back, so make the most of it.'

Thirty minutes later, they left Talbot House. The tranquillity in the garden was replaced by the bustle outside. Horses drew gun carriages past a petrol-engined lorry that stuttered down the street. Everywhere there were khaki clad men, the click of metal rang in the air from their rifles and packs. The two railwaymen made for the engine shed, with Dafydd resolving to hold on to the inner peace in his heart for as long as he could.

Chapter Nine

Josephine

Dear Dafydd

Thank you for writing back to me. I was so relieved to hear from you. I hope they aren't sending you to the front, it sounds so terrible. Are the trains better than the Cambrian? What is it like as a driver?

Things have been so quiet here. I had an argument with a woman trying to give white feathers out. If I wasn't unpopular already, I am now! The house is so busy now, as so many men have gone to follow the master across the channel. I am thinking of what I can do to help the war. I may even go and drive some trains!

Anything to bring you all home quicker. Sioned still won't talk to me, but your little sister smiles at me. I think she must see the best in everyone. Mrs. Owen told me to pack you her socks. I've added the cocoa. It will keep you warm.

Keep your head safe.

Gwen

Tom had said he'd be waiting at the shed, but something must have delayed him. *Probably the Captain on another of his wild goose chases, dressed up as orders,* Dafydd thought sourly. *Why else?* Tom was never late for firing up. He liked his engine smoking and hissing, well before time.

'Because if she's broke, I want plenty of time to change her,' he'd say and Dafydd never argued.

He reflected on how the two had been paired up. A driver of twenty years' experience for the Lancashire and Yorkshire Railway before he had joined up, it took a pompous ass of a training CO next to no time to demote the best driver in the link to fireman. Having been promoted solely due to administrative apathy, Dafydd could clearly see how easy it was for the Army to screw things up. *Never mind* he thought *we've got an agreement that suits us both and I'll be the better for it.* The footplate hierarchy may have been blurred, but Dafydd wouldn't have it any other way.

Dafydd moved to his engine for the day. This time, it would be a Scottish Jumbo, a foreign beast but not one found wanting. The shed itself was surprisingly empty, bereft of the normal bustle of men raising the engines to life or dropping them to slumber. There was no bubbling, hissing steam engine waiting to be let off the leash and this morning, even the distant gun batteries were silent. It made Dafydd uneasy as his footfall echoed. It was as if the land was holding an uneasy breath, bracing itself for the next salvo of shells to violate its surface.

Dafydd could hear his own breathing as he moved along. The cleaners should have been on hand firing up his engine. At least they had better been.

'No time like the present,' Dafydd thought. *'I'll do it myself, then I'll kick their arses from here to Ypres and back.'*

He climbed up to the cab, hung his lantern up, and reached for the shovel. Then he stopped to listen. In the six months he had been supporting the army on the Western Front, he had not heard such silence. A few minutes indulgence wouldn't hurt. He closed his eyes and tried to remember fonder memories of firing a train along the banks of the Dyfi Estuary, all those months back.

He became aware of a sound, a whimpering like a puppy, but muffled as if stuck in a box. The echoing nature of the shed made it difficult to pinpoint and Dafydd went down to track level to listen.

The sound stopped and Dafydd held his breath to focus on the sound. He jumped as the shed door opened roughly and Tom appeared.

'Sorry I'm late, son, I was told to report to the CO, but the man wasn't there. Bloody typical lark, what's up with yer?'

'There's a sound in here somewhere, whimpering like a puppy. I can't find it.'

'You think we've got ghosts?' Tom said with a chuckle, but Dafydd stopped and reached out to grab his arm.

'Listen, there it is again.'

This time it was a distinctive low moan and Tom stiffened.

'That's no puppy. That's someone trapped in a firebox. We'd best shift, for if it's one of the ones that's been working overnight, they'll be baked alive.'

They moved quickly to the front of the stack of engines and Tom cocked his head to listen as they slowly walked down the row. At the third one, he leant close.

'She's in the firebox of that Dean Goods, come on!'

'She?' Tom just glanced back, and realisation hit Dafydd. 'Jo!'

Josephine was a young Belgian woman who always hung around the yard begging for scraps or money, pleading to do any work that would bring a few centimes into the household. In the few weeks that they had been there, Tom had doted on her, as he said she reminded him of his daughter.

Dafydd leapt into the cab and slammed open the firebox door, a warm blast of air greeted him.

'Jo? Jo! Ok, I've got you. Reach for my hand, that's it.'

He began to drag the hapless girl from her prison, reaching for her waist to pull her clear. Dafydd held onto her as she clung to him sobbing. Her clothes were damp with sweat, as he gently stroked her hair and tried to sooth her. Tom passed over an open canteen.

'Here lass, drink some water. It will help.'

She drank heavily, but the relief was short-lived, as she crumbled once more into Dafydd's arms. He felt his face begin to flush with anger, as he smelt her singed clothes.

'Who did this, Tom?'

He spied a face appearing at the steps, one of the firelighters.

'Get our engine ready,' Tom shouted at him. 'We'll be over now.'

Josephine still trembled as she managed to whisper a name to them and then she collapsed. They had to carry her gently off the footplate, as she drooped like a dying flower. In the end, Dafydd took her in his arms out into the cool morning air. Tom tapped his shoulder.

'She'll chill soon if we don't keep her warm. Into t'sand house with her, I'll join you after I've had a few words.'

Dafydd kicked open the door of the small hut used to dry sand. The fire blew a warm air of greeting, more welcoming now as Josephine had started to shiver. Dafydd laid her gently close to the fire and looked for something to cushion her head. The best offer was a sandbag, which he flattened in the middle with a few slaps. Her eyes flickered open as she lay and gazed at him, sending a wave of anger and protectiveness through his body.

'I'll get us a cup of tea, Jo *bach*,' he said. 'We'll have you rested.'

He rushed away, but soon returned and began to help her sip the hot drink. Without warning, the door burst open and Sergeant Macrae walked in. He stopped and sized up the scene in a blink of an eye.

'Captain Curran,' he shouted. 'You'd better come in. There's more to this affair than meets the eye.'

The Captain soon appeared in the small hut and crouched down to Josephine's side.

'Is this why I have just caught your fireman brawling with Cartwright?'

'Yes sir.'

'Who is this woman?'

'She's a local, came around first begging for food. The boys started letting her do odd jobs for a few centimes, whilst the brass hats weren't watch… sir.'

Dafydd bit his lip, Curran's eyes had narrowed at the remark.

'Do the men use her, Thomas?'

'Not in that way, sir. She's been treated well, up to now. Lucky talisman she is, in our eyes.'

'Bring in the brawlers, sergeant.'

Tom marched in with Cartwright. Tom sported a bruise around the eye, Cartwright had a bloody nose. The gleam in Tom's eye spoke of an inner strength still untapped.

'Mademoiselle, which of these men hurt you?' Curran asked Josephine.

She hesitated.

'It's alright, *bach*,' Dafydd soothed, 'Nobody's going to touch you now.'

She pointed to Cartwright and her voice trembled as she sobbed. 'Ee locked me in ze firebox. I only wanted to 'elp.'

'Cartwright?' Curran asked and the man cast a sour look towards Tom as he stroked his fattening lip.

'I wanted the firebox clean, the brick arch was heavy with clinker. She said she'd help me. I must have forgotten she was there when I closed the firebox up.'

Dafydd snorted his derision. 'She's got burns; her clothes are singed. The engine was too hot to work on.'

Curran said nothing, but his keen blue eyes looked at each of the loco crew in turn. Finally, Cartwright puffed out in exasperation.

'Alright, it was a joke. We always do it to new staff in loco sheds, you ask them all here. Wasn't going to be for long.'

'On a colder engine and <u>new</u> staff,' Tom replied. 'You've had it in for her for a while. Always griping about her being around here.'

Curran held up his hand for silence and for a while they all stood and waited until he finally said.

'I've had enough of this. Cartwright, go prepare the engine, you're taking the run.'

'It's not my run, it's theirs!' Cartwright retorted.

'I'm swapping you with Thomas's crew. Go.'

'But sir…,' Cartwright began to protest.

'That's an order, get on with it. We will talk about this on your return. Sergeant, get him out of here.'

Cartwright curled his lip in contempt. 'She had it coming. Little gutter rat keeps hanging around, getting in the way…'

He stormed out. Curran didn't flinch as he looked at Tom and Dafydd.

'She can rest here and then go home. We cannot allow civvies in here and this is no place for a woman.'

'She's the daughter of an engineman,' Dafydd replied. 'She knows what she's doing. The boys struggle to prepare and service our engines as it is. She gives them more time to do stuff by filling in with the easier work. The locos run better because there's time to sort them. We'd be breaking down all the time, else.'

'That's enough, Thomas,' Curran said softly but firmly.

'Permission to speak, sir,' Tom said.

'Denied, Hebdyke,' Curran snapped and moved to the door.

'If we don't keep her on, she'll be penniless,' Dafydd interrupted. 'She'll be just another street whore for the tommies. Do you want that?'

'Last chance to shut it, Thomas,' Curran said curtly at the door.

Tom moved to hold the door open for the officer.

'Do you have a daughter, sir?' He asked calmly. Curran stopped and gave him a curious look.

'Why do you ask?'

'I do and that age, sir. How do you think I feel, letting her on the streets, when I know I can help her? We'll keep her safe here and no-one will be the wiser. I promise.'

Curran looked at the pair and then sighed. 'If I thought there was anything untoward, you would be with the redcaps now. Yes, Hebdyke, I do have a daughter that age. I know what we are here for and what I see in the town distastes me. Very well, keep her out of my sight and we'll say no more of it.

His eyes suddenly hardened. 'One more thing, you're lucky you are a good crew. Don't push your luck though...'

The door swung shut with a sigh of cold air, almost as if in satisfaction. Tom grinned.

'He's a rare one, that's for sure. I had him down as a stuffed shirt, but I reckon he's top notch now.'

'Why? Because we got our way?' Dafydd asked.

'No. Because he knows when to be human in this shithole. Come on Dai, she's off sleeping now. We'll leave her a while. There'll be enough work waiting for us all a bit later today, I'm sure.'

Chapter Ten

Captain Price

Dear Dafydd,

I hope you are well and keeping warm. I have sent you a scarf to help you. It must be so terrible having to sleep in that cattle wagon. How could they do that to you? I hope you get to sleep. Do you get leave? Will they send you home? Please tell me if you do. I would be so happy to see you again.

It seems like forever since I seen you last. I wish it all had been different. I am sorry I have been so unfair, so cruel. I pray I can do something, but fear nothing I do ever goes right...

'She's laying it on a bit thick, son,' Tom said, handing the letter back. Dafydd stopped walking to fold it and place it inside his working jacket. All around were the wisps and sounds of steam from the line of engines kept ready for action. A long line of sleeping, wheezing giants, waiting for their next turn. The crews had settled into sleeping on the cab floors. It was warmer, smelt less and they were ready for the short notice when their engine made the front of the queue and they were needed.

'She's almost panicking.' Tom continued. 'Do you think she's been reading t'lists of dead and wounded in t'papers?'

'You are right, Tom,' Dafydd replied. 'Though I can see there is more here than meets the eye. She's struggling.'

'How's that?'

Ni all neb wasanaethu dau Arglwydd.

'What's that son?'

'You can't serve two masters. Sorry, welsh proverb.'

'And you're her master?'

'Tom…'

Tom flicked up his hand

'I know son, I just don't want you thinking it's all rosy, when t'clouds are still in t'way o't' sun.'

'Lancashire proverb?'

'Common sense, son.'

They were two engines away from their charge, a Scottish engine with a square cab, keeping the warmth inside for them. Dafydd remarked on that, for Tom to grunt in approval.

'Aye, God bless the North British Railway. I'll be spoiled before I get back to me Aspinall engines.'

'The penultimate engine was a large tank. Dafydd could see Cartwright's cap peaked up in the cab window. There was no acknowledgment, but Dafydd could guarantee they were being observed.

'Right, we'll see how Josephine has done with our engine.' Tom said.

'Aye and we'll make sure nobody has been bothering her,' Dafydd said it louder than needed. Tom did not reply, but in the glow of the engines, his mouth could be seen in a crooked smile.

They swung up into the cab. 'Morning love,' Tom said. 'Are you sure you don't need a sleep?'

'No, eet ees fine,' she replied, rubbing her nose. It left a darker mark on her already dirty face. 'Your fire is well.'

'You go home and sleep girl, I am sorry you've been dragged all the way over the yard now to this siding.'

She shrugged. 'The horse must graze where eet ees tethered'

Tom groaned. 'Not another bloody proverb.'

'You 'ave a letter,' Josephine said to Dafydd. 'A loved one?'

'A friend.'

'Ah…'

Dafydd removed another letter. 'But this is from my sister.'

'Eet ees good to 'ave family,' she said with a smile. Tom gave her some coin and she nodded before disappearing. Tom watched her walk down the path, past Cartwright's engine. Then he turned. 'She'll do. She's a tidy fire raiser.'

Dafydd looked up from his letter. 'It's Sioned. It's not good.'

'Not this bloody woman, Dav,' Tom snapped suddenly then sighed. 'Look son, it's not my place, but I think you're being led.'

Dafydd sighed and stopped at the steps, one hand on the rail. 'You may be right, Tom my friend. This is different. My father just died, and I'm stuck in this shit-hole...'

Without further word, he hauled himself into the cab and stared forward, slamming the gear into forward. His father had been a good man to him, but Dafydd wished he had been around at the key moments when Dafydd had needed him. Like now. Sioned had said his father had been at peace. He had enjoyed Dafydd's letters and was happy he was safe. They were looking after the cat, who was giving them comfort.

Dafydd blinked away the tears as he looked forward. An animal was more use than him! He wished he could be there for his little sister. 'Harri was always the vulnerable one. He hoped they would protect her.

'Crossing ahead. Clear.'

Tom's voice broke through the mists.

'Come on son, keep focussed.'

Dafydd did not reply. It was a line of closed wagons that waited for them in the yard and as they backed up slowly, Tom let out a curse.

'Bloody tender's leaking | !'

'Get us over to the water crane,' Dafydd replied and Tom jumped off the train. Dafydd felt happy to have the cab to himself, so he could lose himself in the noise of steam. There was more in the letter, about Gwen, but he didn't want to believe that Sioned was giving more than gossip. He had had enough for the day.

Dafydd watched Tom as he harangued the ground crew. Finally, he waved Dafydd forward and he sounded the whistle in response. As the engine moved forward, Dafydd felt with relief the wiggling motion as it rode the points. He reached the small water tank and Tom moved over to pull the feed across.

Dafydd looked at his gauges. The boiler pressure was fine, but the water level in the tender had fallen to a point he wasn't comfortable with, given the journey ahead. He needed to keep the water feeding to the boiler. No water meant no steam. No steam meant the pistons were not being active and the engine would not be going anywhere. Or worse, he would have to drop the fire for fear of the boiler exploding. Tom raced up the ladder on the back of the tender and opened the cap for the water tank, waving Dafydd into position. Then he jumped down and heaved at the counterweight of the water tank. The water feed was welcome, but nothing like the torrent at Poperinge. It stopped too soon for Dafydd; he had expected them to take it to the brim.

'That's our lot!' Tom shouted. 'Bastard tower is leaking as well! Wipers station has copped it again.'

'And this girl is leaking steam. We're in a pickle.'

Tom gave a rueful smile and checked his firebox. 'Still, the sun's shining. It's a lovely warm day for it. If the water gets too low, we'll have to slow us right down.'

'You two, get your train moving. You should have gone twenty minutes ago.'

It was the Railway Transport Officer, probably one of the RTO's lackey's, Dafydd thought sourly. He stood below the cab with clipboard in one hand and whistle in another, pointing stiffly in the direction they were due to go.

'She's sprung a leak in her tender, lieutenant.' Tom replied. We need water or we'll not last the journey and the tower's empty.'

The officer's stony expression did not change, and he jabbed his hand to emphasise each point, the white armband flashing with each movement

'I don't care! YOU need to get your lazy arses out of here now! YOU are late and are holding up the whole bloody network! Pick up water on the way from shell craters.'

'How?' Dafydd asked.

'Using a suction pipe, like the narrow-gauge engines. Don't tell me you've got it rough. They have to perform bloody miracles each day. Now shift!'

Dafydd shrugged and looked at Tom, he tapped the water gauge and shrugged back. With great reluctance, Dafydd lifted the regulator and they started forward.

'What bloody suction pipe?'

Tom shook his head. 'You see them on the back of some engines. They can pick up water as they go.'

'Isn't it muddy?'

'Aye, just like the thinking of that bloody officer. Must have shell shock. Boilers get clogged with mud that way.'

'Bad enough with the chaos on the line. Does he know how far we have to go?' Dafydd asked.

'He doesn't care once we are out of his section. That's t'bloody army for you.'

****

Five hours later, they were back at Poperinge. A journey normally good for a fifth of the time had been brought down to a level where each stretch of track became a struggle to make it to the next loop. At one time, they were kept waiting as three ambulance trains passed them. It gave them a chance to top up the dwindling water from a stream with a bucket. The last two hours had been spent waiting for other trains to depart, allowing them room to pull into the station.

This time when they finally finished with the engine, neither had the energy to leave and both just collapsed to the cab floor.

Dafydd liked the little North British engine for its square cab. It gave them more shelter than many, allowing the fire to keep them warm from the cooling night outside.

Josephine's head appeared at the steps.

'May I come?'

She quickly climbed into the cab with a billycan of tea and a few cans of McConnachies bully beef. Dafydd did not ask about her resourcefulness, he was just grateful as she passed the steaming tin cup to him.

'This was a bad day, yes?' she asked.

'It's the better for seeing friends,' Dafydd murmured.

She glowed with a smile of satisfaction that touched her lips.

'I talk to ze mess and zey let me bring you food. Cook is nice boy. He wants to take me into Poperinge for tea.'

Dafydd gave a smile. He wished his father was there to give him advice, he hated the fact their time together had been so short. He wondered where Gwen was and if he could keep her attention. He had written a few letters back to her and hoped they would get through.

Here was a woman who was young and pretty in some ways reminding him of Gwen. He knew she had a rough life, but still smiled through the hardship. If there was any chance of happiness, he wished she could have it.

'Jo, if you like him, you should let him take you. You deserve some happiness, especially after the stuff you've been through. You've been so good to us helping and all, I just want you to have something back out of it. But, if he hurts you, you tell me, and I'll lump him one!'

He could hear her laugh and she squeezed his arm, but he was already dozing off. He almost felt that his head was on her shoulder, her hair stroking his face. He even fancied something brushed his lips. He woke with a start and only Tom was in the cab, snoring gently away in the other corner. Someone climbed up the steps and put his head into the cab.

'Thought I heard that whore here with you.'

'Piss off Cartwright, before I give you something to think about' Dafydd
muttered.

He could hear a snort of derision in return, then he was fast asleep.

Gwen,

I been scared since I heard you been having problems, what with Price over here and the like. Don't worry. If you're stuck, go talk to Donato. He will help. Sioned will help also She will if I tell her too, Dafydd thought. *Keep smiling and stay strong. It won't be like this forever and maybe when I come back, we can talk…*

It sounded lame, but Dafydd did not have the words. He did not know how things could change, but he sure as hell wanted to make it happen. He sent the letter to Mrs. Owen. Then one went to Sioned.

...You have to help me, I think Gwen is in trouble, what with Price gone. Can you keep an eye on things and help her on my behalf if she needs it? I know you think badly of her, but you can't be totally convinced. Most of her life recently has been a case of survival and what it takes. I just want to make sure she is safe. I know you will help me and I'll make it up to you. Darling sister, you have been such a pillar of strength for me since we met up again. Please help me now...

'Water's down again!' Tom shouted.

'Better get the bucket. If we are kept here too long, we'll blow.'

The RCO popped his head into the cab almost immediately, although he acted as if he had not heard. Perhaps it was for the better.

'Proceed to the station and await further instructions.'

Another five-hour stop-start nightmare appeared to beckon to Dafydd, as the dark clouds above him seemed to caress his gloomy mood. They sat in the station and waited.

Although set in a loop, he felt in the way as incoming trains flashed past, full of empties. A large tank engine moved slowly to the east, Cartwright taking the opportunity to look across and leer at their predicament. Then another train came in, full to the brim with Tommies. Amid a chaos of screaming NCO's and massed ranks shuffling like a herd of goats, the station cleared. Dafydd could only watch it all impassively.

'You two! I need you to take me to Audricq immediately. Priority one. Step on it!'

Another officer had filled the void left by the RTO on the footplate. A Captain's badge on his epaulettes. Dafydd closed his eyes for a silent prayer to deliver him from the ignorance. He took a deep breath.

'Captain, we cannot just go where and when we choose. Our destination, our journey - is all controlled by the RTO of the area. The ones with RTO on the armband. If I were just to take off I could...'

'Stop complaining and carry out your orders, man,' the captain snapped.

Dafydd slammed open a bleeder valve to drown out the man with the hiss of steam. When he shut the valve, the captain was trembling with anger and fright.

'That's a court-martialling offence, driver,' he shouted. 'Now you have been given an order.'

Dafydd gathered a deep breath.

'I mean no disrespect, captain, but railways don't work that way. Please look ahead with me. See that point where our track joins the other? It's against us. It means if I ride over it we will derail. Which is also a court-martialling offence.

If I were to change the point and go without permission, I will likely meet one of the approaching trains head on. That will cause a crash with casualties and block the line. That is also a court-martialling offence.'

Dafydd stopped. He knew he had gone too far, but he had really had enough of military ignorance for the day. He let the words sink in, as the captain turned red about the ears and he waited for the roar of anger.

'When is the next train back west, corporal?' Tom asked.

'They've been running every twenty or so minutes, sapper,' Dafydd replied.

'Respectfully sir, me corporal is right. We can't just take off when we like, but they have been loading regular on that platform over thur You could get a lift on one of them. Check with that RTO and he'll see you right.'

The captain stared coolly across at Dafydd for what felt like a long time and then gave a curt nod and departed. Tom let out a low whistle of relief.

'Watch yourself, Daf, that one was a loose cannon. You need to pick your fights.'

Dafydd shook his head. '<u>You're</u> telling me?'

Tom smiled and reached for his shovel.

'Take it as one who found out th'hard way, son.'

Two hours later they were sat in sidings at Ypres, waiting for return orders. Whistles suddenly started being blown and nearby clods of earth began to fly up in a plume.

'Here we go again,' Tom muttered. 'Raining bloody shrapnel again.'

'Thomas! Thomas!' Dafydd could hear a voice shouting urgently in the background. He tried to ignore it. Normally it was easy, but this one nagged at him, with its Welsh lilt. He tried to doze and dream of bacon sandwiches.

'Thomas!' The clouds of his slumber could not disguise the calling voice.

'Thomas!'

''Oh, not another bloody one,' Tom muttered and Dafydd snapped fully awake. It was his surname being shouted and now the man was climbing in the cab. Dafydd watched as the khaki flat-topped officer's hat rose higher. The leather gloves, baton in one hand despite the exertion. Another bloody officer looking for a taxi service. Then the slim newcomer stood in the cab and looked up, making Dafydd's mind freeze with the shock of recognition. Despite the thick dark moustache and the hint of a scar by the right eye.

'Captain Price.'

Price turned to acknowledge Tom in the cab, standing with a firm grip on his shovel, as if he was ready to use it as a weapon. Tom looked at Dafydd, who calmly waved back.

'Check the oil and grease the links, Tom. I'll handle here.'

It's the man who took Gwen to mistress. His unspoken words hung in the air. Somehow Tom appeared to hear, he nodded and moved off.

As Tom disappeared, Price turned and stepped forward to grab Dafydd by the throat. The attempt was quickly slapped away.

'Don't try that again, Mr. Price. Officer or not, I'll not be manhandled by you.'

Price held the stricken hand, as if nursing a wound, but then flicked the pain away and held his hand back up, palm out, to acknowledge he had stopped.

'I'll not fight you,' Price sighed. 'I'm just... What the hell are you doing here?'

'What?' Dafydd spluttered, holding onto the cab in surprise. His legs felt weak.

Price reached inside his tunic for a silver cigarette case and then lit a pre-rolled cigarette. He did not offer one to Dafydd. The red tip glowed wildly, as he took a large drag and blew out a cloud of blue-grey smoke.

'You work in a restricted trade. You could have sat out this wretched war with impunity or disgrace.'

'Do you think so?' Dafydd replied coldly. The white feather still hurt. He was only doing his damned job.

'Well, better than most. You should be at home.' Price gnawed the first knuckle of his cigarette bearing fist and then blew another drag.

'Well, I'm...'

'Somebody needs to survive this war. For Gwen.'

The words cut across Dafydd's slow response. The finality of them were overpowering, leaving a silence that both men were swallowed into for a while. Dafydd could not fathom what Price was trying to say, before he continued.

'You've not been in the front line. It's a bloody lottery. If you get the nod to go over the top, you're dancing to death's tune, as the red-hot bullets come at you knee high. Taking you out as you fall. I... I don't know if I will survive this war.'

Price looked at the dials of the pressure gauges. Dafydd ached to tap them, but he felt frozen to the spot.

'I don't care what you think of me, Thomas. But I love Gwen and I want her safe and cared for.'

'Well you done that good and proper,' Dafydd muttered. He expected a backlash, but Price had gone back to biting his knuckle.

'My wife threw her out the day I left for war.'

'She was with child,'

Price grinned bitterly. 'She told you that? It was not true. A false alarm. Perhaps she needed a reason for you to let go.'

He finished his cigarette and flipped it out of the cab.

'Stay alive, Thomas. If I cop it, you go find her and keep her safe.' Price began to climb down. Dafydd sat and watched him go, succumbing to the urge to ask.

'And what if you survive?'

Price stopped and looked up. His cold expression returned, but the haunted look behind his eyes made him less than convincing. He was scared for the future. Even so, he said.

'If I survive, don't bother to come looking.'

Dafydd looked over to the army of valves, levers and dials of his workplace. The warmth thrown from the open firebox door. He tried to carry on as if nothing had happened, but his stomach felt heavy with fear. Tom came back and looked at his mate.

'Everything alright, Daf?'

Dafydd looked at his friend, shovel at the ready.

'Of course,' he lied.

Tom's shovel was lowered so the tip touched the floor.

'You don't con me, son.'

'Gwen's been thrown out.'

He could hear his own voice, but it felt faint.

'What of...?'

'There was no child.' Dafydd felt his words were like a hammer slamming into a large bell, tolling his misery. He sighed.

'I feel helpless.'

'Daf, you're not. No chance, son. Cut the guilt and stop moithering me with it. You're stuck out here, but you've got family back thur, you know they'll do owt for you. You've got a landlady who thinks of you as a son. You've written to say what you want. They will sort it out. They will help you. You know they will.'

Dafydd sighed. 'Tom Hebdyke, you are right. How's the engine looking?'

'This will be a slow turn again. That bloody tender's leaking so bad, we will have to run it proper slow.'

'Get this bloody heap out of here now!'

A helpful RTO bawled from outside. Dafydd released the brake and put the engine to forward. He slammed the regulator open, causing a wheel slip. A single act of defiance that caused Tom to chuckle by his side. The train picked up speed and Dafydd stared ahead, still trying to make peace with the ghosts of his past.

Chapter Eleven

Punishment

It was a Crewe Goods. In its heyday it had been a reliable workhorse, but now was a bit past its prime. However, Dafydd took to the old engine, which Tom referred to as a 'game 'owd lass'. The train limped through the morass that was once Belgian countryside. Already late again, due to congestion and a previous breakdown, the crew worked hard to try and bring back some semblance of timing, as they steamed through the remnants of fields.

'Reminds me of Capel Bangor,' Dafydd mused, trying to lighten the mood. 'All mud and broken trees.'

'Nonsense Daf,' Tom's bluff northern tones came from the tender, as he attacked a large lump of coal with a pick. 'It's Accrington, clear as day – or my name's not Tom Bickerstaff.'

'Sure, Tom <u>Hebdyke</u>,' Dafydd said with a laugh. 'This old girl's taking forever to get anywhere. She's leaking more than she should.'

'She's ailing,' Tom replied. 'Should know, I drove enough buggers like this. Some of t'boiler plates have shifted, we'll have to get her seen to when we finish this time.'

'If we get there,' Dafydd replied, tapping a gauge. 'We're losing so much steam here; we'll bleed dry soon. Perhaps you should take over, it might be my driving...'

Tom shook his head. 'Told you before, Taff. You'll have to fight me for t'shovel.'

Tom hung out of the cab a bit to take a quick look at the tender and swore.

'We been handed a real mess. We've done a good job, for now, but if anything, them holes in the tender are worse than bullet holes. I'm thinking she's rusting away rather than full of shrapnel. Cut your speed.'

'We'll be shot for that,' Dafydd said cynically.

'Better than stood standing in the middle of Belgium with a dry engine about to blow.'

Dafydd made a face, then cut the regulator. This was going to be the longest trip yet. They approached the water tower at a crawl. The engine wheezed like an asthmatic, as it clawed its way slowly up the track.

'Load t'tender up by half,' Tom said once he set the feed off. 'Until them holes start leaking. I'll just be a minute.'

'Where you off to then?' Dafydd asked.

'Repairing t'bloody engine!' Tom shouted, jumping out of the cab and over a fence.

Dafydd shrugged and kept the flow going. Nothing surprised him anymore.

A sharp voice shouted from the lead carriage. 'You there! What's the delay?'

Officer, Dafydd thought gloomily. The tap of a baton on the carriage door confirmed his fears. The same officer who tried to cadge a lift the day before.

'We're running short of water sir!' Dafydd shouted.

'Well hurry up man, we're far too late. You should have driven faster,' the curt reply was followed by the slam of the window.

'*Who needs Germans?*' Dafydd muttered in Welsh, jumping down to stop the water flow. Tom had reappeared clutching a handful of eggs.

'Traded them for your baccy,' he said with a grin. He put the eggs in his tea can, opened the firebox and put the can on the door. 'You never use it. Let the brew heat a while,'

The carriage window slammed open. 'Is this going to take long?' The vexed voice snapped again.

'Five minutes sir,' Tom replied. The officer grumbled and the window slammed once more.

'Right,' Tom said. 'Wish me luck. 'He took the eggs and broke them into the tender. Then, he went to each hole as the leaks slowed, covering the gap with a greasy handful of mud.

'Fill her up now lad,' Tom shouted and Dafydd let go the counterweight once more on the water feed. The tender filled and the holes were now no worse than a trickle.

Tom chuckled as he climbed up to the cab, producing two of the eggs. 'Eggs'll take care of top holes and t'clay will do them I can't reach. And here's breakfast.'

'You there!' The voice of the officer roared from the foot of the cab. 'I've seen you. We've been waiting thirty minutes here and I find you skiving. You're both on a charge and I'll have guards posted on your engine. If you don't work your hides off now, it'll be worse for you.'

'Right you are, sir,' Dafydd snapped and in quick motion released the brake and set the engine in motion. The officer barked at a soldier who had to sprint to make the cab, whilst the officer jumped back in the coach.

'A boy playing soldiers,' Dafydd said.

'Aye but he'll be trouble,' came Tom's glum reply.

The two worked hard at coaxing the engine to work, whilst the poor soldier lurched about on the footplate, not knowing where to put himself. Tom made to look out and the soldier barred his way.

'Do you think I'm going to jump?' Tom snapped. The soldier backed down.

The engine began a climb and Dafydd made for the tender. Again, their guard jumped up.

'Do you want this bloody train to run or not?' Dafydd shouted. The soldier licked his lips in uncertainty, looking at the two and gripping his rifle. Dafydd sighed.

'Look, if you're really worried, sit in the corner. You can see what we're doing and there's plenty of room for a clear shot if you're desperate.'

The soldier moved away. Dafydd grabbed the spare shovel and started helping Tom build up the fire, keeping it roaring white hot to coax power out of the engine. It responded slowly, leaving both men out of breath with the effort as they approached the station.

'Ramsbottom was no fool when he built her,' Tom wheezed, patting the gauges almost reverently. 'We've nearly caught up from t'water stop.'

There was a commotion on the station, as a few soldiers ran to the cab.

'You two, off the cab this instant!' A corporal roared.

Dafydd frowned, but Tom just shrugged and dropped his shovel.

'I have orders to punish you for your insubordination,' the corporal said as they stepped onto the platform. 'Number one field punishment for two hours.'

'Told you I should never let you drive,' Tom muttered dryly.

'That's double time!' the corporal snapped, with a nasty grin.

The pair were quickly hustled to the back of the platform. A fence lay in shreds, complementing the pock-marked brickwork buildings. The place had seen its fair share of shrapnel. Choosing two fence posts, Tom and Dafydd were tied – their hands crossed behind their backs. The height of the crossbeam meant their feet were raised to tip-toe.

Dafydd's shoulders began to burn with pain, he looked at Tom and saw his friend had started to grimace. The sun was climbing now, and it was going to be a hot day. Satisfied with his work, the corporal took the hats off the two railwaymen, making Dafydd gasp at the change.

'Best enjoy the scenery, gentlemen,' the corporal hissed into Tom's face. He punched the bound man's stomach, making him gasp and cough. Dafydd's head dropped and he closed his eyes to shut out the pain. His jaw was grabbed roughly, and the Corporal's rotten breath filled his nose.

'Heads up, chap,' the Corporal hissed. 'Don't want me putting a spike under your chin.' He blindfolded them and walked off chuckling.

Dafydd stood still, desperate to keep as quiet as possible. His back was on fire now, but he didn't want this to last any longer than needed. He could hear the soldiers detrain, though Dafydd was not certain if any had been left behind. Slowly, the noises faded, leaving the gentle hiss of the engine and a chirp of a bird nearby. he tried to lose himself in the birdsong, trying to find a way of shutting out the pain.

Time seemed to drag, and the heat made Dafydd's legs feel weak. His bound arms forced him to stay upright and he began to hover between putting the weight on his toes or shoulders. Neither gave him anything but agony.

He could hear singing in the distance, the voices rough. There was laughter as the men walked closer, a lot of banter drawled between them. Dafydd's mind begged him to scream for help. He didn't dare.

The voices had stopped and all around suddenly felt silent. Dafydd felt like it was a dream, one in which he was blind. He heard a quick rush of footsteps and then felt his bonds being cut. With a groan, his legs buckled under him, but he was caught carried and set down. The blindfold was ripped off and the bright sunshine made Dafydd screw his eyes shut again in pain.

'Got you, mate,' came a voice, full of concern.

97

Water splashed Dafydd's lips and he sipped greedily until he felt sick. He stopped and took deep breaths to steady himself. His arms were being assaulted by pins and needles.

'Take 'em to the shadow of the coaches,' came the voice.

Dafydd's vision was coming back into focus now and he looked at the men's insignia.

'You're Australian,' he gasped.

'Strewth mate,' said the soldier with a grin. 'You just might be right,'

'Oi!' A voice broke through from the station. 'Leave those men alone now!'

Dafydd watched in dread as the corporal who had punished them stormed up towards the Australians.

'He do this to you, mate?' Dafydd's rescuer asked.

Dafydd nodded. 'Train late,'

'Boiler in danger,' Tom groaned. 'Got to get to engine.'

'Got that covered mate,' said the Australian. 'Jonesy, Craig. See to it. I've got business to sort here.'

'Corp,' came the reply.

'Don't you worry mate,' he said to Tom. 'Jonesy's a driver in Oz.'

'These men are on field punishment and you have interfered with my orders,' the corporal shouted, pushing his way through the crowd of soldiers. It was hard work, as the Australians were taking his manner less than kindly and the bully was being buffeted as he waded through.

'Last time I heard, crucifixion wasn't in the field manual, Corporal Tucker,' somebody muttered to Dafydd's rescuer. Dafydd noticed the Australian holding him had two stripes on his tunic. *Three corporals in conflict*, he thought. *Who needs the bloody Germans?*

'Shut your mouth!' The English corporal said.

In one swift movement, Tucker stood, turned and landed a punch on the man's jaw. It took him clean off his feet.

'Get that pommy bastard off the bloody platform,'
Tucker muttered, flexing his hand.

Dafydd sat back, his hands still shook with the tension.
Jonesy came off the engine and offered him some chocolate.
'Here, get some of your energy back, mate.'
Seeing that Dafydd couldn't even open the wrapper, Jonesy
quickly did so. 'How long you driven this crate?' Dafydd began
to explain but was interrupted.

'My name is Smith, I want to see your commanding
officer immediately,' came the unmistakable tones of the English
officer. The man stood bristling with rage.

Tucker nodded 'We won't detain you too long, sir.
Private Mortimer, see the Captain is made comfortable.'

'Sure,' came the reply and then to the Captain. 'Would
you like to wait in the carriage or stand where you are?'

The looks of the men made Smith quieten, but he stood
his ground fuming, whilst Tucker returned with his own Captain.

'My name is Maclelland,' he said nodding
acknowledgement of Smith's salute. What is your problem?'

'These men were being punished by my order, following
a breach of discipline. Your men have interfered and have also
assaulted my Corporal. I demand that you intervene.'

'I am intervening,' Maclelland replied patiently. 'That's
why I'm here. What is the crime?'

'Insubordination and dereliction of duty,' Smith replied
stiffly. 'They have run this train late and I caught them eating
eggs at the water stop. When I intervened, they tried to leave
without me.'

The hint of a smile appeared on Maclelland's lips. 'Eggs,
you say. Well that certainly is insubordinate. Why not shoot
them?'

Smith's eyes bulged, though he kept his composure.
'There is no need to trivialise this sir, these men needed swift
disciplining whilst we rest, before re-embarkation. I would have
flogged them had there been time.'

Maclelland briefly closed his eyes. 'All right. You've had your say. Now you're not going anywhere.'

Smith frowned. 'Why is that sir?'

Maclelland sighed. 'You've made these men unfit for duty by your torture. Jonesy?'

'Sir,' Jonesy shouted from the cab.

'The state of the engine?'

'A bloody mess, sir.' Jonesy shouted.

'Is that so?' Maclelland asked.

'Sure sir, how these boys got anything from this old girl, I don't know. She's crook. They used the eggs to plug the holes in the bloody tender. Eggs, grease, dirt. Bloody miracle she's still steaming, must have dug their way to Queensland to fire her.'

'Thank you, Jonesy,' Maclelland said quietly.

Smith looked on defiantly. 'It is my duty sir, to ensure the discipline of my men. My men are tired and in need of rest. Your men have no idea of what we have been through. This crew have not the mettle of my men.'

'Driver,' Maclelland asked Dafydd. 'Why did you join up?'

'To fight, sir,' Dafydd said wearily.

'No problem with mettle there,' Maclelland muttered. He took out his pipe and began to fill it. 'We'll relieve you of this train, Captain Smith. You can have ours when it arrives.'

'On whose authority?' Smith spluttered.

'Oh, on mine,' Maclelland replied nonchalantly, waving away the smoke. 'Smith, I'm tired so I'll make this brief. Let's just say that your dutiful actions have ensured that there are no fit crew for this train. I thankfully have men skilled in such matters. We will be taking this train and luckily for you, I will not be relieving you of duty and court-martialling you for attempting to crucify two soldiers trying to do their job.'

'Captain,' Smith hissed, now white with fury. 'I insist you stand by and let me continue with my duty. Discipline may not be an issue in the colonies, but His Majesty's Army it is paramount.'

The atmosphere chilled and more than one soldier tensed. One took a step forward, making Smith raise his baton in anticipation of a fight.

'I'll ignore that last slur,' Maclelland said calmly, waving his men back from Smith.

'You have held up the whole railway network with your trivial spiteful punishment. If these men are not deemed doing their duty, we would welcome them in **His Majesty's** Australian army. Anyone who slogs their guts out to get the job done is always welcome. Now Smith, I suggest you walk away and make plans to billet your men before I order Mortimer here to shove that baton up your arse.'

There was no menace in his voice, but Maclelland's eyes were cold. 'One more thing, Captain Smith. When your boys next go over the top, make sure you lead from the front. I have a feeling that you won't last this war and I'd like to think it's because of a Jerry bullet putting you out of your misery.'

Smith stared back for ages, before he snorted and turned to walk away stiffly.

'Jonesy, can you get this girl working.' Maclelland shouted

'Sure, Mortimer will help. He's a good man with a shovel. We'll take the driver with us, he can sit back and show me the road.'

'Christ that was harsh,' Dafydd said as Jonesy came to pick him up.

'No worse than the bastard deserved, mate,' Jonesy replied. 'Don't you worry about us, we're in clover. I miss working the old engines and besides,' he winked at Dafydd. 'That Maclelland's a wily bastard. He knew damn well we were due to spend five hours in cattle trucks. We've got ourselves luxury now. It'll be like Blighty and a leaky engine means we can enjoy the scenery as we go.'

Chapter Twelve

Transfer

Dear Dafydd,

I get so worried when you don't write. I worry that you may have got caught in trouble. I am so happy you got back on the small engines again, like you used to do in Aber. I hope this makes you safer. I know you can't tell me where, but I hope it's green like the hills back here.

I had to move, but Mrs Owen have taken me in. Donato helped get my belongings from the house. I know that was you that done it. I'm happy being a Turkey girl once more. I'm trying to get a job that helps the war effort. I'll let you know as soon as I can…

'I've got no choice, corporal,' Captain Curran said, trying to offer sympathy in as much as his position allowed. 'Sapper Hebdyke has been referred to field hospital with his chest. You're only half of a team and it makes you spare. War Department Light Railway Company are crying out for men and I have the CO breathing down my neck to supply them.'

'Thank you for saying that sir, I appreciate that your hand is forced. It's just I feel like I'm being punished for that leaky boiler.'

'You have experience of Light Railways,' came the curt reply. Dafydd knew the Captain had taken it a bit personally. 'The WDLR would have taken you even if that farce had not happened.'

Dafydd swallowed hard. 'Yes sir, I didn't mean...'

'I know you don't want to go. I'll be fighting to get you back as quickly as I can. You're my best crew and since Geddes has come in to direct the ministry of transport, things are finally starting to work properly here.'

Dafydd stood to attention and saluted. Curran was being too decent by half. Dafydd liked the man. He had not forgotten his civilian past and the men respected him for that. It made him a leader to the irregular locomotive crews. It was obvious Dafydd did not want to go and Curran did not want to lose him. That was acknowledged and nothing would change.

Curran nodded a dismissal and Dafydd moved out of the hut. In the dark, the foreground was pitch black, but the glow on the horizon lit up the shadows to reveal the line of engines, waiting for their duties. The war seemed never-ending, and the result was a faint orange glow on the horizon. That and the constant rumble was as normal to Dafydd as a rain shower.

For a moment, his mind drifted to a normal day as he moved towards the nearest engine. He prepared to jump for the cab steps. Tom would be around oiling the motion, feeling out the points by touch. Josephine would be tending the fire...

Josephine.

Dafydd began to worry as he walked. She would struggle without them around. Both financially and... Dafydd tried not to think of it. He needed to find her. He sped up his pace, walking the side of the line of engines, using the faint firebox glow as beacons. The large Dutch tank engine was next in line and he knew without any light that Cartwright would be there. He prayed the man was not there. Not the night for another of his incessant snide comments.

He couldn't see him, but could feel the sullen presence, the air of gloating.

'Got rid of yer at last,' the malicious whisper sizzled through the air. 'You and that northern bastard!'

Dafydd kept walking, he was not going to be riled this time. The unevenness of the ballast had given way to a smooth dusty and flatter ground. A result of the months of ash being raked out of the engines, cooled and trodden into the ground.

'We'll sort out your whore when you're gone and all…'

Dafydd took two quick steps and jumped. Cartwright's last barbed comment had seen him lean too far out of the cab. Dafydd wrapped his arm around Cartwright's neck and used his momentum to pull him out of the cab and to the ground.

'Corporal!'

'Sergeant Macrae's voice broke through the red mist and within a few steps he was standing between the two men who had rolled apart and were on the trackside.

'Leave him, Thomas!'

'He's busted me shoulder, Sarge!' Cartwright moaned.

'Shame it wasn't your gob,' Macrae snapped with a singular lack of sympathy. 'On your way, Thomas!'

Dafydd moved on without another word. He had to find Josephine. He had to make sure she was safe.

He reached the end of the line of engines and was none the wiser to her whereabouts. Dafydd looked around for a glimpse of light to help him. Perhaps a moving shadow. The yard was full of sidings lined with trucks. Some were static storage units, whilst others were ready or being made ready to move east along with coaches and ambulance trains. Dafydd did not know where to start·thinking of where she might be. He had no idea of where she stayed in the town when she was not at the yard.

The engine shed was off limits to her, so he moved from the damaged building. It had suffered recent attention from a stray bomb from one of the huge German Gotha aircraft. It had been a lucky hit, in that it glanced the side, damaging two engines. Probably the action that holed the tender of the North Brit.

Dafydd sighed. Where to look next? A slight movement to his side took his attention towards a stack of coal. The edge of it was stacked like a dry-stone wall, a testament to the craftsmanship given the time and availability of men in quieter times.

There was a flickering shadow and he knew he had found her. It was a terrible state of affairs that she needed to hide, but it would seem she would risk discovery for the chance to say good-bye.

'Corporal Thomas!'

Sergeant Macrae had followed him over.

'Sarge, I…' Dafydd stopped as his superior placed a hand on his shoulder. This was not normal behaviour for the normally taciturn Scot, but there was something close to an apology in his manner.'

'I didn't mean to be rude to the Captain, I was just upset.'

'Aye, I ken that. Captain kens that. You should have heard him. He tried to give them Cartwright, but they'd no take him, being the loud-mouthed shit stirrer that he is.'

'But I can work these engines here. Me and Tom took that leaking North Brit to Ypres and back twice.'

'You did. I'm a North British man mysel' and I saw you treat that one well and she gave you back in kind. But Tom's awa' mending. When he's back, we'll have you home. Look son, you need your wits about you on them engines. The tracks are put down in the mud when needed and off they go. You need smart thinking and some experience of the wee engines,' he stopped to laugh softly. 'And you want me to send Cartwright?'

Dafydd sighed. 'Alright, Sarge.'

'That wee girl? We got her a berth as an orderly in a field hospital. She's better off there, son. They'll look after her there pay her and feed her too.'

Macrae moved off and Dafydd watched him go. For now, there was no movement at the coal bunker. Dafydd felt the first strands of panic as he thought of Josephine. Where could he find her, to make sure she was all right?

He moved to the coal bunker, but there was no sign of life. If she had been there, she was long gone. His heart was heavy. Josephine and Tom were the two lights in this muddy darkness. Now they were gone. He looked around and realised he had nowhere to go. His orders were to catch a troop train west and there was nothing on until the morning. There was no billet for him, as for the past few months his bed had been little more than a warm cab of a stationary engine.

Talbot House may as well have been a million miles away in Poperinge itself, but he decided to go and beg a floor in its adjoining warehouse. It was always peaceful there. He was certain that he could be spared from having to wait on the off chance of a lift on an earlier train. It was as if he had been forgotten.

For a moment, he looked longingly at the engines. Maybe one of them could spare him a berth? Then he shook his head, with both crew on each side, there would only be the floor directly in front of the fire. Only the big tank engines would have given him space and Cartwright's engine was not on his list of welcome places.

He moved off before he fell afoul of the RTO and jumped as a shadow loomed in front of him from behind a wagon.

'*Iesu Grist*, it's you!' he gasped and then grabbed Josephine in a fierce hug.

'I wanted to see you,' she whispered in his ear. 'To where do you go?'

'To the front. I have been sent to drive engines there.'

'Oh,' she buried her head in his shoulder to suppress the sobs.

107

'It's alright, I will be on smaller steam engines. Closer to the front, but if they used them engines too close, the enemy would see the steam and point their guns at it.' He stopped. His chattering was just making her sob even more.

'Hey, don't worry *cariad*. They take these big engines to a yard like this. Then they unload onto smaller engines, like they do here, who take them to another depot. Then they get petrol tractors to take them to another depot. Then there's horse and finally men. I'll be a bit away from the front line… '

He stopped, in his nervousness, he was more likely to poke her eye with a stray finger, as gesticulated wildly. The sensation of loss was unnerving him too. He was really going to miss her.

'Why can't zey let you work on ze small engines in Poperinge?' She asked with a sniff.

'They need people further up the line. Look, I don't want to go neither, but the army doesn't care about that. I've been told they have got you a place in a hospital. They will look after you there.'

'I will 'elp Tom get better?'

'No, but he will be better soon enough.'

He stopped again as he felt he was hitting another subject that would only bring pain.

'Ee will be better and zen you can come back, Daveed'

Dafydd bit his lip. 'I don't know. I hope so'

He felt her fingers on his cheek. 'Believe it, mon ami.'

She grabbed his hand and started to pull. 'You must come. Now.'

'What?'

'When do you leave?'

'Tomorrow morning, about half seven.'

'Zen you must come.'

'Why?'

She paused and leant forward to kiss him on the cheek. 'We must say goodbye.'

Dafydd's heart sank. 'No, no girl. Don't do this. You don't have to.'

'I love you Daveed.'

A shock at the base of his spine made him jump at the words.

'No, you don't. You're just grateful and... we're friends and all, but...'

She hit his arm with a grunt of disapproval. 'No, I do. I'm not a child.'

'I am thirty-six, car... bach. You are, what? Seventeen?'

'Nineteen!'

'But you do not need to do this.'

'I want to. You think I do not care? I would not stay if I do not care.'

'I...' Dafydd felt the tears in his eyes, as he took a shuddering breath. 'A long time ago, I loved someone. She was all to me. I went away to work and did something I regret. I cannot do the same again.'

'She waits for you?'

'Well not as... I don't know.'

His sigh was met by a sob.

'I'm old enough to be your father, girl.'

He felt her long hair flick his face as she shook her head.

'Eet ees no matter. You are kind. You care. Come to my home. To rest, no more. I will let you sleep, then in ze morning you will catch your train and I will say goodbye.'

'Home?'

'My 'ouse. It is ruin, my family dead, but yes, eet ees 'ome. Eet ees warmer and there ees a bed. You can sleep as I watch over you.'

His resolve gave way. Too much had happened and whilst he still could not lose Gwen from his mind. There was a feeling that he could not just walk away. The back of his mind still held fast the dream that Gwen would come back to him. He had failed before, but even if she did not wait for him now, perhaps thing could change.

Yet the beauty of the young Belgian girl did not go unnoticed and he suppressed the desire to succumb to her offer.

'I will come.'

She led him down the narrow dusty streets. The houses were mostly intact, but after they passed the front of Talbot House, some were less so. Josephine disappeared, but soon, the soft glow of a lantern appeared. Dafydd gasped as the light cast a darker complexion on her face, making her more alluring.

He could not.

She moved back into the damaged building and he followed her, until he found what was a small room in surprisingly good condition. A mattress had been placed in the middle of the room, another appeared to plug a gap in the room. On a small wooden table was a candelabra and a jug of water.

'You live here?'

'Yes, I don't keep food 'ere. Ze rats would come.'

'Where shall I sleep?'

'On here with me. Do not worry, we will not undress.'

A wave of fatigue swept over Dafydd and he sat down to remove his boots. She moved to help him.

'My feet stink.'

'I do not smell zem. Do not worry, ze air is dry with dust, but I have water in a jug.'

Dafydd lay back and felt sleepy. He wanted more time to talk to Josephine, but he was soon lost to slumber. In the background, he could hear her soft voice.

'You are safe.'

He felt her head on his chest. It made him feel warm. Her hair tickled his chin, as she murmured.

110

'Do not worry, *mon cher*. Tonight, we sleep as friends. Tomorrow we say goodbye.'

His arm reached to curl her shoulder. It felt good and a wave of calm swept over him. She lay across him, avoiding anywhere that might stir him. He knew this was respecting him, but part of him wished he could get past the shadow of Gwen.

Just this once.

He was woken by a wail that made him start. He realised it was Josephine. She was still asleep but frowning. Her voice had begun to grow slowly upwards into a wail. He stroked her back and whispered soothing words and she bolted upright. Then there came a big sigh and a shudder, and she fell back into him. He reached forward and felt the sweat on her brow. She was sobbing.

'I am sorry,' she whispered.

'What happened?'

'A dream, no more.'

'Tell me.'

'Must I?'

'If it helps.'

She took a deep breath. 'Then 'old me, please.'

He could not refuse, and she seemed to relax.

'My family. *Ma mère, papa*, my *grand-mère*. Zey were killed in a bomb blast. My sister was murdered in ze fields. My brother in ze army, was killed in fight with Germans. I am left alone.'

'You are not alone,' Dafydd whispered.

She squeezed his arm.

'If zis love of yours is no more, come find me and I will be 'ere.'

He stroked her back and stared into the darkness until he felt the rise and fall of her deeper breathing and knew she was back at rest.

Chapter Thirteen

The Scarecrow

Dear Gwen

I'm really worried now that something's happened. I've not heard from you for over a month. Please send word of what is happening. If you need help, tell me. I will get it all sorted. Please let me help. You've suffered so much in your life and I'll do whatever I can to help you with better times. Go to Sioned and Donato, they will help you. Please let me know.

I'm being moved further up the line, but I will be fine, don't worry. I feel more pity for them who have to go further...

Dafydd's new posting was a dugout, somewhere in the wastelands of what had once been Flanders farmland. It had been fought over time and again, suffering greatly from the ministries of artillery from both sides. Small hillocks, created by shellfire, peppered the landscape, flanked by stark ruined tree trunks in permanent silhouette. Their lofty ambitions now literally reduced to cinders.

There had been no time to prepare for his new assignment. On arrival, he was put straight on a large narrow-gauge Pannier tank engine and told to head off onto the eastward tracks, a large train of bogie wagons, laden with shells in tow. The fireman was to show him the lie of the land as he went.

But his new colleague had said next to nothing, focussing on lobbing in the occasional lump of coal taken from the small bunker behind him. Then he started chuckling and Dafydd guessed it was at his own expense.

'What's so funny, Sapper?' Dafydd shouted. 'Me banging my head on the roof as I came in? Not used to low roofs. That funny, is it?'

'Nah, that's normal. It's just you, corp, asking for some time to learn the road.'

'Standard practice on all railways."

The response was just a shrug of shoulders.

'What do you mean by that?'

'Outside of hell, yeah, it's standard practice. Here, the track isn't permanent. When the army moves, the supply depot moves, and we move with it. Every bomb blast just gives us a new direction. Nothing's permanent, we go where we are needed. So don't expect the road to be learnt, you learn as you go.' He laughed. 'Go on, next you'll be telling me you've never driven narrow gauge.'

'I've handled better than this, sapper!' Dafydd snapped. 'These Baldwin engines are sound enough, but lack of a back truck makes the bugger waggle around like a puppy dog's tail when excited.'

The fireman looked across from his perch by the cab front. The firebox protruded back enough to make a barrier between the two of them.

'Ah, you get used to that, Corp. Feed between two tanks gets blocked with the mud in the water making her waggle. If you don't keep an eye out, your water tanks aren't balanced, and the engine will fall off the track where it ain't so level. Look, give me a break. We're all on the same side here. This is how you operate. You keep your wits about you, trust in me as your look-out, adapt and just forget anything you was ever taught.'

'What is the hose on the back for?'

'Water feed. We got to take it from where we can. Even bomb craters.'

'Are we supposed to dig coal from them and all?'

The fireman guffawed. Dafydd didn't know his name. He wasn't in the mood to find out. This was hell. A dreary, damp depressing land that he loathed for every minute he was in it. The people that he now realised had kept his spirits up had gone. He didn't realise how dark a mood he had fallen into until that moment. There appeared no future outside this miserable existence.

'Hand brake off,' his new crewmate called. 'So, what do you really think of her, Corp?'

Dafydd didn't reply save to acknowledge the hand brake was off. It was an American Baldwin 4-6-0 tank engine and he was secretly impressed – at least when going forward, with her power and the room in the cab. The windows gave a great view forward over the pannier tanks but were slightly too low and he had to stoop. A clear view from behind was to be had as it was only a half cab at the rear. In spite of that, he really wasn't in the mood to share his thoughts.

'Suit yourself,' the fireman said. 'Mad Jack coming up.'

Dafydd spotted a scarecrow at the track side, stuck in a flooded crater. The wind appeared to be blowing one arm from side to side. As they neared, he saw it had been dressed in an army khaki uniform and then with a shock, he realised it was a man.

'Morning lads!' The scarecrow shouted. Dafydd could only stare in horror at the man as they moved past. He was now waving to the guard at the back of the train. It all felt woolly, like a bizarre dream.

The rest of the journey was held in silence. Dafydd had nothing to say, he could not stop thinking of the scene he had just witnessed. He had been so far behind the lines that he could not take in the true horror of what was going on. The ruins of Ypres were removed from the conflict.

The pain showed in its scars of violence, but seeing this man was different. A human being left to perish. Ignored by those who could help. What had happened to the world?

They had arrived at a marshalling yard, a temporary feature of huts, rails and rows of trucks. Dafydd could tell how new the place was by the sleepers and the ballast bereft of oily patches. Many shells were stacked in square rows, similar to how coal was stacked in Poperinge They uncoupled and ran around the train, to allow a small green petrol driven blob of an engine to move into their place. It blew a curtain of blue-grey smoke as it disappeared towards the front line. The soldier driving sat sideways twisting to look forward, which Dafydd found odd. He looked bored and Dafydd was happy to couple up to a train of empties and move off.

'I'll give Lloyd George his due, ever since he put Geddes in charge of war transport, we've been bloody moving.' Dafydd's fireman had started talking again, to break the tense silence. 'North Eastern man. Worth his weight in gold.'

Dafydd was inclined to agree, the whole process was less chaotic, but he really didn't want to talk. A movement caused him to look up and he saw an aircraft nearby.

'Is it one of ours?' He asked finally.

The fireman pushed back his cap and peered upwards for a while. 'No idea, corp. We'll know soon enough if he starts firing.' He moved back to the water feed. Dafydd remembered the man ahead with dread. He could soon make out the silhouette.

'Sound your whistle!' the fireman shouted.

'Why?'

'Because we'll say hello and keep his spirits up.'

'How does that work?'

The fireman suddenly snapped.

'Because the bloke's a goner and we're all he's fucking got! Don't you know nothing?'

The build-up of tension had got too much. Dafydd looked away and blew the whistle.

Mad Jack turned and straightened as they passed, and a flicker of a smile came across his face. He was stuck up to his knees in yellow Flanders mud.

'God bless you, lads!' he shouted.

The train was past and Dafydd did not look back. The view from the open back cab was clear and he wanted to look at everything apart from Mad Jack.

They marshalled the trucks and stopped for their break. The fireman disappeared, leaving Dafydd on his own, chewing his knuckles in frustration. His dark thoughts were broken by a metallic tap and his guard appeared with two steaming mugs of tea.

'Here, corporal, get this down yer neck. It will help thee.'

The broad Yorkshire accent and the man's broad shoulders had Dafydd thinking of him more of a miner than a railwayman.

'Cheers, um…?'

'Oswald Clarke, so I reckon as it'd be Sapper Clarke round these parts. You're new here, arrived just this morning, eh? You must think we're mad or summat. We're a rough lot alright, but we're used to adapting – laughing off the jeers.'

'What jeers?'

'From them we are taking forward to t'front line. They're just frit, that's all and we're in t'right place for them to vent it. It's why we are blunt and your fireman, Johnny Thompson, talks to you like you are dirt. Give it some time and you'll get accepted.'

Dafydd could feel the hairs on his arm stand up in indignation.

'What? Let him walk all over me?'

Clarke gave a wry smile. 'It may look that way, but no, he's not doing that. You tell him what to do and he'll do it. Just don't pull rank too much and it'll work alreet.'

Dafydd nodded slowly. 'All right then, we'll see what happens. If he tries to take over, I'll sort it out with my fists!'

Clarke gave a vicious grin. 'You're talking like a coal miner, lad.'

'My family are lead miners in Wales.'

'That's reet grand.'

Dafydd took it as approval. Feeling more relaxed, he decided to probe for information and asked about Mad Jack.

Clarke sipped his tea and stared at the remaining liquid, sighing through gritted teeth.

'Aye, he's been there a while, that one. Carried a machine gun and he slipped and fell off t'duck board. T'mud's evil here. It sucks you down and takes a reet long time about it.'

'Why hasn't someone pulled him out?'

Clarke raised his eyes to stare at the heavens.

'We can't. Army orders, them that's stuck can't be rescued. Waste of time and resource. They even built a bloody railway past him.'

'That's inhuman!'

'Aye and best we can do is to greet him and show him some dignity.'

Clarke threw away the dregs and nodded. 'Well, welcome anyroad. Don't worry for the billet. It's damp but covered.'

'I've been sleeping in a cab these last few months; I think I'll manage.'

'Then welcome to t'Ritz, corporal.'

Dear Dafydd

I know we're always saying this, but I hope you are safe, and this letter gets to you. It's a mad world we live in now and most kindness have gone away. Aber is such a sad place without its men. We try hard to keep happy because we know what you boys are doing is worse. I hope we can win soon and bring everything back to normal.

Not back to where it was, you deserve more than that. When you come home, things will be different, I promise.

I am moving to another job. I am a XXXXXXXX and have moved to place in xxxxxxxxxx. The address I will get to you as soon as I have it….

'Bloody censors,' Dafydd muttered. 'Don't they know when there's good honest people involved?'

'Surprised there's censors that can read Welsh, corp,' Thompson replied.

'Probably just picking up on names of places and jobs.'

'Maybe you'll get more in the second letter.'

Dafydd frowned as he read it. 'Well, it's my sister. I can smell the coffee.'

… everything is fine here. We haven't seen Gwen around for a while. But you know her, she's always good at finding a safe port in a storm…

It had been only a week and the work was constant. Rumours spread quickly, that now was the Big Push. Dafydd had heard those words so many times before. It just meant more shells; more men forward and more turns up and down the line on the lumpy ballasted track.

Everyone was giving off so many negative emotions, that the air was thick with fear, depression and resentment. Yet nobody could do anything about it. There was a feeling of an inevitable end to a journey, like being at the whim of a cat's paw.

Dafydd waited while Thompson coupled up the engine to another train of bogie wagons. The rain was driving down and Dafydd felt lucky to be only an observer of the action from the cab. The open back to the engine, whilst giving glorious views, left their backs exposed when the rain was driving down. Still, it could be worse, Dafydd thought, watching his cargo arrive.

A sodden company of soldiers marched to the trackside and prepared to entrain. Each one, a helmeted head sticking out of a balloon of canvas cape. The rain dripped from the rims of their helmets. They stood forlornly waiting their turn, a wretched group of saturated humanity.

A sergeant barked out a command and the front line stepped into the open trucks, followed by the next line. This carried on until the train was full.

Dafydd watched as the men settled. Some tried to sit on the edges of the wagon. Many had taken to lighting pipes or roll-ups. Behind the nonchalance was an air of apprehension. There was a lot of banter as people tried to hide their fear and laugh away the atmosphere.

'Oi!' one voice called out from the front truck. 'Why don't you two stop playing trains and come and join the scrap?'

Thompson smiled as he looked back. 'Too busy sorting out you boys. Someone needs to get you there in one piece.'

'Well, when you get us there, you can hop along with us. Do a man's job. Do your bit.'

The reply was followed by a cacophony of laughs, jeers and catcalls. Dafydd turned around and the number of faces gazing back at him as the train moved, made him feel as if he was followed by a pack.

'Don't worry boys, we'll be damned sure we'll be around to take you back in one piece.'

There were more jeers, but in approval of the banter.

'I'll keep you to that, see as you do, Taff.'

Dafydd locked gazes with the soldier who started it. He was a small man with a lopsided grin and a nearly clean-shaven chin. Dafydd felt a flicker of understanding had passed between them, then he turned and looked forwards.

The rain had made the ground sodden and the lightly laid track was now quite uneven. The Baldwin bounced its way down the track, forcing the soldiers to hang on for dear life.

'Oi Taff, do you know how to drive this bloody train or what?'

'Do I know how to drive this train?' Dafydd asked Thompson.

'It's bloody going in the right direction, innit?'

Dafydd grinned at his fireman's reply.

'Diversion!' Thompson shouted and as Dafydd slowed, he could see a group of engineers around a bomb crater. Halfway inside was the upturned back of a small tank engine flanked by the torn and mangled remains of track. The railway line had been diverted around the carnage, but it was a sharp curve and the soldiers yelled their anger at their discomfort.

'Hold on tight you real men!' Dafydd yelled.

The response was less than complimentary. They moved on up the line and Dafydd could see Mad Jack in the distance. He took a deep breath and pulled the whistle chain. Jack seemed to come to life and wave in response. As the engine passed, Dafydd could hear Jack begin to sing a hymn popular in the army

'Onward Christian Soldiers, marching as to war…'

The soldiers in the trucks started cheering and waving in response. Many started to join in the hymn. Then they were past Mad Jack and the singing began to die down. It was if they had suddenly become aware of the reality of it all. The army was happy to leave someone behind. Dafydd glanced a look back and saw the concern on some of their faces. He racked his brain desperately for something to break the gloom and then cleared his throat and began singing.

'Roll out the barrel, let's have a barrel of fun…'

The tune seemed to break the spell and slowly the men came to life joining in. As they reached the transfer depot, they were embarking on the chorus of 'Goodbye-ee'. Thompson gave him a nod and Dafydd was happy that he had managed to do something for them, albeit briefly.

They watched the detraining of the soldiers. The cheeky one gave them a wave and a lop-sided grin. 'I'll bring you a Jerry helmet back, boys' he shouted.

'Why aren't we taking them further?' Dafydd asked.

'They are probably giving them a break, stretch their legs.' Thompson replied. They watched the men gather ready, as a small green petrol engine lined up a train of flat bogie wagons. The men were soon back on their way, the ones on the edge desperately clinging to the chain running between posts at selected intervals.

'They'll have a job standing still on them bogies,' Dafydd muttered to nobody.

Pretty quickly they were met by a Railway Transport Officer. The RTO was curt in his orders. Move the train. Take a break. Spend the day shunting. Go back with the train later in the day.

The rain had mercifully stopped. Dafydd turned to look out the back and let the open firebox dry his back, which now felt numb with cold. Although he had now appeared to have earned Thompson's respect, it seemed that this did not increase the level of conversation. As the day moved on, Dafydd had watched the trains come in with more men, as he shunted the wagons of supplies into trains for the front. He thought they were there for the night and a mist was beginning to rise as the temperature dropped with the sunset. Initially, Dafydd had thought it was a gas attack, but then he grew to embrace it as a cocoon from the emotion and pain of Flanders.

He was on the makeshift station when he heard a roar of diesel engine and one of the small engines broke through the mist with a train of flat wagons and closed vans. There were silhouettes of figures of various heights and as the train approached, the cargo came into focus. There were men, but fewer than they had delivered. They were lying down or sitting, some were on stretchers, the poles sticking out from the vans.

Medical orderlies were running up to the train and road trucks were arriving, together with horse carts. The train came to a screeching halt and there was a rush of activity, as the men were despatched as quickly as possible to the waiting lorries.

Dafydd wondered why they were covered in red poppies, until he realised that it was blood. Now he could hear the cries and groans and with a sudden shock he realised he had to walk past this scene to get to his engine.

He stumbled and checked his pace. Stretchers were pushing past, but the congestion left the stretcher bearers forced into a sprawling queue. Dafydd jumped as a hand brushed him and he muttered his apology to the wounded man. There was a lop-sided grin and a familiar voice replied.

'There you go, Taff. You kept your word. Sorry I couldn't keep mine. I didn't get you a bloody helmet.'

'Christ, what happened to you?' Dafydd asked without thinking.

The man's broken body seemed incomplete or shrunk. Dafydd wasn't sure which it was, but it didn't look right. He was a mix of colours khaki green mixed with light brown and red, his flesh tightly wrapped in white bandages.

'Someone forgot to tell the Jerries to have the day off', the soldier replied.

Dafydd patted his pockets for a cigarette. He didn't like the smoke, but the ration was good for bartering. His hand shook and the packet spilled open. Dafydd lunged forward to stop the cigarettes dropping onto the man. An arm leant over and stuck a roll-up in the man's mouth and then produced a Lucifer to light it. The tip glowed faintly, and the man coughed slightly, but nodded his thanks. Then he was gone in the scrum of humanity around the canvas-roofed trucks.

Dafydd and Thompson looked on at the procession of stretchers and walking wounded. The worst of those with some mobility, were being guided by others who were themselves wounded. Dozens of RAMC were in the mix, together with a clutch of corporals bawling out orders. It looked chaotic, but thankfully the most wounded appeared oblivious to it.

'Poor bastards,' Thompson said. 'They get screamed at and treated like shit on parade. Screamed at to put their lives on the line. Then when they are lying half-dead or blind on a stretcher, there's still some bastard screaming at them. It's no wonder they take weapons off the wounded...'

'And we have to walk through it. I wish I'd stayed on the engine.'

'Steady on, corp,' Thompson said, but Dafydd had stalked off towards his guard who was walking towards them.

'Easy lad,' Clarke said, seeing the storm in Dafydd's furrowed brow. 'There's thunder in thee, but there's nowt you can do here for 'em.'

Dafydd brushed past him without breaking step. 'Twelve hours ago, we were taking these poor sods up to the front.'

He stormed off towards the glow from the cab of his Baldwin. It seemed like a haven that he needed to reach to avoid this madness. Head down, dodging through the throng, his path was checked by a line of soldiers.

The leading man had his arm in a sling and a bandage wound over his head and one eye. He looked straight ahead as he walked, not caring he had cut across Dafydd's path. His dirt encrusted face was blank as he stumbled forward with agonising slowness.

With a hand on the man's shoulder, the next soldier behind appeared to have a bandage over both eyes and looked down as he shuffled to follow. The next in the line was similar, though his head was raised and twitching from side to side, as if scouring the area for sound. The one following him was hunched and trembled with pain as he dragged his feet to follow them. The hand on the shoulder – a lifeline for them all. Dafydd was numbed by the pathetic scene.

The back-marker's hand slipped, and he flailed out in desperation to find his comrades without the benefit of sight. He stood helpless, with his hands by his side, until one of the depot's corporals grabbed one arm and roughly pulled him back to the line. The hand was slapped on the next man so hard that both jumped. As the line moved past him finally, Dafydd could see the backmarker was crying. He wanted to kill the corporal.

He stepped back and stumbled, making him move quickly to retain his balance. A soldier had collapsed to a sitting position, a blood-stained bandage strapped over one shoulder. He was staring as if in a dream, muttering to himself. With his good arm, he hugged one knee as he shook and talked continuously.

Dafydd stopped to bend forward to the man, but stopped, as he realised the soldier had no idea Dafydd was there. The soldier's words started to take form in his mind, again and again, like a mantra.

'Good dog. Good dog. Don't come near me. Go away, there's a good dog. Bark, boy. Bark. Don't lie down, just bark. Bugger off, there's a good boy. Good dog. Good dog…'

Dafydd stepped back again, losing his footing as he tripped. A firm hand gripped him and in slow motion, he turned to find Clarke pulling him back, then hustling him on to the safety of the Baldwin.

'Alright son take it easy. It's not pretty, but it's part of life here. You know that.'

'What bloody dog?' Dafydd asked. 'He's so far gone that he can only think of his bloody pet now?'

Clarke patted his shoulder. 'RAMC have tracker dogs, lad. They are trained to search old battlefields for the wounded. If they are wounded, the dogs bark to bring the stretcher bearers over. If the blokes are goners, they lie down to comfort the poor bastards as they die. That one lost it when he saw a dog come to him. He must have thought his number was up.'

'I feel sick,' Dafydd muttered and promptly obliged on the ballast.

'You crew, get that bloody train out of here, then we need you straight back,' an RTO bawled at them

Dafydd closed his eyes and mouthed a prayer. He wanted to get back and tell the soldier the dog had gone. It was all alright. Only it wasn't all right. None of this was right.

There was little said as they travelled back in the dark. Mad Jack loomed up ahead and as they passed him. He was certain the man cried 'lucky buggers.' It made him angrier. It all seemed so senseless.

On arrival back at the base, he went straight to the RTO.

'We've been ordered straight back to pick up more wounded. We'll water on our way.'

'How are you going to get coal?'

'From that derailed engine. There's enough there.'

'See to it,' came the swift reply. Dafydd turned and shouted as he strode towards his crew.

'Thompson, ready the engine. Clarke get me some good long thick rope. No time for a brew, there'll be more buggers up there needing our help. We'll stop for water on the way.'

The other two looked at each other blankly until Dafydd shouted at them.

'That bloody hose on the back. You know how to use it, there's enough private lakes created by German guns. Get a move on!'

125

Dafydd ignored Clarke raising his eyebrows when he thought it was safe. His plan involved speed with no time for arguments.

He set off at a fast pace, peering forward into the gloom ahead. He knew they would need the Baldwin's generous lamps by the end of the day, so stopped and lit the front lamp himself. Pretty soon, the forlorn figure of Mad Jack came into view and he slowed the engine.

'Thompson, get ready to water the engine.'

Dafydd stopped the Baldwin and grabbed the rope to begin to tie a loop. He was thankful that was one skill his early years at the lead mine had taught him.

'What you up to?' Thompson asked warily.

'You heard. We need water, there's a pool. You know how to use that bloody hose. Off you go. How are you, Jack?'

The stricken man shrugged his shoulders wearily. He had managed to sink lower to the middle of his thighs.'

'Not too bad, corporal. I am glad to report I don't make such a splash now when I pee.'

'Catch this rope,' Dafydd said, tossing the loop across. Jack caught it clumsily.

'What do I do with that, sir?'

'Put it over your head and under your armpits.'

Dafydd moved back to tie it to the side of the engine.

'What's happening, corporal?'

'Nothing to worry yourself, Clarkey. Go and make sure the train is sound.'

'I've uncoupled the engine,' Thompson said as he appeared from under the leading truck. 'You know we're all up for the chop, corp?'

'You boys are all right,' Dafydd replied. 'Tell them I pulled rank on you. I'll back you up.'

They stood in silence, save for the rustle as Jack dutifully put the rope around his shoulders. Dafydd sighed.

126

'Look boys, we've just brought a train full of men out and a load of walking corpses home. We can't save them, but there's one at least we can save.'

'I don't want to get you boys into trouble...,' Jack began to softly speak, but Clarke muttered over him.

'The suction of the mud, it could pull them legs out of their sockets.'

'Do you want to live?' Dafydd shouted. Jack could only nod, tears welling in his eyes. He managed to whisper 'Please.'

'Then make damn sure that rope is tight under your armpits, boy. Thompson, how are we for water now?'

'Enough to get us to the hub, I am certain.'

'Are you sure the knot will hold?' Clarke asked.

'I worked in a lead mine and for a ropemaker, Clarkey,' Dafydd replied. 'I'm happy it will hold. It's going to be a bit painful for a while, Jack.'

'I'll manage,' came the reply.

'What do you want us to do?' Clarke asked.

'Thompson on the cab steps, Clarke at the edge of the pool, but for God's sake don't fall in. We've not much time, there'll be another bloody train along soon enough.'

'Jack...?'

The look that was returned, shocked Dafydd to the bone. A mixture of contrasting emotions; relief mixed with pleading, overwhelmed but firm. Jack nodded back to him.

'Whenever you're ready. I'll be ready too,' the wretched man whispered.

Dafydd hopped into the cab and wheeled the hand brake off. He gently nudged the regulator open and the Baldwin gave a gentle hiss of pleasure. Slowly, she built up steam and the pistons began to pound slowly. Then with a gentle nudge, the engine lurched forward. Dafydd watched the rope go taught, for a second, he felt as if the engine was stalling, but with a minor lurch, the engine moved forward quicker.

Thompson shouted and Dafydd slammed the regulator shut and wound down the brake. Thompson was already running to Jack's prone body and removed the rope. Dafydd jumped down and ran over.

'Jack, can you hear me?'

Jack's eyes were screwed shut and for a moment he didn't move. Then there was a small tic at one side of the mouth and his nose wrinkled, before he coughed.

'Thank you, gentlemen,' he whispered. 'See, I was having a bit of gyp in me right shoulder and you've straightened it out good and proper.'

'Screamed blue murder, the poor sod,' Clarke said.

'Not surprised, considering,' Dafydd replied. 'Hoist him on the truck, couple up and we will be off. We'll lose him among the casualties.' Out of impulse, he grabbed Jack's hand. 'Jack bach, I can't guarantee you're going to be safe when they've fixed you up. But then, you might have a blighty one and be sent back home. If not, well, you've cheated death once already.'

Jack squeezed his hand in reply, then whispered.

'God bless you all. I won't tell if you won't.'

Thompson and Clarke took Jack to the leading truck and then prepared the train. As they started moving, Thompson turned to look at Dafydd. 'That was well done, Corp. but somehow I think we really are all for the chop now.'

****

There was not much time for sleep before they found themselves standing in a cramped dugout. The corrugated iron walls felt clammy and oppressive in the light of a slender candle decorated with rivulets of wax which had fallen onto the upturned crate below. Next to it was a tin cup and a sheet of paper with a pen. Behind this sat the burly lieutenant, built like a prize fighter and with a nose to match.

128

'Now, you lads care to tell me where Jack has gone?' the lilt in his voice unmistakeably Irish.

'No idea sir,' Thompson said quickly. Clarke moved around with discomfort and muttered.

'Begging your pardon, Lieutenant Connor, the man were half sunk in t'mud.'

'Well he's not now, is he?' The men stared forward in silence. 'Somebody pulled him out.'

They continued to look ahead, though the atmosphere felt considerably chillier.

Connor leant forward, his dialogue slowing as he emphasised every word. 'He's languishing in jail now. The redcaps arrested him for desertion. And there's a rope missing from the stores.'

Dafydd shuffled nervously. 'Alright sir, I ordered these men to do it and I take responsibility for their actions. The rope is back in the store if they'd care to check.'

Connor scratched the edge of the paper with his pen. No ink appeared to be coming out.

'I could not just leave him to die like that, sir' Dafydd said.

The pencil hit the table with a thud and Connor looked up.

'You two, bugger off. Me and the corporal's got some talking to do.'

With faces of both gratitude and sympathy for Dafydd, Thompson and Clarke saluted and left with indecent haste.

As the shadows of the two men disappeared from the candlelight, Connor reached for second tin cup and produced a large green glass bottle, which he uncorked and poured a measure of a clear brown liquid in each cup.

'He's not on a charge, is he, sir?' Dafydd asked. Connor did not reply but gazed into his cup before taking a sip.

Dafydd continued. 'Too many people have seen him, and it demoralises the men as they go past. I've seen it. No.... you just did that to force the confession?'

Connor pushed across another upturned wooden crate and nudged the spare cup forward.

'Sit down Thomas.'

Dafydd took the cup with a degree of uncertainty. It was whisky. The spirit warmed his stomach, and a smoky taste hit the back of his throat as he breathed out in shock.

'How did you make Corporal, Thomas?'

'No idea sir, I turned up in France and was told to sew on the stripes.'

Connor snorted and then rapidly checked the outside of the mug to make sure he hadn't lost any of the precious liquid.

'You're an honest man, Thomas. A bright one in some ways. Now myself, I came here as a lowly Paddy. An Irish sapper, lowest of the low in the British Army and I worked hard. Bloody hard until they commissioned me up to this rank. That and a few fatalities along the way allowed me to jump the queue. You haven't seen much action here, but the Jerries like us so much they regularly insist on sharing their ammunition our way. Now, if I was a raw, public schoolboy, with no bloody experience in the front line, I'd have you court-martialled, flogged and everything else under the bloody sun.'

He drained his cup and then poured some more.

'Before I came here, I was Royal Irish Rifles. I had a few adventures of me own over the top and I saw how men are just thrown away over here in senseless attack after attack. I've learned a good man is worth saving.'

He tapped his leg gently with a stick.

'Only decent thing Jerry did was give me leg a ton of shrapnel. Enough to knacker me for the front.'

He took another drink and then waved at Dafydd's still full cup.

'What's the matter with you, boy? Are you a Methodist or something?

'I've visited many churches, sir. The last one was a catholic with my sister and her Italian husband. They all have the same man up top.'

'Jesus, Mary and Joseph!' Connor muttered. 'Jack is in a field hospital with trench foot and shell-shock. He'll survive, nobody there knows he's been a bloody scarecrow for a while. How do we explain his disappearance to top brass? They would prefer to have him there as a lesson.'

'*Iesu Grist*, if you saw the soldiers after they went past him, sir… It makes them think the army doesn't care.'

'The Army doesn't, son. How did you get involved?'

'We were sent straight back to the hub, refuel on the way. I used the shell crater for water supply. Jack helped us.'

Connor's fingers tapped on the crate for a while and he reached for his tobacco pouch, then he nodded. 'That will do. They'll probably move you on. Can't have lower ranks coming up with inventive ideas. Shame, they say you are one of the best from the broad gauge. In the meantime, you get one of these sterling ideas again and you come to me first, right?'

Dafydd nodded and took a large sip of his drink, instantly gasping out his regret.

'I got angry. We'd taken a load of decent blokes up and then were shipping bits of them back. Jack's a man, he deserves a bloody chance to do something. To die fighting Germans, is what he came to do, not in some bloody pool.'

Connor smiled. 'I agree. But this is a friendly warning; next time you do something like that without me knowing, I swear to God, I'll break your bloody jaw. You'll find it difficult to speak any defence at a court martial, you hear me?'

Dafydd nodded. There was nothing to add.

'Now down your drink and feck off, corporal. I've got a bloody story to concoct to those fecking arses in HQ. Don't worry about Jack, I'll write him a bloody chit to get him out of any trouble.'

****

'You alright, corp?'

Thompson and Clarke fell in step with Dafydd almost immediately after he left. Dafydd wondered how they would be feeling, if they knew about the large shot of whisky that warmed his stomach.

'No, he's good is that one. Fair and reliable.'

'Your nose is still intact. He must have agreed with you,' Thompson said.

Dafydd grunted. 'What now?'

'Sleep, lad,' Clarke replied. 'There's plenty waiting for us tomorrow.'

'Yes, I'll just go check the engine first,' Dafydd replied. 'At least it's warm.' He stopped, feeling he had been ungrateful to the other two. 'I'm glad you boys are with me, that's all.'

Clarke nodded. There were no words, the bond was complete.

The back of the cab bowed out like a 'v', to allow a small spot for Dafydd to snuggle down in front of the open firebox door. The fire had long dropped, but the metal still radiated a great degree of heat. He was glad the canvas flap wasn't down. It was raining, but the direction allowed him shelter under the half cab of the engine. He didn't care, if it got wet, he would move to one of the diesels. Anything to have his own space tonight.

He knew he'd been close to trouble for his action, but he'd had enough of the pain and suffering around him. Not for the first time, he wondered about the dubious sanity of his move to join the Army. Once again, he wondered if he could have helped Gwen and he even wondered how Tom fared. Whether Josephine was safe. Despite the troubled thoughts, fatigue won him over and he slept.

He was woken by a loud buzzing sound. Without thinking, he swatted about. Damned bee! It sounded angry as it approached, his hand moved again then stopped. A sudden dread gripped his throat as the reality sank into his waking consciousness. A shell from a howitzer, maybe even something larger, like a railway gun. It was incoming.

The blast threw him forward and he banged his face on the regulator. The recoil made him hit the floor hard and he sat up quickly, only stopping as the sudden blood rush made him sway with dizziness. He tried to brush away the mists that threaten to engulf him into unconsciousness. Grabbing the engine side, he forced himself upwards. The open back of the cab made him feel as if he was standing on a veranda looking out at the scene.

His vision remained foggy and his ears seemed to buzz, as he watched small figures racing to fight a few small fires illuminating the yard. The area where Connor's dugout lay appeared to be in a circular shadow. A dark spot of nothingness. Dafydd suddenly realised why. It was a crater. He hoped it was a trick of the light.

There was a sudden flash of flame, as the fuel dump went up. Dafydd gasped as the wave of heat blew over him. The shock wave had his engine rocking. The sidings full of engines and wagons appeared untouched, but now the dugout area was fully illuminated and the twisted metal amongst the churned-up soil of the crater was exposed. An awful hole in the ground.

133

From his vantage point, Dafydd felt distanced from the roaring fires and the shouts of men. It was like watching a training exercise.

'Corp, we have to move now!'

Thompson was at ground level by the cab entrance.

'Come on, all hands to the pumps. We have to get moving.'

'Where's Connor?'

'Direct hit. Him and a few others.'

'Who's in charge?'

'You until we find someone higher.'

Dafydd shook his head slowly as it all sank in. 'Bloody railway gun. Has it fired again?'

'Yes, but far away now. We was unlucky. You up to this, corp?'

Dafydd's head whipped round as he seemed to wake up. 'Course I am, *bach*. We go and all muck in where we can. Let's go.'

'It took no time for them to send the bloody redcaps to patrol the base. We should have got a dozen useful men instead. Ones who know how to douse them bloody fires!'

Clarke's words undervalued the contempt he felt for the situation. They were all hurting from the attack and were coping in different ways. Thompson had gone silent. Dafydd was looking for something to hit, although he was distracted by trying to hold the other two together.

'War's got to go on, else what use are we?' Dafydd's feeble smile attempted to take the sting out if his words. 'I'll tell you what we'll be doing now in a minute, but I expect it'll be us down the line on a new base. I don't see us staying here, anyhow.'

He walked off around the side of the Baldwin and nearly straight into an approaching officer. The man's brown eyes spoke of boredom and indifference. His uniform was clean with a minimal of creasing.

134

Dafydd instantly loathed the man, he had managed to avoid getting his hands dirty. The report was carefully rehearsed in his mind. All fires put out; all possible stock saved. All pieces of humanity collected and buried. Dafydd took a sharp intake of breath. This man would probably blame them for the acrid smell that still hung in the air and on everyone's clothes.

'Thomas, you're being transferred. The unit is being disbanded and all available resource relocated. You will probably be off back to HQ to train people how not to derail these engines. You appear to be reasonably good at avoiding it, the least incompetent anyway.'

'Sir. Respectfully.' The officer seemed to tense at the word. 'If I'm the most competent at keeping these engines on the rails, shouldn't I be staying here and running them?'

The officer blinked in response. 'You leave tomorrow. Orders to follow.'

He turned and walked off without another word. Dafydd threw daggers at the departing man's back with his gaze.

Later a young Sapper brought him a telegram. His brisk salute was not returned. Dafydd ripped open the envelope and sat down as he digested the words. Then he crumpled the telegram and sighed. He needed to give the information to his new commanding officer, but he could not be bothered to find out who his command was. Dafydd would say goodbye to his crew and show them the telegram. All he had left was to say his good-byes once again and write letters. For a short while, there was at least time to do that.

Chapter Fourteen

Tin Turtle
(1917)

Dear Sioni

Tell Angharad not to mix with any of them soldier types! They are all up to no good and she's so delicate! If you get any problems, go to the Miners Arms and get word to Dai Cochyn. He's getting on a bit, but I would trust him as Dad done before.

Is it Summer already? I honestly lost count. of the months. Mackerel season soon, get Johnny bach out on the beach with his Dad. If it's warm enough, they will catch them by casting from the shore.

I seem to be telling you everything to do. It's like being over here. There's no problem of thinking what to do next. There's always someone to tell you!

I'm sorry you think I sound so English. I suppose the language is all around me now. It's a surprise I haven't started talking all Northern like Tom.

I haven't heard from Gwen for weeks, has she disappeared again? I know you think I'm a fool asking, but I just like to hear that all I care about are well…

Dafydd had had enough. A week into his new posting and he loathed the railhead and everything he saw. The distribution depot, the rows of sidings laden with trucks of all shapes and sizes. He hated them all.

The constant barking of NCOs, pushing, cajoling and bullying ordinary soldiers about, irritated him. He hated the yellow-brown mud that could not be cleaned from boots or uniform.

The rain had been constant, turning Flanders into a land of brown unsavoury toffee. *Like my Mam used to pull*, he thought. *Just as tacky at that.* When the clouds broke, the sun bore down, making Dafydd sweat and his clothes smell of damp. The overload of rainwater oozed into the soil. The remains of trees stood around like crazy gibbets. Dafydd hated it all.

But the thing that he hated most, was the olive-green monstrosity before him. Not for him the training behind the lines or the imparting of knowledge to the uninitiated. Instead he had been dumped further forward with a new noisy harridan of an engine as partner. A lump on rails, tattooed with a number on its side. The number on the inside of the door also. *To remind me of my prison*, Dafydd thought. It was the beast he had as master — or was it the other way around? Dafydd's tin turtle.

It was an odd box on wheels; a thick steel carcass, sloping at the front and back, with letterbox holes at the top for vision, making it claustrophobic at best. It became bedlam when the engine was on, with the pungent smell of petrol, and the noisy vibrations. Everyone drove with the doors open, for fear of fainting with the heat or choking on the fumes.

1914 and I was on the footplate of a glorious steam engine in the hills of Wales, Dafydd thought. *1916 and I'm sitting in this mechanical donkey.* He missed the smell of a coal fire, the cooking of food on the shovel. What was even worse, was that some genius had used old jerry cans to store the drinking water. The effect more than lubricated his insides.

'Morning, bitch,' he muttered, climbing on board the beast. He'd given up slapping the engine. The armour was too hard for his hands. A whistle sounded from farther down the line of static wagons behind him. The guard waved frantically at Dafydd, who rolled his eyes in disgust.

Climbing inside, he fired up the engine. The gears crunched to his satisfaction and then he depressed the throttle. The turtle throbbed in approval and began to lurch forward, coughing up a belch of black smoke. The axles screamed in protest and Dafydd knew his ears would be ringing by evening.

He looked out through the sight-holes, his brow already beading with sweat as the engine warmed up the inside. Dafydd noticed the group of soldiers unloading trucks nearby. They formed a line to gently manhandle shells across to waiting carts pulled by tetchy mules.

'Unlucky bastards,' he muttered to himself. 'Human production line. Wouldn't like to be around if one of them things was dropped.'

Duw! He had signed up to work steam engines, not sit on a mobile trolley all day. He sighed and gloomily drove off to the main rail head for more ammunition. Where the real trains were.

Perhaps he would write to his sister again. She kept on saying how thankful she was that his duties were behind lines. Somehow, Dafydd didn't see it as a blessing.

He returned with some closed wagons of shells and was making ready to take another batch of empties, when he noted everyone starting to run. He cut his motor and could now hear the drone of aircraft engines. Dafydd looked up through the open doors of his vehicle and froze, as he saw two olive green monsters wobbling towards him in the sky, their crew sat awkwardly at the front, almost like on the hide of a dragon. Gothas! He knew of these bombers and the realisation of his position so close to an ammunition dump made his mouth dry with fear.

The ground shook with an explosion, yet Dafydd could not take his eyes away from the Gothas. He had not seen many aircraft and these looked massive compared with the rest. The wings sandwiched the fuselage, seemingly held in place by matchsticks and string.

Another explosion happened, close enough to drop grains of mud on the engine. A few things had launched into the air with the mud. One looked like a body. Dafydd hoped not, it appeared to be in pieces.

The explosions continued, each resounding like a giant drum and each getting closer and closer. Dafydd could only watch with horror. Suddenly a great pressure on his chest threw him back into the turtle and darkness.

He awoke with a pain in his forearm, like it had been seared by flame. The darkness still enveloped him and from outside, he could still hear the thunder of explosions, now farther off. He was being shaken gently by the shoulder and someone shouted to him over the noise.

'Hey, wake up, come on boy.'

The accent seemed familiar, but with an overseas twang.

'Where the...?' Dafydd groaned and then stopped. He realised he was still in the turtle. Light was streaming through the sight-holes above. The doors had been closed.

'That's ok,' came the voice. 'You swear if you need to. You got a shrapnel wound, blast knocked you about and all. I patched you up best I can.'

Dafydd didn't know the man, but he felt he should know the accent.

'They're still bombing?'

'Pretty much, you been out only a short while.'

'The depot?'

'It was fairly empty, but there's still danger.'

'We've got to get out,' Dafydd thought he could still hear the hum of aircraft engines.

'Yes, but how?'

'Help me up,' Dafydd said as he scrambled to stand with difficulty. The pain in his arm as he knocked it made him scream. Slowly, his eyes readjusted to the light and he looked out. 'Rails are good, we could drive out the depot. Just need to change the points and uncouple.'

'Why? We'll be targets.' The man paused. 'Then, if that's the case, maybe we should take the train with us?'

'What?'

'Well, firstly, it'll save time, second perhaps they'll leave the dump alone. This tub is armoured enough.'

'What if they don't follow?

The man laughed. 'Then we're away and safe.'

'You're mad,' Dafydd said as the man opened the door and jumped out. He briefly saw 'Canada' on his lapel. Somehow it didn't feel right.

'And I'm mad to listen,' he muttered to himself.

His arm quivered now with pain, as he tried to stand wrong side, to use his good arm on the levers. He prayed he didn't slip; his injured arm wouldn't hold him.

The Canadian burst through the door and slammed it shut again, cheerfully exclaiming, *'Duw,* that was close. One of them Gothas is still around. I think he's dropped his bombs, but he fancies his chances with his guns.'

At that moment, the hum grew louder, and a thudding sound started on the shell of the turtle. 'Get us out of here!' The Canadian yelled.

Dafydd didn't need telling twice. He rammed the engine into gear, and it quivered into motion. A single explosion came close, making Dafydd duck, as a combination of soil and spots of red-hot shrapnel shot through the visor.

The noise made his ears ring and Dafydd tried to shut it out. He reached out for fond memories and fell back to a time when he was growing up as a boy. The service in chapel, everyone in their Sunday best. The grown-ups looking on with nods of approval or stern stares. He wanted to step into the dream and leave this hell, the images increased. The congregation were singing happily. He began to mouth the words and soon was singing 'I bob un sydd ffydlon'. He opened his eyes briefly and caught the Canadian moving his lips, almost as if joining in.

Slowly, the noises began to fade, down to the loud drone of the diesel engine of the turtle. It was hot and clammy and Dafydd sighed as the Canadian slowly opened the door and cool air flooded in. He looked for bullet holes but saw no chinks of light.

'You can stop now,' the Canadian shouted. 'Our fly-boys have come and chased the Huns away. Bout time too. Come on, let's look at that arm.'

Dafydd stopped the turtle and went to step out. His legs buckled and he nearly fell. His comrade helped him to sit by the track. Dafydd winced at the sharp pain, whilst the dressing was replaced.

'Looks as if you still got a piece in there,' the Canadian said. 'Might be a blighty one if you're lucky.'

'Looked as if you were singing in there with me,' Dafydd muttered. The Canadian laughed.

'Course I was, I'm a Henllan boy, up near Denbigh. Billy Evans. Thought you'd know, we've been talking Welsh since I arrived. You were all shot up and cursing, and you a chapel boy and all.'

'It's a strange war this,'

'Tell me 'bout it. I emigrated in 1911 and joined up to fight later. First thing they do is ship me to Kinmel Bay, only a bicycle ride from my Mam. She nearly died when I turned up in uniform.'

His voice faded into the background as Dafydd fainted.

He woke in a dressing station. A small canvas tent, with the flap flicking in and out with the breeze. Dafydd slowly looked around, wincing with the pain from his back. There were two rows of camp beds all with injured occupants. All was quiet, bar the flapping canvas and the gentle clicks of metal as nurses tended to a man. One saw Dafydd stir and came to him.

'Awake now? Good. Doctor will be around in a while. Your arm may take time to heal, but you should keep it.'

'Billy...?' Dafydd asked. 'There was another soldier...

141

'Back in his unit I expect. You'll see him soon enough when you get back.' The nurse smiled. 'Rest first and heal.'

Dafydd lay back and a tear formed. He never got to say thank-you and he never would. Of all the injustices of the day, that seemed the worst.

Soon, he had recovered enough to be shipped out. Dafydd was transferred to hospital to remove the shrapnel that still burned in him. He prayed it would be fast, the pain still stopped him sleeping.

He found himself at the rail hub once again, in a line queuing for the hospital train. As he waited his turn, he looked around and spied his turtle in a corner. He broke the line and moved to her and gasped at how forlorn she was. Caked in mud and riddled with pock marks, she looked spent. He reached out and gently moved his fingers over the jagged entry of a shrapnel-hole, marvelling at how shallow they were in the thick iron skin.

Her number was obscured by dirt and Dafydd began to clean it away with his good hand. It felt like the least he could do.

'Oi! You! Get away from that!'

Dafydd continued to work away the dirt. His hand trembled, he almost imagined the turtle giving a purr of pleasure and he smiled sadly. Footsteps rapidly approached and Dafydd turned to stare down the angry non-com.

'Shut it soldier, I heard you first time. Don't you shout at me, I've still got one good hand and the other's causing me so much gyp as to give me a temper with it. Don't you insult my girl either; she's the best damned turtle in this army. Bombed to buggery and she's still sitting proud on her axles. You best look after her, for if you don't, when I'm back, I'll want to know why.'

Chapter Fifteen

A Blighty One

Dear Dafydd,
I am so sorry I haven't written. I'm so tired these days with the work in munitions, doing my bit to get you boys home as soon as possible. I'll try and write again when I can, but I'm thinking about you, cariad. I'm always thinking about you...

For a moment, Dafydd expected Tom to be at the clearing station, waiting for him with a cheery smile, a shake of his head as if in disbelief, and a mug of tea. It was all a dream in the fog of pain, surrounded only by strangers. His arm throbbed, as the shrapnel lodged therein kept reminding him of the Gotha raid. It was tantalisingly visible, but its vice like grip was too deep for him to rid himself of the shards.

There was no preamble, he was marched in, given limited local anaesthetic and the operation began. He tried to forget how they cut into his flesh and levered out the metal. He tried to ignore the metallic clunk, as the pieces were dropped into a kidney shaped metallic dish. Dafydd sneaked a look at the shrapnel, it had felt ten times that size. The anaesthetic kicked in late and as the pain in his now bandaged arm dulled, he was shown to a bed. As sleep crept up on him, he began to wonder what would happen next.

There weren't many bandage changes before he was in front of a doctor for review. The man had no time for pleasantries and gripped Dafydd's hand briefly after the bandage was removed.

'That will heal. I'm sending you out, I need the bed for worse.'

'What?' The confusion was numbing in Dafydd's mind.

The doctor scribbled on a paper.

'I need the bed. Here. Two week's leave, then report back to base.

He handed it to Dafydd.

'Bugger off, corporal.'

Dafydd was lost. 'Where?'

The doctor looked over his glasses. 'Up to you. Go find some estaminet somewhere. Get drunk. Find a whore. Or go home. You have two weeks. Nurse will give you some field dressings, keep the damned wound clean or next time they'll just chop the bloody thing off.

'Home?'

'Yes, you should manage a few days. Go, Thomas. You're a lucky bastard. Copped a blighty one and you're not even close to the front…'

Dafydd looked around the tent that acted as a makeshift ward. Over the past few days, he had learnt to shut out the moans of pain and the screams of the tormented. He had got used to the comfort of a camp bed, instead of the spartan existence of the inside of a truck or the wooden floor of an open cab. The noise, the unexpected arrivals, the constant rumble of shellfire in the distance. It was all normality to him now. As normal as the fields of mud, criss-crossed with duck boards not far enough outside his canvas haven. He was even used to the sight of blood now. Lots of it. Sometimes dripping from detached limbs, waiting for the furnace. It was all disturbingly normal.

Now he had a ticket to leave this madness and reacquaint himself with reality. It made him feel paralysed with indecision. A step into the real world felt like a step into a far-off dream.

And dreams never came true, Dafydd knew that from experience.

'Taff. Fuck off out of here, before I kill you for your pass.'

The groaning words came from a body wreathed in bandages. He was minus one leg, possibly two. Dafydd had never wanted to go close enough to check.

He felt stupid. The confusion of transferring and then his injury had meant he had lost all his precious letters. Here was a golden opportunity to find out what was happening. A dream he had cherished for such a long time, was presented to him but the reality had him rooted to the spot. He wanted to see his family and check that they were fine. *Perhaps, just perhaps, he could find Gwen and see…* He quickly dismissed the thought. That path only ever led to pain. He went to sit at the wounded man's bedside. He'd never even bothered to ask his name…

'It's sorry, I am, *bach*. I just got startled for a minute there. I forgot what it was like back home.'

'Now's your time to find out, chum.'

Dafydd thought about his fortune, as opposed to that of the mummified man in front of him. What future lay ahead for that poor sod?

'Look, do you want my chocolate ration or some Baccy?'

The reply was akin to a gurgle.

'I don't have the taste for chocolate anymore, or the mouth for Baccy.'

'Can I get a message out to any…?'

'No.'

The reply was curt and final, the sound hollow within the bandages. After a few moments, he continued with a forlorn tinge to his voice.

'What you can do for me is to make every moment count.'

Dafydd stood up, but the man made no movement. However, his eyes peered through the bandages like dark pools of sadness.

Dafydd saluted the man, it was the least he could do to acknowledge the wish. Then he grabbed his kit bag with his good hand and stepped out of the tent. At the flap, he looked out on the camp, watching the orderlies milling about like worker ants.

A pair carrying a stretcher sidled past two men on crutches, sharing a smoke. Nurses looked busy, walking fast to their posts, as if to avoid any bawdy comments.

An ambulance lorry pulled up and Dafydd made for it. There was a chance of a lift back to the hub if he helped. Two weeks leave? He'd be home in a day or two.

Chapter Sixteen

The Runners

Rain, nothing but rain, Dafydd thought, as it lashed in from the sea and gently melted the salt crusts on the carriage window. He could not remember when he had last seen a dry day. *At least the mud on my boots is different*, he thought - Flanders brown replaced by Dover chalk.

He had his home leave, even though the fourteen days had been cut to seven, as he worked his way out of the chaos of Flanders. Four days of that would go on travelling in smoky carriages like this. Three at home with luck, probably two given the way things ran these days. *Perhaps they would let him sleep in carriages in the sidings on the way rather than rough it on the station?* He didn't worry so much now about going back. As long as he was back across the channel before the pass expired, he could blame the delay on congestion. He had seen it enough from others and nobody seemed to challenge it.

Dafydd wiped the condensation from the window and looked across the platform at the soldiers waiting for another train. Little red glows of tobacco occasionally lit up all around the gloom of Dover Harbour. It was almost dark enough to be night, but Dafydd thanked God that at least he was dry for once.

A mixture of dust and damp filled his nostrils as he looked around the carriage. The windows had been left open allowing the seats to dampen and fester in the rain. The musty aroma kept Dafydd awake, even though he had smelt far worse during his army service. The carriage was a sea of khaki, all carrying rifles except for him.

Many had thrown disdainful looks at him since he had arrived, those who could not sleep off their months of trench life, death and destruction. It was like he was RAMC perhaps, one above a Conchie, a shirker from the real man's job.

The soldier opposite him had not stirred since they had arrived in the train. From the smell on the man's breath, Dafydd guessed he had reacquainted himself with a distillery of old. The kilted uniform implied a man who had tasted home before he could touch it.

The woman guard slammed the doors and called out, one soldier stirred in response perhaps hoping she would be a beauty. A scowl from the lady made him move back to the comfort of his pack.

'There's a fishwife I wouldn't wish anyone to have as a mother-in-law,' he grumbled, making Dafydd smile.

The train jerked and they began to head off north - a step closer home. The journey was not fast and they stopped constantly, but that was just a normal day for Dafydd. The amount of movement to the front meant the railways were always a test of patience, especially for a driver.

****

The carriage rattled as each train passed, making the soldiers in the compartment edgy. All bar the Scot who was still sleeping in the corner. The windows steamed up again. Nothing was said as the train moved on, but the occasional cough and splutter broke through the silence. All the while it grew warmer and the air grew stale.

An hour passed, although it felt like five to Dafydd, then they finally pulled into a station. Soldiers started to shuffle like cattle and word began to spread, as the windows facing the platform were opened. It appeared there were volunteers on the platform serving tea.

The man in the corner woke at the jolt and yawned and stretched the feeling back into his limbs, rubbing the stiffness from his neck. He looked over and said something that Dafydd could not understand. The harsh Scottish accent and dialect was too much for Dafydd's ear, so he nodded back to the man politely. The man stood up and stretched again then said something else with a questioning glance, which just made Dafydd's brain whirr with confusion even more. Seeing the blank look, the Scot repeated himself, pointing at his kit and the seat. Dafydd nodded and smiled.

The man walked over to the carriage door, through the tangle of unyielding legs. He turned and looked at Dafydd and spoke once more. Seeing yet another polite but blank response, the man rolled his eyes. He then spoke in slow measured tones that Dafydd finally understood.

'Ah sed wud you laik ah tea, yer Weilsh bastard!'

Dafydd laughed and nodded, the Scot smiled, shook his head and was gone. After a while, a soldier standing in the corridor saw his chance of a seat and moved in. Dafydd challenged him politely enough, but tired and weary as he was, the soldier was past caring. When he saw the Railway Corps badge on the lapel, he was less than polite about what he thought of it.

'White feather's not good enough for you bastards, hiding behind the lines. Keep your nose out of it, before I knock it off.'

The door of the compartment slammed open, kicked by the returning Scot with two steaming mugs of tea. He looked at the scene and just said one word with the flick of his head. 'Shuft!'

The bullying soldier stared back angrily, but he could not match the glare from the Scotsman's piercing blue eyes for long. He grabbed his pack and shuffled off muttering curses.

Dafydd rolled up his sleeve, the shrapnel wound now healing but still angry, which matched his humour. 'Oi!' He shouted at the departing back. As the man turned, he thrust his arm up. 'See this? That's from rescuing the likes of you, now piss off!'

'He'll no be back,' chuckled the Scot, handing a mug to Dafydd. He turned to address the compartment in his brogue before opening the window.

'We'll close it when we get going,' said Dafydd helpfully to the wall of silence. There was no acknowledgement. Dafydd shrugged to the Scot.

'Chus that,' came the reply, as he settled down in his seat. Dafydd breathed deeply, as the cool fresh air flooded in.

The rain spat drops onto his face, but he welcomed the feeling, it was like being on the footplate again. A shiver went through him as his senses caught up with the change of temperature. The train jolted once more, spilling the Scotsman's tea. It made him lean forward with a tirade of curses, as he held his mug out and brushed off his kilt. Tipping some out of the window, he sighed and scratched his greying hair.

'I ken ye wudnae do that yersel', Taff,' he said acknowledging the Railway Corps badge. Dafydd shook his head and smiled politely, he wasn't really in the mood for talking.

'Ye cannae unnerstand a word ahm sayin, can ye Taff?' rasped the Scot.

'I can a bit, Jock,' Dafydd said with a grin and the man nodded sharply.

'Ah'll try and slow doon a wee but,'

'That's good, *boys bach*,' Dafydd replied and he got a toothy grin back.

'Wharr's do frae?' Jock asked and rolled his eyes at the puzzled look once more.

'Frae? Frem? Ahm frae Shetlan do kenst?'

Dafydd was struggling, but slowly the man was making sense to him. The accent was broader than he'd ever heard, but words were coming through. *Do kenst? Must mean chi'n wybod? Do you understand?*

'Shetlan',' Jock was saying. 'Kenst doo Shetlan'? Da isles north o' Aberdeen?'

'Yes,' Dafydd was almost sure, but he knew Aberdeen was far north. 'I'm Welsh,' Jock gave him a look of the bleeding obvious, so he went on. 'Aberystwyth - on the West Coast?' He took out a notepad and pencil and sketched a bad outline of Wales with an 'x' at the centre of the Cardigan Bay coast.

The train jolted again, and Jock swore and made as to hurl his cup out the window with a curse. 'Had better sailing on Da Roost,' he snarled.

Dafydd calmly pulled the window strap to close it. 'Getting a bit wet now.'

'Damn!' Jock cursed, looking at the wet patch on his uniform. 'Wud ye drive like that?'

'Dafydd shook his head. 'He's hardly making friends now, is he?'

'Can ye no tak his place then?'

Dafydd just laughed. It was nice just to have the break from the cold metal handles, oily rags and coal dust. Just for now, he didn't miss it for the world. Especially not at the front.

'Hoo lang wul it tak ye tae get back?'

'Ten hours, maybe twelve. Overnight if I miss the last one from Carmarthen. Hope not, mind. Want a few days with the family and all. Fishguard train should get me there on time. Here's hoping anyway.'

He could always travel the Cambrian route that he knew so well, but Dafydd wouldn't take it. The memories still hurt, and he couldn't face his old friends just yet. 'Where you going to?'

'Ach, Fishguard,' came the strange reply. Dafydd was surprised, the man had sounded as if it was a sudden decision. He let it pass, the Scot knew what he was doing, Dafydd was sure. Besides, it wasn't his business.

'My name's Dafydd, you?'

The man smiled and took out a hip flask, unscrewing the cap. 'Ahm Jock, you're Taff.' He made to pour into Dafydd's mug then stopped. 'You're no wee free are ye?'

'Chapel? Well yes but,' Dafydd smiled with a mock sigh. 'This is war.'

'Guid. Family back hame?'

'Two sisters, eldest and her husband have a café in Aber, Italiano.'

Jock nodded. 'Ah have the five sisters mahsel'. Ah can sleep a night o' Jerry's barrages, fer it's no such a din as ma hame. Ken what ah miss the most?' Grass, fine green grass.'

'And trees,' added Dafydd, but Jock shook his head.

'Trees dinnae grow weel on Shetlan', no so much grass as well, too damn windy. The merry dancers in the sky on a moonlit night the view frae the Soond doon tae Bressay in the simmer dim. When the dawn comes no half oor past sunset, ah miss that as well.'

'I miss the sunset over the sea, I miss the sea and all,' Dafydd said wistfully looking out the carriage. He hadn't an idea what Jock had just said, but he guessed at the sentiment.

'Ach, nae need frae comin all maudlin,' Jock said and took a swallow from his flask before passing it over.

Dafydd took a swig, surprised at the warm apple flavour in the fire. 'Calvados?' he croaked.

'Aye, them Frenchies have a horrid fine way wi' Brandy.'

The conversation slowed, as the warmth of the brandy had them both dozing. Another jolt woke them, and they looked out on the bustle of Victoria Station with everyone around grabbing their packs in a rush to get out.

'Hoo do ah get tae Fishguard?' Jock asked suddenly and Dafydd frowned.

'I thought you knew? Paddington: bit of a walk it is. Wonder if we can find a bus to ride?'

****

This they managed easily, transport for soldiers being free in wartime London. Sitting on the bus as it lurched its way down the street. Dafydd spied a young woman immaculately dressed standing up as if to get off. She moved towards a pale youth who sat nervously in front of them and offered him a white feather.

'Here, take this for the bravery you show in letting your friends do the fighting for you,' she said sweetly.

Memories of a similar scene on Aberystwyth station stung Dafydd into action and he angrily leant forward snatching the feather from her hand.

'How dare you?' the woman hissed but he was past politeness.

Good dog, bugger off dog…

'Who the hell are you to judge?' Dafydd snapped.

'Just doing my bit for the war,' she replied sulkily. 'There are people running from their duty.'

'It's all a bloody game to you lot!' Dafydd shouted. 'Get another poor soul sent out to be blown to bits for no reason. Talking about running, when are you going to get **your** hands dirty, eh? To work in munitions until your fingers bleed? To go out and nurse the poor bastards who survive their limbs being blown off by shrapnel? That's when you can start judging, girl. That's when you're allowed to say your piece. Not now. Leave him alone, he's scarce a boy and there's enough of them buried in the mud already.'

'Shuft!' said Jock jerking his thumb and the woman obliged rapidly, her departure being greeted by a few choice comments by others. Dafydd tapped the youth on his shoulder.

'When you're old enough butty, make your own choice not because some stuck-up tart tells you to,' he growled. The youth said nothing, but clearly looked upset and left at the next stop.

'Another soul that'll be bullied into an early grave,' Dafydd muttered. Jock shrugged.

'S'life.' Came the taciturn reply from his Scottish friend.

At Paddington, Dafydd spied something that had him racing down the road into a shop, reappearing moments later with two newspaper covered portions of chips.

'No bad, Taff,' said Jock in between chews. 'Nearly as guid as da Belgians.'

'Filerstine,' came the reply.

The South Wales train pulled out and the two settled down for the long trek. The bustle of the station was quickly lost in a forest of bridges and tracks. Jock had obtained a bottle of whisky and he uncorked it without ceremony as the train gathered pace.

'There's no toilet.' Dafydd warned and Jock shrugged.

'Ah'll puss out the windae if ah have tae,'

A woman was the only other passenger. She was already uncomfortable with her proximity to the pair and now she got up to move further down the small carriage. Jock shrugged again. 'Ah've done wurss. So, yer a driver?'

Dafydd nodded. 'Fireman by trade all told, but army thinks I'm a driver and I'm not one to disobey orders even if the desk boys can't fill in forms. I can drive and all, been taught well.'

'What does yer fireman think?'

Dafydd's thoughts fell back to Poperinge. In all this war, it had been home. Tom and Josephine, keeping him sane.

'Tom? He's quite happy, fair play. He's a driver broken by some ass of an officer and he took me under his wing. He gets no grief from me and I learn from him. I was firing on the Cambrian, up Oswestry way at first, but some bloody passenger decided they could afford to give some men to the war and gave us grief. Well, I joined up, so it must have worked.'

'Ye said ye were Aberystwyth, Taff?'

Dafydd nodded. 'Aber boy to the bone, worked my way up from track to shed. Then Oswestry was short and well, I did go back home to work, but got to do my bit, an I?'

The taste of bitterness still hung in Dafydd's mouth as the memory flooded back. Price. Gwen.

'Someone didnae like ye?'

'You could say that…'

Jock started to roll a cigarette, causing a polite cough from the timid lady, who nervously indicated the no smoking sign. Jock smiled 'Nae bother ma'am, ah'll make 'em ready for later, ye ken. Was it a rival?' He said to Dafydd as he licked the papers.

'Oh yes.'

'Love?'

Dafydd glared at him. 'You're a sharp boy Jock and no mistake.'

Jock chuckled.' Weel we're no hermits in Shetlan' oorsels, ye ken.'

Dafydd accepted the whisky bottle and took a sip, then a larger one. 'Alright then, seeing as we've got time on our hands. There's this girl, right? I known her since I was fifteen. She's a fair-haired beauty, Gwen is her name, she's well you know - the kind of girl you just want to be with.'

'Fall in a pit o' muck and come up reekin o' roses? Aye ah ken.'

'But she had ideas above her station that one and she took up as mistress with a rich man in the town. She likes being bought things and she's a kept woman that way, more than I ever could. He has influence on the railway, him and his big house and all. It's why I ended up in Oswestry...' The bitter thoughts of the injustice of it all could not leave him. Would they ever?

'She's no oot yer life then, Taff?' Jock said, though it was a statement, not a question.

Dafydd sighed. 'I don't think she's ever been. When the call came to release more men from the railway to Haig's army, I was breaking down the door to enlist. I got lucky and was posted to the Railway Corps and even luckier that they can't fill in forms, making me a driver when I wasn't.'

'Nae so lucky with yer arm,' Jock said nodding at the bandaging.

Dafydd snorted. 'Lucky I'm still here, mind. Driving one of them turtles at the front, I was. Petrol things, all armour plate but no-one told the German Air Force who used me for target practice.'

'Oh aye? A Blighty one?'

'Perhaps for now. But it's healing fine and I'll be back soon enough. More's the pity; it's only bought me seven days leave in the end.'

'Tough.'

Dafydd was getting used to Jock's way, a man of few words, but he made them count. Dafydd thought back to the time he got the move to Oswestry. He had sent a message as quick as he could back to his love. He had been desperate to see Gwen, to beg her to come with him. She came but only to say goodbye. Not even to see him off, as the train departed.

It was still raining as Dafydd stared out through the streaked window. He had been set up. She had sent him there to start anew, that much was true. His rival had even admitted it, when the fortunes of war had brought them together in a bizarre set of circumstances.

'Do you know, I met Price on a goods yard in Flanders of all places?' Dafydd said, looking for a reaction and getting none. 'Captain Price by then. He was an officer waiting with his men. He just about ran to the engine, so red with anger he was.'

'If I survive, don't bother to come looking.' The words still echoed in Dafydd's mind. He recounted the story to Jock who listened patiently as Dafydd poured out his tale. He hadn't meant to say half of it, but like uncorked champagne the contents rushed out to greet the warm air.

****

They had reached a station and the lady had departed quickly from the carriage, glad to leave. A few civilians stood ready to board, but Jock quickly uncorked the bottle and started to sing loudly, making them all have second thoughts and move further down the platform. Their carriage now empty, Jock grunted in satisfaction.

'So, why dae ye hide, Taff?' Jock's voice broke through Dafydd's thoughts.

'Not hiding from anyone pal!' Dafydd snapped.

'Yer bonnie lassie walked oot yer life then?'

Dafydd laughed. 'War's a funny thing isn't it? I get sent away and she starts pining for me. I got a letter soon after I joined. Cambrian sent it down to my training camp. We been writing ever since. She's warm but...distant I suppose.'

Jock looked long and hard at Dafydd, then leant forward. 'Ye ken when we were in London did ye no see the railway map? I looked fer Aberystwyth an' it sets me wondering why ye travel this way?'

Dafydd looked out the window. 'I'll not travel the Cambrian. I feel ashamed I walked out on them,' he said lamely.

'Ye think they'll no be proud o' ye? I'll wager they'll wannae have ye driving tae see hoo ye fare.'

'I expect you're right,' Dafydd said, his tone unconvincing.

'Where's your lassie jus noo?'

'She said she was going to do her bit, in munitions somewhere. She hasn't written a while since. I don't know when. There's no munitions down our way, she could be anywhere. Wrexham, Hereford, Cardiff even…'

Jock put down the bottle and pointed his finger at Dafydd.

'Ye listen here, Taff. She needs ye noo mair than ever before. Yon man may be rolling in gold, but he'll never make her mair than an unmarried mother and ye ken what yon chapel folk think o' that. Ye find her, ye tell her and ye marry her afore ye regret it.'

Dafydd still stared at the window, biting back the emotion.

'D'ye no love her?' Dafydd nodded. 'How hard wul it be without a man by her side?'

Tears rolled down Dafydd's face, he took a swig of whisky, but the pain didn't go. It felt like an age, but he finally managed to whisper. 'I'll try.'

'That's guid enough frae me, Taff,' Jock said with a smile. Dafydd loosened the strap to let the window down and let the cool air dry his face. He knew it was time to face his fears.

They didn't talk, as Dafydd watched the fields pass them by. He shuddered in the end and with a sigh nodded an acknowledgement to Jock, who smiled and took another swig. Dafydd noticed the smile never reached Jock's eyes. It was common these days, many people had seen too much suffering not to build a wall to protect their feelings. Dafydd looked at his friend and knew Jock was no different.

158

'So,' Dafydd said finally. 'You have a woman in Fishguard?'

Jock shook his head as his eyes took on a haunted look. 'She's at ma hame, North and too far awa fer me tae reach her.'

'Then why are you here?'

'Ah've nowhere tae go and with the time ah have, ah may as weel be in Fishguard than anywhere else.' Jock sighed. 'I just need tae travel and besides ah like yer company.'

'What's haunting you Jock?' Dafydd asked, but Jock sat back and took a long swig.

'Nothin''

Dafydd leant forward. 'Jock, you've just opened my soul and tried to heal it. We've both seen things in this war no man should have to see. I've been shot up. I've driven through gas and I've helped load the wounded onto hospital trains. I know one thing now, you can't hold it inside you, you'll go mad with it and it'll break you.'

Jock's mouth tightened and Dafydd smiled sadly. 'You got to trust me, like I just done to you.'

Jock stared a long while at Dafydd then. His steely blue eyes glimmered with anger and then something seemed to give.

'Ah've killed men I shouldnae,' he said softly. Dafydd let him talk but failed to stop a nervous look and Jock swore. 'No like that, Ah'm no monster, least I dinnae ken ah'm one.' He took another swig. 'We were o'er the top, bayonets an' all tha', moving across No Mon's land waiting fer the bullet wi yer name on,' he swallowed. 'Ah spied a crater and as ah passed it, ah saw it was jus a sea o' mud. A mon was there up tae his shoulders in it, must hae tak oors tae get that far. He couldnae lift his hands, wus a goner. Ah couldnae stand it, ah raised mah rifle and oor eyes met. Ken what he said?' Dafydd shook his head.

'*Danke.*'

The silence was oppressive, both lost in their thoughts.

'I rescued a man once from the mud,' Dafydd said softly. 'Had to use the engine to pull him and broke most of his ribs. Nearly killed him to save his life, that mud was lethal. You did that boy a favour.'

Jock took a swig of whisky, his eyes gleaming. 'Aye, that's right, a favour. But then here's something ye'll not have done wi yer damn engine. When the mist covers the damn ground on a cold morning and ye've been chosen frae one of the firin' squad. D'ye ken what that's like? When it's yer ain pal being tied tae the stake? D'ye ken that?'

Dafydd stared at Jock and watched as the barriers came tumbling down.

'Ye ken he looked at me as they marched him past and he nodded and smiled. Smiled! We'd been shelled frae thirty-six oor and it could hae broke ony of us. They needed one tae punish and Joe was he. He refused a blindfold, dinnae tell me that mon wasnae brave, he faced death an' smiled.' Jock's hands were trembling and his voice hoarse. 'Ah cannae face ma woman after what ah've done…'

'Some of the squad have blanks,' Dafydd said softly and Jock's raw red eyes locked on Dafydd.

'Dinnae patronise me ye Weilsh bastard! Ye/ ken damn well blanks fire different tae bullets. Ye ken when ye fire a blank.'

Dafydd sighed. 'Alright, I know I learnt to fire a rifle too. I'm sorry.'

'Jus dinnae give me yer sympathy,' Jock growled and returned to the bottle.

Dafydd looked on helplessly, he could see the torment. He wished there was some way that he could make it right, some words that would mean something to Jock as the Scot had done for him. Then he knew what he needed to do. Swiftly, Dafydd snatched the bottle and threw it out of the window, ignoring Jock's curses and the raised fist. He stared back at him eye for eye.

'Know what I think? You need your woman now, not some bloody bottle.' Dafydd said firmly. Jock's eyes narrowed.

'Oh, is tha' right?'

'You know damn well it's right.' Dafydd snapped. 'Get your arse off this train and head north fast as you can.'

'Yer pushing yer luck pal,' Jock said evenly. He was standing nose to nose with Dafydd now, but the engineman was past caring.

'You send her a telegram if you need to get her to come to you. You go to her and you tell her all. It will let you live again.'

Jock was livid now and he grabbed Dafydd's roughly. He raised his fist as he yelled. 'D'ye want me tae plant ma fist in yer face?'

'If it helps, yes!' Dafydd shouted back.

Silence fell again, bar the clatter of the train. Jock stared at his hand for a moment, then simply turned away. 'She'll no understan'.'

Dafydd sat down again. 'She will if she knows you and you need her now more than ever. That's why you got home leave, right? Officer had more sense than an army of red tabs.'

Jock sighed. 'Aye, he knew the score, ah was close tae breaking mahsel'.'

Dafydd opened his hand, to show he still held the bottle cork. Jock laughed without mirth, he took the cork and put it in his tunic pocket.

'It'll remind me,' he said.

Dafydd leant forward. 'I understand now, Jock boy. You and me, we're two of a kind. We're both running from our fears, running from our responsibilities. It could all end bad, we could both fail. But we've got to face up now. We got no choice or how will we ever look ourselves in the mirror again? At least we'll know we tried. Both of us, we've got to stop running. It's time to move on.'

Jock went to the window and lit up, leaning out to smoke. He stayed there a while just looking out, then with a long drag, he threw the butt away and came back in.

'Yer right Taff, whisky's a bad mistress and she does nothin but nag ye come the mornin'. Ah'll tak yer advice and ah'll mak ma way North. She's come over tae the mainland jus noo. Cannae survive wi out ma money. Works in a factory, Ah'll maybe not reach her, but ah'll damn well try, and ah'll write it all doon, jus in case ah need tae send it.'

Dafydd scribbled quickly on his notebook. 'That's where you can find me if you need. My sister is Sioned.'

'Bonnie, is she?'

'Married she is, my boy, like you, remember? Though the young one is not and friends of mine are welcome to call - but have to be introduced first naturally.' Dafydd finished in a mock accent. They both chuckled.

'Aye weel, a single man and aal, ye'll no be worried boot that. We'll part as pals an we'll both be off on oor journeys tae find oor own peace. Pray God we both find it...'

Chapter Seventeen

Canaries

'Would you spare a cup of coffee for an old soldier,' Dafydd muttered. The years of training and operations meant he could quite easily fall into the brogue of an English Tommy Atkins at will.

'Sorry, we're closed,' said the woman as she continued to polish a table with her back to him.

Dafydd smiled at the way his little sister had grown up, even in the few years he had been away from Aberystwyth. He looked around the small cafe, the yellow glow of electric light casting long shadows in the now empty room. Dafydd swallowed heavily as the familiarity of it all swept over him like a wave. He had been away too long.

'I said we're closed,' the woman said as she turned, then her mouth opened in surprise.

'Hello, Angharad *bach*,' Dafydd said with a smile. 'I'm back.'

'Oh Dafydd!' She said and ran to his arms.

'I came as quick as I could, that Milford train's always late, mind.' Dafydd muttered, half to cover his embarrassment.

'Oh, I don't care,' Angharad sniffed. 'I been so worried.'

A rustle of skirts followed, and another woman appeared from the back, older and still dressed in her pinny from the day. Her hair was longer than Dafydd remembered and pinned up in a bun. She carried a tray of cups, fresh from washing and put them down as she saw the scene.

'*Pnawn Da,* Sioned,' Dafydd called to her. 'I'm wearing your socks, special.'

'I should think so too,' came the soft reply as she put down the tray and rushed to him with a warm smile. 'Took ages to knit. Where's your rifle now? Can't be a real soldier without a rifle.'

'Well, I'm not a real soldier now, am I? Just a railwayman, same as home.'

'Not quite, is it? You were only a fireman here; army saw enough sense to make you driver.'

'Daveed!' A familiar man's voice sounded out, the unmistakable Italian lilt of Sioned's husband, Donato. Fifteen years in Wales had done nothing to soften the staccato of his native voice. 'Sit down, Daveed. You have come a long way, no? We make some food, Sioned? And I will make some coffee also.'

Dafydd slipped off his pack and gratefully sank into a chair. It had been a long journey from Dover, and he would have to return far too soon. Now he was home, which gave him a warm glow in his body, tinged with rumblings of hunger.

Angharad was talking ten to the dozen, but Dafydd wasn't listening, his mind distracted by the heavy coughing from the counter. For a moment, he thought of his father, living out his last few years here, before a life in the metal mines had taken its final toll. However, the dream died as Donato re-appeared with a jug of steaming coffee and Dafydd was reminded of the Italian's journey in life.

Once one of the men from Bergamo sent over for work at the Frongoch lead mine and had fallen for Sioned. However, the relations between the Italians and the Welsh in the hills had soon descended into violence. On discovery of the liaison, the couple were sent away, with a blessing, for their own safety. Donato now paid the price for his time underground, as many men had in the wilds of Ceredigion.

Dafydd looked at Angharad, who had stopped talking, waiting for a response. On impulse, he reached out and touched her cheek. 'I missed you too, *cariad*,' he said, gaining the desired response as she beamed back and squeezed his hand.

'Angharad's got a sweetheart at the front,' Sioned said as she brought a plate of sandwiches. 'Philip Jenkins? Jenkins, butcher's son? She writes to him every day.'

Angharad flushed. 'Not every day, mind. Have you seen him, he's with the Royal Welch? You must tell me all about it.'

Dafydd thought of the muddy wastelands of death and carnage, the clouds of gas and the screaming wounded on the hospital trains. He closed his eyes.

'Perhaps later, I'm a bit tired.'

'How long can you stay?' Sioned asked.

'A day, maybe two,' Dafydd replied, nervously meeting his sister's eyes.

'She's gone,' Sioned said, firmly but gently. 'She left town a while back. I'm sorry Daf.'

'I know,' Dafydd replied. 'She said she was working in munitions, but she didn't say where.'

His hope of extracting more information came to nothing. No matter how much he tried, she would not be drawn further on the subject and the feeling of a heavy weight settled on Dafydd's heart. He had been lifted by finally being home, but the lack of news of Gwen had knocked him back down.

'How's the boy?' He asked Sioned.

'Doing well, he's looking to join a ship soon enough. Reckons it will be the Cambrian. He just needs to grow up by a few years or five.'

'Naturally,' Dafydd said with a smile.

Dafydd was pushed for questions about the war, especially by Angharad. It was almost as if they felt it was a great game to them, he thought. Detached from the pain and suffering and not having lost any kindred, it probably was.

Hours later, Sioned yawned and got up, ready for bed. She kissed them all and bade them good night.

'So, have you seen him?' Angharad asked softly.

'Who?' Dafydd replied.

'Philip Jenkins,' she said flushing.

'No,' he paused as her face fell. 'Well actually there was the one time. I was taking a train through a station and it was full of troops, Royal Welch, I'm sure.' Dafydd lied. 'Reckon young Phil was there, leaning on a lamp post, lighting a Woodbine. Isn't he an officer?'

'Lance Corporal,' she said proudly. 'Field commissioned only last month. I do hope he's alright.' She rose and kissed her brother's cheek. 'Lovely to have you back, *cariad*,' she whispered and left for her bed.

Donato sighed and slowly got up. He went to the counter and came back with a bottle of brandy and two glasses, pouring two measures. Dafydd downed his in one gulp and Donato refilled the glass.

'They do not understand of war,' he said softly. 'They have not seen. In my country, before I came to Wales, when we became free from Austria, much trouble, we were very poor. They do not understand.' He sipped his brandy and gave a flicker of a smile. 'It is good to see you, Daveed. You remind me of your father.'

Dafydd chuckled. 'I feel at home, my friend.'

'This is always your home,' Donato swept his hand out. 'Always. If the railway let you go, you can always come here. There are dishes to wash,' he added with a twinkle in his eye and Dafydd smiled.

'Your woman, she moved to England, to work a factory.'

Dafydd frowned. 'Why? Where?'

Donato looked in his glass and sighed. 'I think she wants the war to end and everything back where it was.'

'That will never happen.'

'No,' Donato agreed. 'Even this town is not a happy place. Too many have gone. I must ask, why you chase her when she favours another?'

'Because I must.'

Donato tapped his glass on his cheek. 'I have lived long, Daveed. It has been hard. I have seen hurt. I do not want you hurt. Sioned, she does not want you hurt.'

Dafydd sipped his drink. 'Some things are worth fighting for.'

'And if you lose?'

Dafydd shrugged. 'I will have tried.'

Donato sighed. 'She went to Hereford, to a factory making the bombs.'

Dafydd nodded his thanks. 'I will leave in the morning.'

'I know, I will tell your sister.'

'She won't be happy.'

'No,' Donato smiled. 'But once I had a choice to reach for what was not for me. I know how it is and why now you must try.'

'What happened?' Dafydd asked and Donato spread open his hands and smiled.

'Your father was a fair man. I married your sister.'

****

'Is that you Dai Bracchi?' the deep voice boomed and Dafydd's heart sank.

Since the day he had been given leave, he had feared this meeting. He felt ashamed that while his colleagues on the Cambrian were stretched running war traffic, he had left.

'So how is it with those French girls then?' The voice boomed again and Dafydd turned to find Old Man Jenkins walking towards him in oily grey overalls, carrying a rag and a billy-can of tea. Dafydd had had his ear bent on many occasions by the crotchety old bugger, even having earned the man's respect. Now the barrel-chested man puffed and panted at his side and looked him up and down. Dafydd waited for the mocking tones that were inevitable to follow.

'Army done for you, boy. Driver now, is it I am told?'

Dafydd shifted uneasily. 'Well, petrol engines and narrow gauge most recent. They had me on the little armoured turtles last. I just went and reported for duty and next thing I know, I'm a driver.'

Jenkins' eyes gleamed with mischief and his eyes narrowed, 'Think you could handle the old Coffee Pot now, is it?'

Dafydd swallowed. 'I think so, but they have had me driving main line. Dean Goods, North British, Lankys, bit of everything.'

'DEAN GOODS!' Jenkins boomed with a laugh. 'Well, now there's a thing. Where you off now then?'

'Moat Lane,' Dafydd said. 'Need to get to Hereford.'

'Well, you can give us a hand then,' Jenkins said clapping Dafydd on the back. 'See what the driver of a Dean Goods makes of a large Aston.'

Dafydd started to stammer excuses about permission, but Jenkins waved him away.

'You know the road well enough by now and no-one will care. This is the Cambrian, man! Duck down at the signal box and station. Let's see what the army calls a driver...'

Dafydd nodded reluctantly and Jenkins gently steered him up to the engine. 'New recruit, Johnny *bach*,' Old Man Jenkins called at the cab. 'Giving us a hand to Moat Lane.'

Johnny Harris, one of the boy cleaners looked up and beamed back through the coal dust that covered his face.

'Alright Daf,' he shouted as he stoked up the fire of the hissing giant. Dafydd clambered aboard and watched as they prepared to go. The right away was finally given and Dafydd felt a thrill as the engine pulled slowly out. He ducked behind the cab side as they passed the box and stared at the walls of the shed as the black iron beast he stood on lumbered past it. Slowly, it began to pick up speed and Jenkins shouted over his shoulder.

'Best get your jacket off. You'll be sweating soon enough.'

The train gathered speed as it rolled down the straight to Llanbadarn. The ancient church sped past as they crossed the road and Dafydd stood up ready. Old Man Jenkins stood to the side, holding the regulator and Dafydd took the great lever from him. Trembling, he opened it up and the surge of power made the wheels slip and the engine roar in disapproval, the carriages clanking together as they lost momentum.

'That'll wake them up in first class!' cackled the old driver.

Slowly, Dafydd warmed to the task. The thrill of power from the majestic engine made him smile. For years he had dreamt of this moment and now there was nothing but to do his best and enjoy the journey. At every station and box, Dafydd tried to hide. Those who caught sight of him seemed to smile and wave though, which made him yearn for the older times.

They made good progress and were along the coast and up to Machynlleth in no time. The bustle of the sheds and goods yards, made Dafydd feel exposed, but Johnny took the token from the signalman and nobody seemed to complain. Soon they had passed Cemmaes and were thundering up the climb to Talerddig. Dafydd knew he had his work cut out, for if he lost power, he could stall the engine. Johnny had given him a good head of steam though, so he opened up the regulator and attacked the bank.

The fields and valleys below sped by as they made good time. Dafydd looked around to complement Johnny and found him leaning against the tender, rolling a Woodbine. Instead, and much to Dafydd's surprise, Old Man Jenkins was hard at work with the shovel, showing his experience of years on the footplate. With a wry smile, Dafydd tapped the glasses and peered at the blazing fire.

'Not a bad job that,' he shouted.

The response was covered by Dafydd whistling his approach to the summit, but he got the gist. Jenkins shook his head and muttered as he worked, but there was a hint of a smile.

Moat Lane was reached with ease and the signalman took the token from Dafydd with a friendly greeting, as he stepped down to the platform.

'There you are, boy,' Jenkins said leaning out from the cab. 'People been asking of you for ages now. Word got round how you been taken off the standard gauge.'

'I felt humiliated...' Dafydd said and Jenkins nodded sadly.

'When this is all over, you be sure to come back and if they don't make you driver, you get word to me. You just took this lady up Talerddig Bank without any help, didn't you see the banking engine waiting to assist?'

'No,' Dafydd flushed. 'I forgot to check.'

Jenkins laughed. 'You come back when you're ready boy, we'll see you alright.'

The words were like a tonic for Dafydd and he carried on his journey with a warm feeling within. Perhaps his good fortune would continue? The train ambled its way down the Welsh Marches, constantly stopping to let past the Jellicoe Specials -the large coal trains that carried the fuel for the Navy from the pits of South Wales to the very North of Scotland for Scapa Flow. The journey seemed to take forever and Dafydd did not finally reach Hereford until the end of the day.

He stepped off the train and looked down the platform in the greying gloom. Steam swirled around in the cold air and through it he saw the silhouette of a woman walking towards him in the mist. For a moment, Dafydd's heart leapt as he thought of Gwen. He quickly realised this was not his love but stopped her and politely asked directions.

'Rotherwas?' She said with a frown. 'Well it's a fair way from here, best hurry if you want to catch the change of shift.'

She gave him directions and Dafydd rushed over to the factory as the day came to its gloomy end. A soldier stood on sentry duty at the gates and Dafydd approached him hesitantly.

'I'm looking for a woman, here,' he started, but the soldier cut in rudely.

'Know her section?' His eyes looked bored and it made him sullen.

'No, I don't,' Dafydd said carefully. 'Her name is…'

'Don't bother, if you haven't a pass, you aren't coming in,' the soldier snapped.

Dafydd noticed people were beginning to stream out of the buildings like ants. The shift was ending, men strode past in caps and mufflers, the women with their hair tied up in cloth. Many were on bicycles. All wore coats to provide some warmth from the cool grey evening. Very soon, the place was a mass of humanity, buzzing with conversation and Dafydd wondered how he would ever find her, as people jostled past him in their quest to escape.

'If you don't have a pass, *soldier*, you best scram, before I have you arrested.' The bored voice sounded again.

Dafydd was tired and upset and the rudeness finally got to him.

'That's Corporal to you, SOLDIER and if you don't want that rifle shoved up your arse, you'd best remember it!'

'Coo-ee!' A woman's voice called from behind him. 'You looking for your girl now?'

Dafydd turned to see three young girls smiling back. Dark haired beauties, all of them, though their teeth were browned and their eyes red with fatigue. He nodded and the girls giggled.

'Well,' the leader said with the local lilt. 'We'd best see if we can find her. Don't you worry over him, he just thinks there's German spies everywhere. We get you love-struck Tommies all the time, trying to catch us girls.' She laughed, clear as a bell and Dafydd began to warm to her.

'Her name's Gwen. Gwen Jones.'

The girl frowned. 'Jones? Don't know a Gwen Jones. You know any?' She said to her friends who shook their heads.

'Oh well, there's many people here after all. You tried our sister factory down the road?'

Dafydd's shoulders sagged. 'Oh, don't be like that,' said the girl giving his arm a squeeze. 'She's bound to be here, let's think. Night shift or day shift? Supervisor? Is she in the munitions shed?' She stopped. 'You don't know, do you?'

Dafydd shook his head sadly. 'I don't know, just got told Hereford.'

'But you come all the way for her, so she must be worth it. She a Welsh girl?'

Dafydd nodded. 'Aberystwyth. Not too tall and thin, fair hair.'

The girl looked around at the departing people and spied someone she knew. 'Gladys!' She shouted. 'You know a Welsh girl? Gwen Jones from Aberystwyth?'

The woman came over and shook her head. 'No, I do know a Gwennie Thomas though from Mid Wales. She's just behind us. Got a husband in the war.'

Dafydd's heart sank at the news, his throat felt dry.

'Yes, David is the name. Engine driver or something.'

Dafydd's head spun with the news. The girl looked at his lapel and noticed the words on his badge. 'You're her husband! Oh, that's wonderful. Go get her, Glad, there's a dear. She'll be so happy, I'm sure.'

'I will,' the woman smiled.

Minutes later she was back with an extremely nervous looking Gwen and Dafydd gasped at the change. The girl with the shining blue eyes had gone painfully thin, her skin had yellowed, and her eyes looked bloodshot. He had the urge to throw his arms around her, but he had a feeling she would recoil by the way she stood.

'We'll get you back on the train with us,' the girl was saying. 'Railwaymen are alright,' she giggled. 'Well, you'd know that, wouldn't you?'

172

Gwen went on ahead as the group made their way down the narrow pavement to the station. The friendly girl, whose name as Rosie, chatted happily away to Dafydd. Gwen was smiling, but her voice was low and Dafydd knew she was avoiding his gaze.

Once on the crowded train, Dafydd looked around and in the reflection in the window, he caught Gwen looking at him. He knew she would turn away if he tried to meet her gaze. What was with her?

Dafydd felt weary. The long travel and the frosty reunion had been too much, and he began to doze. His mind swept through the last twenty years. Gwen's letters had been friendly but distant. Then she had stopped. Now he had found her over a hundred miles away, living under his name, whilst treating him as an unwelcome stranger.

'Can he stay with you?' He heard a voice.

'I don't know where he'll stay,' Gwen replied and Dafydd felt wretched.

'He can stay with me if you like,' Rosie said with a giggle. Dafydd began to drift once more, planning his journey back.

'Are you coming then?' Gwen's voice cut through his thoughts and he awoke to find the train stopped and many people leaving. He followed her out of the station and down the road in silence. There seemed nothing to say.

Without warning, Gwen turned into a small café, nearly knocking into a man coming out. Dafydd heard the man mutter something, it sounded like 'canary'.

Gwen moved to a booth and took off her coat, but kept her hair covered. Dafydd moved to sit with her and nodded when she asked for tea. She looked jaundiced and tired as she took out her purse to get coins to pay. The teas arrived and they sipped in silence.

'Haven't heard from you in ages,' Dafydd said finally.

She sipped her tea slowly. 'It's the war. I'm so busy here, I'm afraid.'

'I don't know where to start,' he said nervously. She smiled but not as far as her eyes.

'You're looking well.'

'Why are you like this?' Dafydd said. Gwen looked away.

'I can't stay long,' she muttered. 'Mrs. Green looks after baby.'

'Whose baby?' Dafydd asked calmly, his mind screamed though for the answer. Price had lied! The child had lived.

'What business is it of yours?' Came the sharp reply and her face flushed.

Dafydd sighed. 'You're using my name and we had our time, once?'

Gwen closed her eyes. 'Well, I can hardly name him after Mr. Price, can I? Think of the scandal. Besides if you were...well unlucky, then at least he would grow up with a hero for a father, not as a bastard. This war makes us close to starving here at times.'

She looked at him. 'Don't worry, I'm not expecting it to happen, you're well behind the lines anyway. Don't expect you can even hear the Germans, you're far too safe running errands for the French.'

'Gwen,' Dafydd said leaning forward. 'I may not be your brave soldier, but I been shot up and all.' She looked back blankly at him and he sighed and rolled up his sleeve. The skin under the bandage was still clammy and wet in places and he knew where the piece of shrapnel was still lodged, tiny to all but his nerves.

Gwen's eyes widened in shock, as Dafydd said softly. 'You don't have to wave a gun to be in danger.'

'I'm sorry, I feel foolish,' she said.

'Am I the father?'

Gwen shook her head, saying. 'No, it was the master. You can't think much of me and my loose morals.'

Dafydd shook his head and closed his eyes. He'd been practising a speech all journey, but it had left him in an instant. He took her hand and felt the trembling there.

'I had it all planned what I wanted to say, girl and …well, there we are. I think that you have love for two men, one who can keep you in the life you wish and the other who can't. I'd like to think you love them for different reasons. I'd like to think you can't decide between the two and that your coming here is a cry of help for an end to this wretched war and a return to how it was.'

He stroked her hand, but she still wouldn't look at him. 'I came here to tell you of my love, *cariad*. I loved you since the first day on the harbour wall. I don't want to frighten you,' he soothed quickly as her hand tensed. 'I'm not here to push you into anything. I just had to tell you what I felt the once. I wanted to be sure you know. Take my name for the child. I'll make sure the army thinks it and then if anything happens, you'll get a pension.'

Her eyes had closed, but the tears still ran as she bit her lip. Gently she pulled away and shook her head.

'Remember that man we passed on the way in and what he called me. Know why they call us munitions girls, canaries?'

Gwen slowly undid her headscarf and shook her hair down. It was yellow, but the powdered yellow of sulphur. It made her skin look yellower and her eyes dim with their redness. There were streaks of green in the hair and Dafydd guessed that these must have been hairs that had gone grey.

All the sorrow and hardship of the time had taken its toll. She smiled at him through trembling lips and whispered. 'The explosives do this; you can't wash it off. Tell me, who would want someone like this?'

He took her hand gently once more and looked deeply into her eyes. 'You're still Gwen, you'll always be Gwen.'

Her eyes closed and her shoulders began to shake. They didn't speak for a long time, and Dafydd felt a lump in his throat. Finally, she sighed and sniffed.

'What do you want of me?'

Dafydd gave a small smile. 'Write to me, keep writing. I need to hear from you. I need to hear a voice of sanity in this madness. One day it will end and when it does, then is the time to talk of other things. Just don't cut me out of your life, not now. Not while I'm so far away and alone...'

He tried not to think of Josephine. He tried.

Gwen smiled and nodded. 'I will.' She looked at the clock on the wall and her face dropped. 'I have to go, Dafydd,' she said, but this time he could feel the warmth return in her voice. 'I have to get my boy.'

'I would like to see the child,' Dafydd said and she rose up.

'He may not be asleep yet. We're not far. When must you leave?'

'First train in the morning, I reckon,' Dafydd replied.

'Perhaps Mrs. Green will give you the couch,' Gwen said as she gathered her things.

'That would be good,' he said, reaching out to stop her as she went to tie up her hair. 'Don't. Take my arm and walk with me with pride. Let me show you off and let others think what they will. It's something I wanted to do for ages girl, show you off and I got a few streets in Hereford to do it. Let me promenade you to them.'

****

'Dafydd! *Codwch rwan! Wyt ti'n moen panad?*'

The harsh whisper broke through into the darkness of his sleep. He regretted hearing the sound, it had been such a refreshing change not to be troubled by dreams.

He was grateful for the tea that was offered, it seemed to cure all ills these days. For a moment, he thought of Tom and Josephine. He hoped Cartwright wasn't causing any problems. There had been some order over there amidst the chaos of war.

The sound of Gwen moving about in her factory clothes broke his thoughts and he looked up. She looked tired, more so than he had ever seen. The combination of munitions work and being a single parent seemed to have taken their toll on her. Her weariness made her look more vulnerable, the free spirit of youth gone. He remembered the early days when things were easier.

'Life hasn't been good to you,' Dafydd said.

She smiled. 'Do I look that bad?'

He hadn't meant that, perhaps not consciously.

'Not what I meant.'

She leant forward to give him tea and toast, then kissed his cheek.

'A lot has happened, *cariad*. It changes us all.'

'I have to go,' he hated the words. 'If I don't cross the channel before my pass expires, it's a deserter they'll have me as. I can say I got lost on the railway network after, but...'

'I understand.'

'I'll send you some of my pay, help you out and all.'

She sat next to him and gently shook her head. 'Keep it, *cariad*. Us canaries get paid reasonable.'

'I want to do something.' He was desperate.

'Near on twenty years ago, what would have happened if we just lay on the beach that night and the ropeworks hadn't burnt down? If I'd stayed or if I had...'

Her hand caressed his, her voice gentle.

'You are a good man, Dafydd Thomas, but we can't live in the past. This war – you just cannot plan for the future.'

She seemed agitated and one hand was tapping the chair and she looked around.

'What is it, *cariad*?' Dafydd asked.

After a brief silence, she sighed.

'I have to go, to work. They are extremely strict on time and you get punished.'

'I understand.'

He stood to leave and turned back to find her in tears. He quickly drew her close and let the storm of anguish subside on his shoulder.'

'It's just…' her voice had subsided to a shuddering whisper. 'I have nothing for you to remember me by.'

'I don't need tokens, I just need your love.'

'You have always had that. We can't plan for the future, but we can hope.'

'Look girl, I know you are torn between me and Price. Just keep writing, that's all. What will happen, will happen.'

She sobbed again, but it ended with a kiss.

'Thank you for understanding. It is cruel on you. If anyone comes along… you know…'

An image of Josephine swept into his mind, but it did not stay long.

'It's dark out there,' he said.

'Yes, the streetlamps are out. Save fuel and to stop zeppelins finding us. Stay close.'

'Because there are many bumps on the road…'

She smiled and his heart was lifted in the way it was all those years before.

'No, because I want to feel you near me. I want your touch.'

Chapter Eighteen

Meetings

'You're late, corporal.'

'Begging your pardon, sir. I was signed off on blighty leave and then told to report back to the corps I had been attached to. Went all the way to the tin turtles on the front to find they'd sent me back.'

'You don't know how much bloody work it took getting you back, Thomas.' Curran was never going to be the model officer. Dafydd liked him all the more for it.

'Glad I am for it, sir. It's not been the same at the Light Railway Corps.'

It's been hell in parts, Dafydd thought. *Good dog…*

'Well, you're back. My gain, their loss. I would warn you, Thomas. Things have changed around here. There's a sort of peace broken out among the crews. They finally knocked themselves into shape. And that girl has gone, she's a medical orderly now. Should never have let her stay. I want you to start on ambulance trains, give Cartwright a break. Get some food and settle in. We'll see you at the shed in the morning.'

****

As he walked through the narrow-curved streets of Poperinge, he was sure it hadn't changed. The large mass of soldiers in various states of distress, drunkenness of just aimless boredom.

The village - or was it a town? Dafydd never really cared, looked as if time had stood still. It was surely one of the best-preserved places left in Belgium. Being behind the lines, it had not had to suffer the full front of war, as seen by neighbouring Ypres.

Although there was damage, somehow Pops retained its bearing and stood proud. Yet somehow, he could no longer find the crumbling building where Josephine had lived.

It seemed bizarre not to be able to find it. Dafydd guessed it must be one of the piles of rubble behind the ramshackle street market, where lines of poor locals on the road, tried to sell what little wares they had for some coin. Most could not sell from a table and used boxes, cases or even flat stones to lift their wares from the ground. With one last look for the ruin, Dafydd moved off on his next errand. To see if Tom was off duty.

It never mattered how many times that he crossed the threshold, Dafydd would never get over the wave of serenity that washed over him at Talbot House. A clutch of soldiers stood around a map on the wall at the entrance, their conversation being punctuated by constant jabs at towns and villages on it. Even their discussion was muted. Dafydd wandered through the French windows into the garden and the sun began to shine in greeting. For a moment, he lifted his face to greet the warmth, before moving forward to the garden, and a solitary figure resting against a tree. Dafydd sat down next to him and sighed.

'Thought I'd be finding you here, you lazy bugger.'

Tom gave a small warm smile and blinked open his eyes in greeting.

'You stopped playing with your toy trains now have you, lad?'

Dafydd looked upwards, the sun was beautiful and warm. The world was a muted murmur beyond the walls.

'Know what, Tom? Think they got fed up of me. Everything I touched turned to shit or so it seemed.'

Tom laughed. 'Bloody war, never any bloody sense anywhere.'

They sat and enjoyed the sun. Water was slowly pouring out of a small fountain. He felt a brush of fur, as a cat lazily sauntered past him. It was all too peaceful by half.

'They had me down for training drivers until Curran intervened and recalled me.'

'Bout bloody time if you ask me.'

'It's mayhem out there, Tom. I seen some bad stuff. Got the scars to show for it and all.'

Tom didn't reply and Dafydd closed his eyes to rest for a while.

'You never made it back to driver then, Tom?'

'What? Nay lad, I'm better off where I am. Teaching you bloody young drivers how to bloody drive. That Cartwright's the best for it. It's taken the chip off his bloody shoulder.'

He waited for the answer, but Dafydd had none, Tom continued almost by apology.

'Well, I had to do something while you were gone, didn't I?'

'Me?'

'Well, at least you know which way to point the bloody engine.'

****

'Nine months and you haven't changed a bit,' Dafydd muttered to himself, as he stared at the line of dilapidation on the siding. *'Same old coaches, same old damp and rot. Welcome to Poperinge."*

The steps down from each of the old carriages looked as if they were propping them up. The middle of the floor sagged towards them. To move them would probably achieve their demise. Smoke wafted gently from the middle carriage, from which ran a line of rope festooned with clothing, like khaki bunting. Dafydd sighed. Sleeping in the cab of an engine was much more comfortable than the cramped, smelly, damp hovels that he would now call home.

Whilst he had no fondness of the smell of unwashed bodies and clothes, or the massed choir of snorers, there was one good thing about sleeping in the coaches. When the door shut, the war was outside. He could almost remember what it was like before the world went mad.

He wondered what fate had befallen the Nottingham Pals he had met on the boat. He was desperate to imagine positive outcomes, but his mind kept flying back to the detrained wounded and the words of the shell-shocked man.

'Good dog. Bugger off dog…'

Reaching the steps of his designated billet, he unslung his kit bag ready. The letters SNCB were faded on the side of the dilapidated coach. The Belgians were happy to provide the coaches - it was after all, easier than scrapping them.

A shape moved from under a khaki blanket, as Dafydd walked through the door. The man propped himself up on one elbow and then he sighed.

"Oh, it's you Taff. There's a brew on the stove.'

The familiarity baffled Dafydd when he recognised the bleary-eyed figure, who turned back over as if to sleep. Dafydd rustled up his tin mug and moved to the stove to pour a tea. The bitter taste made him wince. It was so long since milk had been there add to it, A second sip made him ready for conversation.

'Nice tea that. So strong you could stand your spoon in it.'

There was no response.

'You ill, Cartwright? You're normally one for sleeping on the engine.'

There was still no response and Dafydd sighed. Nothing had changed. He moved to his bunk and dumped his holdall.

'I've got leave and I'm better sleeping it off than drinking it away in Pops.'

Cartwright's tone was flat. Gone was the malice. In its place a dark and hollow ring to his words.

'What's up with you, Cartwright?'

Cartwright raised himself up again, punctuated by another sigh.

'To be honest, I'm tired of all this, Taff. Seen too many ambulance trains.'

'What? You been using them nice big Dutch tank engines. With enclosed cabs so big you could dance with a woman in them?'

'Maybe I should of looked less at what was on them. Maybe I should of let the engine blow off steam to drown the cries.'

'Good dog. Bugger off dog…'

The echo stayed in Dafydd's mind. He loosened his kitbag to reach deep inside for a small bottle. Pouring some of the contents in his mug, he offered the bottle to Cartwright, who took a swig. The gasp of satisfaction was nearly a sob.

'Thought you'd copped it, me old China. Curran said you'd been in a raid and got caught in a blast.'

'Shrapnel in the arm. Army says I'm fit now.'

'How about here then?' Cartwright touched his temple.

'Should've let my engine blow off steam and all,' Dafydd replied.

Cartwright stared for a while, then sat up slowly.

'This bloody war. I should be at home with my missus and the young uns. Bloody war gets in the way. I misjudged you, Taff. Should of left you alone.'

Dafydd took a sip. 'Long time ago, Cartwright.'

'Well we need you now. Plenty of work around here. Troops, ammo, goods, ambulance, more troops…. Your French girl's still here.'

'What do you mean French?'

'She's from France. Moved up with the Tommies in the race for the coast and stayed here ever since.'

'And how do you know that?'

'Because Tom Hebdyke's been looking after her and I've been paired up with Tom until now.'

'You're pulling my leg! You and Tom and all? He never said.'

Cartwright gave a rueful grin. 'Currans' master plan. We had a choice - beat each other stupid or work together. He loses one team at worst, instead of two.'

'And?'

'Too little time to fight. We had to learn to get on.'

Dafydd gave a short laugh. '*Duw, Duw*. Well I never.'

Cartwright settled back down under his blanket. 'Well if you go back out, you'll probably catch that girl soon enough. Stop her pining after you at any rate. Told you, I'd look after her...' A half smile. 'It's the least I can do after being such a dick. Now, bugger off corporal, I need my kip.'

'Seems that's all everyone tells me these days.' Dafydd complained.

'One day you'll get the message,' Cartwright muttered, turning over to make the point.

Dafydd looked at the door. 'She's too young for me, anyhow.'

'Well that's up to you. But soon we'll up sticks and be on our way to Germany and she won't be coming with us.'

****

Dafydd was troubled by those words as he started the shift. He had reported to Curran and although Dafydd was rusty, the Captain still felt that he would be all right with Tom firing. Sure enough, he found his mate on the engine at the back of the endless queue for rostering.

'Here he is,' Tom said. 'Great Central engine today. You been on a Pom-Pom? You'll hear why it's called that soon enough.'

Dafydd was suddenly enveloped in a hug and found his head buried in the softness of a shawl and a mass of curly dark hair.

'I 'ave missed you, mon cher,' Josephine whispered as Tom chuckled in the background.

'You'd best be gone girl. We'll see you when we get back.'

Josephine nodded and after a squeeze of the arm and a peck on the cheek was gone.

'She stills preps an engine good an' proper, that one,' Tom said.

Dafydd made no attempt to reply. His mind had felt a shock that had him rooted to the spot. He could still imagine feeling her touch and his mind swam to get back to reality. He stared at the controls of the strange engine and tried to work out what was what. His mind was blank, and he needed somewhere to anchor his thoughts and drag himself back to reality. But his hands still tingled.

'We've got the signal,' Tom's voice broke through his dithering. 'You can go. Brake is off.'

Dafydd opened the drain cocks, moved the gear to forward and gently lifted the regulator a notch and the engine hissed its approval. In his current state, it was impossible to resist opening the regulator further and the engine gave a throaty staccato chuff as the wheels slipped.

'Out of practice!' Dafydd shouted. Tom patted his shoulder in sympathy as he adjusted the regulator.

His confidence began to flow back to the extent that they reached Ypres in good time. There appeared more organisation to how the trains were run now, as opposed to the chaos of earlier years.

'So why is this a Pom-pom?' Dafydd asked,

'Did you not hear it? The cylinder beat is like one of them guns. Them's great engines. I'm not so sure I want to go back onto Mr Aspinall's engines on t'Lanky.'

'We do go through them all, don't we?' Dafydd said. 'North British, Caledonian Jumbos, Dean Goods. But I do miss my Jones Goods on the Cambrian.'

'Or them big Dutch tank engines or them Belgian antiques?' Tom replied. 'All that air braking, much more efficient.'

'I'm sorry, Tom.' Dafydd blurted out. 'I'm all in a tiz today. Don't know what's wrong with me.'

'Aye Dav. It's getting back into big engines, I'll be bound.'

Dafydd wished it was, but his mind was hard pushed at keeping Gwen in focus, amid images of dark curls and foreign voices.

On the return, they were held up for hours, whilst train after train passed them.

'Looks like empty shell casings are not as important as troops,' Tom remarked. 'Or hospital trains.'

'I'll buy a pack of cards next time. We must be up for the Big Push.'

Tom groaned. 'Not another bloody Big Push.'

As if on cue, an ambulance train glided past. The big 4-6-4 tank engine effortless in its motion. The driver gave a slow solemn salute.

'What happened to Cartwright?' Dafydd asked.

Tom shrugged. 'We had words, exchanged blows while Curran looked the other way. Then we decided it was enough wit' Jerries bombing us an got on with it. I'll call it an honourable draw.'

Dafydd's shocked expression was not helped by Tom punctuating his words with a wink.

'Ah, your face, young Dafydd. Curran got fed up of us, so he put Sergeant onto the case. We was sent to the back o' th' billet coaches and told to sort us selves out. We traded a few blows, then started talkin' like. Well, cursing and stuff for starters.

186

He thought we were in favour with Curran, until I pointed out that his turn were mostly ambulance trains and me a long-standing top link on t'Lanky working as a fireman and all. I hit him hard when he said we had our own little harlot. Told him not to speak bad of someone younger than me own daughter.'

Dafydd looked ahead as he listened. They were still stuck, in a side loop, even though there was no sign of a train in front or behind them. The Belgian countryside was green at least, proper living trees rather than black skeletons of them.

'So, what happened then, Tom?'

Tom took his broom out and started to sweep the loose coal from the floor. 'We talked a bit better, while he rubbed his jaw and me knuckles ached. He misses his wife and bairns and he sees Josephine all friendly and it makes it worse fer 'im.'

'There's nothing going on!' Dafydd snapped. Tom arched his eyebrows and opened the firebox door to feed the fire.

'Tom, she's lovely and all, but I'm nothing to her!'

Tom seemed to be choosing the right shovel load of coal before he placed it in the fire, adding a few more without speaking.

'Tom, you know the tale, I've bored you enough with it. Gwen is the woman I love, and I can't change.'

There was as much silence as the hissing steam engine would allow. Dafydd noted an RTO appear from a dug-out and wave them on.

Above the noise of the starting engine, Dafydd managed to shout.

'I'm sorry Tom, I'm not trying to be an oaf.'

'You're not, lad, just take a look at yourself sometime. Cartwright started talking. He locked her in t'firebox as a joke, one of them pranks they do on some sheds. But then was called away sharpish and forgot her. He felt guilty but too damn proud to admit his mistake when he saw her.

He's just a man, all defensive and trying to avoid punishment. Them were his first thoughts, that's what th'army's done to him. He's not that bad now. Looked out for her wi' me whilst you been gone. He's forgiven now.'

She's not my girl, Dafydd muttered through gritted teeth, 'Crossing clear.'

The shout from Tom brought him back to his senses and he acknowledged the call. The train gathered speed, as Dafydd focussed ahead. He'd only been away for a few months, but it felt like the whole world had changed around him. He pushed the turmoil out of his mind and concentrated on the line ahead. Somehow it made him feel worse.

****

The approach to the depot at Poperinge was attempted at as slow a pace as possible, due to the plethora of hazards not found on a railway back home. Men walking across tracks without any sense of awareness, cargo stored too close to the trains and a lack of signals were all bad enough during the day. At night, they were nigh on impossible to detect, where lighting was kept to a minimum. Moonlight was a godsend to the crews, unless you were one who saw German spotter planes and bombers in every cloud.

It wasn't the loop around the town that Dafydd feared, it was a useful way to bring the engines round so they always faced towards Ypres in the east. Whether it be the entraining station, the goods yard or the running queue of engines, it ensured that they were able to run forward, at maximum speed when called upon. The approach to this maze was easy, the points were not. The night was pitch black and Dafydd and Tom, exhausted from a long trip, riddled with delay, now had to navigate without light. The hope was that everything was in order.

'A man with a lamp would be handy,' Dafydd muttered. 'Even just to flash the light once to show the points.'

'Th' army is just paranoid about zeppelin raids,' Tom replied. 'Because they happen every night, of course,' he added with dripping sarcasm.

'Well, they are not as loud as bombers, I suppose, and the lights may as well be a flare, so normal routine. Canvas covers across from tender to can roof and don't open the firebox unless you really have to.'

'With a lack of light to read the gauges, I'm unlikely to know if we are stopped. I've done this before you know…'

'Every bloody night. Sorry, old man, tired, I am.'

There was a clump and screech of the wheels as they ran onto the points and the engine slewed to the left.

'Now what I could do with is a bloody signal, to know which damn siding this is,' Dafydd muttered.'

'Red and green lights would have Jerry thinking we were a canal boat,' Tom replied. 'Or a railway…'

A shout from the trackside had Dafydd reaching for his brakes, as an RTO jumped onto the cab steps wreathed with steam. They were instructed to uncouple and go forward for coaling.

'Me, I love coaling in t'dark,' Tom grumbled.

'Water is worse,' the RTO replied. 'especially if you miss.'

He directed Dafydd forward and told him to wait, whilst he secured the points. Tom was pacing up and down the cab until Dafydd called him to stop.

'What's with you then?'

Tom moved his hands in agitation. 'In case you don't realise, he's left us on the throat of a point. Anything going past us will tear a strip off us.'

He stopped as he heard the throaty exhaust of an engine close by. Tom grabbed the side rail and peered out.

'Damn! Bloody engine sounds too close and it's too bloody dark to see owt. Dafydd watch your side. Get ready for anything.'

'It's too bloody dark,' Dafydd agreed.'

'Aye. Too much cloud. Too much bloody gunpowder dust in the air. Keep your eyes peeled.'

The mystery engine was gathering pace. Dafydd was hanging out of the cab, straining his eyes to find any shadow within the darkness. It felt impossible, but he began to be certain of a movement, however improbable the vision. It began to take the form of a cylindrical shape.

'Shit!'

He yanked the chain that sent the whistle echo into the night. Alerted to the danger, Tom stepped back and threw the firebox door open, flooding the cab with orange light. The response was a screech of brakes from the oncoming train, sparks could be seen as the brakes locked the wheels. Dafydd was mesmerised as the sparks provided a flickering image of the large driving wheels as they slid closer and closer, almost in slow motion.

The impact threw Dafydd and Tom backwards against the tender, as the two engines groaned in their metallic embrace. Live coals flew out of the firebox and danced around their feet. Then the engine lurched forward with a crash and the world appeared to be silent. Tom swiftly threw the live coals back in the firebox and slammed the door shut.

'Now let's see who's bloody come over to say hello.'

There was a clamour of voices in the darkness

'I'll be down checking the wheels, make sure that our engine's still on the rails.' Tom said.

'How?' Dafydd shook his head. It felt like there were cobwebs inside.

'With my bloody hands. Come on son, we need you alert.'

Dafydd widened his eyes and blinked. He had been dreaming of a girl, he just couldn't see her face and couldn't work out who it was anymore.

Chapter Nineteen

The Hearing

'Sit down Sapper.'

It was an order, not a request from a voice weary of asking. The military policeman escorting them was clearly tired of life.

'Tom, you'd better sit down.' Dafydd soothed.

Tom glared and stormed across to sit on a chair in the small room, furthest away from everyone else.

'Bloody court martial for doing my own job. I'm fed up of it. I'm fed up of sitting wit' meatheads in small rooms, waiting for someone to lecture me on me own job.'

'If you don't button your lip, Sapper, you'll be in the block house, guilty or not.'

'Sapper!' Dafydd snapped. 'You will refrain from talking unless you are directly asked a question.'

Tom's head snapped around as if he had been hit. He glared at Dafydd for a moment, then gave a sigh and a slight nod and went to sit down. Relief flooded through Dafydd, at the acknowledgment.

'Thank Christ for that.' The policeman muttered.

'Same goes for you, butty *bach*,' Dafydd snapped. The silence was therapeutic.

They were marched into Curran's office, a small hut next to what remained of the engine shed. The Captain sat behind a desk with two other officers. After Dafydd, Tom and the MP, there was little room for anyone else. It was made extremely claustrophobic when another MP arrived with Cartwright and his fireman. Cartwright looked straight ahead and scowled into the wall.

'Corporal Thomas,' Curran said carefully. 'In your own words, describe what occurred last night.'

Dafydd cleared his throat. 'Sir. We returned with a train of empty wagons from Ypres. It took five hours as we got bumped down the line. We were brought around the loop into the goods sidings and told to run forward ready to coal up. It was dark. We were held at the throat, waiting for the all clear. Next thing we knew, another train was coming towards us. I threw the engine forward quick as I could.' Dafydd looked over to Cartwright. 'Corporal Cartwright applied his brakes on our warning signal. The contact was less than it could have been. Both engines stayed on track.'

The officer in charge was a colonel, who looked to Dafydd, as if he had been stuffed and mounted. He peered over his half-moon glasses. 'Did you not omit something, Corporal?

Dafydd blinked.

'That your fireman threw open the firebox door, in breach of blackout regulations?'

'It was to alert the approaching engine, sir,' Dafydd replied quietly. 'We have no lamps due to blackout. It was pitch dark and we could hear the engine approach. He couldn't see us.'

Cartwright cleared his throat. 'Begging pardon sir, it was the light that alerted me to the engine. If he'd not done it, I'd have derailed us both.

'Corporal Cartwright, please remain silent until you are asked to speak,' Curran said quietly. 'Now, Thomas. You said you had a long journey, lots of congestion and delay. You must have been exhausted. Did you not hear the order to move?'

'No sir, because none was given,' Dafydd replied.

'Corporal Cartwright,' Monroe continued. 'You were also tired, being on your second turn with the ambulance train. Not as if you can be reckless with that cargo. Need your wits about you at all times. Are you sure you were given the order to leave?'

'Definitely sir, the RTO stood on the cab steps as he told us.'

The tribunal officers leant forward to confer in soft tones. Then Curran stroked his drooping moustache and sat back.

'Alright men, thank you. You can leave.'

As they turned to go. Dafydd stopped. 'Sir? If I may ask. How long had the RTO been on duty?'

There was a gleam in his eye and a hint of a sardonic smile, as Curran answered. 'You are dismissed, Thomas.'

****

Confined to the barracks in the damp coach, Dafydd lay on his bunk and stared up at the one above him. Although exhausted, anger still forced him awake. Whilst not blamed for anything, they had still found themselves confined, when all he wanted to do was get back out on the footplate.

'Psst.'

A fly, nothing more. Dafydd closed his eyes and tried to urge sleep on. He began to drift.

'Psst.'

He waved his hand to swat away the fly.

'Daveed.'

Dafydd woke up sharply and looked around. Nobody moved. The three other enginemen inside were snoring away quite happily. Dafydd lay back and stared at the wall. Then he jumped. The wooden sides of the carriage had plenty of gaps and through one, a pair of brown eyes stared back.

'Josephine?'

'Daveed.'

The brown eyes seemed to soften. 'I came to see zat you were all right.'

'Yes, yes. And you?'

She snorted. 'For sure. I 'eard zere was accident?'

'Nothing really. But they have us staying by here for now.'

There was a brown curl of hair close to one eye that he wanted to push away.

'I will give you some money. It's not fair you cannot work, just because we're stuck like this.'

Her glare complemented the look of derision. 'You think I do zis just for money? Am I your camp follower?'

Dafydd sighed. 'Look, I didn't mean… I just didn't. I mean I…'

The look was cool, Dafydd was sure she didn't blink.

'I came to see you. To cheer you up, Daveed.'

'Okay, I'm sorry I said that. It's because… because I care.'

The brown eyes blinked slowly; the apology was accepted.

'Okay, zat is different.'

Dafydd checked his pockets for franc notes, which he passed through the gap. There was a rustle and then the eyes returned to stare at him.

Her voice was now low, tinged with amusement. 'You will be out soon. Then we can talk about how you c…*Merde*! It is Curran. I must go.'

Dafydd had not realised the light was so bright outside, until she had disappeared.

'Boys. Curran is on his way.'

'Ow the hell do you know that, lad,' Tom muttered, as the sound of boots thudded on the steps outside. The wood creaked in protest. Then the opening door created a curtain of light through the dust of the carriage and two men walked in.

'As you were,' Curran said, and the four incumbents settled to sit on their bunks after rising to attention.

'I want you gentlemen to rest and recuperate. Officially, you've been suspended for two days, but I cannot afford for you to be impounded. You're back on the engines tonight, I'm having them prepped for you.'

Cartwright's words became higher pitched as he spat out his indignation.

'Hang on sir, we've been stopped two days' pay for something that's not our bleeding fault.'

The insubordination appeared to be overlooked by Curran or at least outwardly, bar his gaze, as he spoke slowly.

'I've got them to keep this off your record and I'm paying your wages. As soon as the colonel is back up at HQ, we'll be back to normal and delivering a service this Army doesn't deserve. So, rest and you'll be back on the line soon enough.'

He tipped his hat and then stopped. 'Eighteen hours, Thomas. That's how long the RTO had been on duty. Fifth day in a row. Now they are sending me some cover. So, some good came out of this. Shame it cost me two engines in the process.'

The door closed after him quietly, his departing steps on the staircase making more sound. Tom sighed and turned over.

'So, that's me back to me bed then.'

Chapter Twenty

Rescue

Pops was a haven. Pops was a nightmare. Pops could be a breath of sanity or a drop into hell. Dafydd knew it all depended on who was in town. What they had faced and for how long. Men drank to celebrate – or to forget. Anger or sorrow – it was all pain that needed to be acted on and cleansed from the soul.

Dafydd thought about his base, as he made his way down to the square. The problem was that there were some around who wanted to pass on the hurt to others.

The centre was a mix of faded grandeur and dereliction. Poperinge had remained in a degree of order, but there were still buildings that seemed to have melted into a pile of rubble. The town had suffered damage, from the uncertainty of war, but he lack of repair materials and labour had left a sorry status quo.

The square was a tide of khaki, ebbing and flowing as necessity or drink dictated. Those back from the front mingled wearily with new recruits, eager and feckless. Khaki packs lay strewn everywhere there was a wall to lean on or slump against. People were constantly on the move. Some just sat drinking from coffee mugs in silence. Others staggered with unsteady feet to some meaningless anthem. By night, the bustle was more boisterous. Alcohol fuelled the volume and aggression, leaving a drunk and stubborn rabble. The redcaps had their work cut out to keep order and had fallen to turning a blind eye unless the situation became serious.

Dafydd fancied a bag of chips. He needed it. Fish and chips was the food that linked him with Aberystwyth. It was a psyche that the Belgians had learnt quickly from the Tommies and had adapted their fare accordingly. Even if fish was an unlikely commodity, the chips were not.

Dafydd had managed to get a day pass. He refused Tom's offer of going to relax in the serenity of Talbot House. He needed chips. So, it would seem, did the rest of the British Army that day. Dafydd thought he could eat early and beat the rush. Then perhaps he might find his way to Talbot House and see if he could sleep in some relative silence.

In the fading evening gloom, many of the small side streets were already in shadow. As he passed one, he caught the faint sounds of a struggle. A quick glance saw a few squaddies wrestling over a sack of wool. Dafydd kept moving. They were obviously up to no good and it was better to mind his own business than take on some battle-weary crazy men.

Then he stopped, as the reality dawned on him. It wasn't a sack of wool. It was a shawl and earthen skirts. Long curly hair. He knew what was happening and hoped she was getting paid for it. He hated the callous thought, but against three the chances were stacked for a knight in shining armour.

A flashback came to him of a time in decades past. Three young miners had lined him up for a beating in a long-lost industry in his home amongst the hills. He had never known what chip shops were in those days. Potatoes were there, but even in Aberystwyth vinegar replaced the mayonnaise the Belgians sometimes offered. Meat was a rarity, just as now. Dafydd grunted, it was why the cats in Poperinge were very careful not to be seen. Dafydd missed cats.

A feeling of anger began to warm the edges of his dream. He had managed to dislodge the stick held by one of his assailants and used it to beat them. It had left a bitter taste in his mouth, not of blood, but of wrong. He could feel it now.

'Daveed!'

He heard his name as a gasp. The sound rooted him to the spot. He reached for his breast pocket and took out a small spanner he always carried for work. It would do for now. He turned back to the alley, where the woman was still fending off her assailants. His mind froze in dark fury. No guilt, no wrong. These men had forfeited the right for doubt.

He ran to the first soldier and jabbed his kidneys with the spanner. The man yowled in pain and fell to one knee. Someone grabbed his arm, but Dafydd went with the force and led with his fist. The man fell and Dafydd followed up with a kick.

White stars exploded around him as he fell to his knees. His head felt light and the world seemed to slow, as he turned toward Josephine and saw her face upturned in fear. Dafydd saw a movement and turned to see a blade moving towards him. White fury took over and he moved towards the threat with a roar. He felt a burning pain but carried onwards. His assailant's eyes widened with surprise and then fear, before glazing over from Dafydd's punch and kick to his descending head. A glint of metal spiralled away from his hand. Dafydd kept on moving as the man tried to rise.

He became aware of the noise around him. There was a lot of shouting. Dafydd no longer knew if he was the one doing the yelling.

Then his vision was clear. So suddenly, that he felt as if he was teetering on a ledge. The white anger receded and Dafydd turned to see the flash of khaki disappearing around a corner. A soft, urgent voice slowly pierced through the noise in his mind.

'Daveed. Daveed You must come, before they call the gendarmerie. Come, I must bathe your wound.'

The mists had nearly vanished. The noise mere echoes. A nagging pain grew in his side. He looked into the eyes of a woman. It was Gwen and she was crying.

'*Parry*,' he muttered. '*I knew I'd never be done with Parry.*'

198

Gwen's features seemed to meld and as he blinked, she grew into Josephine. Her hair darkened as her image came into focus. Her voice was taut with emotion. The pain was growing, and he felt weakened.

'*Iesu Grist*,' he whispered. '*Iesu Grist yn Arglwydd Dduw.*'

It was all a blur, as he staggered along, his weight supported by Josephine. He vaguely admired her strength as she gently but firmly steered him along the path. His head was buzzing. His side hurt and felt wet.

'What is wrong with me?' he muttered out loud.

'You were 'it. Many times,' Josephine replied. 'But you saw zat bastard off, like a true Welsh hero.'

Is this how a hero feels?

They had reached shadow, a smell of damp, the taste of loose cement in the air. Dafydd stiffened as they shuffled through a doorway and then he was dropped onto a bed.

'Sit zere.'

The urgent scrapings of flint were followed by a faint flame. Josephine's face was in silhouette as she gently blew into a tinder box. He could not help admire her, but he resolved not to say anything.

'I would not let them harm you.'

She stopped and he felt her touch his cheek.

'No, you were very brave. *Maintenant*, we must take off your tunic.' She moved off to grab some cloth, which was studiously ripped into strips. Then she was back to help him slowly move the clothes away from his side.

'Eet ees not so bad.' She said.

'Easy for you to say,' Dafydd muttered and she snorted.

'*Enfant!* 'Ee missed and zere is some skin cut, but I can bandage. Your tunic I will sew now. Drink zis water.'

'Why?'

'Before you faint, we will talk now, yes? Oo ees Parry?'

Dafydd shook his head. 'A memory. A bad one. That's all.'

She said no more as she began to bandage the wound and Dafydd continued.

'When I was young, I was attacked at the mine I worked on. There was this man who was all a bullying me and one day he lined up with two others. I could take no more and I hurt them back.'

She grunted and continued to work. Then she smiled grimly.

'Zis may need a doctor. Do you 'ave any things at work zat you can blame for zis wound? No, don't move. Stay still.'

He winced, but did as he was told, as she put some bandages around him and tied them in place.

'You are as bad as French men.'

'Why French?'

'I am from France, of course.'

Dafydd frowned 'So it is true. I thought you were local until Cartwright told me.'

She gave a short cry of surprise. 'What is wrong wiz you English? Do you not see zey speak a different language – or 'ave you been 'it on ze 'ead too many times?'

'I am Welsh,' Dafydd replied and was met by a snort of derision.

There was a silence and she set to work sewing his clothes. 'I lived in ze valley of ze Marne river. Ze Germans came and murdered my family. I had to run North and North until I could run no more. I found my place 'ere in Poperinge. Ze people allow me to live and I beg what I can like everyone does. Zey are good people, ze Flanders. I... ach!' She spat the exclamation and sucked her bleeding finger.

'Take your time,' Dafydd muttered. She shook her head.

'You need to go or zat is what you were saying as we walked. Your duty begins soon. Sit, drink and do not sleep, for sure.'

He watched her work deftly repairing his tunic. He liked the way her brow kinked when she frowned and then gave a half smile when she had solved the problem. There was intensity and focus. There was life and lots of it. Dafydd realised he liked being around her. He had no words, but he enjoyed watching her.

She put the tunic to her mouth and bit into it. Then spat away some thread.

'Zere you are. Zis will do.'

He took back the proffered tunic. Her hands were shaking gently. On impulse Dafydd took her hand and stroked it. Her eyes were now pools of sorrow. She bit her lip. He said one word.

'Come.'

She moved to his arms and began to sob into his shoulder. Dafydd held her close and gently stroked her matted curls. It was not so long ago that he had done the same when he had rescued her from the firebox of an engine. It felt like a lifetime ago. Then she was a girl to him, now she was a woman who he could never see harmed.

'Nobody will touch you again, cariad,' he whispered. 'Not while I'm around.'

He turned to gently kiss her hair and felt her freeze.

She looked up to him, eyes wide with wonder and with trembling lips reached out to touch his cheek. Then slowly she moved forward to gently kiss his lips. The thrill was almost too much for Dafydd, but as she leant forward again, mouth opening in anticipation, he stopped her.

'No, I cannot, girl.'

She looked at him in confusion.

'I have another at home.'

Her smile was tinged with sadness. 'But I am here. She ees not.'

'You don't have to do this.'

'Zis I want. Do you not also?'

He looked away and sighed. 'A while ago now, I met a girl in Aber. She was the one for me. I had to leave for work, but she promised to wait. And when I was away, I did something I regret even now.'

There was a pause. He could hear the gentle hiss of the lamp.

'Did she wait?'

Dafydd gave a start. 'What?'

'Did she wait? Your woman.'

He sighed. 'She had to go and work in a big house to make money.'

'*Bien*, but she came to you when you returned?'

'No, she was her master's mistress. She found me better work in a big engine shed in England. She put me on the road to become a driver.'

'And when you went to England again, she went also?'

He looked away. 'I went and came back. I thought I were over her, but when I came here, she started writing and when I was on Blighty leave, I went to see her. She's struggling as a munitions worker and the house have tipped her out. She has a son and…'

'What ees 'is name?' She asked gently He stopped, and she sighed.

'What is ee like?'

'I never seen him.'

She frowned. 'But you went to see 'er. No picture? Zat ees strange.'

'I don't know if he's mine. We had a time once'

'It does not sound eet or you are very fertile.'

Dafydd looked as if he had been slapped.

'What was ees name?' Dafydd floundered to respond and the questions came fast.

202

'Ow old? Can you describe eem?' There was a pause. 'Was zere a child really?'

'She never writes of him.'

'Strange do you not think?'

A storm was gathering in his brows and she put her hand up. 'You 'ave your dream, I cannot change that.'

He reached to clasp her hand. 'I am sorry. I just did not want you to be… grateful.'

Her eyes widened and her nostrils flared in a puff of outrage. 'Mon Dieu. Do I open my legs every time I am *grateful*? I am so much stronger zan zis. 'Ow do you zink I 'ave survived?'

She sighed and looked at him. He drowned in her large brown eyes.

She reached to touch his cheek again. 'You 'ad a time when you were young. She has moved away from zat. You 'ave not.'

Dafydd's eyes had filled with tears. 'I cannot change.'

'Tonight, I can 'eal your pain.'

Dafydd winced. 'This is not right.'

'War is not right. Ze world is not right.'

'But…' he started, and she stopped him with a short cry. 'If you do not wish you can go. You were very brave today and eet does not make me love you more or less for eet. I want you, zat is all.'

'But she…'

'She ees not 'ere. I am 'ere. Zat is enough, no?'

Dafydd felt the anguish born of betrayal and she smiled. 'Zere is no guilt. Zere is only us.'

'If I kiss you, it will not stop there and then where would we be?'

She smiled and whispered one word. 'Appy.'

He could not resist her.

The road from the church in the town square was not long enough for Dafydd, as they walked down towards the station. He could not walk as slow as he would wish, to let the moment last to his satisfaction. Josephine was by his side, dressed as a medical orderly. She would return to the hospital as soon as they parted. For now, the warmth of her touch on his arm was enough to keep his breath in short bursts.

They arrived at the station complex. Dafydd realised straight away that there was trouble.

'They've posted extra guards. I don't recognise them.'

'What ees wrong?' Josephine asked.

'I don't know. Although I may have an idea.'

'Are you een trouble?'

'No and don't worry about me, there's plenty of ways into this place, as you know. Tom will have the engine ready, he said we were on an Aspinall and what he don't know of them is not worth knowing. I...' he stopped and held her gently away. 'I just wish we had more time.'

She smiled, the warmth made him flush with pleasure. 'Zere will always be time. When I have ze time to come, I will be 'ere. And you can write to me and I will write back. Badly...'

He held her close then and kissed her. 'I have wasted too much time.'

She puffed her cheeks slightly in expression. 'We 'ave had time. We 'ave time and we will 'ave time. For now, we do not 'ave much time, that is all.'

'*Cariad*,' he whispered. Her eyes glinted with emotion, then she fiercely pressed her lips on his for a long time and stood back.

'*Je t'aime.*'

The thrill was back again. The tingling down his back that made him gasp. Gwen was banished from his thoughts. Almost.

Josephine walked away and then stopped to look back. Dafydd saw her shoulders rise and fall in a sigh, then she put her hand to her mouth and blew him a kiss and carried on walking.

As Dafydd had said, getting into the railway yard posed no problem, especially given the chaos of constant groups of soldiers entraining and detraining.

The unloading and transfer of goods gave him enough room to reach the line of coal stacked like a dry-stone wall. He used it as cover, as he made his way swiftly to the end and looked at the line of engines waiting. There appeared to be a group of soldiers nearby. Dafydd found his engine, third from the front.

He elected to wait and moved around the other side of the coal bunker, so he could reach the line of engines from the rear. Waiting patiently, he watched the train movements. When one started to roll past the line of engines, he sprinted across to the back of the line.

Crouching low, he made his way down the line. He was a few engines away when a firebox was opened slightly ahead, casting a gentle glow around the engine. There was a pall of steam and within a silhouette of a soldier.

'Oi, Taff. Get up here sharpish!'

Cartwright's voice came from the footplate of the engine next to him. The silhouette appeared to be getting larger, then the light was gone. Dafydd did not give it a second thought and grabbed the rails to pull him up to the cab. Cartwright grabbed him as he reached the top and threw him inside.

'Redcaps on the prowl out there. Searching the engines. What the bleedin' 'ell you been up to, Taff?'

'What you on about, Cartwright?' Dafydd grunted, rubbing his shoulder where the tender had met it.

'Talk of some transport boy pulling a knife on someone in Pops.'

Dafydd cursed. 'Not quite. I caught three bastards trying to rape Josephine. One had a knife...'

Cartwright's gaze could bore a hole in Dafydd, but then he picked up a rag and wiped his hands.

'Thompson,' he said to his young fireman. 'Get up to Tom Hebdyke and be his fireman for a while.'

'You'll be seen,' Dafydd said.

Johnson smirked. 'No, I won't, mate. Watch me. Meatheads are only looking down one side of the track. Pillocks!'

Dafydd watched, as Johnson deftly climbed along the engine, holding onto the rails on its boiler side. For a moment, he ducked low and then stood and hopped onto the front of the engine, then leapt for the tender of the engine in front. Hauling himself up, he rolled over into the coals. He disappeared only to bob back up with a shovel and started shovelling. He stopped and looked down at someone below the engine.

'Shovelling coal!' he shouted. 'What do you think I'm doing. I'm a fucking fireman, aren't I? Well if you want me to, but the bleeding engine will go cold and we'll stop all the others in the line while they move us out of the way. Do you want to be responsible for stopping the trains? Yes, you need coal, to put in a fire. The coal is here, the fire is there. What do you think?'

'Don't you worry about Johnson,' Cartwright said from behind Dafydd. 'Tilbury man. Brought up on the docks. He can look after himself.'

'There was a group of them.' Dafydd muttered. 'They had her down an alley and when I waded in, one of them pulled a knife.'

'What did you do?' Cartwright asked.

'They ran.'

Cartwright chuckled. 'You're dangerous, Taff.'

Dafydd did not reply, as three men quickly climbed into the cab. A redcap soldier with bayonet drawn, followed by an officer and finally Sergeant Macrae If Macrae was surprised by seeing the two men together, he showed little sign.

'Stand back, soldiers,' the officer snapped. 'Have you men been here all day?'

'Sir, we have to be ready at a moment's notice, we gotta stay here to keep the engine in steam.,' Cartwright replied.

'Fireman,' the officer said. 'You are injured. How?'

'I got caught on the edge of a tender, sir,' Dafydd replied.

'Are you sure that isn't a knife wound?'

'Begging your pardon,' Macrae said. 'but the report was of an attack by a man with a knife. The only one with a knife. So, that man wouldn't be the one with a knife wound or he'd be the one attacked...'

The glare in reply spoke of an acknowledged defeat.

'At ease, men,' the officer said and climbed off the engine. Macrae's look to Dafydd was long and piercing as he descended the steps.

Cartwright smirked. 'He knows. Smart one is our Sarge. He knows them villains have gone running to the redcaps. Best get some shovelling done, Taff. You're with me now. Don't worry, I'll go easy on you.'

Dafydd looked troubled and Cartwright went back to wiping the oil of his hands with a rag.

'She's safe, mate – or you wouldn't be here.'

'It was luck I was walking past.'

'Well, I always had you as a lucky fucker. Don't go spreading the word around, a there's a few Tommies out there would want your luck.'

Dafydd paid attention to his shovel, but as he built up the fire, his mind kept racing back to the evening. The woman of his dreams still haunted him, but strangely, he could no longer see whose face it was...

Chapter Twenty-one

Borre

'Borre? Why Borre?'

'Daf, pal. It's 1917, nearly 1918. Us don't ask; we do.'

'I know Tom, but it's not just taking all the crocked locos away. Feels like they are giving up on Wipers and preparing to retreat.'

'I don't see us giving up, but I can see them Jerries giving us hell before them Yanks come.'

Dafydd looked back at the line of engines, streaked brown in rust. The driving rods taken away to allow freer movement.

'I think if t' billets get towed away, then we should start fretting,' Tom continued, giving the all-clear without breaking step.

'I suppose so,' Dafydd replied glumly. 'But then you're fonder of the cabs.'

Tom attacked the coal in the tender in reply.

'I hope you're still writing to her pal.'

'Which one?'

Tom smiled. 'That's up to you. I know who I would have my eye on.'

'Yes, but she's not down Borre way,' Dafydd muttered.

Tom stopped to look up from his shovelling. 'What's up wi' you? We're at Borre and Hazebrouck all t' bloody time.'

Dafydd peered out at the dark shadow of Messines Ridge in the distance. He could swear that he saw puffs of smoke, every time he looked.

The sound of constant firing had diminished from there a long time ago. Now it just blended into the land. He sighed.

'Not sure, Tom. There's been things we've been asked to do which make me wonder if we're not preparing to withdraw back.'

Tom turned back to the pile of coal on the tender. 'Look lad, you write and tell her where you are and she'll find a way of getting there.'

'Letters get censored…'

'Then tell her you won't bore her with any details, and she'll know.'

'Maybe it's for the best,' Dafydd said.

'Think you just like being miserable, pal,' Tom replied.

'That's not fair, Tom. I'm torn. Besides, you'll be missing your tree at Talbot House.'

'What I won't be missing is them debates. Every year, they have a debate. Is t'war going to end? Every year, them nays get larger in size at the vote. Look lad, I can see you're torn between two lasses that have you in raptures. Don't let it get to you. Stay in touch, Keep your spirits up. The time will come when you need to make a decision. That time ain't now, so don't do owt that will cause you any more grief than you already got.'

'It's a blessing having a barracks, not a mouldy old carriage.' A voice piped up from a distance.

'What you on about Johnson? | We're living in a fucking tent!'

'Yeah, but it's new and clean.'

Dafydd could hear the debate as they came closer to his cab. The pair climbed up and Johnson produced a bottle.

''Ere, this boy's only gone and got himself some brandy,' Cartwright said gently cuffing his young fireman's head.

'Went and helped the station master out on some repairs,' Johnson said with a smirk. 'He responded with some good old French hospitality.'

209

'Yeah, we've been celebrating it with this calvados. And then we thought we haven't been round the neighbours for a while, so 'ere we are, sharing our bonus. So, the old redcaps don't see us as drunk, we'll all have a nip.'

Dafydd took the proffered bottle and took a swig, gasping as the spirit burned down his throat. His taste buds appreciated the apple flavour as he breathed out.

Gone was the animosity of old, replaced with a camaraderie as warm as the spirit in his belly. They had been through too much together, bearing the brunt of the nomadic life the army had doled out to them.

The square cab of the North British engine allowed Dafydd and Tom to sit with their backs to the cab sides and the other two to sit with their backs to the tender, the roof providing relative cover for all. The firebox was partly open, to provide warmth as they passed the bottle around.

"They say the Jerries are getting restless,' Johnson said. 'One last push before the Yanks arrive and tip the balance. Try and force us to terms before they get slaughtered.'

'Oh, they do, do they?' Cartwright's biting scorn was never too far away.

'They might be right,' Tom said. 'Us being pulled back to Borre and all'

'Yeah, but we're still running the bleeding trains through to Wipers,' Cartwright replied.

Dafydd was paying little attention to the debate. He focussed on the glow of the fire, mulling over his life and getting no answers.'

'You be back on those Lanky Yorky expresses?' Cartwright asked of Tom. 'Me, I'll be looking forward to taking a Claude Hamilton out of Liverpool Street station. What about you, Taff?'

'What?' Dafydd stumbled back into reality.

'I said what you gonna be up to? I mean you got to go back...,' Cartwright continued, as Dafydd shrugged in reply. 'Do you think that Welsh bird of yours will be there for yer?'

Dafydd took a letter out of his pocket, which he threw at Cartwright. 'You decide, boys *bach*.'

He hadn't drunk for a while and the brandy had made him dozy and a little irritable.

'Ann will Daffid...'

'It's in Welsh, innit,' Dafydd snapped, reaching to snatch it back.

'Well bleeding hell, how am I supposed to bloody read it?'

Dafydd sighed and began to translate.

Dear Dafydd,

I hope you are still safe. God knows, it is bad with me that you are in harm's way at this terrible time. I am happy that you friended a girl. Happy and heartbroken. Funny, isn't it. The way I behaved to you, I do not deserve you waiting for a change in the wind, as they say down the harbour.

I'm sorry I lied to you about the child. I didn't in a way. The poor thing died long before term. Much to my lady's relief. And satisfaction. She could not wait to see me out of the house when my Master had gone to war.

I expect I kept talking to you about it, because I wanted to keep you at arm's length. I didn't want you to feel hope, when I knew not my own heart or what I wanted to do.

When the war finally ends, I may stay in Hereford. The life is harder now, but I do have friends, and nobody sneers as I walk down the road. Perhaps this will be for the best.

Please know though, that despite everything, inside my breast beats the heart of your Turkey girl and she still loves you from afar.

Gwen

'Turkey?' Johnson asked.

'It's what we call people from her part of town – Trefechan Turks,' Dafydd replied his eyes not leaving the glow of the firebox. 'It's like *Twr Cei*, the harbour of towers, with all them industry around.'

'Sounds as if she's given you up,' Tom said.

'I suppose,' Dafydd said softly.

'Have you given her up?'

Dafydd shrugged. 'If I were to say Josephine, I'll be trying to drag her to a place she don't know and a language she don't speak. If I were to say Gwen, I'd be pulling her back to a place where she's not always welcome or fighting for her hand from a rich lover, with me a fireman and a few years off driver.'

Cartwright gave a quick look out of the cab. 'RTO. We'll slip off the other side. I'll leave yer the bottle, as you need it more than us. At least tonight, it'll take the pain away.'

'Best hide that bottle,' Tom said as the other crew left. 'He'll want us on duty, not drinking.'

The RTO jumped up to the cab and stopped.

'Where's the bottle, gentlemen? I can smell the spirit, so don't hide it.'

Dafydd produced the bottle and handed it over. The RTO looked at the small amount of liquid inside, uncorked the bottle and drained it in a gulp, gasping with satisfaction.

Opening the firebox, he slung the empty inside and slammed the door shut, to stifle the cracking noise as the bottle exploded in the inferno.

'That's better. Cold night tonight and a run to the front for you boys. Ammunition train to Pops and await instructions. They might unload there or go to Wipers. Depends on how hot Jerry's been making things. Be careful. It's a dark cloudy one and there's a lot of unlit traffic on the tracks. You're clear for Hazebrouck.'

'Taking ammo towards a German advance,' Tom muttered.' Bloody great.'

212

The realisation hit Dafydd once more. Tom was right when he said it would all wait. It would have to, there was too much going on where they were.

****

Dafydd felt a grim satisfaction, when it became clear they had been moved to Borre, by the repair workshops. Every day now was a blur, tinted around the edges with fatigue. The cargoes now all looked the same, or at least felt so to him. Even tanks and ambulance trains. He felt numb. To lose one sweetheart was careless. Now to lose two was unforgivable and Dafydd's mood sank like the muddy brown morass that lay around the railways.

In this bleak moment, he was grateful to the crew around him. Tom especially kept him going, even though he probably had his own demons to overcome. But he felt constantly haunted by the image of the man cowering in fear by the light railway.

'Good dog, bugger off dog…'

Dafydd had stopped admiring the scenery. Especially around Ypres, it now appeared no more than mud and haphazard stone silhouettes that were once houses, and the occasional blackened skeleton of a tree stood sentinel. Church spires that desperately clung to something close to their original shape. He felt a large weight on his head and his breathing was laboured as the words came through his fog.

'Tell us summat good, pal,' Tom's voice rang out over the creaking and clanking of the engine, as it lurched onwards.

'What?'

'I said tell us summat good that happened today.'

'Cake,' Dafydd snapped back. 'My sister Sioned sent me a cake. Not only did it arrive, but it was fresh and all and hadn't been pilfered.'

213

'All right lad, so every day you'll be telling me something good. From now until th'end of t'war.'

'To what end?' Dafydd snapped.

He moved the regulator a bit too far and the engine responded with a noisy wheel slip, as if in reproach.

Tom didn't break step from shovelling coal into the fire. 'I'll tell you, shall I? it will slowly get you out of this sulk. You've had a rough hand dealt, but God knows there's some had rougher that we've seen over here. You let this drag you down and you'll be the poorer for it. T'railway engine needs you to treat her right and you'll not be doing it wi' your chin in t'gutter.'

Tom stopped to tap the pressure gauge before grunting in satisfaction. 'Besides, she's a Lanky and Mr Aspinall had them built so likes of us could get a good run out of her. You treat her right and she'll be your pal back, won't you love?'

'So, we'll have you perk up and say no more about it.'

'Yes Dad,' Dafydd replied. 'Now you give me one back.'

'Simple,' Tom replied. 'Over here, you're a driver, not a bloody fireman.'

He slammed the firebox door shut and moved into the tender, to shift more of the coal forward, so as to make it easier to carry to the fire. Tom worked hard in spite of the downpour, that left rivulets of water mixed with grey coal dust trickling into the cab. Dafydd felt bad as he saw how his friend's body language spoke of irritation.

Dafydd sighed and checked ahead. The road was clear, and the rail was straight and level for a mile. He called Tom forward and held out his hand.

'Tom, I'm so sorry, I'm such a *Twpsyn*. I could not have got this far without you there and I'm punishing you for it.'

Tom took the proffered hand. 'Don't use all your good fortune in one go.'

'You get up and drive, Tom. I'll go and sort out the coal. Reckon the rain will cool me down. You get some time sheltering under canvas.'

The portable canvas stretched from the cab roof to the tender and invited shelter from the rainstorm. Yet it provided only basic relief and the rain streaked down the lines of Tom's face.

'I won't ask twice,' Dafydd said with a smile.

'We don't need too much, son,' Tom said. 'Just a bit more, close to t'cab and even out t'weight a bit.' He patted Dafydd's shoulder as he went past.

Dafydd made short shrift of the task and, as the cooling rain broke through the mists of his musing, he looked around outside. They were on the flat approach towards Poperinge. Dafydd had become quite fond of the place and it had hurt to leave. Even without Josephine, the town offered a relative serenity from the madness surrounding it. Talbot House in particular gave him a feeling of inner peace and he missed the simple garden.

The flat fields lay untended, pock-marked and forlorn, criss-crossed by drainage ditches, in an attempt to run off the ever-present water from the clay soil. The approach was lined with red-roofed houses and he sounded the whistle at every crossing they passed on their journey to the bustling station.

As always, it was a mass of activity. Men detrained, cargo was unloaded – this time, mainly shells. At the far end, a few narrow-gauge Baldwin engines were simmering, as they waited for their trains to be filled. Dafydd tried not to think of it, but the scene still brought back the voice of the man shooing the dog away...

Bugger off...

He noticed quite quickly that a village of canvas had been set up nearby and he called Tom over to look. His mate wasn't there long before he returned to watching his side of the train.

'A new CCS - Casualty Clearing station, that is,' Tom replied. 'Looks as though front has come closer to us than we realised.'

Dafydd slowed on arrival, close to the CCS. He didn't have to wait long before his new orders were received – proceed to Ypres with extreme caution.

'And no further,' the RTO said. 'We lost a train recently. Aussie crew and Canadian pioneers. They crossed the front line without realising it.'

'You're serious?' Dafydd asked.

'Don't prove me right.'

He eased up the regulator and the engine crept forward. The CCS was becoming more pronounced and the activity fascinated him. Orderlies moved forward and back carrying stretchers which were bearing men in various stages of mummification. Those who could walk were being helped. The doors of the largest marquee opened and closed like they were being used for ventilation.

Dafydd watched a young female orderly, dressed in brown, as she helped a man with an arm in a sling and a bandage covering half his face. The good arm held a crutch to aid his walking, the whole of one side of his body had suffered a great trauma.

Dafydd became captivated with the scene. The orderly's long hair was kept up under an un-peaked canvas hat. The erratic movement of her charge knocked the hat slightly off centre and she was desperate to correct it but needed both arms to help her patient. Every time she reached up, she had to hurriedly return it to provide assistance.

Tom leaned forward and pulled the whistle chain. The blast of sound caused the orderly to look up and pause, then wave madly in delight. It was Josephine.

Dafydd felt a thrill of pleasure. He could not stop the train, on any pretext, all he could do was watch and wave. He felt trapped. There was so much to say, and it would appear, no time to say it. The slow movement of the train was torture. In a sudden rising panic, Dafydd leant out to shout. The flashback was still raw in his emotions.

The train that took him out of Aberystwyth to a new life, that moved slowly enough to allow him to watch his love sitting in the nearby avenue. She didn't look up,

Dafydd never got to say what he needed to say. He could not let it happen again.

With all his might, he yelled, 'I love you!!'

Josephine gave a happy reply, lost in the sound of the engine, the bellowing of an NCO nearby and a cacophony of jeers, catcalls and mock protestations of love from nearby soldiers.

She stood for a moment and watched, then seemed to respond to someone and moved off. An NCO appeared to follow her. Dafydd wanted to jump off the engine and punch the man.

'Well, that's settled then,' Tom said. 'Just need war to end, then you get demobbed and go back home. Then you find where she is, come back for her or send money for her to travel. What could be simpler?'

Dafydd said nothing. The Messines ridge glowered on the horizon reflecting his frown of uncertainty.

Chapter Twenty-two

Green Mist

Dear Dafydd

I was glad to hear from you so quickly again. I hope the new base is warm and comfortable, better than it has been. It seems so long now that this all started, and I hope it gets finished for all our sakes.

The café is quiet, people are not buying coffee so much now food is so scarce. We get by, growing what we can. Donato has managed to get a small patch of land near the Lein Fach. He goes fishing of an evening at the harbour and those normal things occasionally grace our plates from time to time.

Harri still writes to her young man at the front and I am so happy she keeps smiling. I hope he comes back, and I do hope they keep their feet on the ground and their heads out of the clouds thereafter.

My little boy grows every day. He still wants to join the Navy like his cousin Huw. He helps carry the fishing rods for his father as they go to harbour. Maybe when you are back, you could take him on the Rheidol engine up and down the harbour, like you done with Nat Treveglos them years back.

Your Uncle Gwil brought Dai Cochyn over the other day. I tell you this, Cochyn has as much hair as Gwil these days. There's no red hair left for him to be a Cochyn no more.

That driver Jenkins asks after you. I don't know why people are feared with him, as he's like a gentleman with me. He said he's foreman now and he's holding your place open for you when you get back. That's good news, isn't it?

Donato was told your Gwen is coming back to Aber. I don't know how, as she's apparently bad in bed and under the doctor...

They were stood down at Ypres for a rest but remained in the cab after refuelling. Gone was the desire to wander the shattered streets. The town now felt closer to the front than it ever had. It was under bombardment even as they watched. The cab of the little North British engine was warm when they put the canvas over the gap to the tender. Outside was grey, cold and suffering an almost constant downpour.

'It could be worse,' Dafydd ventured to Tom. 'There's more activity going on south of here around Amiens, they say. Jerries trying to get the edge before the Americans arrive and turn it for us.'

'Tell that to their bloody gunners, so I can take me tin hat off,' Tom grumbled. 'It's like t'buggers have been told they aren't firing enough.'

The zooming sound of incoming ordnance suddenly grew louder and Dafydd ducked. The whole engine shook as the shell hit the ground. He heard the drumming of millions of pieces of soil on the canvas roof and cab and spat out some dirt that had suddenly gathered in his mouth. His hands felt as if they had been slapped.

'You all right, son?' Tom had jumped to his side and helped him up.

'That was close,' Dafydd replied. 'I'm still here, mind.'

'Not too far off by half. I'm going to check us to make sure there's no shrapnel damage. Not having that malarkey again. You sure you're with us?'

'Just fine, Tom. I used to work in a mine, remember? Got used to explosions all the time. '

'Well, you'll not be back there in a hurry, that's for sure.'

An RTO suddenly appeared in the cab, as if he had leapt onto the steps. His face was brown with dirt and fixed like a mask with strain.

'Get over to the closed wagons. I want you and them out of here now. The Jerries have got the range of the station.'

'I'll just check us out...' Tom began.

'No, you won't,' came the terse reply. 'This is your order. Get those bloody wagons on the back of this bloody train and piss off out of here. And take these buggers with you.'

The RTO pointed at a forlorn group of four men dressed in field grey. They were smeared in mud and their uniforms were ripped and shabby. One had a head bandage; another had an arm in a sling. The handlebar moustaches made them look an even more pathetic sight.

'Germans?' Dafydd gasped.

'Captured a while back and have been acting as non-combatant servants. Take them with you.'

'Where?'

The RTO shrugged. 'Fuck knows. But if they stay around here, someone is going to get trigger happy with all this shellfire. Up to you, corporal.'

The RTO swung off the engine and started running across the yard to a dugout. Dafydd looked at Tom, who shrugged and went to the side.

'You'd better shift. *Komm.*' The men moved up unsteadily and Tom pushed them into the corners of the cab back, pushing them down. Then he picked up his shovel and pointed at them menacingly. 'Any funny business lads and I'll throw you in to t'bloody firebox meself.'

The men let themselves be manhandled into position, showing little interest. Dafydd felt immediately uneasy, having enemies so close. He had never seen a German before, but these men looked so ordinary. A far cry from the arrogant postures of the Hun soldiers in the posters.

Nevertheless, he could not help feeling a touch of anxiety. The shelling continued and Dafydd decided that following orders was the correct course. His doubts would have to wait. He had no desire for another episode like that in the tin turtle.

He blew a sharp blast of the whistle and lifted the regulator sharply. The wheels slipped on the wet rails. The rain had got heavier and Dafydd glared at the sky.

'Tom, check the canvas.'

'Why's that?'

'Because our guests will get this bloody rain else.'

'Should be used to it in t'bloody trenches,' Tom grumbled. 'Sod 'em, they can rot.'

Dafydd sighed. 'And it keeps our backs dry...'

Tom said nothing, but he went and pulled the canvas tighter.

'Please, may we stand?'

One of the German men spoke in perfect, if clipped English. 'The water from the coal runs under us.'

Another explosion happened nearby, followed by a puff of smoke in the air.

'Shrapnel shells, none of your bog-standard whizz-bangs. Get us away from here, Daf.'

Dafydd already had the regulator far open than he had in the past. The wheels slipped in protest again, before he pegged it back and the train lurched forward.

'Do you have helmets?' Dafydd shouted to the German.

'*Nein*, they were taken. As souvenirs...'

'Well, you're bloody lucky you weren't taken.'

'I am of Hanover. My grandfather fought with Wellington at Waterloo.'

He was stopped by Tom's glare. Dafydd lifted the regulator up another notch, the train was wobbling from side to side.

There was an explosion ahead in the far distance, but for now they seemed clear. Dafydd wiped the sweat from his brow and eased the regulator back, checking the pressure gauges.

'We've pushed her, but I think we're through the worst,' he said.

Tom did not reply. Dafydd had a sudden panic that his mate had been hurt by their guests, but he was relieved to find Tom tapping the pressure gauges by his side.

He turned quickly to look behind, but the talkative German was standing in the corner staring out on the passing land. Subconsciously, he reached into his empty top pocket, patting it to check. Dafydd thought he must be looking for his cigarettes. Probably also taken as souvenirs.

He could not get past the feeling of uneasiness, that behind him stood an enemy. The German seemed quite pliant, nonchalant, or passive even. *But surely, he would want to escape? Surely, he wanted to get back to his own people? What would stop him jumping Dafydd from behind.* Dafydd's anxiety increased. *Wouldn't they want to run than to stay the wrong side of an attritional conflict, where the front line constantly oscillated, but only by small distances?*

He started taking small breaths in his panic and suddenly that did not feel enough. There was an itch at the back of his throat, and he gasped. It was as if a bar had slipped across his windpipe and was blocking his breathing. His nose was sore and his eyes began to stream with tears. There was an overpowering smell of bleach, making Dafydd want to gag.

Terror gripped him as he was grabbed firmly from behind and a hand slapped over his face. The German shouted something urgently, as he held Dafydd like a vice, then he spoke again.

'Breathe, quick. We must share.'

Dafydd felt grateful for the air, as his lungs opened up.

'Now you must hold your breath.' The words came as if forced.

Dafydd took a deep breath and the hand was removed. As he turned, the German had a gas mask held over his face. With the dawn of realisation Dafydd rushed past and grabbed a small canvas bag. Desperately wrenching it open, he removed a gas mask and placed it over his head.

His lungs were burning with the desire to breathe, but he managed to keep from inhaling the gas, until - on his knees and moaning with the effort, the mask was fitted, and he could take long deep breaths.

The smell of rubber was powerful, but he ignored it. The glass eyeholes were misting already, but he felt alive. He rolled over to sit with his back against the cab side and looked up at the German who nodded back, his eyes looked humane within their glassy prison.

'*Es ist gas. Chlor.*'

The words were muffled from within the mask. Tom was on his knees, shaking his head, but nodded back. His gas mask gave him a hang dog expression as he gave a thumbs up. Then crawling forward, he threw open the firebox door. The fire normally brilliant yellow in its roar appeared to be slightly subdued before returning to normal. Dafydd noted the attempt to flush the cab by drawing air into the fire.

He pulled himself back up and looked out. The land looked churned, blasted and pock-marked. Looking back, in the depths of a cutting, there was a light green hue to the low-lying mists,

Dafydd looked back to the end of their train and sighed in relief, as the guard poked his gas-masked head out of the van and waved. The tension broke and he quickly lifted the gas mask to vomit over the side.

'The danger is past. You can breathe again.'

The German looked on and Dafydd nodded in thanks. It was all unreal. The German continued.

'The water is good for the gas – and the vomit.'

He took a proffered canteen of water and sipped to rinse his mouth. Then he took a long swig and his throat began to cool its ardour.

'One of yours?' Dafydd asked.

'Nein, our chlor gas has more blue in colour.'

Dafydd stared at him and he shrugged.

'I try to joke.'

Dafydd began to notice the urgent swaying of the train. He quickly looked to the front and eased off the regulator. The crisis had passed, there was no need to create another one.

****

'Jerries in the cab? Bleedin' 'ell Taff!' Cartwright's young fireman, Thompson had an opinion that belied his tender years. Looking no more than a tall, skinny teenager with an affable grin, he had caught many people out by his nonchalant appearance.

'Weren't yer thinking them buggers were going to attack you?'

Dafydd shared a wry grin with Tom. 'I did Thommo, but there was no reason why they would. Captured, they were and had been working as orderlies at an airfield.'

'Didn't they want to go back then?'

'They probably had a guts full of being on the front line and the main man talked of food shortages.'

'Cowards then,' Cartwright snapped.

'Not in my book,' Dafydd replied. They rescued us from the gas.'

'Why was the gas around then?' Thompson persisted.

'Stray shell – or a dud that went off late.'

'What? That never happens!' Thompson's ironic reply made Dafydd smile.

'I tell you what, my *Tad-cu*, my grandad, was done in by a hang fire blast down a mine. He put his chisel in the rock and boom. Just needs a slow fuse, or a bit of pressure or shock and the charge wakes up and remembers what it's to do.'

Thompson stopped and thought for a while.

The one main benefit they had in Borre was facilities. The four had time off and were sitting by the mess. This time, the fluid being drunk was nothing more dangerous than tea.

'Was it a Jerry shell? Probably,' Dafydd said. 'I don't know though, them German boys was, I don't know, just normal, like.'

'What you saying, Taff?' You swapped addresses, pictures of sweethearts? They all gonna get the bloody iron cross?'

Cartwright's venom was fresh, he stared into his mug of tea, both hands holding it for warmth. The knuckles appeared white.

'Don't know what you mean,' Dafydd replied evenly. 'The man saved my life. He didn't have to.'

'Yeah right, like you picked up a group of train drivers,' Cartwright snapped back. 'They needed you to drive. They was looking after themselves, like always.'

'Dafydd's right,' Tom added. 'They was captured soldiers, put to work as stretcher bearers and some bright spark had th'idea to get them away before some bugger used 'em as target practice.'

'Conchies, then.'

'No, Cartwright. Just men. They then got us out of a mess. We saw them safe at the next camp and that's done with it. Can't help thinking we are all just ordinary boys here.'

'They're all murdering bastards,' Cartwright's voice was almost a growl. His face was a mask of hatred as he spat out the words. 'Huns murdered Charlie Fryatt. Great Eastern man through and through. All he done was protecting his ship and they shot him like a dog. Don't you **ever** tell me they're human, cos they're bloody animals. They was lucky you picked them up, I'd have thrown em in the firebox.'

He got up and walked away. Thompson rolled his eyes and made a face, his arms open in a shrug. Then he followed, speeding up to catch his mate. Dafydd sighed and looked at Tom.

'What's up with you, butty?'
'It just got me thinking, that's all, pal.'

225

'Well, those tank things will clear the Germans out in no time.'

'If their engines' don't break down.'

'Come on old man, you'll be home in no time. Back to normal.'

'Will I?'

Tom sighed and got up to leave. 'This war's just been gone on so long now. I don't know what is normal no more.'

Chapter Twenty-three

Retreat
(1918)

Dafydd was left on his own. He retrieved his mail from his pocket and started to open the envelopes.

The first was from Sioned. His smile warmed the pages as he read through his loyal sister's prose. She tried to make everything seem normal, but a hint every now and then made him aware that things were getting harder for them.

Would you believe, we actually had a full house on Saturday. Some of the wounded men turned up in their hospital blue uniforms. One started playing a harmonica and the others joined in song, brought in people from all over. We ran out of cake, as the rationing didn't allow me to make enough, but nobody seemed to mind.

Donato works hard, but someone had a go at him for being foreign and not at war. Tried to give him a white feather. Luckily, he was with Dai Cochyn at the time, so that was that, pretty sharpish!

I've not heard about Gwen for a while. She's gone into hiding again. I will go ask Mrs Owen now in a minute. She'll know something. I heard that Captain Price come home wounded and all. Lucky bugger.

Dafydd started to feel down, so he moved to the other letter. He did not recognise the writing and there was an illegible postmark that didn't show its origin.

Dafydd,

I write to hope that this reaches you. I cannot write the English well, so this will be small. I want you to remember me and if you can find me when all is calm, this will be good. I will leave word at the Talbot House where I am.

Je t'aime

Josephine.

Dafydd had a third letter which was a shock. *Aberystwyth? Probably Harri? Had I seen her sweetheart or whatever nonsense.* With a fond smile, he opened it and stopped.

...I know you must think bad of me, but I have done what I done to stay alive. I never meant to hurt you and I wish it could all go back to cooking potatoes at the lime kiln, but there we are. I am back in Aber; my lady took me back in and I cook and clean and do whatever I am asked because I am grateful for the chance. You are a special man, keep your head down and away from all the fighting and try and look for me when you come home. I promise I won't be so snooty this time round!

Cariad 'ti

Gwen

The dark cloud had now reached Dafydd. He put his letters away and sighed. He reached for his tea, wishing there was rum in it, just this once. Just enough to take away the hurt. Tom was right. It was difficult to tell what was normal anymore.

They were all summoned to one of the larger locomotive workshops. Dafydd had never seen so many of the crews together in one place.

Monroe was on edge, as far as Dafydd could see. He stood still with his arms behind his back. In the shadows, his baton could be vaguely seen switching up and down

Monroe waited for Sergeant Macrae who came in with a nod, then cleared his throat.

'All here, Macrae?'

'All bar those out on trains,' came the reply.

'Right chaps, I'll be brief. You know the Jerries have been making things even warmer than normal. Word has it that they are trying to make a break for Wipers. But the only way to do that is to circle it. That makes them bloody close to Hazebrouck and us. So, we're going to have to move.'

There was a silence. The sounds of work outside provided echoes like ripples on a pool.

'When sir?' Tom's voice scythed through the silence.

'Now. We start immediately.'

'How much do we leave behind?' came another voice.

'Nothing. We take the lot.'

The silence reclaimed the room like a wave crashing through.

'Everything?'

'Everything, Thompson. Engines, tools. Even the bloody coal. We don't leave anything the Germans can use, except the bloody track – and we'll nobble that. I'll brief the others as they come in. But for now, we are moving the works and its engines back to Audruicq and the front base for us will be Hondeghem.'

'Begging pardon sir,' Cartwright was scowling already. 'there's nothing in bloody Hondingam. Where do we stay?'

'You'll be sleeping on the engines, waiting in line. Come on chaps, settle down. You've done it before.'

Monroe held up his hands for calm. The number of voices grew until Macrae bellowed.

'QUIET!

'Thank you, Macrae. Right, men keep calm here. You know the score; Jerries been making some serious attacks this year and it's been getting steadily worse. If they do make the breakthrough, we can't be leaving them a supply of engines, parts fuel and a railway to chase us all the way back to Dunkirk.

General Haig has told the Army we've got our backs to the wall and that is all of us; the poor sods at the front and us playing trains. But we've been dealt a rough hand. No rougher than anyone else over here, but we can't let our heads drop. The only reason we're still where we are is because of the work we've done getting things back and forth. However, it's crunch time now and we've got to stand up and be counted. Any questions? No? Good. We need to get going. There's 9000 tons of coal here. That's a few trains for us to fill.'

Dafydd looked around. Tom was normally by his side, but this time he was already halfway out of the door. He found him at the notice board, checking the roster. The list, pinned to a board, was surrounded by a scrum.

Tom looked over and spoke with a voice of stone. 'We've a Central 2-8-0, taking crocked engine's back to Dunkirk fur shipping out.'

He set off at pace, leaving Dafydd struggling to keep up. Dafydd was nervous. He'd been on one of these lumbering beasts before, albeit briefly. He preferred one of the new Baldwin Spider engines that had just come in from America. Now he had a heavy unbraked train to manage carefully along a long stretch of track, to stop the dormant engines from taking over and pushing them beyond every stop. Between him, Tom and the guard, they had their work cut out. Tom obviously felt the same.

'Tom, I know it's a tough link, but we're good enough, you and me.'

Tom said nothing and Dafydd tried again.

'Heads up, Tom bach. We'll be alright.'

'Aye.'

230

'We've been in worse scrapes before.'

'Aye. If it weren't for your bloody women, it'd be a party.'

Dafydd reeled as if slapped across the jaw. Although there was no physical hurt, his eyes welled up with pain.

'I'm sorry,' was all he could manage in a hoarse whisper.

They prepared the engine in silence. Dafydd still smarted at the comment. He felt embarrassed and ashamed. For so long, he realised he had opined his lot to Tom. He had not thought it might be trying his friend's patience.

Tom for his part seemed to be studying the art of coal firing with an intensity, borne of keenness to blot out the world. He examined every inch of the firebox before he shovelled in an extra load of coal and shut the firebox. As they moved to form the train of its component loads, the communication began to flow, but it was still curt and distant. Each comment, a simple observation of the task, the line ahead or just an acknowledgment. Each time, the voice cut through a cab bereft of the normal noise of jovial conviviality.

They set off to the west. It was a route that was as pleasant as the mixed-up world would allow. It was at least away from the signs of carnage that marked Flanders. However, the atmosphere in the cab was still tense and the engine made full effort to hide the silence behind its own exertions, as they slowly made their way forward.

The congestion had begun to build up on the line and they soon found themselves slowly limping from signal to signal, as a constant stream of traffic went past the other way.

Guns, ammunition, troop reinforcements, even the new secret weapon that they were calling the tank. All had passed on long, noisy trains to shore up the front. Dafydd watched them go by, spending the time in-between gazing at the green rolling French countryside. He marvelled at the houses sitting proud and undamaged in the land – unlike the ruined dwellings languishing in light brown Flanders mud.

231

It was like a pleasant dream, but it made him feel dirty and in need of a decent wash. He sighed.

'Looks like we are backed up following ambulance trains and empty shell casings,' he said in an attempt to restart the communication.

Tom was busy lighting a pipe and he nodded while the tobacco in the bulb glowed with every breath as he held a match over it.

'Reckon you're right there, son.'

The words came out of the side of his mouth, with the popping sound of some preliminary puffs. Dafydd took a deep breath.

'Look Tom, I'm sorry. I don't know...' he stopped to claw for the words. 'It's probably since I ran away as a boy that I been chasing security and never finding it neither. I fall for girls too easily and then I can't let go for trying. It's because I want to feel secure and happy and I want that warmth in my life. You're kind and a good pal. You listen to me, as I get this stuff off my chest and you let me go on. I never thought I were one for moaning, but I must sound like one. I never realised it would be annoying. I'm that sorry I am.'

Tom stopped brushing the coal dust from the floor of the cab and leant on his broom, taking the pipe from his mouth to emphasise his words.

'You're like a son to me, Daf. You're a good and honest boy, like I would want a son to be. Problem is, you've too much love in your heart and you're desperate for it to be given back. This Gwen's had you tied round her little finger for so long, you're doing a merry dance in your sleep. It's not healthy, you daft apoth. You were going t'right way with young Josephine, but life's not dealt you an easy hand there.'

Tom gave a sad pat on Dafydd's shoulder to acknowledge the confusion in his face.

232

'But what are we doing now? Retreating, that's what. It might be short term, tactical and all, but its bloody obvious. All of a sudden, we're losing this bloody war. Four years and we're bloody losing and for what? So that's what we've been dealt. All you can do is see which way the cards go and pick up the pieces when it all ends.'

'Son, it's not that bad, I can see your heart's in t'right place, but I hate to see you suffering with it. Don't worry of my mood. This bloody war gets to me sometimes and I just got so bloody frustrated.'

'Well at least you've got your wife at home writing to you,' Dafydd replied.

Tom laughed, but the tone was hollow. 'Well, son, all's not as it seems.' He produced a crumpled letter from his pocket and held it up.

'Missus? She's gone off wi't'lodger. I didn't even know we had a bloody lodger. He copped a blighty one and went home to cuckold me. Apparently, she wants to be with a real soldier. Doing her bit for t'country, it would seem.'

Conversation died, leaving the hiss of steam and crackle of the fire to fill the gap. Tom screwed up the letter into a ball and lobbed it into the fire.

'Tom...'

'Leave it, son. It's what it will be. Your romances give me hope so don't give up. You're not a fickle lad, you're just confused. It will pass, you'll see. Just talk to me if it helps.'

He looked out of the engine to the fore and smiled.

'We're pegged to go. Best get this moving or we'll be holding up t'army in its retreat. We'll say no more of it for now.

'We'll turn it round Tom. Everything will work out, you'll see.'

There was no reply.

Chapter Twenty-four

Exhaustion

Dafydd placed his head against the cab side and let the shock of the cold steel course through his temples. He hoped it would break his feeling of his head in a vice. They were approaching Hazebrouck junction. Not only was there a complicated series of points ahead, but also, the Germans had not been idle and had been attempting to breakthrough by circling the town. If they could take Hazebrouck, they would cut off the artery that kept the Allies going at Ypres. Lose that and Dafydd felt they'd be carrying the British Army back to the French ports with their tail between their legs. For the moment, it meant that Hazebrouck was warm with activity.

There was no choice, but to keep going. Dafydd had been working flat out for a month since the German attack. Keeping warm was only made bearable as they slept on the footplate, by the issue of a greatcoat. The fire only dried off one side at a time, so the coats were hardy, but reeked of damp. Dafydd thought that could only add to the overall smell of the great unwashed that they had all become. Perhaps it didn't matter. They were hardly needing their Sunday best for chapel.

He was mentally exhausted. With the concentration needed to focus on the hours of driving; checking the gauges, listening as the engine told you how it was coping and always looking ahead to see what was coming. Tom had been taking turns at the regulator. Dafydd appreciated watching him work in the job he was born for.

Fatigue washed over him. It wasn't a night run, when he felt his eyes ache through the focussing outside, of constant changing from the bright firelit cab to looking out into black nothingness. It wasn't as if they had been warmed up by German guns or even a plane attempt to bomb them – One had tried, badly, not even reaching the track, before being chased away by a Sopwith Camel.

It was nothing like the issues they had come through. Today was calm and quiet. Bright, warm and sunny. Perhaps all this had caused his body to relax and the sleep he had been cheated of for so long crept up to embrace him. Now he put his head to the metal to help him focus. It was either that or ask Tom to slap him. He'd try the easier option first.

'You're tired.'

'What makes you say that Tom?'

'You've been staring at the signal for five minutes and its set for us. We've been given the road.'

Dafydd shook his head with embarrassment as he opened the drain cocks and unwound the reversing gear.

'Forget my name next,'

'Maybe we should try and get some kip when we get back.' Tom said with a huge chunk of irony.

Dafydd snorted. And then shook his head ruefully.

''Maybe when they put the fire out and take the engine out of service.'

'You're right Daf. In-between changing to a new engine, we should get a few minutes nod.'

Dafydd couldn't reply. He had lost the words. He had a few letters unopened in his pocket. But he had not yet penned replies to the last batch, let alone having the energy to even read the ones with him now.

They limped into Poperinge, Dafydd refusing to go faster than a snail's pace for fear of not seeing dangers in the mayhem of the station. They were flagged down by an RTO with a clipboard.

'Are you carrying shells?'

Dafydd's mind went blank. 'I don't remember sorry.'

'You having a laugh, Corporal?'

Dafydd shook his head. 'No ammunition, shells. That's what we got. Sorry *bach*, I just had a moment. Cup of tea will solve it all.'

'Well, you've a bit of a wait. We'll get you into siding as soon as we clear the troop train.' The man stared at Dafydd and frowned. 'Leave your train here and go to that tent. Drink the strongest tea that you've had in your life.'

'But what happens if you need to shift the train.'

'I'll know where to find you…'

The unloading of the cargo took an age. The coaling and watering of the engine felt the same and by the time they took the engine to the back of the queue, Tom was leaning on his shovel and Dafydd grabbed the cab window for support. Ahead was one of the Dutch large tank engines, probably off an ambulance train. Cartwright was possibly driving. For a moment, Dafydd felt like going over to share the cab with that crew. It was larger and more enclosed. The thought disappeared as soon as it came. He was too exhausted to move. He'd probably fall off the engine and then wouldn't get back on. *Just one small rest – back to the tender pack against his head for cushioning. Just a small rest…*

He awoke in a half world. His vision was blurred and for a few moments he didn't remember where he was, what he was doing or even who he was. Then he looked around. It was night, cool air was rushing in from outside of the cab. The area was still noisy. An officer stood at the regulator looking ahead. Dafydd's heavy eyes closed again.

He awoke with a jolt. There was an officer in his cab. The urgency woke him, and he shook his head to clear the cobwebs. Then the engine shuddered, they had hit something ahead.

A chorus of disapproval broke out ahead. *He had been right; Cartwright was in the leading locomotive.* Dafydd peered around the engine. *They had moved up the queue quite considerably. How had he not noticed?*

Realising again there was an officer on board, he scrambled up. The officer stood up and turned around. It was Curran.

'Sorry, Thomas. I'm a bit out of practice.' The ghost of a smile played on his lips. His eyes were also hooded with fatigue.

'What are you doing, sir? Begging your pardon.'

'Giving you both some rest before you collapse. You needed some sleep.'

'So, does everyone.'

'Yes Thomas, but you've been suffering more than most. People have been concerned.'

'Who?'

'Your colleagues. You need leave, but I can't give you any. I'll get you off the roster as soon as I can.'

Dafydd hadn't the energy to argue.

'Sir – are we losing?'

The Jerries have been pushing to take all this for two months now and we're still here. So, in my mind, we're not losing.'

'Shame we had the Portuguese up there. They broke the line; the Germans went through them...'

'Don't be too critical, Thomas. The Portuguese army were thrown in unprepared by people who should have known better. They hadn't the right kit and were gassed out of their trenches. There's plenty that stood their ground where they could and a few of their gunners saved our bacon. A bit more thought about preparing them for this hellhole would have helped everyone.'

'I hope it's all worth it in the end."

'I don't know anymore,' Monroe's voice was soft, wistful. 'Is killing a man worth it? Maiming someone so he will never be looked at the same again or can't do what he could before? Killing husbands and sons? Everything is war. We work for war, back home they make things for war,' he chuckled cynically. 'Yes, I hope it's all worth it too. Perhaps one day we'll find out.'

'Well, they have an annual debate at the Talbot House. Is the war going to end this year? The no's increase every year. They now outnumber the ayes by two to one.'

'All the more reason for me to make sure you don't fall apart. I'll have you rest and no looking for your French girl whilst we're here. She's busy and the compound is off limits. I need some trains going forward to Ypres and beyond and you just volunteered. Now get some sleep.'

Dafydd's eyes closed. He began to drift but his mind was filled with Josephine. For a moment, she had Gwen's face...'

Chapter Twenty-five

Armistice

Dawn broke and a cold breeze woke Dafydd from his slumber. He had slept on his seat, slumped with his head against the cab side of the steam engine, his body giving in to seventy-two hours of being on duty. Now his neck was telling him all about it, as he desperately tried to rub the stiffness out.

Tom was slumped in the tender on the coals and a sudden panic arose in Dafydd's mind. He was supposed to wake him to change watch. Nervously, Dafydd scrambled up to look out of the cab, but they were lucky. The signal stood firm, red for danger. They had been kept waiting overnight. Whoever was screaming for the shells was obviously in no hurry to help in getting them there. The guard hadn't been over to check on them; probably happy enough to stay in his cosy van. *Probably asleep too*, thought Dafydd with a chuckle. Somewhere in the damned Belgian mud, an artillery battalion would probably be cursing their names. Dafydd didn't care, not anymore. Too much had happened over the past three years.

Tom stirred and stretched, groaning at his back pain brought on by the bed of coals.

'You're a lucky bugger, Tom. We'd have been shot for that back in '15.'

Tom hawked and spat out of the cab. 'Dropping that signal arm would have woken me, should they have got round to letting us move.'

He stood up and stretched again, moving forward to tap the pressure gauge. Then he moved over to the cab end and emptied his bladder on the embankment below. A grunt of satisfaction and he reached for his trusty shovel, kicking open the firebox door to light the cab with a yellow glow. The shovel went roughly into the coal as Tom started building up the fire again. Happy with the result, he grunted again and kicked the door shut once more, turning with a wink to Dafydd.

'Got a surprise, Daf.'

He carefully retrieved his pack and pulled out a small linen bundle, which turned out to be a few slices of streaky bacon, almost fresh.

'How the bloody…' Dafydd began, but Tom just tapped his nose with a grin.

'Never you mind, Daf. We'll mix it with bully beef and wash it down with black tea. It'll give it some taste.'

Tom tapped his shovel on the cab floor, shaking some coal dust onto the floor.

'It adds to the flavour,' he said, running his finger over the back and holding up the smutty digit to Dafydd.

Dafydd nodded. 'A railwayman's breakfast, shame about the eggs.'

The firebox door was wedged open and the meat placed on the back of the shovel and rested it on the entrance. Very soon, the crackle of fat and a wonderful aroma of cooked meat filled the cab.

They ate their food and as the last piece was eaten, the signal arm obligingly dropped to green.

'Jolly decent of them,' Tom said, his broad Lancashire still singing through the mimicking an officer's clipped tones.

The next station was manned by a Railway Transport Officer. He flagged the train down, and Dafydd slowed them to a crawl, so as not to lose momentum. The man was almost dancing with joy.

'You 'eard? They reckon they'll be signing a ceasefire tomorrow morning. Jerry's caved in, blooming marvellous! We'll be home by Christmas.'

'Bloody heard that before,' muttered Tom, as Dafydd opened up the regulator and they took off for their destination.

Standard gauge work normally brought them to a yard, where the goods would be unloaded to go forward via narrow gauge railway or mules. The front, which had been so static on this blood-soaked, god-forsaken quagmire, had advanced so quickly over the last couple of months. Now they had moved beyond the morass that had taken so many lives and were well forward, as the German Army fell back with increasing rapidity. The ammunition depot had been brought forward to make it closer to the front, although out of reach of the more accurate German guns. Not that many seemed to remain. As the train pulled in, Dafydd could see trains of mules standing patiently waiting to be loaded up for the end journey.

'Decouple your engine and move forward,' the officer in charge commanded. 'I'll not have sparks set off these munitions.'

Dafydd just nodded and Tom moved off to uncouple the engine. No need to speak, it was always the same. Same old bloody officers who haven't a clue. What about the sparks the old girl had puffed out over the last hundred miles? The pair bit their tongues and got on with it. No need for hassle either, the memory of being punished for late running still cut deep.

Thank God those Aussie soldiers had cut them both from the stakes they were tied to as punishment.

Now the talk of an armistice, perhaps this time it was true, Dafydd thought. He moved the engine forward as the officer held up his cane and lowered it when he was satisfied.

'Shall I throw out some hot coals when we run th'engine round t'back of t'wagons?' asked Tom slyly.

'Best leave it, eh?' Dafydd replied.

'You'd have thought time over 'ere would have removed that stick from up his arse,' Tom shouted as he shovelled more coal in the fire and kicked the door shut once more.

It was a cool day, but so clear. Dafydd was sure he could hear a bird singing in a nearby charred hulk of a tree. There were certainly no sounds of war. No barrages and plumes of mud on the horizon, mixed with the detritus of battle; mud, water and lost equipment together with the dead carcasses of souls lost to their comrades. Never to be found, but still to be mourned over. Dafydd had heard tell of bones sticking out of trench walls, picked clean by rats the size of cats. He had heard of dead bodies being treated as part of the trench, until borne away by stretcher parties. He thanked God daily that his lot was the iron road and not that hell upon earth.

'Penny for 'em?' Tom said and Dafydd shrugged.

'Just thanking my luck.'

'You men help us unload,' the officer was at the footplate. Dafydd sighed; he'd been there so many times before.

'Respectfully sir, we have to remain here to keep the fire up and the steam pressure level. Leaving the engine would be dangerous, see. Engine could get too hot or the fire could go out and that's four hours to raise steam once more for starters.'

The officer looked sharply at them with suspicious eyes.

'Honestly sir, I have the regulations in my pack. Railway Corps orders say never leave our engine unattended. Especially in a munitions depot.'

'Humph, well don't move this damned thing out from my depot until I tell you,' the officer said flicking his hand with undisguised contempt.

'Right you are sir,' Dafydd opened up the regulator, sending steam rushing through the pistons, making the officer back off quickly.

'Nice man,' Tom remarked dryly.

Moving to the end of the compound, Dafydd set the engine to rest and looked back. 'Well, that's a busy afternoon we have ahead of us.'

Tom smiled, 'Your turn to sleep or mine?' They settled down for a welcome respite.

'Aye, aye! Here's the sleeping beauties.' A rough voice broke through their dreams. Dafydd looked down at the weather beaten, grubby face of the soldier who gave the chirpy greeting from the engine steps. It was a face that had lived through a lot, his smile contradicting the pain in his eyes.

'Morning Corporal, off to kill Jerries?'

The man snorted. 'No, I'm wondering if you boys have a kettle on, so I can service the King's army with tea. You look like a pair of old maids; I had you for the Red Cross.'

'Well, we may not be able to be your old maids, but this old girl's the largest kettle you'll ever find. Have a cup, courtesy of William Dean.'

'I will that,' the Corporal replied, turning around quick to bark orders to a group of soldiers, who began to offload and rest nearby and outside of the depot.

'Can't make them all a cup,' Tom said handing him a tin mug with black tea.

'They'll live,' the Corporal replied dryly. 'Thanks for the brew, William.'

Tom hid a smile, 'My name's Tom. It's William Dean who built this beast. A Swindon girl she is.'

'Ah, a West Country wench then,' came the reply as the Corporal sipped his brew.

'You off up to the front?' Dafydd asked and the Corporal nodded.

'Aye, I've been three days now without the lice and have a need to scratch.'

'Well, that's all you'll be doing if this talk of a Ceasefire is alright.'

'Yes, I heard that too, that'll pee off some of His Majesty's *orfficers*. Some won't get too far without the chance of a field commission. Still, until they get around to telling us to stop, we have to keep giving it to those poor bastard Jerries. Poor buggers, they're getting a pasting now like we used to. Some don't know when to give up though.' He stopped and sipped his tea a while. 'You know one day; I would think they'll need a few gardeners to come and put back some green in this mud bath. Maybe I should volunteer. I'd like to make this place beautiful again once we've stopped messing it about.'

'Are you a gardener then?' Tom asked and the Corporal smiled and sipped the last of his tea. 'No chum, I'm a postman. Funny innit.' He put his hand in his pocket and took out a crumpled paper, which he gently smoothed. 'Look, you boys are all right, perhaps you could do me a favour. Get this sent back to Blighty, will you?'

'What happens if you come back?'

'Well, that'll be a bonus' came the soft reply.

Dafydd nodded and took the note. The man clapped his shoulder and started shinning down the steps. 'You lads keep your heads down and if you do get lost, keep to the duckboards!'

'God go with you,' said Tom quietly. The man looked up and nodded curtly.

'Keep your heads down, boys.'

****

The day was lost at the depot, but it gave Dafydd time to dream. What if they were right about the ceasefire? Dafydd dreamed everyday of going home to Gwen. But more recently those dreams had clashed with finding Josephine once more in Poperinge. Now the talk was of an end to the war, Dafydd could hardly imagine his dreams coming true. A new beginning, a new life back home to look forward to. When the time came, he would make the right choice, he knew.

They ran the engine back in the depot and coupled up the empty trucks. Tom even managed a sloppy salute, insolent enough to annoy the officer without fear of reprisal. They moved off back down the line, as the light began to fade. It was cold out there now, as November always was in those parts. Short days and cold breezes. Dafydd tried to avoid sticking his head out of the cab for fear of freezing his face.

Perhaps that made it more difficult to see the track or the fatigue just made him lose concentration. More than likely, he would never have seen the broken track anyway. A few miles out of the depot, the train ran off the rails and fell on its side.

The first Dafydd knew of it was a violent lurch that took the engine left and then it began to lean at a crazy angle. The sound of gravel was like an avalanche and in Dafydd's mind the world was all in slow motion as the engine bucked and threw him from the cab. It was a strange feeling as he saw the red glow of the fire below and he passed through the engine smoke.

The worst thing was he knew it was not worth struggling for there was absolutely nothing to do about it. He hit the ground and skimmed across the muddy surface, the pain making time speed back up again. Onwards he sped, until he was brought up short by some wooden boarding laid across the mud that knocked the breath out of him, making his ribs creak.

His legs were sinking now in the sticky mud, slowly but enough to make him grab the board in wild panic and hold on for dear life. He'd heard enough about Flanders mud. He remembered Mad Jack, it made him frantic. It felt like forever, but then the boards thumped, and Tom was by his side.

'Come on you Welsh bugger, I could hear yer crying a mile off.'

'How the hell did you get here?' Dafydd groaned.

'Don't ask me, I got thrown off the footplate and found myself in a tree. Scratched to buggery I am. Now, let's see if we can't get you up.'

'Don't stray off the boards.'

'I'm not daft Daf, right let's lever your leg up a bit with me shovel'

'You and your bloody shovel.'

'Well, it's instinct; in times of peril I grab hold of what's close and hang on for grim death. Anyway, it were like a shield and it got me wedged in that tree. It stopped me getting flung in t'firebox for a head-on. Now, try and pull your leg up.'

Between the two of them, they managed to free Dafydd's legs, the ground giving them up with a mighty squelch.

'Alright now, lad?'

'My ribs hurt, and I took a crack on the jaw. How's the shovel?'

'It'll live,' Tom replied dryly. He looked around as best he could, for it was pitch dark. 'Can't see bugger all here.'

'How do we find the track?' Dafydd said

'God knows, track must have been blown by a shell.'

'A German bomber perhaps, more like one of our stray shells. Told you they were cock-eyed...'

'Can you see the engine?'

Dafydd peered into the black. 'Not a chance, but I can hear her over by there. Look, I'm not wanting to stick around by here, them boards have sunk since we arrived, and I'd rather not be swimming at dawn. Let's make for the sound of the engine. It might be drier further on.'

'Aye,' muttered Tom. 'If such a place exists in Belgium. We'll follow t'boards until we're closer to th'engine then.'

Tom started wandering off and still dazed, with his head buzzing, Dafydd was forced to follow. As they moved, Tom became less and less vocal and before long, he clammed up all together. Shovel on his shoulder, like a common soldier.

The hissing of the stricken engine began to fade and Dafydd realised they were moving away from it. However, the boards still felt as if they floated on the mud and he was worried about losing Tom, so all he could do was follow.

Dafydd wondered what had happened to old Smithy in the guards' van, but as he couldn't get Tom to stop, he just followed, praying the old boy was safe enough.

'Can't bloody wait to get home now,' Dafydd grumbled. The cold and the shock had started him shivering. 'That derailment is the last straw, even shunting at Aberdovey on a freezing January morning is better than this.'

Tom just walked on in silence. It felt as if they had walked all night, carefully moving along the muddy duck boards. Each step sent the board further down into the mud, oozing fresh muck into their boots and ankles. On and on Tom moved relentlessly.

'Stop, you old bugger!' Dafydd finally cried.

'Engine's just off this corner,' Tom muttered faintly back.

They walked on in the dark. For a fleeting moment, the moon broke through the clouds, giving a monochrome sight of desolation that made Dafydd shudder.

Silhouettes of shattered trees amongst the watery pools of old shell craters. It was like nothing on earth. Dafydd saw the remains of carts and equipment and what he prayed weren't dead bodies.

It grew darker again and on Tom went. Finally, Dafydd realised that the path had sunk down to become a trench. It seemed empty, until his boot came into contact with a large fur ball that disappeared squeaking with a scrabble of claws. He realised he had met the resident rats.

The trench zigzagged on and Dafydd lost his footing a few times, he knew his trousers would be caked with the yellow mud now, if it ever dried. Still Tom moved on ahead, until a rough voice called out a challenge that made him stop and Dafydd finally catch up with him.

'Don't shoot,' Dafydd cried. 'We're British. Railway Corps.'

A dim light appeared, and a soldier peered forward, the silhouettes of rifles either side of him.

'What the hell are you doing here?'

'Train derailed, tried to make our way back, followed the duckboards.' Dafydd stammered. The man swore in reply

'Do you know how many miles that is? You sure you're who you say you are?'

'They're covered in coal dust, beneath the blood and mud, Jim,' another voice piped up.

'Well, I think we best send them on to the Corporal, he'll know what to do. Medics up there and all, to see to your head, mate.'

Dafydd looked at Tom and saw for the first time the trail of red from a head wound.

'Come on then lads, lucky one of you's a Taff or we'd have had you for Jerries."

They followed on farther into the trench complex, this time with the benefit of light. The mud looked like yellow-brown porridge and Dafydd was surprised that when rats came into view, they needed a kick to shift them, rather than scuttling away in a panic. The soldier was scratching his side and Dafydd started worrying about catching lice.

'What the hell are you doing here?' It was the Corporal they had met at the ammunition dump, looking stunned at their arrival, *as well he should*, thought Dafydd. Bandaged up and given a tot of rum, the railwaymen began to warm up and their cuts and bruises started to register in their brains.

The Corporal laughed, but without mirth at their story. 'Get yourselves some rest boys, as best you can. Come dawn, you can make your way back and find your engine."

The railwaymen settled down on a fire step, but had difficulty sleeping in the cold and with the activity that was beginning to start around them. Soldiers were cleaning their rifles and checking their kit. In the end Dafydd asked what was going on.

'We're over the top and at Jerry at dawn, Taff,' came the gruff reply. 'Second wave. If you stay long enough, you'll have a grandstand view through them loopholes,' he gestured at the covered spy holes at the top of the trench. 'See how the real army works.'

Dafydd was shocked. Seeing the Corporal, Dafydd rushed to him. 'Is there news of the armistice?'

The Corporal spat. 'Word came through the trench quite fast; it was signed at five this morning. Word also came through that it starts at eleven o'clock and up to then, we're still at war. So, until I get told different, I've got to get my lads ready to kick Jerry up the arse.'

'What's going on?' Tom groaned from the step and Dafydd rushed to him.

'They've signed the ceasefire Tom *bach*, but it's not until eleven and the boys are still being sent over. It's madness!'

'Officer's over there,' Tom said with a nod as the man worked his way through the trench. 'Maybe he hasn't heard.'

'Well, I'll damn well make sure he does.' Dafydd growled.

'Rum ration distributed, Corporal?' The officer asked. 'Are the men ready?'

'As ready as they can be, sir,' the Corporal replied without emotion.

'Right then, best get started. Get them ready to move forward.'

The Corporal started barking orders, as Dafydd approached the Officer.

'Sir, isn't it true that a ceasefire has been signed?'

'It is,' the officer replied coolly looking Dafydd up and down. 'The war ends at eleven, but these are our orders, so we have until then to punish them. Corporal, who are these men?'

'Railwaymen, sir. Got lost last night after a crash.'

'RAILWAYMEN! I think you need to make yourselves scarce,' the Officer said with contempt. The horror of it all began to sink through to Dafydd and he began to panic.

'Sir, please. I have to ask. What is the point? It's all going to end soon. A new beginning, we can all go home.'

'Because those are my orders. Until the ceasefire, we are still at war.'

'What the lad is trying to say,' Tom's voice sounded out, clear as a bell. 'What he means is, why are you trying to get your command killed when we could all go home from this hell?'

The silence was overpowering, making Dafydd sway with shock. The officer went stiff and his eyes cold.

'Lieutenant? These men are under arrest for insubordination. Keep them here, so I can deal with them on my return.'

'Shall I post men sir, as guard?' The Corporal asked quickly as the Officer brushed past. For a moment, an understanding passed between them.

'Two would be enough, our young ones. Need the beef up at the front.'

The officer's eyes locked on Dafydd's and the railwayman felt a wave of sadness in the stare. Then he was gone, the men filing after him. The Corporal nodded as he went. The two to remain were boys in Dafydd's eyes. Boys with the lined faces of old men. They stood down and started rolling cigarettes, their shaking hands belied their nonchalance.

'Shall we run for it?' Tom whispered, colour had returned to his face, but he still looked weak.

'Best not,' Dafydd said with a smile. 'We won't get far the way we're feeling.'

Dafydd sat down next to Tom on the fire step and sighed. It would be an uneasy wait; home suddenly seemed a long way away.

The whizz of shells had begun, as if the guns were trying to work off all their ordnance before the end. The ground began to rumble as they landed. It felt like an age, before the world suddenly fell silent once more. Far off Dafydd could hear a yell, like a far-off football game, then the faint crack of rifle fire and the bombing started again.

The two young soldiers had taken up position at one of the loopholes and looked on in silence. One of them shook, as if sobbing. Dafydd gently made his way up to the other loophole and gazed on the scene of the battle. The view seemed to be for miles and the British soldiers looked like ants. Dafydd watched in horror and then stumbled back.

'What's up?' asked Tom, scrambling forward.

'Like bloody dominoes…' Dafydd whispered. Tom stepped up to look and then recoiled as a particularly large explosion took place.

'My God,' he whispered. 'It's like watching a pack of bloody cards being thrown up in th'air.'

Dafydd heard a movement and looked at the lieutenant as he calmly walked down the trench, occasionally pulling scraps of paper from the sandbags. He looked up at the two stunned railwaymen.

'If I were you gentlemen, I'd bugger off now.'

'Won't you get into trouble?' Dafydd stammered back.

'They won't be back,' was the simple reply. 'Jerry's got that line sewn up tighter than a virgin.'

It was too much for Dafydd, he couldn't stop himself.

'Then why send them?' he yelled. 'There's no point, they should be packing for home, not being led like lambs to the slaughter. What's the matter with you red tabs? Don't you know when to stop? I felt this morning like we were all ready for a new beginning, but some of you don't want it. Don't you feel ashamed?'

The lieutenant calmly walked over, straightening the papers. 'Listen chaps; you've had it easier this war. I'm not saying it has all been easy, for I'm sure you have tales to tell also, but here you're out of your depth. Here when you receive an order, you carry it through. A hesitation could kill you. Top brass may have signed some paper, but how do we know the enemy will do their part or even know that it has happened. Those Jerries over there are a stubborn lot; they've been fighting to the death. What makes you think they will just lay down their arms?'

Dafydd just stared on as the lieutenant walked up to him, his voice still calm.

'I would say most men went by choice; duty, honour, revenge, a chance for advancement, even if most know that they don't stand a chance. To show that it's useless to resist or gas us, to stop the German High Command having second thoughts. I hope our boys return, I pray so. But I've been here a while now and there's a lot I will have to live with until the day I die.

He slapped the paper on Dafydd's chest.

'This is all you can do for them now, get these letters sent home. Let their loved ones know they died with courage; let them have a chance to weep. Give them a new beginning.' He looked at his watch. 'It'll all stop soon. The war will be over, then at least we can celebrate. And we can grieve.'

Chapter Twenty-six

Talbot House

It had been a week since the armistice. Dafydd had been given leave, to allow him to recover from his accident. He had not been allowed permission to return home, so he had gone back to Poperinge, where the town appeared to have received a giant wave of celebrating Tommy soldiers. Dafydd was there for another reason, he wanted to get Tom into Talbot House, in the hope that the place would heal his soul. The injuries, the exhausting days on regular service and the general air of morose fatalism in the place was bad enough, but Tom's wife had been the icing on a forlorn cake, and his fireman looked ready to crack. Dafydd had managed to get them lodging there for a short while.

He left Tom in the garden and moved towards the great French window doors leading in from the garden. Stepping across the red brick patio, he moved inside past the kitchens, in the hope of finding a seat in the snug. Perhaps he could snag a copy of the Wipers Times, the gallows-style humour appealed to him these days. Or maybe just snag one of the highchairs and sleep.

The downstairs was busy, so Dafydd moved up a floor to the library. In another room, a table tennis game was going on. Good-natured by the sounds of approval, emanating down the corridor. The small white ball bounced out of the doorway onto the landing towards Dafydd and a soldier burst through after it. Tunic missing, his shirt sleeves rolled up, Curran did not look like the officer he was known.

'Hello Dafydd.'

'Hello Sir,'

'My name is George, Dafydd. At least here it is. Fancy a game?'

Dafydd shook his head. 'Can I watch?'

'Certainly. Off we go, Hamish.'

Curran's opponent was Sergeant Macrae. His walrus like moustache looked out of place anywhere near a sport.

Curran served and the two set off on the battle for the first point. Dafydd felt there was a certain rhythm to their play. One bounce, hit, one bounce hit. Very relaxed and calm, not that they looked capable of upping the tempo. Curran spoke to Dafydd as he played.

'So how do you feel after your leave then Dafydd?'

'I'm feeling more tired, sir…'

'George…'

'George. I been sleeping for ages but feeling the dopier for it. I'd forgotten what sleep was.'

Macrae laughed at that.

'That's what happens. The body relaxes and you're a sleepy head all the time. I suppose you ended up sleeping on the floor?'

Dafydd coughed in surprise. 'How did you know?'

'Force of habit, son. We've all done it.'

'How's Tom?' Curran asked.

'He's alright really, considering,' Dafydd replied. Curran nodded

'He's been through a lot recently. Look, there's a spare bat here. Come and join in.'

'Alright.'

It was awkward, Dafydd learned quite quickly the delicate nature of hitting ball with bat, after a few efforts sailed past the table. He focussed on making the ball reach the table. Every point was lost, but each time the ball bounced on the green table, it was a victory for Dafydd.

Soon they were all grinning like schoolboys and Dafydd followed his officers to the kitchens to get a pot of tea. The weather was unseasonably mild, so they moved outside to the garden and found a bench. Tom got up from his customary position at the base of one of the larger trees and came to join them.

'I think your arse will be a wee bit damp now, Tom,' Macrae said.

'Aye, you're right there Hamish. Ad worse though.'

'Listen.' Curran held up his hands for silence. The land replied with an equal lack of sound.

'What is it?' Dafydd asked.

'Nothing',' came the reply. 'Magical, isn't it? All the way up to armistice they were firing anything and everything they could find. *Pom Pom Pom!* Then it just stopped and when the echoes cleared, you could hear the birds singing. There's more noise at my solicitor's office in Edinburgh than there is here?'

'Was that your job?' Tom asked.

'Aye, It was. Another world of pompous circumstance.'

Macrae smiled. Dafydd felt he had missed the joke. Macrae continued.

'I'll be back tae St Rollox fer the workshops on the Caley.'

'I'll be firing on the Cambrian,' Dafydd said glumly. 'Unless they recognise my experience here.'

'I'll write them a letter,' Curran said. Dafydd nodded his thanks.

There was a moment's pause, as everyone looked at Tom. He was staring at the high garden wall opposite.

'I'll be staying 'ere.'

'You've mair experience than any o' us,' Macrae said. 'Even mair than Cartwright. You'll be walking back into your job on the expresses.'

Tom shook his head. 'Nowt for me back 'ome. I'm staying put. Cartwright too. We'll pair up if we have ter.'

'Look, Tom. We don't know when we can get demobbed. It could be tomorrow or next month or whenever. You don't have to make your minds up now.'

'George, yer right in a way. But trains still got ter run. Belgians won't do it, not yet, don't have enough folk around. Th'army 'll need transport into Germany. But if there's nowt to do, me an' Cartwright'll be running trips fer folk ter see t'battlefields. There's a few already come over like, ter see where thur loved ones fell.

'I'm staying with you then!' Dafydd snapped.

Tom smiled and shook his head. 'Nay lad, you can't be stopping here. You've got a girl to go home to.'

'Thought you had one here?' Macrae said and Dafydd flushed.

'She's gone. She said she'd leave word, but she hasn't, and no-one's seen sight or sound of her in Poperinge since she went to the field hospital.'

'Sometimes it can take time for messages to come through.' Curran remarked.

Dafydd said nothing. The mug of tea was tart, but he was used to drinking whatever he was given. He watched the vapours skim off his mug and his mind drifted into blankness.

'You got a letter from Gwen?'

Tom's voice burst through the silken threads of his daydream. Dafydd nodded glumly. He didn't want to get it out and show the men. They were probably fed up of it, he was certainly. He couldn't go on deciding his love life by committee.

But even now he remembered the words.

...I been so lost since I last wrote, and I hope I'm not too late. It's all done now and all I can say is I been a fool. I want to make it up to you. I want you with me so much it hurts to think of what is gone. I wish it were different.

256

Come back as soon as you can. I am feeling better every day and I'll be your lovely Gwen again by the time you get here. Come soon, I miss you....

Dafydd looked up at the grey sky. He wished the sky was blue and the sun was warming his face, but it was November and the world was still half there and half suspended in the air above. There had been enough explosions over the years, that he wondered if it had all managed to come back down yet. He knew the others were watching, but he didn't feel like talking to them.

'It's alright lad, I understand.'

'Do you, Tom?'

Tom's look was a picture of sympathy. His dark eyes reflected like pools of sorrow, both for himself and his mate. He knew the pain. He knew the frustration and he knew the limitations of the support that could be offered. What he could give, he gave freely.as he always had. To support his friend and comrade. Dafydd felt humbled that he could not give as much in return.

'We don't know when we can go home,' Curran said. 'Probably in small groups. All I can do is recommend you to be one of the first, Dafydd, although it may depend on how long you've been out here.'

'Thank you, sir,' *I think*. Dafydd muttered. Then he gave a deep sigh.

'It's crazy, but I'm thinking I'll miss all this, in a way. Not the lack of comfort, the smells or the tiredness. But us, together. Working through the problems. Getting the trains running.'

'When are these back on duty Hamish?'

'In an hour, George. I got them a bit of more rest by having some sappers raise the steam and prepare the train.'

Curran smiled and tipped the dregs out of his tin mug. 'I'll miss all this, men. I may not have been born into this work, but my job is so clinical and boring compared to it. I'd wish I had more time. Perhaps I could even drive one of the trains before we left.'

'I'll not be doin' with that work.' Macrae said with a laugh. 'I had enough of footplate work on the Caley.'

'You gone soft, Hamish?' Tom said with a lop-sided grin.

Macrae guffawed. 'Oh, I can turn a decent shovel if I have to. And you'd best put in a good performance, my laddie, for we'll be travelling on your next train.'

'Well,' Tom said with a grin getting broader as he spoke. 'Maybe you should come on t'footplate and show us how it's done?'

Dafydd clicked his fingers. 'Here's a thought. You two on the footplate. Hamish, you do the firing and George, I'll teach you to drive. It's about 30 minutes or so back now and if anyone asks, you are supervising us on our return to work. What do you think?'

Curran's eyes grew large and he quickly looked to Macrae. The other looked on for a few seconds before he gave a face that had them both laughing like schoolboys.

'Go on, George. You've earned it.' Macrae said.

The two officers moved off to get their jackets and Dafydd looked at Tom.

'Thank you.'

'It were you, lad, not me.'

'No, for everything. For being around. Thank you.'

'I told you lad, it were you, not me. But I'll tell yer this. I have a feeling I will be finding Josephine for you. That'll be my thanks.'

'So, you think I should stay?

Tom shrugged. 'No, I think you should go. Fate'll play it all out fer you. If Gwen's thur for yer, yer best to find her. But only if she's not playing you fer t'fool.'

Chapter Twenty-seven

Home
(1919)

There was an indecent haste in the way that the train started to move. The jolt made him bang his head on the back of the carriage wall, the seats not being graced with cushioning. Dark thoughts flew through Dafydd's mind, punctuated by expletives from the other passengers. Dafydd knew what had happened – greasy rails and a bit too much regulator. He didn't mention it; the audience wouldn't have cared. Dafydd embraced the apathy of the carriage instead.

He had looked forward to this day for nigh on four years, yet it had taken many, many months to happen. He had imagined the time he would spend admiring the green fields of France and Southern England. But now, it was too much like a massive anti-climax.

'Perhaps it's the delay?' He had said to Tom who took a drag of his roll-up and smiled.

'Months beyond th'armistice they've been ferrying troops and equipment.'

Dafydd looked at the lines of men ready to entrain. It was if nothing had changed, but for one key factor.

'Only this time they're all going west.'

'True enough, lad. An' we've been running Belgian trains whilst they wait for their own folk to turn up. Still, you're off 'ome now.'

'It's not fair, Tom. This should be you going back, not me.'

'Told you before, son. I'm staying 'ere. But if yer find a post back 'ome, like, see if thur's one fer me an' all.'

'I will my friend. I dunno what I'll be doing without you '

'You will, son. Yer'll be fine, now bugger off before you get all weepy on us.'

It wasn't the delay. It was losing Tom. He'd been the anchor, the support and strength through the days of exhaustion. Tom was like an older brother, guiding and watching over him. Now Dafydd felt as if he was walking a narrow path above an abyss and the handrails had been removed.

Yet it was more than Tom. The intensity of war had brought with it a kind of security. The circumstances would always change, but there was an order somewhere within the chaos. In a bizarre way, Dafydd always knew where he stood. There was a comfort in the order of command.

'I'm off to a great deal of uncertainty, Tom. I'll be back as a fireman, plying second fiddle to someone else. It'll be hard not being in charge, setting the pace and all. Managing the fire and water. Maintaining the boiler pressure and watching the driver's blind side. Playing second fiddle. How the hell did you cope, Tom?'

'I knew you wouldn't be giving me a hard time and I could nurture you, lad. Turn you into a proper driver.'

That's if they still had jobs. Word was you weren't guaranteed a place, even if it was promised before you went to war. A land fit for heroes was more one of uncertainty and doubt.

It would be good to see the family again. To feel the warmth of his sister's love, the comradeship of Donato. He looked forward to lodging with Mrs Owen. What he was scared about was Gwen. How did she feel? More than that, how did he feel? Time had moved on, the days before the conflict appeared rosy, but his time in Flanders had filled him with darkness. Too much had happened. It was as if he had waited for the sun to rise after a cold black winter's night. But the night had lasted four years.

'Cup of tea, dear?'

The muffled sound came from the window. The WVS lady stood holding a steaming mug. Dafydd didn't know where he was. He hardly remembered crossing the channel. He was sure he hadn't passed London. The carriages were Caledonian, but they were probably lent out to fill the gaps created by sending stock to France. He opened the window and nodded his thanks.

'Where are we, *bach*?'

'I can't tell you, it's top secret,' the lady replied.

Dafydd stared at her until her laughter rang out like a peal of bells.

'Got you there. Ashford, in Kent. I would have tried out my French accent to tease you, but it ain't that good.'

'Ashford Kent,' Dafydd muttered.

'Got far to go?'

'Aberystwyth.'?

'Oooh, that's in Wales, innit? Must be nice.'

'You're right, but I'm used to waiting.'

She smiled and he thought the woman was interesting. Attractive in her way, it occurred to him he could get off the train for a while, just to see her smile. It was warm.'

'It must have been terrible for you. At the front and everything.'

Dafydd smiled. 'I don't know. I only been there once, and that was by accident. I was in the railways.'

There was an edge there, just for a second. He saw it in her look, disappointment, slight condescension. Just a flicker, then it was gone, and the smile beamed like a summer's day. But it felt too glorious, not natural.

'Well, you have a good trip. I'll be off with my tea urn. Cheery bye.'

Without me, your heroes wouldn't have had a bullet between them! He wanted to shout, but then another thought gripped him. *Without me, many of them wouldn't have got to where they fell.*

He sat down and his hand went to his mouth in shock. He needed to get home now. He needed to talk to his family. He needed to confess the awesome guilt of what he had done. The train was leaving, and the land was flashing by, but then he realised he was still holding the mug. He sat down to take a sip; it warmed within but did not stop the numbness he felt without.

****

The tapping on the café window appeared not to work. After a long time of percussion on the glass and the door, Dafydd was ready to vault the back wall, when a glimmer of light began to appear. It was just as well, the pack on his shoulder was now becoming more of a burden than it had ever been. The air seemed cold and the dampness of it caused his body to chill. His teeth began to chatter, as the curtain was drawn across and Sioned came into view, quickly opening the door.

'Dafydd *cariad*, you didn't say you were coming. And so late.'

'I wrote. It's probably not got to you. And the trains are still running to pot over here. Too many trains full of smelly soldiers coming back home.'

'Well you don't smell lovely, but come in, you look blue with cold and I'll make you a cocoa while you warm up by the fire.'

She took him through to the back parlour and started raking the glowing ashes in the fireplace. Adding some light tinder, she began to work the fire back to a red glow and Dafydd went to sit next to the welcoming warmth that came from it.

'It's good to be back.'

'You go easy, you're looking exhausted, brother dear. I'll tidy up Dad's room.' Sioned stopped and sighed. 'That's if you're happy to sleep there. I'll not have you walking across Aber at this time of night. Certainly not waking up poor Mrs Owen for your lodging.'

Dafydd gave a rueful smile, but his eyes did not stir from staring at the fireplace

'I'll be honest, I'm that tired, I could sleep here now.'

Sioned would not stop moving, as she spoke, fussing the room into shape and willing the pot to boil.

'I'm sure you're starving too, I tell you what, I'll rustle you up a plate of bread and cheese and you can go to bed with a fuller stomach. Then in the morning, we'll get Harri to cook you breakfast. I'll see if we can call in any favours for fish.'

'I've got to go and see.' Dafydd whispered faintly.

Sioned paused. 'See what, *cariad?*

'See her. I got to know once and for all.'

Sioned caught a sigh and smiled sadly. 'I think you need some rest first and a bit of a clean-up. Give yourself a day or so. You can stay here - unless you are asking Mrs Owen for her room in Turkey town? Then there's your job. You best go off to the shed and be sure they will take you back as soon as possible. The best thing to do is to be sure of where you are. This must all be so different for you.'

'I've been away so long; I don't know what normal is no more.'

Sioned stopped her tidying and came over to kneel by his side. Looking fondly at her brother, she reached to give a comforting squeeze to his arm and then stopped. She gave a quiet sob as she saw his tear-stricken face. He had already succumbed to his fatigue and was fast asleep.

Chapter Twenty-eight

Endings

The warm letters from Gwen had kept him alive at the beginning of the war. Then they had become distant, making Dafydd fear that she had returned to Captain Price. The torment of her indiscretions with Price over the years had hurt Dafydd. In time, he also had found his solace elsewhere, but he never forgot his Gwen.

He rose early to wash and dress. He chose his Sunday best, rather than the demob suit. It was less of a reminder of his life over the past few years. One thing at least the army had taught him was how to present himself. Today, presentation was important, as he needed answers.

Dafydd had been driven to distraction by her last letter. It prayed for his return, begged him to save her. Now he had made it back to Aberystwyth, with its robust churches and genteel terraces. Far away from the rubble and mud that once was Belgium, back in the land of his birth. He could taste the salt in the air once more. Yet no matter how he tried, wherever he looked, once again he could not find her.

Even Mrs Owen did not know and those he still knew at the harbour just shrugged as if she had disappeared. She was one of their own, perhaps not so much of late, yet their curt responses gave Dafydd no clue as to what had happened. It was not just they didn't know, but they seemed to no longer wish to remember. He had one final place to look and it filled him with dread. He feared what he might find at the home of his rival.

The walk was short, and the years of military service had kept him trim. The weather was dry, although the sunshine was patchy. Grey clouds whispered of rains to come somewhere along the coast. *That sums up my life*, Dafydd thought. *I don't know if it's light or dark anymore.*

He started walking down a leafy road of large houses. Llanbadarn Road, where all those with wealth tended to live. Price was a man of means and Dafydd knew his house very well, it stood out from the rest. The dark local stone blended with the twisted ironwork of its verandas. The pretty garden, like a green velvet scarf caressed the residence.

Dafydd approached with a little trepidation, though he knew he wouldn't turn back. Too many war years had put paid to his fears. He no longer worried about who he spoke to or how, courtesy of his time with Haig's army. Whether a gentleman or a gentleman of the road, he would give the same blunt reception. He knocked and waited for the maid to appear at the door.

'I have come to see Captain Price,' Dafydd said firmly.

'Are you expected?'

'No, but he does know me.' Dafydd replied. 'Please tell him it is Dafydd... David Thomas.'

'One moment please.'

As the maid disappeared, Dafydd admired the décor. The tiled floor formed a black and white mosaic diamond. The carved beasts guarded the banister. He wondered if he would ever afford a house of his own. *A home fit for heroes.* The thought made him snort in derision.

The maid returned. 'Mrs. Captain Price will see you in the garden,' she said, gently ushering him out and round the side of the house.

He was directed to a small circular white pavilion made of twisted iron. A conical roof gave some shelter and sat inside was a small and very slim woman. Her hair was cut short, after the fashion. She had her back to him, making Dafydd uncomfortable. He'd been ready for a fight, but one with a stuck-up army Captain, not his wife.

Mrs. Price did not turn but looked up as he came into view. She indicated for him to sit, a small table between them already bore a teapot and two cups.

'Some tea, Mr. Thomas?' Mrs. Price said with a strong, quiet voice.

'Thank you, ma'am,'

The maid had disappeared and Dafydd felt in no-mans land. Mrs. Price slowly poured out the brew.

'Sugar?'

'No ma'am,'

Then to puncture the silence, he added.

'It's a habit now, I'm told I have tea so strong as to stand your spoon in it.'

There was no response. He sipped his tea, wondering how he was going to manage to keep hold of the tiny cup handle.

'Captain Price…?' He started to ask.

'Is indisposed.' She was polite, yet firm. He wondered what to do next.

Mrs. Price placed her cup down.

'Have you been long back in Aberystwyth, Mr. Thomas?'

There was an edge behind the tone, which made him frown.

'No ma'am,' he replied. 'Just returned. Demobbed last week.'

'The war ended two years ago,' Mrs. Price said, almost disapproving.

'I agree, but the Railway Corps was retained in Belgium to run the trains.'

266

'It looks like rain,'

She opened a silver case and removed a cigarette, attaching it to a holder. He couldn't help noticing the slight tremor in her hands.

'Do you smoke, Mr, Thomas?' She asked politely.

'Can't say I do anymore. Lost the taste for it.'

He'd watched too many men on hospital trains having one last drag before the end.

She lit her cigarette; Dafydd politely cupped his hands to shelter the flame. Mrs. Price nodded and exhaled.

'And what is your business here, Mr. Thomas?'

'I'm trying to find an old friend.'

Dafydd tried to keep calm, though his heart was racing. 'Gwen Jones.'

It was a statement, sending a shock down his spine.

'Perhaps I will have that cigarette,'

A ghost of a smile played on her lips. He gave her an appraising look, noticing that she was quite striking in appearance. For a brief moment, his mind imagined her as a younger woman. The image was not displeasing.

'And how would you think my husband help you with that strumpet?'

'He may know where she is.'

He was taken aback by the poison in her tone. Dafydd began to feel ill with fear, that he would find what he truly dreaded.

'Why would he know that?' Mrs. Price said.

The question seemed innocent, though Dafydd saw the steel in her eyes.

'You're playing games with me,' he snapped back, an irritation beginning to gnaw at his thoughts.

It wasn't his place. *To hell with his place!* Four years in khaki had put him beyond knowing his place.

She pursed her lips. 'Perhaps...'

'You know who I am,' His simple reply was met by the ghost of a smile.

'The man who never won over my husband's trollop. Yes, I know you.'

Although said without malice, the words felt like a cold judgement.

'Come Mr. Thomas, would you really expect me not to know of my husband's misdemeanours? Are you indeed surprised that I am aware?'

He did not reply; the teacup became a source of fascination for his eyes.

'Tell me, did you never find love in Belgium, Mr. Thomas? Or were you restricted to queuing in the bordellos, with the other ranks?'

He ignored the taunts, although the wound was still fresh.

'I did find love, Mrs. Price. A fine woman, I'll not have bad said of her.'

'Yet you chose to abandon her,' the words stabbed at his heart. He swallowed hard at the memory.

'She disappeared. She knew my past and understood me.'

Yes, she read me like a book and forgave her Judas.'

'Understood what, Mr. Lloyd? That you had got bored and wished to return to renew an old acquaintance?' The smile was openly wicked now.

Dafydd took a long drag and puffed it out. Mrs. Price sat with her cigarette hand up, nonchalantly flicking away the ash. Her other hand was locked across her body like a barrier. There was no give in her malice, and it made him angry.

'Look, I'm not taking no more of this. You can play your little games, but you'll not talk bad of her. I would have, should have damn well stayed and all. I had to go. Damn you! You haven't a clue what it's been like over there. Stuck in your fine houses, complaining of the rain.

She's worth a thousand of you and yes, I chose to leave her. She didn't deserve me. She never deserved the likes of me. I don't need some stuck-up Captain's wife telling me what I done.'

He flung his cigarette angrily onto the manicured lawn. There was an uncomfortable silence, before she sighed.

'Don't worry, Mr. Thomas, I'll have the gardener pick it up. He's more than used to my husband's similar antics in the past.'

'I'd have been court-martialled for less,' Dafydd muttered.

'Those who play toy soldiers never did have any ideas about importance,'

She sighed again; Dafydd thought he almost saw sympathy.

'If you loved her, why did you come back to *your* Gwen?'

He reached for his tea. His throat was parched now.

'Let's stop playing games ma'am. It's time you gave me a bit more respect, I'm not your husband and it seems to me that you know everything already.'

'Oh, I know enough of this whole tawdry affair, Mr. Thomas.'

The reply was sad.

'I know of when my husband took a lover and boasted of his conquest, using it as a weapon to hurt me. When he mocked your own attempts to win the heart of this girl and yet raged at the time of your one night of passion with her. When he crowed at how he had you transferred to Oswestry on the pleading of his lover. You'd be surprised how much I do know, Mr. Thomas. Most of it has been flung in my face at some point.'

He got up and retrieved the cigarette butt. It was close to an apology.

'Do you know what he did after he found you had seen her again? He spent days getting you moved to Oswestry. Days. He did nothing else; he was that scared of you. He knew that you had her heart. He tried to lose you, he cursed you. He wished you dead or married to some English working girl. He thought Oswestry would swallow you whole and spit you out of his life.'

Birdsong broke the silence; Dafydd wondered how it could sing so sweetly.

'Have you seen the baby, Mr. Thomas?'

'When I was invalided in 1917. A lovely boy, strong and happy,' Dafydd lied

'What happens if he's not yours?' Mrs. Price asked softly.

He shrugged. 'Boy needs a father. If she'll have me. But if only there was a child. It was a lie. She told me.'

'Yet you still love her?'

There was almost sympathy in the tone.

He nodded. She pursed her lips, then stood. 'Come with me.'

She moved off quickly to the house, not checking whether Dafydd followed. It seemed as though the conversation was at an end. They walked through some open French windows and then weaved through the house to the staircase. She moved up the stairs, leaving him to wonder if this wasn't some bizarre proposition.

Finally, she stopped at a closed door and turned to look at him. For a moment, the mask slipped, and she gave a look of anguish. Then the barriers snapped shut once more, as she slowly opened the door and Dafydd peered into the dark beyond.

He heard a rustle of bedclothes and a figure rose from an untidy bed. From the dim light of the doorway, he recognised Captain Price, although the man's eyes were covered in bandage.

'Who's that?' The Captain whispered dreamily. 'Are you the relief? I hope to God you are! We've been stuck here for three days now. Jerry hasn't stopped throwing everything at us. Come forward man, I can't see you!'

'I'm Railway Corps sir,'

Dafydd managed to mutter, as sick realisation dawned on him.

'Railway? There's sixty of us left. Can you take us out of here?'

'Yes, sir,' Dafydd said with a hollow voice, the lie being played out for the tortured soul.

'Right, we'll start loading as soon as we can. Wish it was light,' Price moved his head swiftly. 'Damn! Jerry's started up again. Whizz bangs and far off. Oh God, it's a gas shell. It's close.' He screamed and scrambled in his sheets. 'GAS, GAS, GAS!'

'Put your mask on Captain.' Mrs. Price said sadly. 'The gas will clear in a moment and we'll commence loading.'

She softly closed the door, leaving her with Dafydd on the landing and the sound of Captain Price sobbing in the room.

'My God!' Dafydd said. 'He still thinks he's there.'

'In a trench in 1917, under an attack of mustard gas,' she replied as she moved away.

'It's the last thing he ever saw. A vain and arrogant man, but when faced with a situation he could not control or resolve...well that is for the doctors to solve. I am a mere woman in this world. Deemed good enough for bandages and comfort.'

'Will he recover?' Dafydd asked. He was unsure of how to react to the bitter cynicism in her words.

'I don't know how much of the man remains,' she replied.

'You know, Gwen Jones was never there to pick up the pieces. He bought her and this is how my husband was repaid. It was all left to me.'

She took a deep breath. '…and I at least know my place.'

'You don't deserve this,' Dafydd said hoarsely and she smiled.

'What I deserve is immaterial, Mr. Thomas. It is my fate.'

Mrs Price gazed at him and her features softened.

'I have done you a grave disservice here, please put it down to my anger. Perhaps, also to my self-pity. I chose to spend my life with this man, not you.'

She indicated for him to follow, but now there was a change of pace. She waited for him as they entered a drawing room. Moving swiftly to a bureau, Mrs Price quickly wrote a few lines on some paper, which she carefully blotted and folded before offering to him.

'I admit it was my thought to torment you, Mr Thomas. I have suffered long from the actions of my husband with his amour and I had a foolish thought that by hurting you, I could somehow hurt that woman. I regret the thought and would ask your forgiveness.'

'What is there to forgive?' Dafydd looked hard at her. 'Perhaps I have never appreciated how it would be for yourself.'

Mrs. Price gave a curt nod. 'Perhaps. One thing you are wrong about though is the suffering of those who were left behind in this land. It is a miracle for a house not to be touched by the slaughter, or unemployment or the Spanish flu that has raged over this land. All beyond our control and then we, the wives and mothers of this land, are left to clear up the mess. To bandage and dress what is left of our kin.'

He nodded slowly and she sighed.

'We haven't deserved this. Yet, this is our fate. It gives me no pleasure to tell you where to find your woman, Mr. Thomas, she does not suffer as you or I any more, or even that fool upstairs. She has escaped the worst, as she has all her life. I'm sorry, Mr. Thomas, the Spanish flu took its toll. Although even that was mercifully quick.'

Dafydd opened the note and gazed numbly at the words. The cemetery was not far from the house he stood in. All those years of struggle, of fighting for his love. Only to have her taken from him by Spanish flu. His legs felt weak and he grabbed for a chair.

Mrs. Price rang the bell and a maid appeared. 'Sweet tea for Mr Thomas.'

He heard her voice, though the words were blotted out by an animal crying. He quickly realised the animal was his own grief and torment, his lifetime of hope and faith. Ripping clear from his soul and released to the world. His head dropped and he wept.

Time passed and a peace settled on him. Dafydd sipped the tea and wondered if he should tip the spillage back from the saucer to the cup.

'I'm sorry,' he murmured, though his voice sounded distant to his own ears. 'It seems you are always left to sweep up his mess.'

She gave a thin smile. 'Sweet tea cures many ills, Mr. Thomas. It will help – for now.'

She moved to sit down by his side. Gone was the game-playing, the distance and aloofness, as she continued.

'I took her back in, after, she came back from Hereford and she was a shadow of her former self. Drawn, thin, very tired. The munitions work had left her yellow. Did she not have anyone in town?'

'Her mother died in childbirth, her father of injuries after his ropeworks burned down. She had no security.'

273

'I let her convalesce, but she was weak. When the flu came through town, she was easy prey. She lasted a day.'

Dafydd shook his head. 'I seem to spend my life chasing after her and she was never around. Even when she died, I wasn't there.'

Mrs Price moved to light another cigarette and place in her holder. She seemed to draw energy from cigarettes, he thought, whereas all he got from them was a bad cough.

"Mr Thomas, you could not have helped. The flu is evil. When she died her face was blue. Would it help to know her last breaths were spent calling for you?'

'Did she?'

'If you want it to be.'

'Please…'

She placed her hand on his. 'It is true. At the end, she was your girl, not his.'

'It seems my journey was in vain.'

Dafydd had to laugh at his own words. They were but a speck of the dark void that he felt swallowing him.

'You know, I loved her since I was fifteen and I tried to win her time and again. I was never in time. Then she wrote and I thought… all those years…waiting. But my journey was a waste. My life's journey has been a waste.'

'Mr, Thomas,' she said softly. 'Go back to Belgium, find your girl. She is waiting for you.'

Visions of Poperinge swam before Dafydd's eyes. Of a young woman, who had pledged her life to his. Her face blurred in the sea of tears that filled his eyes.

'Dafydd slowly shook his head. 'I'm too late….'

'Mr Thomas, please try.' Dafydd looked up at Mrs. Price for the first time since he had collapsed on the chair. Tears streaked her cheeks. 'One of us has to have resolution. One of us at least should gain freedom from this.'

Swiftly he stood and swept her in a huge hug. She felt stiff and struggled, then the pressure eased and slowly she melted into the embrace. Her shoulders heaved with sobs, long held back through the years of pain.

Time stopped for Dafydd, then slowly she pushed away, and he stepped back. She sniffed and touched her hair, giving a trembling smile of thanks. She could no longer meet his eyes.

'Your journey was not in vain. You at least have found the answer, even if it was not that which you sought. Go back, Mr. Thomas. If you can, go back to Belgium. Find her. We both have ghosts of our past. Bleeding us dry, sapping our energy. I want to know that at least you can lay yours to rest.'

'And you?'

She hugged her arms from an imaginary cold. 'I must live with mine.'

Chapter Twenty-nine

The Bet

The early morning knock on the door was the worst part of the day for Dafydd. Even then, he pitied the apprentice whose job was to run around town waking up the engine crews. At least Dafydd got the extra hours in bed. In spite of this, he still felt exhausted when woken by the sound of little stones hitting the window. He leant out the window to quickly and gruffly acknowledge the call. He could have sworn the lad sounded Belgian-French. *I really must be dog-tired*, he thought, *to go back that far*.

The sound drew him back into the war and the shared experiences with Tom. The horrors they managed to see, in spite of their distance from the front line, still bit deeply. Not for the first time, Dafydd felt the pain of loss and the bitter memories of what might have been. To him it had been on more than one front. If he had only known his own emotions earlier. Today he had to put it all behind him and see to the job in hand.

Miraculously, he had managed to secure a job back on the Cambrian Railways. Not only that, but as driver and in Aberystwyth shed. He focussed on today, after links shunting and a few goods turns, it was his first local passenger train and he wasn't going to make a mess of it. Four years of running trains in war torn Belgium had certainly not given him a sense of complacency.

However, there was an important detour that he needed to make. He lit his lamp as he made his way quickly down to find a small amount of peace, though little comfort.

He reached the engine shed just in time to clock on. There were already sounds of activity. Shunting of trucks had begun in the yard and the ringing of a shovel driving home into a pile of coal came from a nearby locomotive.

Dafydd blew into his hands for warmth and made for the mess. His breath was misting in the gloom and his nose already felt frozen. He wondered if he could scrounge a *panad* of tea before his shift began. He was met with a smell of fried food. The aroma of smoked bacon filled his stomach with longing, making his mouth water. The reassuring spit of egg solidifying in the pan was domesticated enough for Dafydd to relax. What shocked him was seeing that Jenkins the foreman was cooking it.

Dafydd remembered his time firing for Jenkins before joining up. He respected the man but was wary of his temper even more.

'I'm a bit late, Mr. Jenkins. Sorry, it won't happen again.'

'That's alright son,' the man replied quickly. 'The men tell me you go off to the cemetery before your shift.

Dafydd stared back, his sleepy state clearing like a morning mist. All he could do was nod, for the pain was too much to bear.

'Ah, I'm sorry, Dafydd lad. People like a good gossip here and there's many who would take delight in storifying your misfortune. Come on, there's a *panad* we can brew. I'm sorry I mentioned it. She must have been someone special to deserve such devotion.'

'She was.'

There was nothing more to add.

'How did she die?'

'Spanish flu.'

Jenkins shook his head slowly. 'A waste. How did you manage to keep in touch with her when you were over there?'

'The post was not bad. Look, do you mind if I don't talk about this?'

'That's ok, son,'

Jenkins scooped the egg from the pan and added it to a plate containing bacon.

'Here, you look famished. Have this on me.'

Dafydd was surprised to say the least, but his stomach told him to be polite. he took the proffered plate and a mug of tea, nodding his thanks. Jenkins threw a few more strips of bacon in the pan and added two eggs.

'Dafydd, we've run a few engines together before the war. I've seen you grow from a green one to a confident man. I know enough of your story. this town's a small place in the end. But I wonder if you'd have had your happy ending had she not died?

A door opened and one of the other drivers poked his head around it.

'Leave us,' Jenkins snapped. 'We're having a meeting.'

The head disappeared and Dafydd thanked the fates for the intrusion that had taken away the angry retort on his lips.

'When I was invalided back to Blighty, I sought her out,' Dafydd took a long sip of his tea and stared at the vapours steaming from it. 'She was working in Hereford, in munitions. We came to an agreement. Her letters never changed from that point.'

The reply appeared to be ignored by Jenkins.

'Dafydd, *bach*. I know she never stopped being his mistress.'

The sound of crackling bacon in the frying pan seemed to envelope the room. Dafydd held the mug close to his lips, though he could not bring himself to drink.

'Why do you tell me this?'

'You've had it rougher than many. The war ended in 1918, but they kept you boys running the trains in Belgium for a year. The waiting you had to go through and then to come back to a land wanting to forget rather than celebrate. I see you each day boy, you been tearing yourself in two this last year.'

Dafydd started on his food, though the taste was lost to him.

'If you don't mind me saying, Dafydd, it's a shame you didn't find someone when you were over there.'

'You're not my Dad,' Dafydd muttered in reply.

Another lull followed before Dafydd continued.

'We were stationed near Ypres. That was our shed for two years. I got to know a girl who we rescued from the street. She used to do odd jobs for me and Tom. Prepare the engine, clean her out and the like. We paid the girl what we could spare. The... I don't know.'

Dafydd swallowed hard.

'I never thought of her as any more than a girl, then a friend. It wasn't until it was later on that I knew. But then I was sworn to Gwen, wasn't I? What could I do? She would be giving up her life of comfort to be a railwayman's bride. If I got her to do that and then cast her away? What kind of man would I be then?'

Jenkins filled the second plate and came to sit by Dafydd's side.

'After all she'd done to you. no-one would feel you were bound to Gwen.'

'Well, it killed me then and it's killing me now. I'm a fool for the loving of two women, when most would take what they could get. Jo gave herself freely and I took, knowing I was not for staying. What kind of man does that make me?'

Jenkins sighed and rubbed his eyes.

'Thank you for being honest. You know if I was a gambling man, I'd have lost money on what you just said. There's a new one preparing your engine today. Go tell them the gaffer's made breakfast as promised.'

Dafydd frowned. 'What's all this about, anyhow?'

'Because someone came down last night and told me all about the war, then bet me a breakfast they couldn't prepare your engine to top notch. Now that's someone I think would make a decent fireman.'

'Is it Tom? Tom Hebdyke?'

Dafydd's mood changed in a flash.

'You've got a fine one there if he's staying!'

'Go tell them to come to breakfast,' Jenkins said with a wry smile.

Dafydd raced out to the main shed. His engine was nearest the door and alive. Steam caressed the funnel, whilst the faint red glow from the fire cast silhouettes that moved in time with the sound of shovelling coal. Dafydd smiled at the thought of Tom. He'd been through a lot with him and it would be good to get the man back on the footplate. If anything, he was the one person that Dafydd could trust. Perhaps together they could work through his pain.

Dafydd felt a sudden urge to surprise his friend, so elected to climb the back-ladder of the tender to surprise him from behind. As quietly as was possible, he shinned up the ladder and stopped when he finally saw the cab through the red glow of the firebox.

The figure at work was almost in silhouette against the glow of the fire. There was black hair, far too much of it. Shoulder length and cascading down to a bunch on one side. The figure seemed to be in very baggy trousers. So much that they should have been skirts, which was crazy. Dafydd was transfixed as he watched the figure stop to wipe their brow, leaving a smudge of dirt on their face. It was a scene he had been party to many times before in Flanders, but one he never dared hope to see again.

Josephine looked up as if by instinct, before digging her shovel into the pile of coal.

'You always were a lazy bastard, Daveed Thomas.'

Dafydd was over the ladder and scrambling down the tender in seconds. So fast that he quickly lost his footing and fell in a heap at her feet. She looked sternly at him, though the corners of her mouth quivered with mirth.

'I was keeping zis tidy. Mr Zhenkins 'as a bet I cannot prepare ze engine.'

Dafydd got to his feet quickly, feeling as if he needed to straighten his uniform in her presence.

'It's alright girl, he knows he's lost already. There's breakfast waiting for you in the mess.'

She gave a tired smile. 'Good. I am a little hungry, you know?'

'How did you get here?' Dafydd asked.

'Tom finds me when I left message in Talbot 'ouse. He knows you 'ave returned, and he came to Pops to find me.'

'He's back at the old shed?'

She shook her head, her brown eyes refusing to yield her gaze on him.

'No, ee came to find me,' she repeated. She finally looked away. 'When I finally came to Poperinge, you were gone, and I did not know what to do.'

'Tom gave me money to come 'ere. He told me your news. *Peut-etre*...per'aps a part of me went wiz you and now... I 'oped you may need me.'

'*Ma chérie,*' Dafydd whispered and stroked her cheek. The embrace was long, fierce and so warm. It was only broken by an embarrassed cough from below, followed by an over-zealous rattling of an oil can. Dafydd's fireman was making his presence obvious.

'I have to go,' Dafydd sighed. 'I have a train to run and if the station master sees us, I'll probably be out on my ear. Go have your breakfast, then get Jenkins to send you to my sister's café, the local Bracchi's. Seek out either one of the girls.

281

If it is Harri - Angharad, the younger one, make sure she is not holding anything when you tell her who you are. She's liable to drop it. They'll look after you until I'm done here.'

'Will zey not find it awkward to 'ave a foreigner wiz zis tale?'

'It's a bit late for that, they know most of it already. Besides, Sioned married one of the Italian miners that came over here. Go on, you'll be fine. I will see you at the end of shift. We will have all Sunday to talk. There is much to say.'

She had always had beautiful eyes, Dafydd thought. *Why had I never seen it before?*

'…and there is much to plan,' he added.

She gave a weary smile that melted away the years of hardship. Then she leant forward to kiss his cheek and climbed off the engine. Her eyes never stopped looking at him as she descended and Dafydd saw his future in them. His cheek felt damp and it wasn't long before he realised it was from his own tears.

Chapter Thirty

Harmonica
(1920)

The weather grew warmer and the town began its preparations for the summer season. The leaves of the trees in North Parade long ago fallen, were now cleared away. The area around the big Seilo chapel was now free from flooding. Sodden ground now a distant memory. Birds sang of hope and the town breathed in this heady optimism. Perhaps this year, people would start to come again and visit. To try and forget the past, the horrors and shadows of the last six years. To escape the tensions of the riot-stricken cities. To come, relax and live for the future. After all, it was the only thing to look forward to.

'The world have not been kind enough to them poor bastards that served,' Dafydd muttered as he sipped his coffee, looking through the window of the café to the street outside. He watched a bedraggled man dressed in a mixture of khaki and grey, slowly take off his greatcoat and lay it on the ground in front of him.

'He is a poor sod,' Donato replied, as they sat at a small table together. Business was quiet and they sat close to the window, to give the impression that the place was not empty, but not too full.

'You work, when?' Donato asked.

'I am on the roster for Sunday,' Dafydd replied. 'I'll be up the coast to Barmouth, so I'll make the most of today.'

'For sure.'

The ragged man stood behind his coat and rubbed his hand over the stubble protruding from the edges of his balaclava. From a side pocket, he produced a harmonica, which he held in his fingerless, gloved hands.

'He comes every now and then. He plays and they give a coin. Sometime.'

'It's not fair, Donato. They gave so much for their country, believed the lies about duty and honour. Then they got fed lies about how the country will be better for them. They go out and do that duty. Some of them don't come back., the rest got shafted. Many don't have jobs, they can't afford rent, so they have no home. A land fit for heroes? No wonder they had them riots in Glasgow. Everyone's angry as hell and there's buggers like him standing on street corners for a few *ceiniog*.'

Josephine appeared from the back and moved to clear a table of empty cups. She gave Dafydd a warm smile and he grinned back. Donato watched her go.

'The war, it made some good.'

Dafydd chuckled in reply. 'Thank you, my friend.'

He took his coffee cup and savoured the liquid around his mouth as he watched the busker outside.

'It's too easy to get angry about how wrong this all is. We've all had it rough, but then them politicians don't make it any easier.'

'You blame the Lloyd George?'

'It would have been worse for us without DLG sorting out the munitions, but he's been no angel since, like them all.'

Josephine appeared again with a cup of coffee and a cake which she served to a waiting customer.

'We got to thank you, Donato. With business being so slow. Are you sure you can afford to take on Jo? Or let us live here?'

Donato shrugged 'Is no problem. She keeps us happy and she is happy here also. She needs friends. It is good to have people in a foreign land. People, they are friendly for the most, but you are still stranger. Different.'

The warbling of the harmonica came through the door. Dafydd's mind sang along with the tune.

Pack up your troubles in your old kit bag and smile, smile, smile...

He realised that Josephine had taken the coffee and cake outside and crossed the road. Dafydd noticed the man's arm was lame and he appeared to have a scar around the balaclava line.

Dafydd started to look for money, but Donato waved the offer away. Josephine took hold of a chair and went out, sitting on it in front of the café window.

'I am sorry...' Dafydd began. Donato ignored him and grabbed a small round table, which he took outside to put next to Josephine. He then went to the counter for a slice of cake, which he took out to her., giving Josephine's shoulder a squeeze.

Dafydd watched Josephine as she focussed on the busker. Her lips moved to the lyrics of the tune.

'She is happy to be here, with you my friend,' Donato said as he returned to sit. 'But in here, she is still sad.'

He patted over his heart.

'This has all been too much to bear. She wants to be happy, but she needs to bring out the bad memories and remember the good. Then she can heal.'

'You are kind,' Dafydd said.

Donato shrugged. 'She is-a family now since you are-a married. I will do what I can to help make her happy.'

Dafydd looked at the busker, as the music had stopped. A man had walked by with a friendly retriever. The dog was keen to make friends with the busker, who shrank back in horror. The image pulled Dafydd back to memories of Flanders.

Good dog, bugger off dog...

'There are many who need to forget the sadness.'

Dafydd rose and went outside. He glanced across to his wife, who smiled back with tears in her eyes. He gave her a kiss and crossed over the road, dropping a shilling among the few coins on the man's coat.

'Right boy,' Dafydd said to the busker. 'You and me are going to give a concert. I hope you know your tunes.'

He launched into 'Pack Up Your Troubles' again. The busker looked on with puzzlement, but soon followed.

While there's a Lucifer to light your fag. Smile boys, that's the style
What's the use of worrying? It never was worthwhile, SO!
Pack up your troubles in your old kit bag and smile, smile, smile.

There was another voice singing now, a man had come and joined them Dafydd knew him vaguely. He worked in the cattle market, by the station. He was normally in a white coat. He smiled a greeting.

'We done that one loads of times in the Royal Welsh. That brought back some good memories! You want to sing another one?'

Another coin landed on the coat with a clink and Dafydd grinned. 'Go on then.'

Goodbye-ee. Goodbye-ee – wipe a tear, baby dear from your eye-ee

The busker again caught up with the tune. The sun had heated the street and even now the buildings radiated warmth, despite them passing into shadow. More people had joined in and Dafydd felt a wave of weariness from it. Donato came across the street and dropped coins into the now decent pile.

'It will look a better and now my café is-a busy.'

Dafydd glanced across the road and was surprised to see the café was hidden behind the number of people standing outside, armed with mugs of coffee. There were silhouettes of people inside. It was all good natured, many were singing along. Space was created to allow Josephine to watch. The smile she gave him had such a glow that he faltered.

If you want to find the general, I know where he is.
I know where he is. I know where he is…

More had joined in. Dafydd did not know them, but he didn't care. They had all been there, that was the bond.

I saw him, I saw him. He's pinning another medal on his chest...

If you want to find the colonel, I know where he is.
I know where he is. I know where he is...
He's sitting in comfort, stuffing his bloody gut. I saw him, I saw him...

Dafydd looked at all the faces. There were many women in the crowd. Josephine was like a beacon to him, as she always would be, but it made him realise. that everyone had been through it, not just the men. Women like Gwen, making themselves ill in the munitions factory. People carrying on at home, to try and keep some semblance of normality and order, whilst losing many friends and relations abroad. Everyone had suffered and everyone tried to work through the pain and smile. That was their bond.

'... If you want to find the sergeant, I know where he is – he's drinking all the company rum. I saw him, I saw him. Drinking all the company rum...'

A policeman had appeared at the street corner, but Dafydd saw the man's stance was relaxed. He may have even been tapping his foot to the tune. The policeman looked over and nodded to Dafydd. *He knew*, Dafydd realised. *He must have been over there as well...*

If you want the whole battalion, we know where they are. We know where they are, we know where they are...They're hanging on the old barbed wire. We saw them. We saw them. Hanging on the old barbed wire...

The words were bitter, but it gave the people a shared outing of a wound. They all showed heartbreak and sadness, but within there was a spirit to keep going. the song was like a talisman and for many, it was a release. A blessing. There were a few tears shed at the end as people applauded, but everyone stayed waiting for the next offering.

'How about *the bells of hell go ting-a-ling-a-ling*?' Someone shouted.

'Something Welsh, how about *Sospan Fach*?' Came another voice.

Dafydd looked at the Staffordshire regimental badges on the busker's coat.

A chorus of boos rang out, though all good natured in tone. A horse and trap was trying to edge its way down the narrow road, through the sizeable crowd. The exasperation of the horse could be seen, as its hooves drummed on the road, the cart juddering behind him. The driver swapped banter with the crowd as he passed by. Then he was gone, and they turned again with expectation for the next song.

The notes reverberated in the air, the audience listened in stunned silence, save a single sob. The tune was simple but haunted the street with its beautiful melody. It was a Welsh lullaby, *Suo Gan*. He wished he knew the words. His Mam had known, for she sang it to him as a baby, back in Trisant. He went over to Josephine.

Some people tried to sing, but the tone was hushed and reverential. Nobody wanted to break the magic. The melody swam gently around the crowd, until the busker stopped, to a ripple of polite applause.

'Zat was nice,' she said. 'You must teach it to me some day.'

There was a lull, as the crowd drank in the sweet memory of the lullaby. They stood waiting for more.

The busker took the harmonica from his lips and surveyed the audience. He put the harmonica away and stood to attention. Taking in a deep breath, he opened his mouth and began to sing.

His voice was melodious, but it sounded as if it might break with the strain of emotion. He had his eyes screwed shut with passion and focus. The notes rang out and echoed off the walls. It was sad and sweet. A woman tried to join in, but choked and stopped, her hand covering her trembling lips.

> *Abide with me, fast falls the eventide*
> *The darkness deepens Lord, with me abide*
> *When other helpers fail, and comforts flee*
> *Help of the helpless, oh, abide with me…*

Tears fell down Dafydd's face. There had been so much pain, more than he could bear. But the sadness was soothed by the melody. The tune echoed in the street. The busker stood straight and saluted, then began to collect the coins and prepared to leave. A stranger approached with a cap of coins and shook his hand. People applauded and then slowly turned to go. Many wiped away tears, but they appeared stronger, happier, more complete.

'Trés bon,' Josephine said. 'Now per'aps people can let go of ze past and live for ze future.'

'I love you,' Dafydd said and she smiled.

'I know, you told me back in Poperinge.'

She stood to embrace him, there was nothing else needed. The healing had begun.

Chapter Thirty-one

Family

'I don't see why they call you all the way up to Oswestry, Dafydd,' Sioned said over breakfast.

Dafydd briefly exchanged glances with his beloved Josephine.

'I have to meet the loco superintendent,' the lie flowed almost too easily. 'There's a chance of Top Link driving, but I need to be chosen and there's many as would like the job of driving the expresses. I need a health check and all.'

Sioned snorted her derision. 'Health check! You had one when you joined the Cambrian. And there's enough of them returning from France with bad lungs from the gas and all. They never say anything about them now, do they?'

'Tables are done,' came Angharad's cheerful voice, as she bustled into the small kitchen. 'I just need help with the flowers.'

'I'm coming,' said Sioned rising. 'And I hope they are paying you for this day off, Dafydd?'

Donato coughed at length and leaned to gob in the fire. The muck sizzled in the flame.

'When they say health, they compare you with what, Daveed? Me? No, no. You are spinning dreams. Sioned she nod and listen, but I see behind your words. What do you do?'

'I want to leave. I am going to see a small railway in Llanymynech called the Shropshire and Montgomeryshire. They may take me on. I want to go somewhere that people don't stop and nudge when they see Jo and whisper about Gwen.'

Donato sighed. 'Does Jo need this?'

He looked across and smiled sadly at the French girl.

'You are strong, I think. To survive war, yes. Very strong.'

'I will go where Daveed is 'appy,' Jo murmured.

Donato raised his hand. 'Ok, I dunno. Here you have friends, you have family. They keep you safe. There, Jo will still be a foreigner. I know of this being foreigner myself. Think carefully.'

'You catch ze express?' Jo asked as she walked Dafydd to the door. 'So, go and see zis place and zen make sure you take ze express back. I know your mind, but I 'ear Donato's words also. I want you to promise not to commit before we talk, okay?'

Dafydd hugged her and kissed her full on the lips. She sighed and patted his cheek.

'Just make sure you behave.'

****

Aberystwyth station was busy with activity. Porters wheeled their trolleys, expertly dodging the groups of excitable or bored people waiting on the platform and guiding their luggage effortlessly to the carriage of choice, leaving the owners rushing behind in their wake.

Dafydd wanted as little fuss as possible, so he hung back as long as he could. Even then, he bumped straight into the guard as he boarded. Thankfully, it was Ed Morris, one of the friendlier crew.

'Where you off to then?' Ed asked.

'Llanymynech,' Dafydd replied. There was no use lying when his ticket would say otherwise. Perhaps he should have bought one to Oswestry? Too late now.

'Alright Daf, I'm not going to ask why, but best we get you out of sight before tongues start wagging here. Jump into the guards compartment a moment and we'll sort you out when we're underway. Quick now!'

Dafydd was almost dragged in. Ed looked out and touched his cap to a passing entourage.

'Earl Vane is taking the through coach to Paddington. God bless all who sail in it. Wherever a director goes, there will always be a bunch of Cambrian lackeys following him, so I got you away before they spied you. He's gone now and you'll not see him again. You can ride the cushions if you want, but there'll probably be a quiet compartment near to the back.'

'The Earl must be doing some business in the capital,' Dafydd said.

'Who knows? I'll call you up if I get a minute and we can chat.'

Dafydd sat on the left of the train looking forward. It was a force of habit and as they started to move out, he regretted the move.

There behind the goods yard was the slender avenue of trees. There was the bench that he had seen Gwen sit when he had been bound for Oswestry. She had chosen to remain a mistress for a richer man than join Dafydd in a new life. Even though they had planned to leave, she had turned her back on him at the very last minute. As the train moved on, Dafydd gazed at the cemetery where she lay after Spanish flu had claimed her. Very soon, Llanbadarn Church came into view, where Dafydd had longed to marry her.

He sat back and tried to shake off the gloom. Too many memories, too many ghosts. He needed a fresh start with Jo, away from the sniping and gossip. He would see how it was with the little S&M railway.

The journey soon became a blur of green hilly fields, crisp in the January morning. The years seemed to catch up with him and he was soon asleep. A jolt made him wake up and he quickly realised they had made Machynlleth.

People milled around, eager to get on and find a decent seat, hopefully without anyone else around, fat chance of that today! The rising column of steam from below the station gave testament to an engine working lazily in the goods yard below.

Ed was walking down the platform talking to people as he went past with his easy smile. He looked across to Dafydd through the window and winked. The buckled strap of his bag across one shoulder and the strap of the ticket machine across the other. *Like a bandolier*, Dafydd thought, as he tried to switch off and fall back to his dreams.

He had spent his adult life in pursuit of the love of a woman, only to find it was never to be returned. Then when all seemed lost, Jo had found him. Even though she had needed to travel across the land from the killing fields of Flanders to do so. He couldn't let her down, not this time.

Machynlleth quickly became a memory and the engine charged forward towards the long climb up to Talerddig. Dafydd closed his eyes again and imagined himself willing the engine forward. He'd worked on a small railway before and he tried not to think of the shabby reputation of the S&M. *No, if it's bearable, I'll live with it for Jo's sake*, he promised himself.

The train was now pushing hard and soon they were past Caersws and Moat Lane. Dafydd checked the time, the crew were doing well. He wasn't surprised, they were the best.

The express came to a stop in Newtown and again, Dafydd watched the world go by. There would be a quick climb and they would be past Abermule and onto Montgomery. Once more, the train picked up speed and Dafydd went back to dozing. It wouldn't be too long now…

A loud blast of the whistle woke him, followed by a very sudden deceleration and the sound of screeching brakes. Dafydd was pitched forward by the motion.

'Christ, we're going to crash!' Dafydd said out loud, desperately looking to the seats opposite to cushion the blow.

Even with that, the impact knocked the wind out of him and threw him sideways towards the window. He tried to reach for the luggage rack to steady himself but missed. An awful feeling of helplessness gripped him, as he felt tossed around in the compartment like a rag doll. Time slowed down and he began to feel numb. Then everything stopped.

He could hear muted sounds from the other compartments. Groaning or was it crying? Screaming or was it shouting? Dafydd's head felt wrapped up in a blanket. He looked around the compartment and then at himself. His ribs felt tight with bruising and there was dampness on his head. He touched it and found his fingers red with blood. The window was intact, and he managed to crawl to it and pull it down with the leather strap.

His first thought was that the valley below was on its side. Then he looked down. The wheels seemed to be at a crazy angle to the coach and the more he studied them, the more they didn't seem to belong. Then he realised they were from the coach in front. He looked up the train, the chocolate and cream Great Western coach for Paddington had disappeared. Where he thought it should be was a tangled mass of twisted metal with a set of locomotive wheels pointing like an accusatory finger to the sky. Dafydd scrambled out, gingerly lowered himself to the ground and started to stagger up to the front.

His back was killing him now and the whole scene seemed so strange. The carriages were like a concertina decorated with matchwood. The contrast between the carnage and the broad peaceful river valley behind could not have been greater.

Dafydd picked his way slowly to where the locomotive should have been. He noticed an engine boiler was thrust at an angle from its wheels. Steam seemed to be still rising from just about every part of the wreckage. It was unreal.

He spied a body close to the line and quickly stumbled over, thanking God the man was still alive. It was Pritchard the driver and he held his neck with fingers that were thick with blood.

'You alright Pritch?' Dafydd said, though his own voice seemed miles away.

'He's gone to get the tablets,' Pritchard groaned. 'I want to know.'

Dafydd looked back to the mangled wreck. 'The tablet that gives you permission to proceed. Christ, it's a head-on, isn't it?'

'I want to know if it was me what picked up the wrong one.'

Dafydd became aware of a movement around the engines and a man staggered over. He recognised Pritchard's fireman, who was holding two large key-shaped lumps of metal.

'It's not us, look. The boys in the other train were carrying the wrong tablet. Come on now, Pritchard. You need to see a doctor.'

Pritchard groaned and tried to rise, while Dafydd saw a few men moving up from the carriages.

'Anyone with medical knowledge?' Dafydd shouted. 'Quickly now, he's lost a lot of blood.'

As the driver was tended, Dafydd asked his mate.

'How the hell did you survive a head-on?'

'We stayed on as long as we could, then jumped off just before impact.'

'What about the other crew?'

'Must have been stoking, the fire's been blown out of the firebox. They're under it.'

Dafydd stopped, there had been a smell he could not place. He hadn't thought much of it until those words began to set in and then Dafydd knew what it was. Charred meat.

He retched uncontrollably. Vaguely he became aware of someone asking his welfare. He tried to answer, but his legs felt weak and white spots had begun to creep into his vision. Dafydd was sure he could fight the giddiness and nausea, but he was falling, and strong arms were supporting him more and more. He began to drift away and the smells and sounds of the nightmare slowly diminished.

****

It was late in the night when the door of the small cafe opened. Long closed for the day but unlocked in hope. The lady of the house sat at a small coffee table, her normally spotless hair bun now dishevelled. The proprietor, old before his time, sat smoothing his moustache with one hand, whilst stroking his wife's hand with the other.

The small bell at the door tinkled and the woman's head whipped up in anticipation. Her emotions moved quickly from despair to hope and incredulity and she stood up so quickly that the small table crashed down in front of her.

Dafydd wanted to smile his reassurance, as he slowly limped into the café, but the pain was too great. He could only focus on putting one foot in front of the other.

'Sioned, Donato. Sorry I'm late,' he muttered.

Sioned rushed to her brother and held his hands, then gently brushed his face with a look of wonder.

'I knew you would survive,' she whispered.

'Did you?' Dafydd asked.

She gave a wan smile and shook her head. Then she gently led him to Donato who held a glass of brandy.

'Here, it helps with the pain.'

Dafydd drank it in one gulp and coughed.

'I needed that. My hips don't work properly, you know.'

Donato nodded. 'I know this from-a the mine. May I?'

He pulled up the back of Dafydd's shirt and gently probed the sides of the spine towards the base.

'Ah, the pelvis. I can do this if you want?'

Dafydd swallowed. 'Do it, I can't take this.'

Donato held Dafydd at the armpits.

'Now I want you to let yourself fall; I catch you. You trust me.'

Dafydd was too weary to care. He fell back and at the last moment, he felt Donato's leg cushion the back with a jolt. Dafydd let out a gasp, which quickly turned into a cry of anticipated pain. He panted breathlessly for a while, until he realised there was none. Although battered and bruised, he could now feel some mobility had returned.

'Thank you,' Dafydd breathed.

Donato nodded. 'In the mine, it was common.'

The door opened and Angharad flew in. She gave a gasp and rushed forward so quickly that Dafydd cried in alarm. She checked herself, but Dafydd still winced at the fierce hug.

'Oh, thank God, thank God,' she cried. 'Quick, you must go to Josephine.'

'No,' Donato said. 'Not quick, he must rest.'

'Yes,' Angharad replied firmly, clutching Dafydd's hand. 'Quick, for she's dying back there.'

She pulled Dafydd gently to the kitchen door and then stopped and kissed his cheek. 'Go you,' she said.

Dafydd opened the door quickly and looked in. His love sat in a large chair next to the fire. In spite of the warmth, she had her shawl pulled across her shoulders. She did not look up.

Dafydd moved slowly to her, picking up another chair to be by her side. She still showed no sign of movement.

Dafydd reached to stroke her arm. '*Ma chérie,*'

Slowly she looked up. Her gaze at first was distant, then she frowned, and the life seemed to rush back into her. Her face did not show any further sign of emotion, bar a single tear falling down her cheek.

'I felt so alone,' she whispered. 'All zose years of waiting and zis…'

'You are not alone,' Dafydd replied, reaching out to take her hand. 'There is family here, they are your family now. I didn't think it was important before, but now I know. I left my doubt outside Abermule this morning.'

'Yes, you 'ave strong family.'

'All this time, I was worried about protecting you from the talk,' Dafydd continued. 'Yet I never looked at what my sister done. She kept strong for Donato, but not by running away. Not from no-one. And she kept her family around her. If you don't mind, we'll stay in Aber.'

Josephine gave a smile. Her eyes were nearly half-closed, though Dafydd could make out the tears.

'Yes, I would like zis. It ees good to 'ave family.'

Glossary (with English language phonetics where applicable)

Aber – local abbreviation for Aberystwyth.

Abermule – a small village station, three miles west of Newtown in Mid Wales

Aberystwyth – (Abb-er-ust-wiff) The seaside resort is the terminus for the Cambrian railways to the West.

Aled – (Al-ed), male name

Angharad - (Ang-harad) Dafydd's youngest sister,

Bara brith – A welsh yeast bread, speckled with dried fruit and soaked in tea.

Bach – (pronounced as in JS Bach, the composer) The welsh word for small, used as a friendly address, especially after a person's name.

Band of hope – a Christian organisation and part of the temperance movement.

Bergamo – (Bare-gam-oh) an Italian mining district north of Milan. A number of Italians were recruited from there to work at Frongoch from 1899-1902, a turbulent time for all.

Blighty – slang for the UK

Borth – a station 8 miles north of Aberystwyth

Bow Street – a station 3 miles from Aberystwyth

Bully beef – corned beef

Cambrian Railways – the local railway company, serving Aberystwyth, up the coast to Pwllheli, across to Welshpool and Oswestry and down to Three Cocks, near Brecon. Also, owned the Vale of Rheidol railway from about 1911.

Cariad – (carry-ad) A fond term of address to one of the opposite sex, meaning darling or sweetheart. 'Cariad ti' means 'love you'.

Casualty clearing station (CCS) – a medical facility behind the front line and out of reach of artillery, for the treatment of battle wounded.

Charles Fryatt – sea captain, formerly of Great Eastern Railway, captured after trying to ram a U-boat with his cargo ship to escape. Accused of being a spy, he was tried and executed, much to the outrage of the British, who claimed he was a civilian.

Chlor –(Klor) German word for Chlorine, used as a poison gas.

CO – Commanding Officer

County – Notts County FC; One of Nottingham's professional football teams.

Cwtch – (cootch, the oo as in 'book') a welsh hug or cuddle, but oh so much more…

Dafydd – (Dav-i-the. -Remember to pronounce 'the' not 'fuh'!!!). The main protagonist. The welsh version of the name David,

Dai Bracci – (Die Bratchy) Dai is abbreviation of Dafydd or David. Bracci's was the welsh slang for an Italian café.

Devil's Bridge – a small hamlet 12 miles east of Aberystwyth, up the Rheidol valley. Used as a hub for freight by the Rheidol railway and home of spectacular waterfalls bridged by a triple spanned bridge.

DLG – David Lloyd George

Donato – (Don-ah-toe) an Italian café proprietor and former miner at Frongoch, married to Sioned.

Dovey (Welsh pron. Dyfi) – the river and estuary north of Borth and Ynyslas and south of Aberdovey (Aberdyfi). The Cambrian coast railway line extends across the Dovey at Dovey Junction, near Glandovey halt.

Duw (Dew) – God, used as a mild expletive.

Frongoch – (Vron-gor-ch, as in loch), A large lead mine south west of Devil's Bridge

Gwilym (Gwill-im) – Dafydd's uncle, his mother's twin brother.

Hisht – a welsh version of 'shhh'

I bob un sydd ffydlon – (Ee borb een seethe fuvlon) – a welsh hymn 'for everyone who is faithful'

Iesu Grist yn Arglwydd Dduw – (Yessy Greest un are-gloo-eeth view) Jesus Christ and God Almighty

Jellicoe – Admiral John Jellicoe was Admiral of the fleet in 1915 and commander at the Battle of Jutland, the only major naval battle in the war. The fleet was based at Scapa Flow, in the Orkney islands and the chief source of steam coal came from South Wales. Large coal trains traversed the country to the tip of Scotland during the conflict, known as 'Jellicoe specials.' A lot of these trains ran on the Cambrian Railways route from Brecon through to Whitchurch in Shropshire, en route to Crewe and beyond.

Lankys – Employees of Lancashire & Yorkshire railway

Lein fach (Line fach) – a welsh nickname for the Rheidol railway. Means 'little line'

Llanbadarn – (LL-ann-bad-arn) a village a mile outside of Aberystwyth town and where the Cambrian and Rheidol railways pass en route to the town.

Llanfihangel – a station 4 miles north of Aberystwyth, now called Llandre

Longmoor – military training camp in Hampshire, specialising in railway operations

Lucifer – a type of cigarette lighter

Machynlleth (Mach-un-ll-eff), market town at the end of the Dovey (Dyfi) estuary and a main station and engine shed. Abbreviated to 'Mach' by most, whether you speak Welsh or not!

NCO – Non-commissioned officer.in the army – Below the rank of lieutenant

Oswestry – A town in Northern Shropshire, the headquarters of the Cambrian Railways and their railway works. Dafydd moved there as a passed cleaner to work and train as a fireman at the end of *By the Banks of the Rheidol*

Owain Glyndŵr – (Owe-ine Glin-door) last indigenous Prince of Wales, who created a nation from 1400-1405, he is reputed to have held his first parliament in Machynlleth or nearby Pennant.

Panad – (Pan-add) A northern welsh slang for a pot of tea. An abbreviation of Panad o de (Pan-add o dare)

Plascrug – (Plass-creeg) an area a half mile from Aberystwyth

Plynlimon – (Plin-limmon) abbreviation for the Plynlimon & Hafan tramway

Pnawn da – (puh-noun dah) Good afternoon

Poperinge – (Pop-er-ing-eh) – 'Pop' was one of only two Belgian towns not occupied by Germany in the Great War. Used by the British as a billet and field hospital, it lies 8 miles west of Ypres.

RAMC – Royal Army Medical corps

Reckit's Blue – a whitener for fabrics, in the form of a blue tablet.

Rheidol (Rh-ide-ol) name of the river valley, the railway and Dafydd's favourite small tank engine.

Right away – permission to move

Road – 'You've got the road', railway slang for permission for a train to proceed along the line

ROD – Railway Operating Division of the Royal Engineers

RTO – Railway Traffic Officer

Rupert - derogatory slang for officers of the British army,

Sioned – (Shon–ed) Dafydd's eldest sister, but younger than him. Married to Donato. Dafydd refers to her as Sioni (Shon-ee)
'

SNCB – Belgian National Railways

Square bashing - derogatory term for military drill on a barracks square

Talerddig – (Tal-air-th'ig) the highest point of the Cambrian Railways line, a challenging climb for crews when heading east of Machynlleth.

Talybont (Tal-ur-bont) – a village near Llanfihangel

Tommy – slang for a British ordinary soldier

Top Brass – higher ranking officers

Top Link – the engine crew duties were referred to as links, ranging from shunting duties to express trains. The latter were the highest duty and referred to as 'top link', reserved for only the best crews and mostly took many years' experience to achieve.

Trefechan – (Trev-eh-chan, with the ch as in 'loch') the industrial side of Aberystwyth harbour, the inhabitants are referred to as Turkeys or Turks, possibly as a corruption of Twˆr Cae (pronounced Toor Kie)

Twpsyn – (Toop -sin, the oo pronounced as in book) stupid person.

Vale of Rheidol railway – a narrow gauge line from Aberystwyth to Devil's Bridge, initially built to tap into the freight trade for the local metal mines and forestry. Now a tourist railway with a soon to be museum

WD – War Department

White feather – given to people perceived as cowards for not joining up to fight. Whilst not official policy, the government did not discourage the practice by civilians.

Wipers – Tommy slang for Ypres

Ynyslas (Un-iss-lahs) – a small halt 9 miles north of Aberystwyth on the Dovey estuary

Ypres – (Ee-per) also called Ieper in Flemish and 'Wipers' by soldiers. The city at the front line in Belgium throughout the Great War. Captured by the Allies in late 1914. The city survived for the rest of the war, despite the Germans surrounding it on three sides.

A few words on Welsh pronunciation

The Welsh language appears a minefield at first to the uninitiated, but it's a beautiful language and there are some simple rules in pronunciation. The main rule of thumb are all the letters should be pronounced hard. In modern appliance, this does not always happen, but in early 20th century parlance it would. Of these, this is a list of the main ones to consider:

A – is hard like 'apple'

Ch is a guttural word, like the Scottish word 'loch'

Dd -is pronounced like 'the'

E is hard, like 'egg'

F is pronounced hard, like 'Of'

Ff is soft, like 'Off'

I is like 'igloo'

LL is unique to Welsh and so should be approached by placing the tongue behind the front teeth as you exhale. Yes, it does work, so repeat after me… 'Llanelli, Llanelli, Llanelli…'

O is hard, like 'Of' or 'Off'

Rh is like exhaling an R

U is like the I in 'irrigation'

W is a vowel, pronounced like 'oe' in 'does' but with northern English flat vowels

Y is a vowel, pronounced like 'us'

There is no J, K,V,X or Z

There is one circumflex. Called a 'to bach (little roof). It extends the sound of the vowel, thus:

Â is like 'ah'

Ê is like the ai in 'air'

Î is like 'ee'

ô 'is like 'oh"

û is rather like the French 'u', as in 'menu'

ŵ is pronounced 'oo'

ŷ is pronounced 'ee'

There are also mutations. After certain words or in context, the first letter of the next word may change. This is completely alien to those who think or are used to the English language, but are quite natural to fluent speakers of Cymraeg.

Over the years, I have encountered many occasions of the language being seen as a threat or an inconvenience, or casually dismissed as an irrelevance by people who should know better. As a non-fluent Welsh speaker, I can confirm it is a living language, used in everyday life. It is not merely used 'when English people step into shops' (yep, been told that). Neither is it a disadvantage for children to learn. Surely children growing up multi lingual is a positive and unlocks their potential, if only in the study of other latin influenced languages

It has relevance in the culture and communities in Wales today, as it has and will be in the future. Please don't see it as a threat, see it as an opportunity. But do remember that all languages have different structures, tones and pronunciations. Attempting even to rectify the latter of those shows a basic respect to the land and its people.

Author Biography

I grew up in Aberystwyth until the University of Leicester beckoned with a course in Mining geology, which led to nothing pertinent, but a wealth of experience in standing in the rain in remote parts of Britain.

After many years of working and living in Milton Keynes and Northampton, avoiding using the words 'me duck' and 'where you frum?', I returned to live to a village near Aberystwyth in 2008. After working for a bank for many years and then British Telecom, I finally managed to do something useful, working firstly for a rehab clinic and then in solar energy. I now currently work for the Vale of Rheidol Railway.

This is my third novel, the other two being:

- By *the Banks of the Rheidol* (Y Lolfa) ISBN 9781784615598 - the prequel to this novel
- *Forest Brothers* (Circaidy Gregory press), ISBN 9781906451691 -which is set in WW2 Estonia.

In his spare time…who am I kidding? I have no spare time. I have kids…